SAMUEL BEST

MISSION ONE

For my bright little star

CONTENTS

PART I

LAUNCH

_DAY 1

Jeff Dolan squinted and shielded his eyes as he looked up at the 61-meter rocket. The 2700-ton Neptune III solid-fuel colossal towered above him on launch platform LC-44 in Cape Canaveral, silhouetted by the glaring morning sun. Two smaller solid-fuel boosters clung to the sides of the world's largest privately-built rocket.

The support scaffolding of the gantry hugged one side of the white rocket from the ground up to the door of the tapered command module, just below the dart-like tower jet on the nose. Humid Florida air condensed against the liquid-cooled shell. Thick steam rolled slowly down the exterior, dropping past the blue Diamond Aerospace logo and over the tri-finned solid rocket booster, into the three-story engine-wash space below. In less than twelve hours, four nine-engine Hydra cores at the bottom of the Neptune III rocket would blast that empty space with the exhaust from ten million pounds of thrust and torch it with heat in excess of 2000 degrees Fahrenheit.

Jeff admired his bright orange Mark IV Constellation Space Suit and couldn't help but smile. Thinking back over the past few days, there wasn't more than a minute when he didn't have a stupid grin plastered on his face. He felt like a little boy on Christmas as he stared up at the rocket. This wasn't just a simple unearned gift, however. Jeff had worked hard for the opportunity to be on the launch pad right then, at that exact moment. His entire adult life had been focused on breaking out of Earth's atmosphere.

Now he was on the threshold. He would finally be amongst the stars, instead of merely staring up at them in wonder.

He laughed. Six months ago, he was just one applicant in a crowded pool of more than three thousand, each more eager than the last to claim a seat aboard the Neptune III for its inaugural launch.

But that was six months ago, Jeff reminded himself. That was the past.

Today he would be going into space.

Jeff stepped into the industrial elevator at the base of the support scaffolding. A young ground crewman in a white jumpsuit and hard hat pulled the door down behind him.

"One pumpkin, goin' up," the crewman said with a grin, referring to Jeff's Constellation Suit. "Morning, Mr. Dolan."

"Hey, Danny. How's your mom doing?"

Danny thumbed a green button and the elevator lurched upward. He tilted up the front of his hard hat and scratched at the hair plastered to his sweaty forehead.

"Much better, thanks. Doctor thought she'd be stuck in bed until the end of the year, but she's a tough old bird. Third time with pneumonia in two years, and she's already back in her garden."

"I'm glad to hear it."

Jeff watched the smooth side of the rocket as the elevator ascended the scaffolding, passing the seam where the lower booster connected with the upper. He always forgot the sheer size of the rocket until he was close enough to touch its cold metal exterior.

The elevator passed a clean hull panel and Jeff smiled. He remembered joking with the other crew members about spray painting *TITAN OR BUST* on the outside of the rocket. It would have gone a long way to add character to the overused Diamond Aerospace logo the company tried to slap on every available surface.

Titan.

Even the mere thought of the name sent fresh chills down Jeff's spine. It conjured images of warring gods struggling for dominion over the cosmos – battles on an epic scale, stretching back to the dawn of the universe.

None of the previous missions to Saturn's sixth moon – from *Pioneer 11*, *Voyager 1* and *2*, and *Cassini-Huygens,* to the most recent Van Schuyler probe – had cast as bright a light on the enigma of Titan as would the team of *Explorer I.*

"How about you?" asked Danny, breaking through Jeff's daydream. "Do anything crazy for your last night on Earth?"

"Just had a quiet evening at home. I have a feeling I'll be missing it more than I expect."

"It's only a few months, Mr. Dolan."

Twelve, actually, thought Jeff. "A year can seem a lot longer when you're leaving someone behind," he said.

Jeff's enthusiasm for the upcoming journey waned briefly as some of the darker thoughts he'd been suppressing seeped into the foreground. If he hadn't just spent such a fantastic night with the woman he loved, he would have no reason to think twice about boarding the rocket. It was too late to turn back now, of course. Every detail of the mission had been planned with four team members in mind. The entire project would have to be canceled if the flight engineer wasn't aboard.

The elevator bumped to a stop and Jeff forced himself to smile. "But like you said, it's only a few months."

He looked away from the rocket, beyond the concrete platforms of LC-44 and over the shimmering waters of the Banana River toward NASA Causeway. Since it was the closest spot from which the public could witness a launch from Kennedy Space Center, crowds of enthusiasts and press would gather along the shores of the river hours in advance.

"Usually a few die-hards on the causeway this early," Jeff said.

He noticed there was no traffic on the causeway, either.

"With a launch this important," Danny said, "they probably have the bridges closed for security reasons."

"Maybe," Jeff said, not quite convinced.

Danny pulled up the elevator door, revealing the open hatch which led to the command module of *Explorer I.*

"Have a good flight, Mr. Dolan," he said. "See you when you get back."

Kate Bishop slammed her palm down on the snooze button of her blaring alarm clock. She swiped back long, dark hair and tried to focus on the blurry red numbers. 7:20am. She had slept through her first two alarms. Apparently, purposely buying one that sounded like an old fire engine klaxon was still not enough to do the job.

Kate rolled onto her back with a sigh and stared at the white ceiling. Seagulls cried on the beach outside her small ground-floor apartment, occasionally shutting up long enough to allow for the sound of gentle waves rushing over sand to drift in. She reached out next to her and felt the indentation in the mattress where Jeff had slept.

Well, neither of them had *really* slept. They had been too busy enjoying the longest goodbye of their relationship. It was a goodbye that had to last them a year, until Jeff's return.

Kate smiled with satisfaction. It had been a damn good night.

A few minutes in a scalding hot shower brought her most of the way back to life. There wouldn't be time to make coffee before she left, which meant relying on the swill at work. Every time she had to drink that motor oil, she swore it would be her last.

After reluctantly leaving the shower and drying off, she riffled through the clothes strewn over her floral-print sofa while brushing her teeth until, miraculously, she managed to find a clean outfit.

The furniture had come with the apartment. Jeff thought the wicker-and-doily decor was tacky, but it reminded Kate of the beachfront timeshare condo her family had frequented when she was a child. Nostalgia was a powerful force, she reflected, perhaps the *most* powerful, and Kate was not immune to its charms.

She got dressed in a hurry, pulling on a pair of gray slacks over what she liked to call her practical underwear, and a white, button-up blouse over her no-nonsense bra. Kate had different themes for different sets of delicates. Last night's theme had been "make him remember you". Today's was "get it done".

Of course, it hadn't been a one-way street during their long goodbye. Jeff wasn't always Captain Romantic, but last night, he had certainly tried. Kate came home to scented candles, a three-course steak dinner, and a bottle of her favorite Merlot. He should have been a chef. At least then he wouldn't be strapping his ass to a space-bound rocket and leaving for a year.

Yet that was part of the job. Kate had known it when they started dating two years ago. He stuck it out when she left for five months to finish her master's degree. She could do one year, right? It was only a slightly longer walk in the park.

She tied her wet hair back in a tight bun, slipped into a pair of black flats, scooped up her keys, and headed out the door.

Jeff squeezed into the command module of *Explorer I.* The bell-shaped spacecraft nested in the top of the Neptune III rocket, which sat with its pinched nose pointing skyward.

Constellation Space Suits with slide-lock joint seals and soft front entry weren't as bulky as the golden-age extravehicular variety used until the early 2020s, but getting settled into the cramped command module was always a fun challenge regardless. Switches and dials covered every inch of the low, domed ceiling. Many were protected with plastic flip guards, but the ones that weren't systems-critical could be tripped by a careless crew member.

More delicate maneuvering would have been easier in one of the comparably flimsy Modified Advanced Crew Escape Suits astronauts used to wear during launch and reentry, but that design had been rolled into the pressure-friendly Mark IVs, creating a hybrid for all stages of a mission – including spacewalks – rendering

MACE Suits obsolete.

The command module had been designed for four, and Jeff was the last one to arrive. While the craft was resting on the pad, the floor was actually one of the walls. All four flight chairs were above him as he stood just inside the hatch. There were two chairs in each row. The front row was for the pilots, closer to the nose of the rocket.

There was only a small space behind the two aft flight chairs. Jeff hunched over and turned around, then, moving backward, used strategic hand- and footholds to maneuver himself deeper into the command module until his head bumped the back of his own chair. Utilizing the crew-patented technique known as "diving ass-first", he hoisted himself up and squatted over his form-hugging chair. He wiggled his hips, squeezed between the narrow, rigid armrests and finally plopped down onto the seat. Sensing his weight, the seat automatically reclined until he was on his back, facing skyward.

The other three astronauts were already settled in and going through their pre-flight checklists.

"Thought maybe you got lost," said Commander Tag Riley from the pilot's chair above him.

"Just smelling the roses," Jeff said.

Riley grunted with amusement. At fifty-one, he was the oldest member of the crew. After thirty years of flying jets for the Navy and extensive space flight training in the resurrected NASA astronaut program, he had accepted an offer from Diamond Aerospace to lead the first manned mission to Titan.

The mission needed someone like him at the helm, said the head of public relations at Diamond Aerospace. They needed someone who would radiate confidence; who would soothe the apprehensions of a public that hardly ever looked up anymore; a public that would most likely wonder why the hell we kept sending people back up there in the first place.

It didn't hurt that Riley still maintained the rugged good looks of his youth. His gold-flecked, dark brown eyes were frequently mentioned by some of his more ardent fans.

He kept the military-style flattop haircut from his Navy days, though his hair was now shock white instead of chestnut brown. His respectably-weathered forehead wrinkled in thought as he read an instruction from his metal clipboard, then he flipped a switch on the crowded control console before him.

Lieutenant Li Ming sat in the co-pilot's chair to his left, scribbling numbers into data grids on her own clipboard. Sitting only a foot away from Riley, she seemed like a child who had wandered in through the wrong door. Her slight frame fit easily in her chair, even while wearing the padded, bright orange Constellation Space Suit.

Her small stature belied a huge talent for piloting any vessel her commanding officers would authorize. She graduated in the top five of her class from the academy of the People's Liberation Army Air Force, and within ten years of service had already racked up more flight time than many retired pilots.

She ticked a box on her clipboard and flipped

another switch in front of her.

The control console covered the wall in front of the two pilots' chairs. The designers of *Explorer I* had been kind enough to add a narrow strip of window above the console to ease the claustrophobic, cave-like atmosphere inside the restricted compartment. For now, it showed only the blackness inside the tower jet capping the rocket's nose.

Doctor Gabriel Silva sat in the seat next to Jeff, tapping on his clipboard with a pencil and humming to himself. The two of them became fast friends at the beginning of the intense six-month training program leading up to the launch after being repeatedly grouped together in the same mock flight team.

Jeff had a fairly conventional career trajectory for an active flight engineer – he cut his teeth on a deep-sea research yacht two years after receiving his bachelor's degree, then followed that up with private contract work overhauling Navy submarines.

Gabriel graduated from the University of Sao Paulo with a doctorate in biology at the young age of twenty-four. He had his pick of jobs after that, and shocked his mentors when he packed up and went to Antarctica, where he spent four years operating an advanced hydroponics lab for an American genetics research corporation. Afterward, the good doctor accepted a comfortable teaching position at his alma mater, occasionally taking time off to pursue his growing interest in agronomy.

"Hiya, Gabe," Jeff said. He pried off his own metal clipboard that had been magnetically attached to the side of his seat and skimmed the first few action items.

"You look tired," said Gabriel, "which means you didn't take my advice to go to bed early." He wagged a scolding finger at Jeff. He already wore his Communications Carrier Assembly, which tightly hugged his scalp. The broad white stripe down the middle and the bulging black ear coverings had led to the CCA being called the Snoopy cap. The crew wouldn't be donning their full helmets until a few hours before launch, but they communicated with Mission Control using the earphones and microphones built into the CCAs.

"Oh, I went to bed *plenty* early. Maybe I just didn't fall asleep right away."

"Well, we're gonna be sitting in this tin can for twelve hours. Plenty of time for a nap."

"Don't bet on it," Riley said. "As soon as we finish one set of checklists, Mission Control will spit up some more. It's half their job."

With all the chairs tilted back, Riley and Ming were several feet above Gabriel and Jeff, closer to the nose of the rocket. Jeff watched the pilots' movements, steady and smooth. If he recorded a continuous video of them over the next twelve hours and played it back at high speed, he bet it would look as if two androids were going to guide the craft into space.

Jeff settled deeper into his seat and went back to the first item on his checklist: fuel tank integrity. He cycled the appropriate switch on a small control panel next to his seat, waiting for a flashing green light. Flashing green meant he was in test mode, and the test was good.

Solid green meant the rocket was in flight and the system remained stable. Yellow and red – well, Jeff thought of those as different shades of impending doom.

The light above the fuel tank integrity switch flashed green.

Jeff ticked the appropriate box on his checklist, then moved down to the next of over one hundred items that remained.

Traffic near the beach always moved slow, and that morning was no exception. Kate weaved her old Mustang safely but steadily between other cars as she drove to work with her windows down, humming along to a nostalgic song on the radio. She was listening to one of those stations that played all the best hits from twenty years ago, when she'd been in high school and had little to care about besides boys and music.

The sun was up and blasting the beach to her right. Soon she would turn inland for a quick jaunt up the highway before a straight run to work, farther north on one of the barrier islands that hugged the eastern coast of Central Florida.

She saw the highway on-ramp ahead, and signaled to exit. Kate was halfway into the next lane when a car horn blasted from behind her. She jerked the wheel and swerved back into her lane, thinking she had cut off another driver hiding in her blind spot. Yet when she craned her neck to look back, there was no one behind her.

An engine revved to her left, and the horn blared again. She jumped in surprise and her car shuddered in response.

An older brown sedan pulled up on her left side. A lanky man in the front seat waved his arms wildly and shouted, but his windows were up and she couldn't hear him. It looked as if he wanted her to pull over.

Kate checked his car – there were no law enforcement markings of any kind. The man himself didn't resemble a police officer in the slightest. A patchy shadow of stubble clung to his sallow cheeks and dark bags hung under his manic eyes.

He blared his horn again and swerved toward Kate, pushing her toward the shoulder. She yelped and accelerated, blowing past her exit, gripping her wheel with both hands to steady her shaking. The other driver accelerated to match her speed, shouting at her the whole time. Then he seemed to realize the problem and reached over to roll down his passenger-side window.

The two cars entered an intersection. Another engine revved and Kate looked over, past the brown sedan, to see a large, black SUV barreling in their direction. The man in the brown sedan must have seen her eyes go wide, because he looked to his left just as the massive silver grille and the black SUV it preceded crashed into his rear-left side panel and spun his sedan away from Kate's car.

She zoomed out of the intersection, leaving the brown sedan spinning. Smoke poured from under the bent hood of the SUV as it slowed to a stop on the other side of the intersection from the sedan.

Breathing hard and still maintaining an iron grip on her steering wheel, Kate guided her Mustang to the side of the road. She turned back to watch.

Two well-dressed, muscular men with buzzed haircuts got out of the black SUV. One of them adjusted a cuff link and cracked his neck. Other cars had stopped before entering the intersection. A few drivers laid into their horns, but the two men paid them no attention.

The brown sedan had spun to a stop a short distance away. The silhouette of the man inside worked frantically to start the engine. Kate could hear the chug-chugging as the old engine tried to catch.

Her heart beat faster as the two men from the SUV approached the brown sedan. She couldn't stop her racing mind from telling her they would kill the driver.

Then the engine of the sedan turned over, roaring to life. The two approaching men stopped as the back tires of the other car squealed in place. Rubber caught and the car lurched into motion, gaining speed as the driver tore off down a side street.

Kate breathed a hesitant sigh of relief when the brown sedan disappeared around a bend. The other two men hurried to the black SUV. The driver hopped in, but the passenger turned to look in Kate's direction. He stared at her until she pulled back onto the road and drove away, heading for the next on-ramp a mile down the road.

The rest of her rushed drive to work was uneventful. Kate was consciously aware of checking her mirrors more often than usual, expecting either the brown sedan or black SUV to reappear at any moment.

She drove onto land at the northern tip of Cape Canaveral leased by Diamond Aerospace and hit the brakes hard in front of the main security guardhouse gate. Her old Mustang groaned at the harsh stop. She peeled off her sunglasses and fished through her purse for her badge, chiding herself for not having it ready – though not too hard, given the circumstances. Humid morning air rolled in through the open window, overpowering her weak air conditioning.

A stocky security guard in a dark blue uniform approached her side of the car and stopped a few feet away.

"Good morning, Ms. Bishop," he said. "You alone in there?"

"Hi, Ed. As always, yes."

"You know I gotta ask."

"Oh, I know." She forced a smile as she became increasingly frustrated with the futile search for her badge.

Ed was part of Blackbird private security, the company Diamond Aerospace hired for the duration of their lease agreement at Kennedy Space Center. Based on his refrigerator-like appearance, Kate guessed he had probably made a good linebacker or wrestler in one of his previous careers. He hooked one thumb in his belt and casually rested his other hand on the butt of his night stick.

"I feel like such a mess this morning," Kate said. "I can't seem to find anything."

"Well, things may get worse before they get better. It's only fair to warn you that the money men are here."

She stopped rooting for her badge and looked at him, then at the square, bulky Launch Command Center on the far side of the Diamond Aerospace parking lot. There weren't supposed to be any representatives on-site, especially not on launch day.

"What money men?" she asked. "From Atlanta? Chicago? Beijing?"

"All of 'em, I think."

She shook her head in frustration and dumped the contents of her purse onto the passenger's seat.

"Ah ha!" she said, plucking up her badge and handing it to Ed.

He produced a hand-held scanner from the back of his belt and swiped her security badge. The device chirped happily and Ed returned her I.D.

"Any idea why the causeway is empty?" she asked. "Usually they start piling up out there before sunrise."

"I heard your boss got the local Sheriff's Department to close the bridge."

"All day?"

"Seems like it."

He turned and nodded at the reflective glass of the guardhouse. The gate in front of Kate's Mustang slowly lifted.

"Don't you and your boys handle crowd control?" Kate asked.

"Usually. But today's different, isn't it?"

"Sure is," she said quietly, picturing the black SUV plowing into the brown sedan's side panel.

Kate looked in the direction of launch platform LC-44, where Jeff and his team were already waiting. She could only see the very top of the distant rocket over the roof of the Diamond Aerospace building. From where she was sitting, it looked like a toy.

Ed tapped the roof of her car. "Good luck in there," he said.

"Thanks. We'll need it."

Noah Bell stood at the large picture window in his fortieth-floor penthouse, overlooking Manhattan. It wasn't a great morning in the lower atmosphere. A wet and heavy fog enshrouded the tall buildings in downtown New York.

Far below on the busy sidewalks, nearly lost in the haze, streams of umbrellas flowed on either side of a blockade of unmoving taxis. Noah wondered if the people on the street ever looked up at his penthouse, or beyond, to the stars. He could remember his days down there on the sidewalks, amongst all the umbrellas. He had somehow always found the time to look up, even if it was raining.

Fortunately, Noah wasn't worried about the bad weather blanketing his adopted hometown. The only thing he had to worry about was if the skies would be clear during the launch window that evening in Cape Canaveral, Florida.

He stretched his back and adjusted the waistband of his three-hundred-dollar silk pajama bottoms.

At thirty-eight, Noah still had a thick, natural head of light brown hair. He was neither overly tall nor unusually short, instead falling into the comfortable, inconspicuous middle territory. Outgoing, yes, but consciously guarded when asked bluntly about the intricacies of his operations. His boyish exuberance masked a razor-sharp intellect and a quick temper, the latter of which he worked hard to unleash only upon ignorant reporters during what he called his moments of weakness.

As he looked at his shirtless reflection in the window, a pinkish scar from a recent shoulder surgery caught his eye. He pressed down on it hard with two fingers, grimacing from the pain. Noah had earned that one by not diligently checking his abseiling harness while canyoning in the Swiss Alps several months ago. He had slipped off his rope and slammed into a couple of boulders on his way to the ground.

Yet, he didn't mind the scar. It was good to have a visual reminder of a past failure. It helped him stay focused while taking new risks.

Thirty-eight years old, he thought, *and today you make history.*

Almost immediately after having the thought, his deceased father's voice barged into his mind.

Don't get cocky, junior, said the gruff voice – gruff, but kind. Even in Noah's imagination, his father's voice still carried a thick Australian accent. *You've put the cart in front of the horse before, and it didn't work out.*

But this isn't losing ten million on a bad stock tip, thought Noah.

You're right. It's actually dangerous.

Noah smiled faintly as he pushed the thoughts from his mind. Today was not the day for hesitations, nor for second-guessing himself.

The massive proverbial ball was rolling downhill, picking up speed. It was impossible to stop it now.

Noah was considered a late-comer to the realm of the nouveau riche. While most young millionaires made their fortunes in Silicon Valley from explosively popular internet apps and data-mining technologies, he had taken his time by playing the stock market as a fresh college graduate, feeding whatever expendable cash he saved from working three jobs into his growing portfolio. He wasn't even a blip on the radar until a small nanotechnology startup in Montana was bought out by an undisclosed computer corporation.

Noah just happened to have stock in nanotech. He made fourteen million dollars in one night.

He rolled it all back into his portfolio, and by the end of the next year was sitting on well over half a billion. His talents were not limited to a preternatural understanding of stock market systems. He also turned out to be one hell of a businessman. Diamond Aerospace was his fourth successful company, and would likely become the world's most profitable if it could be the first to get a team to Titan.

It was launch day, and Noah felt like a million bucks. Several *million* million bucks, to be more accurate.

The company he had built from the ground up was going to Titan after years of careful planning and financial maneuvering. The automated mining stations on the moon and Mars made it possible. Without the financial windfall from those endeavors, Noah would never have made it close to Titan. He had expected the majority of his company's profits to come from the asteroid mining division, but they had yet to secure a cost-effective way of transporting raw ore back to Earth. That department hadn't been able to claw its way out of the exploratory phase, and had been operating in the red since the beginning. Noah was only able to keep it operational due to the success of the other two automated mining outposts.

And now, if he could unlock the secrets of Titan and of the strange object orbiting that distant moon, he could perpetually run all of his gestating pet projects at a financial loss until he dropped dead of overstimulation. Not that that was the goal, of course. Noah enjoyed being fiscally responsible, but he also had to admit that it was nice knowing he would never have to worry about the bottom line ever again.

He struggled, and not for the first time, with whether or not he should tell the crew the supplemental addendum to their mission. Originally, the purpose of the first manned voyage past Mars was to begin construction of an orbital research station around Titan. Riley and his team were to lay the groundwork for future missions, delivering and constructing the skeleton that would eventually become the most distant occupied human settlement in history: Space Station Glory.

Yet informing the crew about the more recent

secondary objective created too much opportunity for an information leak. Noah didn't like handing over critical information to people until it became absolutely necessary. People made mistakes. People blabbed. Riley and his team were still going to deliver and construct the foundation for Glory; that part of the mission hadn't changed. Now they would just be taking some time out of their schedule to investigate the mysterious object one of Noah's deep-space probes had seen in orbit around Titan.

Titan was supposed to be naked. An empty, untouched world, primed for exploration and discovery. And yet the artifact was there, in slow orbit around the moon, defying all attempts at explanation.

Of the competing companies that were capable of sending a craft so far from Earth, only Noah's Diamond Aerospace had an engine that could get one to Titan quickly. He had to concede that it was possible MarsCorp had surreptitiously launched a vessel half a year ago or more, but Noah paid good money to stay informed of his competitors' clandestine actions. If they had launched a ship, he would have known. And besides, without Noah's unprecedented solid core thermal antimatter drive, the journey would take too long. He knew the suits at MarsCorp. They didn't have the patience for that kind of campaign.

Which gave rise to the question: if his own company hadn't put the mysterious object in orbit around Titan, then who had? It was a question he asked himself a thousand times a day.

Noah sighed and rubbed his eyes.

Yes, he decided for the nth time. Better to tell the crew about the new addendum to their mission en route and avoid any potential fallout. He couldn't imagine they'd be too angry to learn they were the first people in human history to personally investigate an unknown object orbiting a body in their home solar system.

A soft form groaned pleasantly in the large bed behind him.

Speaking of bodies, Noah thought as he turned around.

The oversized bed was the main feature of his penthouse. The rest of the sparse furniture was oriented around it, drawing a visitor's attention toward it. Noah did his best not to bring work home. Long ago, he learned the value of keeping the two separate. His home was a sanctuary, and he did his best to eliminate any outside influence. There was no television and no computer. His team of secretaries intercepted all calls and only forwarded the emergencies.

The penthouse was his own personal Zen palace high above the streets of Manhattan.

He walked barefoot across the tile floor and sat on the edge of the bed, admiring the shape of the body beneath the silk sheets.

The body rolled over. Slender fingers pulled down the top of the sheet, revealing forty-three-year-old Elena Riley, ex-wife of the man who would be flying Noah's spacecraft to Titan. She pushed her thick, wavy brunette hair away from her face.

"Are you watching me sleep?" she asked with the slight hint of a flirtatious smile.

"No, but I'm watching you wake up," said Noah. His own Australian accent was stronger than usual because of his imagined conversation with his father. He knew the effect would only last a few minutes. With years of practice, he had become capable of eliminating the accent altogether for brief interviews or speeches – situations where foreign investors might have an easier time understanding him.

"That's not usually as graceful."

"Would you like some coffee?"

"From the cafe downstairs?"

"I can have some sent up."

She thought about it for a moment. Noah recognized the hesitation, but also the eagerness. He usually saw it in people who had spent so long getting their own coffee that it would always be second nature for them to have it delivered.

He smiled. "I'll be right back."

He walked to the other end of the three-thousand square-foot penthouse and opened the door. One of his assistants, a young man so well-manicured he looked as if he were cut from a mold, waited in the hallway with two cups of coffee.

"Thank you, Trevor," said Noah as he accepted the lidded cups.

"Anything else Mr. Bell?" Trevor asked.

"Not right now. Flight's at eleven?"

"Yes, sir. Pick you up at nine?"

Noah glanced back at Elena. "Make it ten."

"Yes, sir," said Trevor.

Noah closed the door with his foot, then went back

to bed and handed Elena her coffee.

"How long was he standing out there?" she asked.

"With these particular cups? Only a couple of minutes. But I had him make three runs earlier while I was waiting for you to wake up."

"You did not," she said playfully. She sat up and the silk sheet slipped off her smooth skin.

Noah admired her beauty and silently thanked Commander Riley for taking her for granted to the point that she left him.

Elena took a long sip of coffee. Her eyes rolled up with pleasure.

"So tell me," she said, looking at Noah coyly, "don't you usually wake up next to gorgeous young models?"

"You're not a model?" he replied with mock surprise. "You have been paying too much attention to gossip news. I prefer women who have a little…substance."

She returned his gaze over her coffee cup. "Just a little?" she whispered.

Remarkable woman, thought Noah. His cheeks flushed with desire. He gently took her cup and set it next to his on the nightstand.

"Trevor can bring more later," he said.

Elena sank down into the silk sheets, her sparkling eyes locked on his, and he followed eagerly.

Kate swiped her badge outside the automatic sliding glass doors that led into the heart of the Launch Command Center building, then pressed her thumb to the fingerprint scanner. The lock beeped approval at her, but she hesitated.

Now that she knew what awaited her inside Mission Control, Kate wasn't in such a hurry to start her workday. Beyond the doors on the main operations floor, several of her coworkers chatted and sipped coffee, enjoying the easy pace before the launch. Three rows of workstations on the operations floor split by a walkway down the middle faced a screen that fully covered the far wall from corner to corner. A grid of virtual panels broke up the screen, each one fully dedicated to a specific feed of information pouring in from *Explorer I*, the Neptune III rocket, the astronauts' Mark IV Suits, and two dozen other monitoring points. Live video, heart rates, fuel levels, temperature – it was all up there. At a casual glance, everything appeared normal.

The room formed a large half-circle, with the monitoring wall on the outer curved edge, the rows of workstations facing it, a raised viewing platform behind the workstations, and a glass-fronted conference room behind the viewing platform.

From where she stood at the security doors off to one side of Mission Control, Kate could just see her boss, Frank Johnson, inside the conference room at the back, laughing with a group of other men.

Money men slowed everything down. They asked too many questions and distracted employees. These were representatives of some of the richest men in the world – men who usually only wanted to know two things: when is more money coming in and why is it taking so long. Noah had been very clear with them that the Titan project was not a typical quick-return scheme. The investors were unlikely to see their money again any time soon. So far, every penny of their Diamond Aerospace investment money had gone toward development of the thermal antimatter drive that would get *Explorer I* to Titan. The project would only become profitable if, and *only* if, the company could find a way to operate an automated natural resource depot on the surface years down the line.

The money men knew this. They had been reminded repeatedly. Yet they answered only to higher powers, and if the higher powers said to get back out there and keep kicking the tires, they flew back to Cape Canaveral and kicked until they needed new loafers.

Kate would have been happy with a new car, but she hadn't gotten into the aerospace industry to buy a mansion. She did it because she had to; because ever since she was a little girl, the mysteries of the stars had been the only thing consistently pulling her attention from the banalities of everyday life.

She stepped toward the glass doors, but they didn't open. She sighed in frustration and swiped her badge and stuck her thumb in the scanner again. The lock beeped and the doors slid open, letting out a heavenly rush of cool air. The Florida humidity had kept her sweating since her interaction with the security guard outside. Kate hoped to God she had remembered to toss a spare stick of deodorant into her desk drawer.

Instead of heading for her desk, she turned left and lightly took the few steps up to the viewing platform, making for the conference room. One of her coworkers down on the operations floor, Rick Teller, caught her eye while sipping coffee at his workstation. His dark, thick eyebrows went up with a warning over the rim of his glasses as he rotated his chair to track her brisk movement.

He wore one of his three faded yellow button-down shirts over one of his two pairs of faded black slacks. He and Kate had been working side-by-side for two years. In that time, Rick had turned forty-five, lost most of his hair, gained a pair of glasses, and told Kate more about his wardrobe than she ever wanted to know. According to him, wearing the same clothes every day made it more difficult for third parties to keep track of his movements. They couldn't be sure if he went to the laundromat on Thursday or to the movies, when in fact he had done both on *Tuesday*. It confused their procedures, said Rick, and they couldn't keep their heads screwed on without their precious procedures. Kate told him that he was being paranoid, and that no one was watching him. She had repeated the same line countless times throughout their relationship, but Rick always just smiled and wagged a scolding finger at her, as if she were a simple child who would never understand.

She caught a glimpse of the large digital clock at the very top of the monitoring wall. It was just after nine o'clock, and the director of Mission Control needed to be out on the operations floor, guiding his crew, not hamming it up with the representatives of investors whose money was already spent.

Kate pushed open the glass door to the conference room with a smile. The five visitors talking with Frank didn't acknowledge her.

The men stood next to a circular, glass-topped table, which took up a large portion of the room. A ring of black, high-backed chairs surrounded the table. Dark wood paneling covered the rear wall, meeting slate gray carpet at the floor. The only object adorning the table was a pyramidal black conference phone in the middle.

Besides Frank Johnson, the mission director, she didn't recognize any of the other five men, nor would she have been able to pick any one of them out of a police line-up – mid-thirties, slim, broad shoulders, average height, thick, full heads of hair, no glasses, clean-shaven, and tan-but-not-too-tan, which was hard to pull off in the harsh fluorescent glow permeating every crevice of the operations center. Frank had just passed fifty yet looked to be in his early forties, helped mostly by his full head of short, black hair, a rigorous workout regime, and a strict diet. He seemed to fit right in with the money men, in cold demeanor if not in the price of his cheap suit.

Frank had been kicking around the private space industry since it was a nascent gleam in the eye of Diamond Aerospace's forebears. He was on the engineering team that had designed the first Hydra core, the descendant of which was now widely considered the most stable and powerful solid rocket engine money could buy. Long before that, he had been on the ground floor of NASA's Mission Control during the brief and disastrous reincarnation of the Apollo program, in which all seven souls bound for the moon's surface were lost when their capsule broke apart in Earth's lower atmosphere.

"And as I mentioned earlier," Frank said, glancing briefly in Kate's direction, "Diamond Aerospace leases this building and the launch pad from NASA. They are contractually forbidden from interfering in our day-to-day operations." He grinned. "It's a perfect relationship. They needed more money to send their toys into space, and we needed the space to send our people and your technology to Titan. That's the reason you won't see any government employees on the operations floor this evening. Diamond Aerospace is and will remain a private company, not beholden to anyone or anything but the clear vision of its CEO."

"And where is Mr. Bell?" asked a Chinese man with a heavy accent. Kate had never seen the actual figures on paper, but she knew that of all the outside investors, the Chinese had the largest interest in the mission.

"He'll be here this afternoon," Frank said soothingly. "As you can imagine, members of the nouveau riche always have a lot on their plates."

Kate had to stop herself from rolling her eyes. She had heard Frank mention Noah's prodigious bankroll to investors more times than she could count. It was supposed to inspire confidence that there was no way they could lose money, falsely hinting that Noah would simply reimburse any lost capital.

Half of the project's investment hadn't come from pure capital, though, as Kate knew. Most of it was in the form of technology that Frank and his team of designers had crammed into every nook of *Explorer I*. The technology was in the walls of the ship. It was in the engine, in the command consoles, and in the sensors. Diamond Aerospace could only build so much of its own equipment before needing to reach out to experts that had been manufacturing specific parts for decades. The prospect of including a few of their products on the first manned mission to Titan was usually more than enough to persuade companies, and the powerful CEOs behind them, to help sponsor the voyage.

Though they sent their money men to hound Frank about the mission's progress, the heaviest investors didn't care about short term losses. Most of them had partnered with Diamond Aerospace and offered Noah healthy percentages of any future profits derived from the exploitation of information gathered by their technology during the mission. They wanted to be among the first to stake their claim on Titan in any one of a variety of fields – a prospect that was worth far more to them than mere capital.

Frank told a well-worn joke, and the money men laughed. Kate finally grew tired of waiting.

"Good morning, gentlemen," she said.

They turned to look at her.

"Ah, at last!" said one of the men in a thick southern accent. "I could sure use a strong cup of coffee, sweet thing."

Kate's smile wavered only slightly and Frank cleared his throat.

"Gentlemen," he said, "Ms. Bishop here is our Ground and Flight Teams Manager."

"Speaking of which," she said, pulling her glare off the man who asked for coffee, "I thought we could get started with the scaffold integrity tests."

"Of course, of course," Frank said, nodding. "Gentlemen, you'll have to excuse me. Duty calls. If you speak with my assistant, Charlene, she can recommend an excellent restaurant for breakfast. There's still plenty of time before the show this evening."

They all shook hands, but not with Kate, and left the conference room.

Frank looked at his watch. "You're late," he said.

"Why do you tolerate those assholes?" she asked.

"Because those assholes are going to keep Diamond Aerospace in the black for decades."

"Oh, come on, Frank. You know Bell could fund a dozen more missions like this one before his wallet felt any lighter."

"The first rule of any venture is to never use your own money. It's good business."

"Not when those guys are the alternative."

"They're not just empty suits. You should give them a chance."

"How can I? They've been here five times in sixteen months and they've never even introduced themselves."

"I imagine we're not the only project in which their companies are involved."

She shook her head as she looked out at the main operations floor. Rick sat at his workstation, watching the display wall and occasionally typing on his keyboard. Most of the other workstations were empty. The room was subdued, almost peaceful – but it was still early.

"Kate, what's wrong?" asked Frank.

She sighed. "I'm just wondering if we got everything right."

"You'll do fine. Your team is ready and you know your job. Don't worry. Now, let's go start those tests, shall we?"

One could only sit in the cramped cockpit of a rocket ship so long before getting twitchy. After hours of systems tests, that moment had come. Jeff adjusted his Snoopy cap, trying to scratch the back of his scalp.

"Damn thing's already starting to itch," he said. He stuck his pencil underneath the cap and scratched hard.

"Well," said Ming from the co-pilot's chair, "you only have to wear it for twelve months."

"I think I'll just leave it off and shout all the time instead."

"Dolan, how's that checklist coming?" asked Riley.

"Nearly finished," Jeff said.

Riley held up his clipboard so Jeff could see all the checkmarks. "Aren't you glad you didn't bet on it?"

Jeff smiled. Riley always beat him during pre-flight checks in the last few weeks of training. The guy was a machine.

"Always," he said. "Besides, Gabriel usually finishes first, anyway."

Ming said, "It helps when you only have fifteen items on your checklist."

"And when all the items relate to the happiness quotient of the plants you're putting into the crew module," Jeff added.

"So we're making fun of the plant guy, now?" said Gabriel, feigning offense. "We'll see how hard you're laughing when I eat all the food and you need to find another agronomist to grow a nutritious dinner."

"You eat all my food," Riley said, "and I will flush you into space."

"Yeah," said Jeff. "Nobody touches my packets of beef whatever-it-is. It's my favorite."

Riley attached his clipboard to the magnetic strip on the side of his chair.

"Three hours and counting," he said. "Private missions. Time to confess."

During their intensive training, the crew had agreed to allow each of the others one personal project they could carry out on the mission, as long as it didn't interfere in any way with their primary goal or smell like dirty feet. They all pretended it was a big secret from the show-runners in Mission Control, but they weren't so irresponsible that they didn't get their projects approved before bringing it on board.

"I'm growing lima beans," Gabriel said.

"Sticking with the plants?" Ming teased. She ticked off the last checkbox on her clipboard and stowed it next to her seat. "I thought we could already grow lima beans in space."

"They would make a nice addition to the

greenhouse. The seeds were sent to me by a primary school teacher in Peru. She thinks she can get her students interested in agriculture if I send back pictures and video."

"*She*, huh?" Ming said playfully.

Gabriel blushed. "What's yours, then?"

"I'm growing lima beans, too." She looked back and winked.

Jeff laughed. He flipped a switch, cycling the hatch that jettisoned liquid waste into space. There was a deep solenoid *clunk* from somewhere in the ship behind him, and a light next to the switch flashed green.

"Good news," he said. "We can still crap in space."

"Hallelujah," Riley joked.

"But seriously, Gabriel," Ming said. "I brought a sealed petri dish of blooming *Caulerpa lentillifera*."

"You're bringing seaweed?" Jeff asked.

"I want to see how well it does up there. As far as algae goes, I believe it's an underrated contender for growth on Titan. It could facilitate oxygen production inside a small surface habitat."

"Yeah, but it's *sea*weed."

She shrugged. "So we can call it space weed."

"Now, now," said Riley. "We don't want to give anyone the wrong impression about what we do up there. For example, I'm testing a new tanning cream for my daughter's best friend. It's completely innocent, and safe for media consumption."

"I thought you looked more orange than usual," said Ming.

"Ha, ha. The girl wants to open her own shop on

Titan. She's another Noah Bell in the making."

"Did you tell her no one is permanently settling on Titan?" said Gabriel. "We're only going to have a research station orbiting an uninhabitable death trap."

"I didn't want to crush her spirits. Glad I kept her away from you, Silva. Dolan, what's your project?"

Jeff ticked another three items off his list. "Has anyone picked lima beans yet?"

"Still not funny," Gabriel said.

Jeff had wanted his project to be a surprise during the journey. He had heard stories about other astronauts who got so tired of eating the same thing all the time that they half-joked it would be preferable to burn off their taste buds.

"Pizza," he said.

Ming laughed. "Yeah, right."

"Not really pushing your mental limits with that one," Gabriel said.

"Hey," Jeff said, holding up a warning finger. "Don't mock the engineer, or I'll sync the ship's remote systems to my suit and pilot this thing into a meteor on my first EVA."

"You can't do that," Gabriel said. "Ming, can he do that?"

She nodded. "He can do it."

"I brought all the ingredients, freeze-dried," Jeff said. "You know how hard it is to freeze-dry a freshly-baked pizza crust?"

"How are you going to cook it?" Ming asked.

"I was just going to take it outside and wave it under the antimatter engine wash."

"Good luck with that."

He smiled. "The method is part of the surprise."

"I think I'm planning to be full that night," said Gabriel.

There was a knock from outside the open hatch. Danny poked his head in, cradling two full-cover helmets under his arms.

"Hi, guys," he said. "Control wanted me to run these up to you."

"Was wondering where those were," Riley said. "I felt naked walking up here without it."

Each helmet was labeled with the last name of the intended wearer above the face screen. He handed them to Jeff, who passed one to Gabriel. Danny accepted two more helmets from another ground tech on the scaffolding behind him and passed them inside to Riley and Ming.

"Thanks, Danny," Jeff said.

"Sure thing. Director Johnson wanted me to remind you they plan on sealing you in before the final round of tests a little early."

"We wouldn't forget something like that," Riley said with a dry smile.

Danny left with the other tech. Jeff turned the full-pressure polycarbonate helmet over in his hands, double-checking the integrity of the locking ring at the neck and of the seal around the clear pressure faceplate. The retractable, gold-tinted sunshade visor was already in place over the pressure faceplate, though the crew wouldn't need it for liftoff at eight in the evening. The last thing Jeff checked was the anti-suffocation valve at the back of the helmet, which allowed the passing of carbon dioxide.

He caught himself smiling again as he held the helmet in his lap.

A pair of ground techs in white jumpsuits and hardhats appeared at the open hatch.

"Gotta seal you in now, folks. It's time."

"Roger that," said Riley.

"Last breath of fresh air for a whole year!" Gabriel said, and breathed in deeply. His cheeks puffed out as he held the breath in, nodding encouragingly at the others.

The ground techs pulled the hatch closed, shutting out the late afternoon sunlight. Small, recessed lamps faintly lit the inside of the command module. Riley flipped a series of switches above his head and more lights came on.

Gabriel released his precious air in a rush, and sighed. "Why do you think they're sealing us in so early?" he asked.

There was a loud series of clunks from outside the module as the ground crew worked to seal the hatch, then a faint mechanical whine as the scaffolding ramp retracted.

"That's just Frank being jumpy," said Riley. "He tends to get a little paranoid the closer we get to launch."

"Doesn't bother me," Ming said. "I prefer hyper-vigilance to him being asleep at the keyboard."

"Get that engine data up *now!*" Frank roared from the viewing platform behind the rows of workstations.

His eyes darted across the wide monitor screen, searching.

Kate's desk was in the second row of workstations, bordering the carpeted walkway that split the two halves of the room. Rick Teller sat at his desk next to her, sweating.

He fumbled for a dial, then pushed a button.

"It's up!" he said quickly.

A panel on the display wall flashed to black, then populated with lines of text and a small graph.

"Uh huh," Frank mumbled as he read the data. "Very good!" He clapped his hands, smiling. "We're right on track, people."

Rick let out a heavy sigh of relief and rubbed his eyes.

"Don't let him get to you," Kate said. She pulled down her wireless headset microphone and took a sip of coffee. "It's going to be crazy for another hour or so, then things will calm down."

He wiped sweat from his forehead and nodded.

"I thought I'd be better under pressure," he said.

"Frank has a way of helping you figure that out pretty quick."

"My other launches weren't so intense."

"Welcome to the private sector."

He eased back in his chair and it protested with a loud squeak. "I thought I fixed this stupid thing," he grumbled, sitting upright. He pulled out a roll of black electrical tape from a drawer in his workstation.

"How was your meeting?" he asked as he worked behind the chair, grunting as he ripped off pieces of tape and rolled them around a loose spring.

"With Frank?"

"Yeah." He sighed satisfactorily and dropped the tape back into his drawer, then plopped down into his chair. He waggled his eyebrows at Kate as he leaned back silently.

"You're just a regular Mr. Fix-it," Kate said, rolling her eyes. "The meeting went horribly. We're under the thumb of evil, vacuous, terrible men. But again, that's the private sector."

Her gaze drifted to the wallet-sized picture of herself taped to the edge of her transparent workstation monitor. She sat at a much smaller desk in a smaller room filled with tables of electronics. Her first job at NASA had been assembling components for the now-defunct Ulysses modules.

It was a personal reminder to keep her momentum.

As long as she continued moving up, she couldn't fall back.

"You could have stayed at NASA," Rick offered.

She grinned. "And miss all the fun? That was six years of sitting backseat to other peoples' bad ideas. At least here I have some input. Oh!" Kate said, snapping her fingers. "That reminds me." She typed on her keyboard and studied a graph on her workstation screen. "Huh. That's odd."

She stood up and looked around the room. All three rows of workstations were now fully occupied by engineers from the departments required to send a crew into space. Her eyes scanned over the hunched backs of her hardworking team until she saw the particular bald pate she was after.

"Phil!" she barked.

The wiry Flight Operations tech jumped in his seat and looked around wildly, finally seeing Kate standing with her hands on her hips.

"Yeah?" he said hesitantly. He wiped sweaty palms on his faded blue collared shirt and adjusted his glasses. Stalwart clumps of black hair clung to the sides of his otherwise bald head.

"I'm three kilos heavy in the command module." She tapped her screen with a pen, but kept her eyes locked on Phil. "The crew didn't eat *that* much for breakfast."

"Uh..." he said. He wheeled his chair closer to his own monitor and typed rapidly at his keyboard. Then he looked up and blinked. "Looks like it's heavy, yes."

"That was me," Frank said, walking over to stand

next to Kate. "I needed to add a piece of heavy equipment from our Chinese friends at the last minute, and that required a bit of clever rearranging."

Kate stared at him in disbelief. "What equipment? We're not supposed to make those kinds of adjustments this close to launch."

"It had to be done per our arrangement with the Chinese, Kate," he said calmly. "I ran the numbers. Three kilos is well within our limits of tolerance. Besides, the crew will burn through that in food stuffs in a couple days. Phil!" he said loudly. "Back me up. Can we still get off the ground with an extra three kilos?"

"Oh, yeah. The Hydra cores shouldn't even feel it."

Kate's jaw tensed up. "Fuel consumption," she said. "Exit trajectory. Ignition pressure after they link with the crew module and the antimatter propulsion system. Did you run the numbers for all of those? Personally, I'd rather not deal in 'should' and 'maybe'."

"And rightly so," Frank said. "But we ran the tests this morning. The paperwork is on your desk. It's been there since before your late arrival. Trust me and over two decades of experience, Ms. Bishop. We'll be fine."

He walked away before she could respond. She dropped down into her seat, fuming.

Rick held out a tin of candy. "Jelly bean?"

"It infuriates me!" she said. "The way he was just so…so nonchalant about the whole thing!"

"Here, this one's rum punch," he said, offering her a red jelly bean.

She took it and popped it into her mouth, shaking her head as she chewed.

"Isn't that better?" Rick asked.

She burst out laughing despite herself, then sighed. A new clipboard holding a thick stack of papers was indeed on her desk, nearly hidden among the collected paraphernalia of her pre-launch preparations.

"You know, Rick," she said, "sometimes I think the place would fall apart if it weren't for the two of us."

"I'm sure of it," he agreed. "We're the only two sane ones here."

Kate looked up at the big red clock over the display wall. Thirty minutes to launch.

"Speaking of which, where's Noah?" she asked.

Rick looked around the room. "He isn't here yet?"

"I don't see him. You'd think the guy who dreamed up this wacky scenario would be here for the launch."

"Probably just now waking up," Rick said. "If I had that kind of money, I'd never get out of bed before noon ever again."

"He didn't get where he is today by sleeping in."

"Then who knows? Maybe in his office, or maybe he has a special room off-site where he's calling the shots. Or *maybe* he's stowed away in the rocket. The guy does enjoy pulling the occasional prank."

"I don't think anyone would laugh at that one," Kate said. She wheeled her chair up to her workstation and adjusted her headset microphone. "Alright, time to get serious. Ground Team, I want to hear from you first. How's it looking out there?"

Noah watched the preparations within Mission Control from his office on the top floor of the Diamond Aerospace building. The wall of monitors across the room from his desk showed him that, ten floors below, the final steps in the launch process were being checked and re-checked, then checked again.

Much like his New York penthouse, his office at Kennedy Space Center was a single room with a large, open floor plan. Subdued lighting gave the office more of a museum feel, with soft highlights throughout the room, unlike the uniform luminescence in Mission Control. Instead of the imposing bed of his Manhattan abode his office was dominated by an expansive redwood desk, behind which Noah sat, leaning back in his chair with his ankles crossed on the desktop. He watched the camera feeds of Mission Control with his fingers interlaced behind his head. On the surface, he remained calm and controlled. Inside, his heart beat rapidly. These were the last moments of uncertainty, where it remained to be seen whether his company would continue in prosperity or crumble into ruin.

He was alone, having sent the investors' proxies downstairs to one of the many empty media rooms – the rooms which, on a launch day of that magnitude, would normally have been packed to bursting with eager reporters clamoring for the best vantage point.

Noah stewed over the unused speech he had spent months honing toward divine clarity, lingering on the final lines: *This first mission must come to represent the ideals that we, as humans, strive daily to uphold here on Earth: Bravery. Loyalty. Trust. Hope. We will carry these hallmarks of our species into the solar system and beyond.*

He sighed. It would have been perfect.

Frank had convinced Noah to wait until the Thermal Antimatter Propulsion System had been fired successfully at least once aboard a manned vessel before shouting their success to the press. Besides, Frank added, it was better to keep their competition in the dark until the last possible moment, considering what they'd discovered in orbit around Titan. Until then, let everyone think it was just another unmanned test flight of the Orbital Launch System. Frank had proven to be very effective at getting local law enforcement to shut down the main roads leading to Kennedy – under the pretense of a Presidential visit, no less. Perhaps Frank had the sheriff on Diamond Aerospace's payroll, or maybe he knew a secret dirty enough to buy him a few big favors.

Noah had been unable to argue with Frank's logic to exclude the press, despite a small bit of his soul shriveling at the thought that the historic launch of *Explorer I* would not be televised in real-time. However, accidents did happen, and secrets leaked. It was best if the company could control the way it revealed those secrets to the world.

Some of his competitors were unfortunately keenly aware of the concept. MarsCorp lost a rocket early last year to a seemingly irreparable booster ignition problem – the very rocket that was supposed to have beaten *Explorer I* to Titan. The negative press surrounding that disaster was monstrous, and had only just begun to fizzle by the time Diamond Aerospace secretly rolled out the gargantuan Neptune III rocket that was planning to follow the exact same trajectory and timeline as MarsCorp's doomed craft.

And so Noah had agreed to prolonged secrecy. It hadn't been easy keeping the launch quiet. There were a lot of rejected applicants who knew about the Neptune III rocket sitting on Kennedy's launch pad. Naturally, the applicants had all signed rigorous non-disclosure agreements – yet there was never any accounting for the tenacity of a particularly pugnacious reporter. Ultimately, there was no way to guarantee utter secrecy, so cover stories were kept readily available. Even without security leaks, people tended to notice large rockets screaming through the atmosphere.

If all went according to plan, the crew would learn of their additional mission mandate around the same time Noah announced the success of the thermal antimatter engine to the press. Frank was certain that Riley and his team represented the best chance the company had of completing its mission, and Noah regretted withholding the true specifics from them for so long. Yet he couldn't risk a leak, not when he was so close to reaching his goal. Besides, they had been well-trained, with an emphasis favoring adaptation over rote protocol. They would hopefully take the news in stride, and focus more on their original goal than on the fact they weren't told the whole story from the beginning.

Noah was confident that the unmanned test flight cover story would hold long enough for him to be able to prove to the world that he wasn't just another rich kid trying to squeeze his way deeper into the space industry simply because he could afford the most expensive toys. He had bigger plans. His toys just happened to be the most well-designed and safest on the market. Beyond that, he was genuinely interested in space – had been since a very early age. He wasn't just fascinated with it from a monetary standpoint, as were his contemporaries, according to their own shameless admissions.

Noah viewed his automated mining outposts on the moon and on Mars as stepping stones to reaching farther into space than had ever been thought possible in his lifetime. Before he died, he wanted to send a mission to the very edge of the solar system, and perhaps even beyond. When the Titan mission succeeded, he would be so far ahead of his competitors that it would take ten generations to catch up.

MarsCorp had wanted Titan – had wanted it almost as badly as Diamond Aerospace. Yet fate gloriously intervened, and it would be Noah's crew who got there first.

He picked up an eight-by-ten inch black and white photograph from his desk. It was the only one of its kind. Noah had ordered the negative burned. He also had everyone who saw it fill out such draconian nondisclosure agreements that they were convinced they would be shipped off-planet on the next satellite delivery rocket if they ever spoke a word about the photo to anyone.

It was a blurry picture, filled from edge to edge by a murky fog. If it were a color picture, the fog would be a smoggy sort of yellow – the atmosphere of Titan. However, it wasn't the weather on Titan that captured Noah's interest when one of his imaging techs first brought him the photograph.

He was more interested in the mysterious object orbiting the moon – the object neither he nor any supposed expert on Earth had been able to identify.

"Helmets on," said Commander Riley.

Jeff unhooked the communications feed from the back of his Snoopy hood. The Constellation Suit gloves weren't as thick as ski gloves, but they were close, having been designed with minimal padding for the manipulation of controls during takeoff and landing while still preserving pressure integrity outside the ship. Jeff put on his polycarbonate helmet and, with minimal fumbling, attached the feed to the back. Then he rotated a metal locking ring where the helmet met the neck of the suit, forming a seal. Next, he unhooked a thin hose from the side of his chair. He attached the locking nozzle at the end to the small, faucet-like air feed input on the front of his suit. There was a slight hiss of cool air, and Jeff shivered. The inner faceplate of his helmet fogged quickly, then cleared. He was now breathing the ship's atmosphere.

Jeff turned in his chair to face Gabriel, who had just finished sealing his helmet.

"Want to check me?" he asked.

"Sure thing."

Gabriel reached out for Jeff's neck, grunting with the effort it took to move more than a few inches while strapped into the chair wearing a thick Constellation Suit. He checked the seal of the locking ring and gave a thumb's up.

Jeff checked Gabriel's seal, while Riley and Ming did the same in the pilots' seats above.

"All good?" Riley asked.

"Seals verified," Jeff answered.

"Excellent. Mission Control, this is Explorer One reporting that we are go for launch. Repeat, we are go for launch."

"Copy that, Explorer," Kate said over the headsets. *"We're wrapping up the final tests, and we'll be lighting the fuse shortly."*

Jeff grinned at hearing her voice. It was bittersweet knowledge that he would still get to hear her on his journey into space. On the one hand, it was better than not being able to speak with her at all. On the other, it was a constant reminder of how much farther away she would be with each passing second.

Still, he considered himself lucky that the new thermal antimatter engine would make the trip to Titan in a fraction of the time it would using traditional propulsion methods. Instead of the three-year journey made by *Voyager 1* in the late 1970s, *Explorer* would tackle the same distance in just under five months.

"Jeff," said Kate, *"we're reading an elevated heart-rate. Everything okay?"*

"Just couldn't help remembering how I spent my last night on Earth. I don't think my heart has slowed down since I left the base yesterday."

There was a conspicuous pause. *"Well,"* she said, *"I hope you didn't go too big. We need everyone on top of their game today."*

"No worries here, Ms. Bishop."

Keep it formal and discrete, Jeff thought as he grinned. *Just like we discussed.*

Of course, that didn't mean he couldn't slip one past the goalie every once in a while.

Gabriel stared at him suspiciously. Jeff winked.

"Got your speech ready?" Ming asked Riley.

He grunted. "I was saving it for when we slid into orbit around Titan. The launch seems routine by comparison."

"It's the first manned flight using a brand-new propulsion system," said Gabriel. "One that will eventually carry humanity farther than we ever dreamed. We have to say *some*thing."

"Sounds like you might have some ideas," Jeff said.

Gabriel shrugged. "Maybe one or two."

"That was a good enough speech for me," Kate said over the headsets. *"Booster ignition in T-minus one minute. We have initiated final launch check."*

"Copy that," said Riley.

Jeff shifted in his chair, settling deeper into the fabric. He checked his restraints, making sure they were as tight as possible. The next part was going to hurt.

Kate rattled off her verbal checks of the various departments within Mission Control, waiting for a *go* or *no-go* signal from each. Jeff had been surprised when he realized how few people Diamond Aerospace employed in Mission Control. If it had been a NASA operation, he would have expected to see a large perimeter crowd of ground techs, engineers, and representatives from all branches of the astro-sciences on the operations floor during launch.

"All stations are go," said Kate. *"T-minus thirty seconds. Hope you all are strapped in."*

Jeff closed his eyes and breathed out evenly, mentally counting along with Kate's steady voice.

"Three. Two. One. Ignition."

The rocket's four Hydra nine-engine cores ignited with a liquid rush and a deep, sonorous *booooommmmm*, shaking the command module.

Jeff's vision vibrated. Above him, Riley's helmet rattled against the top of his seat. Ming shook in the co-pilot's chair, calm as ever.

The pressure started in Jeff's chest, sitting on him like a sumo wrestler as the Neptune III rocket began its ascent.

"We have lift off!" Kate shouted over the headsets. In the background, the other techs in Mission Control whooped and hollered.

The sumo wrestler on Jeff's chest got heavier. Now the wrestler laid flat, smothering his entire body from toes to scalp, and pushed down hard. Jeff groaned and tried to lift his head from his seat-back, just to see if he could do it. He didn't move an inch.

Inside the command module, he and the others were blind to the outside world. He tried to imagine the launch as if he were standing in Mission Control, with Kate.

He pictured the engines roaring furiously, belching flame and exhaust as the launch scaffolding broke away and the rocket climbed higher. A billowing mountain of smoke rose from the ground in the rocket's wake, still glowing orange as it expanded to swallow the entire platform.

"Prepare for Stage One separation," Kate said.

It's too early, thought Jeff. Had they really been in the air for a minute? They would soon be in and out of the stratosphere. It had seemed like mere seconds.

"Stage One separation initiated."

Ponk-Ponk!

The two solid-fuel boosters which had clung to the main rocket like remora broke free and tumbled down toward Earth.

"Hydra array down to thirty percent," Ming said. The sealed Mark IV helmets muffled most of the engine roar. "Twenty."

The nine powerful engines carried the Neptune III rocket higher into the atmosphere. Jeff felt the vibration in his bones.

"Prepare for Stage Two separation," Kate said. Then, a moment later: *"Stage Two separation initiated."*

The roaring engines went suddenly silent and the vibrations calmed to a gentle shake. The rocket was merely a giant dart being propelled out of the atmosphere under its own momentum.

The liquid oxygen booster that constituted the back half of Neptune III ejected backward with a boom of cannon-fire, slamming Jeff upward against his restraints. A split-second later, the secondary engine array ignited, crushing him back into his seat and pinning him there.

Now it was a whole team of sumo wrestlers sitting on top of him, making it damn near impossible to breathe.

In reality, the sensation of being crushed should have lasted less than a minute. To Jeff, it felt like an hour. He shut his eyes against the pressure, grimacing and forcing himself not to scream. He imagined his windpipe flattening and his lungs deflating in a nanosecond.

The techs on the ground told him it would be bad. He had sat in the centrifuge accelerator during training and endured extremely high g-forces for minutes on end to give him a glimpse of what was in store.

This was worse.

"All systems are normal," Kate said. *"Prepare for Stage Three separation."*

The rocket had punched into the thermosphere – the second-to-last atmospheric layer surrounding Earth. The only remaining barrier to cross was the thin exosphere, four hundred miles higher.

"Stage Three separation initiated."

There was a loud *BOOM* as the secondary engine array separated. Four rapid-fire metallic *CLANGS* echoed inside the command module as the side panels of the rocket popped off and tumbled down toward Earth, revealing the orbital engines of *Explorer I*.

The javelin-tipped tower jet shielding the nose of

the rocket popped away like a champagne cork, and the four astronauts could finally see through the narrow strip of a window in front of the pilots' chairs. They all took a moment to peer through the fifty-centimeter-thick fused silica and borosilicate glass, into the featureless dark sky beyond.

Commander Riley reached for the control panel in front of him, his hand hovering over a row of three buttons.

"Explorer," Kate said. *"Prepare to fire retro boosters on my mark. Three. Two. One. Mark."*

Riley popped open the flip guards of all three buttons and pushed them in rapid succession. The small orbital thrusters on the back of the bell-shaped *Explorer I* ignited, giving the craft a final push.

"Well done, all of you," Kate said, the relief in her voice obvious.

The shapeless darkness outside clarified itself into a starry landscape which, on Earth, was called the night sky.

For the astronauts aboard *Explorer I,* it was their road to Titan.

Kate stood at her desk, hands flat on either side of her keyboard, staring up at the display wall.

Everything looked normal. The launch had been executed flawlessly. Commander Riley and his crew were set to dock with the International Space Station, where they would link up with the Thermal Antimatter Propulsion System that would get them the rest of the way to Titan.

So why did she feel the queasiness of uncertainty in her gut? Why did her instincts tell her something was wrong?

"Look who decided to show up after all," Rick said, nodding toward the back of the room. He sat in his chair, rotating slowly side to side and squeezing a small rubber stress ball.

Kate turned around and looked up at the viewing platform. Noah Bell stood in the conference room beyond, wearing his trademark gray tailored suit with scarlet pocket handkerchief, talking to Frank. Noah was clearly excited. He often used enthusiastic gestures when he spoke, and now he was moving his hands so quickly they were almost a blur. Frank nodded patiently, his hands in his pockets, waiting for his boss to take a breath.

He finally did, and Frank said something that gave Noah pause. Then Noah put one hand on Frank's shoulder and pointed at the display wall with the other. He smiled.

"Guess he's happy with how things are going," Rick said.

"So far," added Kate. She turned back to the display wall and checked the myriad of data flowing across the different sections. "Oxygen levels holding?" she asked.

"Of course," Rick said. "We checked that system more than any other."

The air cycling system had given them their biggest headache since day one. Ever since Frank and his team of designers laid out the initial plans for *Explorer I* and began working with the other teams to make sure it was feasible, the air systems had presented a problem. There was nothing to worry about while the crew was still in lower atmosphere, or even while they were docked with the ISS.

The initial problems arose when they were trying to run the fuel lines for the antimatter engine too close to the oxygen compressor. During the construction phase of *Explorer I*, there was an obvious location for the compressor, and, independently, an efficient path to run the fuel lines with minimal directional interruptions – in other words, they wanted a straight line. Directional interruptions were opportunities for integrity failure, so these were always minimized. Yet the logical positioning of the oxygen compressor was in a perfect little hollow right next to a long run of fuel lines in the wall of the crew module.

Instead of breaking up the lines, the design team moved the compressor to the other side of the module, forcing the use of a longer oxygen line to the pump, which feeds oxygen into the cabin. The line cooled too much before oxygen reached the pump, causing it to freeze, so the team installed a smaller secondary pump halfway down the line to combat the problem.

The system was stable, even more so than before, because the secondary pump took a load off the main compressor, noticeably lowering the cumulative power consumption.

The idea of an air systems failure haunted Kate's dreams, no matter how many times she had her team check the equipment.

"Uh, Kate…" Rick said. He spun around in his chair, facing away from her.

"Ms. Bishop!" said a friendly voice. She turned as Noah Bell approached her desk, his hand outstretched. "Hell of a job, getting that beast off the ground. Hell of a job."

She shook his hand, smiling because he was smiling.

"We're just getting started, Mr. Bell."

"How're we looking up there?" he asked.

"We're square," she answered. "Everything's in the green."

"Perfect," he said, looking up at the display wall with a smile. "Absolutely perfect. Did you ever think we'd get this far?"

"Many others have," Kate said.

Noah's smile widened. "Ah, so you're a pragmatist."

"Someone has to be," she joked.

"Well, between you and Frank, I think we have that covered. The rest of us can dream freely."

Commander Riley's voice broke in over the room speakers.

"Mission Control, this is Explorer One. We are settled in and headed for our rendezvous with the International Space Station, over."

Noah clapped his hands and rubbed them together.

"Ladies and gentlemen!" he shouted to the room. "Let's build a spaceship!"

Three hours later, *Explorer* traversed a prograde orbital path at an altitude of 249 miles, directly in-line with that of the ISS. The tapered nose of the bell-shaped command module led the rest of the craft, pulling behind it the cargo hold, operational systems, and orbital engines.

Jeff and the others would have floated out of their seats if they weren't strapped in. He let his arms drift up slowly, enjoying the weightless sensation.

He sat in awe, staring out the window at the blue curvature of the Earth. The surface of the planet rolled steadily beneath him, revealing the African continent, and a few seconds later, the dark blue waters of the Indian Ocean. A faint blue glow emanated from the surface, fading to black as the atmosphere thinned. For the most part, the weather was good, with hardly any cloud cover.

"How we doin'?" Riley asked. He and Ming were kept busy running post-launch checks and preparing the vessel for docking.

Jeff studied his own control panel – green across the board.

"Everything normal," he said.

"Echo that," added Gabriel.

"Good," Riley said. "You boys sit back and enjoy the ride."

A pinpoint of golden sunlight flashed in the distance above Earth – a reflected glint from the space station's photovoltaic arrays. The station rapidly grew in apparent size as *Explorer I* approached, resolving into a sprawling mechanical dragonfly stuck in the blackness of space.

"Fire stabilizing thrusters," Riley said.

Ming set a dial and pressed a sequence of buttons on her console. "Firing."

Three forward-facing thrusters in the nose popped on, and the craft slowed noticeably.

"We'll be in docking range in three minutes," Ming said.

She cut the thrusters, and *Explorer I* orbited the Earth in silence at 17,200 miles per hour. Like the International Space Station, it would see a sunrise every ninety-two minutes if it held its current speed and trajectory.

"I've been trying to get onto that space station since I graduated from college," Gabriel said. "Every project I ever completed was supposed to get me one step closer to a contract. But I never received the nomination from my country. Six other Brazilians have been up here, but not me, and I am left wondering why I was chosen for this particular mission."

"Don't doubt yourself," Jeff said. "We're headed to Titan because we earned the right to be here. This mission didn't need the other six. It needed you."

Gabriel turned to face him. "I have to wipe a tear from my eye, but I can't touch my face." He tapped his helmet.

Jeff shook his head, smiling. "I only said it because I've felt the same way."

"Me, too," said Ming. "Yet here we are."

"Silva, if you're feeling like you don't deserve to be here," Riley said, "I'm sure there's a spare bunk on the station."

Gabriel leaned to the side to get a better look at the space station through the window, then he frowned and settled back into his seat.

"You know, up close it doesn't look like much," he said jokingly. "I can stick with you guys for a while."

Noah and Frank retreated to a darker corner of the operations floor to carry on a hushed conversation, mercifully leaving Kate to do her job without the immediate pressure of two bosses standing right behind her.

She tapped a camera feed on her small transparent monitor and flicked it upward to send it to the display wall. It showed an empty corridor inside the International Space Station. Above it, a separate camera feed looked past the nose of *Explorer I* as it approached the ISS.

Kate was consistently impressed that anyone who spent more than a day in the station didn't go crazy from the clutter. Wires and pipes ran into and out of the walls, onto which had been secured objects ranging from camera lenses to infrared thermometers. The combined effect of such organized clutter was that one felt like they were floating inside a giant computer, where the circuitry crowded every available surface.

Cosmonaut Alexei Orlov floated into view of the camera feed inside the station. He wore a white polo tucked into gray sweatpants and white running shoes. In the wall behind him was a small porthole window showing only the darkness of space.

"Good morning, Kennedy," he said with a thick Russian accent.

He crossed his arms, casually drifting in the middle of the corridor. He was in Nauka laboratory, the Russian segment of the station, and all the labels and instructions plastering every piece of equipment were in his own language.

"It'll be midnight here soon, Alexei," Kate said.

He grinned and ran a hand over the dark stubble on his shaved head, then he yawned.

"Of course," he said. *"We just had another sunrise. Very hard to keep track, you know?"*

"I hope someone told you to expect visitors."

"Visitors?" he asked. *"Up here? But is so boring! Of course they told me. I wear my best pair of sweatpants."*

He pushed away from a wall with a gentle tap of his toes and drifted to a monitoring station secured to a pipe.

"Ah, yes," he said. *"They are soon here."*

Kate scratched her scalp and adjusted her headset microphone. "Is the engine prepped for their arrival? We're trying to get the crew members in and out quickly so they're less of a burden on your resources."

"Yes, yes, don't worry. Everything is ready. I give them a few hours of air, no problem. But I am also happy to move giant engine bomb quickly away from my nice space station."

Kate smiled. "Thanks, Alexei."

"Okay bye-bye," he said, wiggling his fingers at her.

He tapped a button on his monitoring station and the feed switched over to an exterior view of one of the station's photovoltaic arrays.

Kate yawned and rubbed her eyes.

Rick tapped his desk with the eraser end of his pencil. "Do we talk to Alexei instead of the Americans because Russia's still upset they didn't get a spot on Explorer?" he asked.

"They lost a huge bid to the Chinese," Kate said. "Of course it's still a sore spot. Making Alexei our representative on the ISS is a minor concession thought up by someone in Public Relations."

"You mean, just in case we need to ask Russia for any more favors."

"Exactly. Alexei works well with everyone. It's the least we could do."

"Hmm," Rick said thoughtfully. "Ever wonder if his superiors told him not to tighten all the bolts on the antimatter rocket?"

Kate put her hands on her hips and stared at him. "Does your mind always leap to conspiracy?"

"Whenever I smell one, you bet it does."

"Honestly...yes, the thought had occurred to me, but not seriously. Alexei hasn't had direct access to the crew module or to the antimatter engine. The only way to get past the American segment of the ISS to the crew module is to spacewalk from the Russian side, and someone would have noticed a cosmonaut on an unscheduled walk. And besides, you of all people should know what the experts say about conspiracies."

"The chance of success drops as the number of conspirators rises. But still," Rick insisted, "it would just take a single pissed-off cosmonaut with a wrench to ruin everything. That's all I'm saying."

"Well, say it elsewhere. Let's keep things positive, shall we?"

"Yes ma'am."

"Good." She turned to face the display wall. "Now let's get them docked so I can go home and try to sleep."

Jeff leaned forward eagerly in his seat to get a better look at the space station through the narrow window as *Explorer I* approached.

Eight rotatable, rectangular blades stuck out from the 106-meter-long truss, four on each side, covering a total span of 73 meters from top to bottom. The elongated truss was an industrial-looking amalgam of external robotic equipment, cylindrical labs, and critical station components.

The delicate station spun slowly on its primary axis, sunlight glinting off the eight blades of its solar array.

"Thing's the size of a football field," Jeff said, shaking his head in disbelief. "You don't realize how big it is until you get closer. Incredible."

As the space station rotated, it revealed the entirety of what would become *Explorer I*'s crew module and the attached Thermal Antimatter Propulsion System.

"It's longer than the station!" Gabriel said in awe.

"You didn't read the specifications docket before

we left?" Ming asked as she adjusted her controls.

"Of course I did, it's just...it's hard to imagine until you see it up close, like Jeff said."

"There's a better view," Riley said, smiling.

The station rotated, and sunlight hit the docked engine full-on, illuminating the 120-meter-long cylindrical caboose of *Explorer I*.

"Now *that's* sexy," Gabriel said.

"Looks like a donut on a stick," Ming countered.

The 'donut' housed an internal centrifuge that caused the first third of the craft to bulge wider than the main cylinder, like a snake that swallowed a soda can. The crew module and science lab were inside the centrifuge. It would spin slowly as the crew headed for Titan, offering them a percentage of Earth's gravity.

The rear two-thirds of the craft extended back from the center of the centrifuge like a long tube, terminating at a gold, cone-shaped engine wash shield. Inside the long tube section were the inner workings of the antimatter drive and a majority of the ship's systems.

"Lieutenant," said Riley, "take us in."

"Copy that, Commander."

Ming's hands hovered patiently over the controls. The space station grew to fill the command module window.

She tapped a few buttons, and *Explorer I* gently spun on its axis, syncing with the rotation of the space station. There was no sensation of physical movement, only visual confirmation via the narrow command module window that they had changed positions. Jeff felt as if he were watching a television show.

"Explorer One to ISS," Riley said into his headset microphone. "Requesting permission to dock. How's it going in there, Alexei?"

"Your engine is waiting for you, Commander," Alexei replied. *"Are you hungry?"*

"Famished."

"Good! I hear Dolan has pizza." He let out a deep belly laugh.

Jeff said, "That was supposed to be a secret."

"I have many ears, Jeffrey," said Alexei. *"No one brings pepperoni without my knowledge."*

"Two-second retro booster fire," Ming said, "in three, two, one."

The space station slipped out of sight in the window, and what was considered the front of the crew module segment of *Explorer I* slid into view. Ming positioned the command module a few meters from the front of the longer section of the craft, then slowly backed up to it.

"Looking good, Explorer," Frank said over the headset.

Jeff didn't like hearing the director's voice nearly as much as Kate's. It always sounded like he was waiting for something to go wrong. *Edgy,* Jeff thought. *That's the right word for it.*

Riley watched a small monitor on his control panel. The video angle looked past the orbital engines on the back of the command module toward the docked crew module. Ming aligned the crafts perfectly, and the orbital engine at the back of the bell-shaped command module glided into the hollow sleeve at the front of the crew segment. With a soft bump, they came to a stop.

Riley turned three key buttons on his control panel. A red light blinked off. A second later, a green light next to it illuminated.

"Seal is good," he said. "Mission Control, we have successfully linked with the crew module and TAP System."

"We read you loud and clear, Explorer," Frank said. *"Great work, all of you. Get some shuteye and we'll talk to you in a few hours."*

"Copy that, Canaveral. Explorer One, out." Riley unbuckled his safety harness and turned as he floated up from his seat. "Who's ready to get out of these suits?"

"Not me," Jeff said. "I like sitting in a soggy adult diaper."

"You'd think they would have a better system by now," Gabriel said.

"They ran a contest for it a while back," Ming said, "to see who could come up with something better."

"And?"

"The only thing they got was a more absorbent diaper."

"Genius," said Gabriel.

"Commander," Jeff said, "I don't really have to make pizza right now, do I?"

Riley sighed. "No, Dolan, you don't have to make pizza. We'll be fine with rehydrated beef cubes and chunky protein smoothies. Right, gang?"

"Oh, yeah," Gabriel said without enthusiasm. "My favorite."

"Good," said Jeff, ignoring the sarcasm. "You're

going to thank me later."

"Come on," said Riley. "Let's get inside. Four hours of sleep doesn't sound like a lot, but we need as much as we can get before our departure window closes in the morning."

Jeff unbuckled his harness and felt full-body weightlessness for the first time since he boarded the spacecraft. The desire to tuck his legs up to his chest and spin end over end was too much to resist.

"Just like the circus," Gabriel said as he floated up from his own chair. He tapped Jeff's boot to keep him spinning.

Riley shook his head as he grabbed a handhold on the side of a seat and pulled himself closer to the floor. Jeff's elbow bonked his helmet.

"Oops. Sorry Commander."

"Okay, okay," said Riley. "Let's hold off until the adults get through the hatch."

Jeff grabbed the top of his seat and stopped his spin. He and Gabriel floated peacefully while Riley unlocked the floor hatch and swung the lid inward.

"Ladies first," said Riley, gesturing into the opening.

"Thanks," Ming said. She floated past Jeff and went headfirst into the passage that ran next to the orbital engines, connecting the command and crew modules.

Riley followed after her. A moment later, his helmeted head reappeared.

"Don't spin too long, boys. It *is* possible to get dizzy in space, and you don't want to get sick in those suits. Not after you did so well on the first leg of the trip."

He disappeared into the passage. Gabriel grinned at Jeff.

"Two snack rations for the longest spin," he said, tucking his knees to his chest.

"You're on."

The headlights of Kate's old Mustang passed over the front of her apartment building as she pulled into her parking space. Her ground-floor unit was attached to a three-story vacation rental, which made for loud summers and a messy front lawn. If she wasn't a workaholic and didn't spend most of her time at work, she would have looked elsewhere.

She cut the engine, and suddenly all her energy flooded out. It had taken zealous focus to stay awake on the twenty-minute drive to her apartment.

Kate sensed her bed inside, waiting for her. She picked up her purse and grumbled, realizing most of its contents were still spilled across the passenger's seat from when she had hunted for her security badge that morning.

A project for the morning, she decided. She scooped up her phone and got out of the car.

There was no gentle breeze that night, only a stagnant stickiness that glued her blouse to her skin as she climbed the steps of her small porch. Calling the night air of Florida cool in the dead of summer was like saying being a mile away from the sun wasn't as hot as touching its surface.

Her car's headlights illuminated her hibiscus bushes and red front door. She fumbled with her keys and locked the car with the fob. The headlights cut out, and something moved on her porch.

She gasped and dropped her phone in surprise as a dark figure stood up against the porch railing, only a few feet away.

Kate groped blindly for her purse, realizing too late she had left it – and the can of mace she carried – uselessly on the passenger's seat. Her keys rattled as her shaking hands struggled to find the one that opened her front door.

"Please, Ms. Bishop!" said the figure urgently. "I'm not here to hurt you."

Her hands shook uncontrollably and she dropped her keys. The figure stepped toward her and she stepped back instinctively.

"My name is Michael Cochran."

Kate began to creep sideways, planning to leap over the bushes and make a run for it. The man took another step toward her. Light from a street lamp hit his tired, frightened face. He was probably in his early thirties, with thinning hair and a shadow of beard. An oversized coat swallowed his thin frame. He gripped the coat shut with sinewy hands.

"Please listen to me!" he said. "It's about Noah Bell's antimatter drive."

She stopped moving. Unsteadily, she asked, "What do – what do you know about that?"

"Everything!" he said. "I helped design it at the Diamond Aerospace facility in Baikonur. I worked there for three years. The schematics in your current documentation have been falsified."

Her eyes narrowed suspiciously. "There's no D.A. facility anywhere *near* Russia."

"Not anymore."

A car zipped by on the street, and Michael crouched down with a frightened gasp, watching it until it disappeared around a bend.

Realization dawned on Kate, and she said, "That was you in the car this morning! You tried to run me off the road!"

"Please," he said. "If we could go inside, I'll explain everything."

Kate slowly bent down, keeping her eyes on him the whole time, and picked up her keys and her phone.

"We can talk out here," she said cautiously. "But I want to write this down. I'll just go inside and grab a pen." She was thinking about the baseball bat she kept just inside the door. Had she moved it last time she cleaned the place? Did she remember to put it back?

Kate paused when a black SUV with tinted windows rolled slowly into view on the far side of the street, past her front lawn, then stopped. Its headlights were off and it had no license plate. The vehicle just sat there, its driver and anyone else inside obscured from view. It seemed to be waiting.

Cochran turned around when he heard the engine

noise. He stiffened, as if he recognized the SUV.

Kate watched him closely as she unlocked her front door and went inside. A moment later, she burst back onto the porch with her baseball bat raised in one hand and her phone in the other, ready to dial the police.

Cochran was gone, along with the SUV. She had been so wound up she didn't hear it drive away.

Kate breathed out a sigh of relief. She slumped against the wall next to her front door, scanning the dark corners of her yard.

There had been other unwanted visitors on her porch in the past. They were almost always protestors of some kind, railing against the continuous march of technology and the evils it wrought upon the world. Many of them hated the fact that billionaire Noah Bell – along with his other rich, space-crazed peers – was so intent on dumping pointless money into missions to Mars and Titan instead of pouring it all back into what they called the broken society of Earth.

A twig snapped in the yard and Kate jumped in place. Her grip tightened on the bat.

An armadillo waddled out from under a bush, sniffing at the ground. Kate lowered the bat and forced her tense muscles to relax.

"Good luck sleeping now," she muttered.

She called the police and told them about her unwanted visitor.

"Would you like an officer to come by and take a statement?" asked the operator.

"I don't think so. I'll be fast asleep by then."

"We'll at least send a patrol car down to watch your

apartment, Ms. Bishop, just in case."

She hung up and looked around the yard one last time. The armadillo had made a hole and stuck its snout in up to its beady little eyes, rooting for grubs. The damn things were always digging ragged holes in her St. Augustine grass.

Kate got the mace out of her car, locked herself inside her apartment, and pushed an oversized lounge chair in front of the door for peace of mind. Not long after, her bed welcomed her as if it was made from the cloudy fabric of heaven itself, and she forgot all about Michael Cochran as she drifted into a dreamless sleep.

_DAY 2

Jeff awoke wrapped up in his sleeping bag, pinned to the curved wall of the crew module. There were four cramped bunks the crew would use during the journey, but mission regulations only specified they had to be used while the ship was in motion. He and the others wanted to delay being stuck inside the coffin-like bunks as long as possible. For their brief visit to the space station, they opted to sleep farther back in the crew module, where the floor plan was a little more open.

He had traded his orange Mark IV suit for a pair of gray sweatpants and a thin t-shirt before his late dinner last night, and he wasn't overly enthusiastic about trading back. Yet he and the other crew members would soon be on the longest leg of their journey, during which he could stay in his boxer shorts all day if he wanted – except for the video chats with Mission Control, of course. Jeff thought that perhaps seeing an astronaut working in his underwear wasn't much of a confidence-booster for the public.

Gabriel slept nearby, his bag pulled up to his armpits and his arms floating out in front of him. He wore a long-sleeve hoodie, which bore an official mission patch on the left breast. It depicted a cartoonish, thickly-outlined *Explorer I* approaching Titan over a starry background, with the simple, italicized text of the Diamond Aerospace logo beneath it. Jeff had one just like it tucked away in his clothes bag.

The crew module was kept at an even sixty-four degrees Fahrenheit, mostly because that was the balance that had been struck between the cold vacuum of space and the heat generated from the engines and machinery of *Explorer I*. The heat was filtered and recirculated through the walls of the crew module, but there was no dedicated heating unit. If the recirculating motors failed, the crew would have about two hours before the inside of the ship became a freezer.

It was, Jeff thought, one example among many of how thin the dividing line was between staying alive and utter catastrophe.

He unzipped his sleeping bag and floated out of it, then rolled it up and stowed it in the mesh pouch bolted to the wall nearby. Riley's and Ming's sleeping bags were already rolled up and tucked away.

Already Jeff could feel more blood in his head than usual, especially his face. There was no real up or down in zero gravity. No matter how he had tried to angle his body before sacking out a few hours ago, the even distribution of blood throughout his body resulted in a puffy feeling in his face and a slight but constant pressure behind his eyes.

Enjoying the weightlessness, he allowed himself to drift slowly away from the wall. The crew had experienced a few minutes of simulated zero gravity during their training. A Boeing 747 following a parabolic flight path over the Arizona desert was the closest they could get while still on Earth, but the experience paled in comparison to absolute weightlessness. It was like being underwater without having to worry about the nagging requirement for air.

The slightest touch against any surface altered his spin. Jeff spent a few happy minutes floating in the crew module, occasionally tapping a wall or monitor to change his spin direction while he inspected what was to be his home for the next year.

The interior of the crew module was a 30-meter-long centrifuge capable of creating just under three-quarters of Earth's gravity for the voyage to Titan, minimizing bone loss and keeping the crew that much more sane. The centrifuge would begin to spin after the antimatter engine had fired and the ship had passed the moon. Until then, the crew would spend most of their operational time in the command module at the nose of the vessel, sending out status reports and double-checking each other's calculations for errors.

A large central pillar ran through the centrifuge along the ship's primary axis, four meters from the floor. The design team had originally favored a more open floor plan, without the pillar, to ease the inevitable feeling of claustrophobia. It was to be the longest manned space mission, and the company psychologists didn't want it to be compromised because there wasn't enough elbow room. The designers tried to work without it. They thought it would be neat if an astronaut could push off the floor with enough force to float to the opposite side of the centrifuge, spinning in midair to land on their feet. It turned out that someone floating from three-quarters Earth's gravity immediately into a pocket of zero-g almost always lost their lunch, and they could never fully control their direction once they hit that central dead zone. Sometimes they got stuck in mid-air and had to be pulled back down to the floor.

So they went with the pillar design.

The floor plan had been kept mostly open as a result, with only low barriers constructed off the centrifuge wall to approximate sections. The sections of the crew module, moving from forward to aft, were divided into the crew quarters (including a shower and private hygiene compartment), kitchen and dining area, communications systems access and vehicle monitoring stations, the science lab, and space suit storage.

Every interior surface was contoured for maximum efficiency. It had been designed for habitation in space, not on Earth, which meant chairs bolted to the floor and extra straps for securing anything and everything that could float away if the centrifuge stopped spinning.

Now that the command and crew modules were linked, Riley and Ming would be spending most of their time at the front of the craft during the voyage, while Jeff and Gabriel worked in the centrifuge.

"What do you think?" Gabriel asked sleepily. He unzipped his sleeping bag and yawned. "Getting cabin fever yet?"

"Are you kidding me?" Jeff said. "I doubt I could ever get tired of this."

"I'll ask you again on the way home." He noticed that the other three sleeping bags were stowed. "Early risers, I see. Guess we better go check in. We're lighting an awfully big candle today."

"Right."

They pushed off the floor and grabbed the ladder that ran along the central pillar. Jeff followed Gabriel toward the command module, barely needing to touch the rungs to keep his body moving forward.

The crew module tapered down like a cone to an open, meter-wide hatch. Just beyond, in the passageway to the command module, was a docking hatch at a T-junction that led to the interior of the space station through *Explorer's* sphere-shaped airlock.

"They put us on Node 2," Gabriel said as he drifted into the open airlock. "Bet that made the photographers angry."

One of the last major components to be attached to the International Space Station was an observatory module named the Cupola. Its seven windows offered the crew unrivaled views of Earth – a perk that both resident and visiting astronauts declared, without exception, was the single greatest perk aboard.

Docking *Explorer I* at Node 2 effectively blocked half of that view.

Gabriel drifted into the next module, the eight-meter-long Destiny laboratory. The lab's walls met at ninety-degree angles as opposed to the contiguous cylindrical wall of *Explorer I's* crew module, forming an extruded square that ran from hatch to hatch.

Two female astronauts floated in the four-meter-diameter lab. One had a clipboard and scrolled through lines of code on a monitor screen, and the other spun lazily as she sipped from a sachet of apple juice. The ISS had no centrifuge to create a percentage of Earth's gravity; here, the inhabitants spent the entirety of their mission in zero-g.

Both women wore t-shirts under lightweight one-piece jumpers.

"Good morning, ladies," said Gabriel.

"Morning, fellas," said May Harris, the woman with the clipboard. A blue baseball cap with the letters ISS stitched on the front kept her springy dark brown hair under control.

The other woman, Elizabeth McCall, waved and smiled while chewing on her straw. Her curly, fiery red hair floated around her head as if she were underwater.

"What's new?" Gabriel asked.

"Not much," Elizabeth replied with the thick twang of a Texas accent. "Earth's still spinning."

"Your boss called while you were asleep," May said.

"Riley?" Jeff asked.

"No, someone from your Mission Control. Kate Somebody. She wanted to make sure everyone was doing okay. I passed it on to Riley."

"Thanks."

May smiled knowingly and glanced at Jeff. "She put a special emphasis on *you*, space cowboy."

"Me? Huh. Interesting."

"Yeah, right," Gabriel said. "You're good at playing dumb, but not *that* good."

"I'll take that as a compliment."

Elizabeth squeezed her sachet and a stream of apple juice flowed out of the straw. It formed a wavering globe the size of a large marble. Gabriel pushed gently off the wall, soaring across the lab and swallowing up the floating liquid before Elizabeth could get to it.

"Hey!" she said, laughing.

Gabriel bonked into the far wall and coughed, choking on the liquid.

"That's what you get."

"Riley and Ming around here somewhere?" Jeff asked.

"They're with Alexei in Nauka lab," said May.

"Right. I'll go see how we're doing."

Jeff pulled himself past the others and floated to the far hatch.

"I'm going to hang around here a bit," Gabriel said. "See if I can be of any assistance."

"Oh, my *hero*," May said, rolling her eyes.

Jeff smiled as he drifted into the next module. "Just give a shout if he starts any trouble," he called back.

He made a mental map as he went along. Like the others in his crew, Jeff had studied the layout of the station before leaving Earth. Staring at a schematic on paper didn't give him the proper sense of scale that came with being inside the real thing.

Moving from the docked *Explorer I* toward the truss, which was the longest section of the space station, he had passed through two modules: Destiny lab and Unity. Continuing straight from Unity module would take him past the truss and into the Functional Cargo Block. Beyond that was Freedom module, and finally Nauka, the Russian lab.

He decided to take a quick detour on the way to Nauka. Instead of continuing straight ahead when he left Destiny lab and entered Unity module, he hung a right toward Node 3 – Tranquility.

Including the crew from *Explorer I*, there were only seven souls aboard the space station. Jeff had expected the station to be as crowded as the command module of

Explorer I, even considering its larger size. He saw no one as he drifted slowly through the various compartments.

Alexei Orlov had just crossed the halfway point of his year-long habitation, and wouldn't be joined by a fellow cosmonaut for another three months. Elizabeth and May were the only two U.S. astronauts on the station. The next NASA launch would bring a third, along with a replacement for Elizabeth.

Accompanying the two U.S. astronauts on the same launch would be two from Japan. The country was eager to make use of the Japanese lab, which had sat vacant for nearly a year after the quick collapse and slow restructuring of their space program.

Attached to one side of Tranquility module was the Cupola. Ming floated there, her head inside the multifaceted dome created by its seven large windows. Her neck-length black hair wavered around her head. She lifted a DSLR camera to her eye and snapped a picture of the luminous Earth below.

Jeff cleared his throat politely.

"Oh, hi Jeff," she said with a smile. "Want to have a look?"

She pushed to the side as he floated over.

"Taking some pictures for your daughter?" he asked.

"She doesn't believe me that the space station is so high up," Ming said. "She imagines it as a big airplane no higher than the clouds. She's too stubborn for a four-year-old. I thought this would be the best way to show her."

Jeff stuck his head up into the dome of the Cupola. Sure enough, more than half of the panoramic view of Earth was blocked by the nose-end of *Explorer I*.

"Hmm," said Jeff, looking through the windows. "Gabriel was right. That's a horrible place to park a spaceship."

"Still makes for a pretty good picture. Look," she said, pointing. "We're about to pass over Australia."

The largest of the seven windows was the one in Cupola's center, like a large eye observing everything beneath the station. Jeff watched the Earth spin below him, a glowing sphere etched with the patterns of oceans and continents. Australia appeared first as a beige line on the horizon, partially obscured by a great cloudy sheet of stratocumulus.

The tall peaks of the Flinders Ranges came into view to the south as the station flew over. The mountains gave way to the eastern continent – a vast landscape of reds and browns. A minute later, Australia was blocked behind *Explorer I* and Jeff was looking down on the deep waters of the Pacific Ocean.

"Almost makes you sad to leave, right?" Ming asked.

"Well," said Jeff, grinning. "*Almost.*"

They floated in silence, watching the Earth spin, until Ming said, "Something Gabriel mentioned on the way here got me thinking. According to him, he tried for years to get into space."

"Some people try their entire adult lives," Jeff said. "I have friends back home that apply to NASA's astronaut program every chance they get. They're rejected every time, and these are people whose experience puts mine to shame."

"Ever wonder about that?" she asked casually. "All four of us went through training with so many other qualified applicants. You and I weren't the only ones with engineering experience. Gabe wasn't the only agronomist."

"But we were the best. And I'm pretty sure you're here because you're an engineer *and* a pilot. Leaving you back home would have been like benching a star baseball player during the World Series."

"To be honest, I would rather have your job."

"Well, I'd like to be a pilot, so there you go."

She smiled. "Too much pressure."

"I don't think I've ever seen you stressed," Jeff said. "Not even during training."

"Training wasn't real," she said. "This is."

Jeff glanced at his watch. "We should check in with Riley," he said. "Departure window's closing in an hour."

"I'm going to take a few more pictures," said Ming. "Pick me up on your way back?"

"Sure thing," Jeff said as he pushed off toward the hatch. "Get some good ones."

"Ha! That's asking a lot."

The camera shutter clicked rapidly as Jeff left Tranquility module and made his way to the Russian lab.

Jeff coasted through the hatch into Nauka module. Alexei and Riley floated in the middle of the dimly-lit cylindrical compartment, engaged in conversation.

The machinery here was a little older than in the U.S. compartments closer to where *Explorer* had docked. Jeff remembered hearing that the Russian labs felt more lived-in than the rest of the station, mostly because they were the only country to have a continuous on-board presence. It wasn't unusual for a cosmonaut to be on the ISS for weeks at a time without company.

Alexei held a bottle of liquor and studied it with sleep-deprived eyes while he floated in front of Riley. The commander seemed wide awake, despite the puffy bags under his bloodshot eyes. The two of them noticed Jeff coming their way. Alexei greeted him with a grunt, and Riley nodded.

"Morning, fellas," Jeff said. He grabbed a handhold on the wall and floated next to the other two.

"Frank Johnson wanted me to bring that to you,"

Riley said to Alexei, gesturing toward the bottle. "He wants you to know he appreciates all of your help with the Explorer project."

Alexei frowned at the squarish bottle of dark brown liquid. "I thought Americans could not drink in space."

Riley smiled. "This is international territory," he said vaguely. "And besides, it's for you. My crew is bone-dry."

"Usually we only drink after surviving emergency, like a fire," said Alexei. "For celebration. Would take big fire to drink all this. Is not vodka, but should work okay."

Riley reached for the bottle. "Should I send it back?"

Alexei pulled the whiskey to his chest. "Don't be rude. I will redefine the word 'emergency'. Maybe later I lose my towel. That could be dangerous. Would definitely need to reward my bravery if I survive."

Alexei released the bottle and let it float beside him, spinning slowly. He turned to Jeff. "How do you like it so far?" he asked. "Sleep well in tin can?"

"Like a rock," Jeff said.

"A rock that could have slept for another twelve hours," Riley added.

"Sometimes first night is hard," said Alexei. "But maybe now I can't sleep on Earth because too much gravity. Now is natural for me."

"You're not going stir crazy?" Jeff asked.

Alexei tapped the bottle of whiskey, changing the direction of its slow spin. "Not for long," he said.

"How are the others?" Riley asked Jeff.

"Gabriel is flirting and Ming is taking pictures."

Riley nodded. "Well, as much as it pains me to tear them away, we need to start getting ready." He shook hands with Alexei. "I hate to sleep and run, Alex, but it's time. Guess we'll catch you on the way back. Thanks again for your help."

"My pleasure."

Jeff followed Riley as he drifted toward the hatch.

"Commander," Alexei said. Riley paused and looked back. "That is nice new engine on Explorer. Don't burn hole in space station when you leave."

Riley grinned. "You got it."

Kate nervously tapped her pen against her workstation as she studied the display wall in Mission Control. The rectangular section that displayed the crew members' vital signs showed that everything was normal. Heart rates steady, breathing steady. None of them gave the slightest biological indication of fear at being strapped to what was essentially an untested, theoretical energy cannon.

Rick slurped coffee at the workstation next to hers, and she cringed. Noises seemed louder to her, more invasive and distracting, ever since she arrived at work that morning.

"Get any sleep?" he asked.

"Some."

Kate remembered the strange visitor who had shown up on her porch when she got home the night before. Later that evening – or earlier that morning – the police assured her they canvased the area and didn't find anything. They didn't seem too concerned, but a squad car had remained parked on the street in front of her apartment until she pulled out of the driveway in the morning just the same.

She considered telling Rick about the visitor, but she didn't want to get his conspiracy gears turning so early in the day.

"I crashed in the equipment room," Rick said. "Just brought a duffel with my clothes."

"And deodorant?" Kate asked.

Rick sniffed his armpit. "Why?"

She smiled. "No reason."

Kate had skipped a shower that morning. Her hair remained in the same tight bun she had put it in yesterday. She assured herself she would get better sleep and a proper bath after *Explorer* was safely on its way to Titan.

As if on cue, the gruff voice of Commander Riley came in over her headset.

"Anybody awake down there?"

Kate pushed the VOX switch on her console and said, "Barely."

"Well, you might want to put on some coffee, because we're thinking about lighting this candle."

"Copy that. How's the rest of the crew?"

Ming and Gabriel chimed in and said their good mornings.

"You don't sound tired to me, Ms. Bishop," Jeff said.

"Why, thank you, Jeff."

"Any time."

Kate turned and looked back at Frank, who stood

up on the viewing platform with his arms crossed, chewing on a toothpick while he listened to the conversation through his own slim headset. He caught her gaze and nodded.

"What's the plan, Commander?" she asked, turning back to face her desk.

"Figured we'd fire it up at oh-nine-thirty. It's not the last minute of our departure window, but why wait? We're all strapped in up here. Dolan is running the last round of tests on the TAPS and Lieutenant Ming is quadruple-checking our heading."

"Don't want to miss Titan," Ming said.

"You certainly don't," Kate agreed. "Everything looks good on our end. I'm not getting any red flags from the department heads." She paused for a moment to allow anyone that was listening time to interject. "Okay, Explorer," she said finally, "you are go for launch at oh-nine-thirty."

"Copy that," Riley said. *"Ten minutes to launch."*

Kate leaned back in her chair, tapping her pen faster against her desk.

"Oh, hey," Rick said, wheeling his chair over. "What do you think about my new t-shirt? Had it printed up yesterday."

He stuck out his chest to show her the crude lettering which read, "It Don't Matter Unless It's Antimatter". Below the words was a picture of a cartoon rocket bearing the Diamond Aerospace logo blasting off from Earth. A cartoon cowboy with a big grin and missing teeth rode astride the rocket, waving his ten-gallon hat over his head.

"I hope you didn't pay too much for that," said Kate.

"Oh, come on! It's my good luck shirt for this mission. I designed it myself."

"I would never have guessed."

She winked to let him know she was just giving him a hard time.

"It's gonna be a classic someday," he mumbled.

Jeff typed at the small keyboard built into the control panel in the wall next to his seat. The process of simply tapping out a few words was frustratingly slow due to the added bulk of the Constellation Suit gloves. Even though the design team had trimmed the fabric where they could, his gloved fingers invariably hit more than one key with each attempt. Luckily, some genius had thought to make the backspace key larger than the rest. Jeff used it liberally as he called up every sensor that monitored the Thermal Antimatter Propulsion System. He was relieved to see the tidy line of green lights which meant that the ship probably wouldn't blow up during ignition.

"TAPS integrity confirmed, Commander," he said. "All sensor readings normal. We're looking good."

"Copy that," Riley said. "Keep a close eye on it when we push off. Silva, report."

"Atmosphere is stable," said Gabriel, tapping a screen in his control panel. "No change in oxygen levels since we started warming up the engine. There is no draw from the TAP System."

During early tests with the antimatter engine, when the engineers at Diamond Aerospace were still struggling to fit a round peg into a square hole, there had been several instances where oxygen levels inside a closed system near the fuel lines dropped inexplicably. It appeared as if the TAP System sucked the oxygen from neighboring spaces, and either burned it up or converted it into fuel. Heavier shielding around the fuel lines seemed to have solved the problem.

"Lieutenant, what's our status?" Riley asked.

"Systems up and humming, Commander," she replied. "We're ready for departure."

"Excellent." He toggled a switch on his console. "This is Explorer One calling International Space Station. Alexei, are you sober?"

"Of course! I am professional."

"Copy that. We're shipping out."

"Good luck, Commander."

"Lieutenant, if you wouldn't mind?" said Riley.

Ming tapped a sequence of commands on her control panel monitor, then turned a key switch. A hollow *clonk* echoed inside the command module as *Explorer I* separated from the hatch of the space station, drifting slowly away.

"Docking clamps open," she said. "Retracting."

Another turn of the key switch and there was a high-pitched, mechanical whine as the docking clamps retracted into the hull.

Gabriel sighed. "And what a bittersweet goodbye it is."

"I have a feeling we're going to be hearing about Gabe's undying love for those two women for the rest of the trip," Jeff said.

"Open your heart, my friend," said Gabriel. "You will find plenty of room for love."

Jeff laughed. "Did you steal that from a poem?"

"I plucked it from the very soul of the universe, as if pulling down a star from–"

"Okay, okay," Riley said, holding up a gloved hand. "Just go write a sonnet or something, Shakespeare. Lieutenant, please get us into position."

"Firing atmospheric jets now."

Ming deftly manipulated the controls in front of her. A series of quick hisses from small jets embedded in the hull pushed the *Explorer* farther away from the space station. She angled the nose of the craft away from Earth.

Jeff watched a small screen on his control panel, which showed the ISS drifting farther into the background until it was the size of a jellybean.

"We're at minimum safe distance for engine ignition," Ming said.

"Copy that," Riley said. "On my mark, Lieutenant."

They both reached for their controls and settled deeper into their seats. Gabriel checked to make sure his harness straps were as tight as he could make them.

Jeff thought about Kate. If he blew up when the engine ignited, he wanted her face to be the last thing he pictured. He admitted to himself that it was a grim way to think about things, but the cold hard reality was that every breath he drew inside *Explorer I* could be his last.

"Initialize antimatter system," Riley said.

Ming pushed a button. "Initialized."

"Activate fuel pump."

Another button. A mechanical hum grew louder from the back of the ship.

"Activated."

"Here we go," Riley said. "Engine ignition in three...two...one. Ignition."

He and Ming pressed buttons on their respective consoles at the same time.

Nothing happened.

"Lieutenant?"

"I don't know what happened, sir."

"*Nothing* happened," said Riley. "That's the problem."

"*Everything okay up there?*" Kate asked over their headsets.

"You sold us a lemon," Gabriel said.

"Hold the chatter," said Riley. "Lieutenant, I've reset the ignition sequence. Let's try it again."

"Copy, sir."

They went through the process again. Riley counted down, and they both triggered ignition.

Silence.

"Uh, Canaveral?" Riley said. "There might be a *slight* issue with the TAP System. We have ignition failure on the main engine. Lieutenant Ming and I have tried resetting the sequence and going again from scratch, but that was unsuccessful. Please advise."

"*Copy, Explorer,*" Kate said. "*We can verify ignition failure. Sit tight up there and we'll get back to you.*"

Kate peeled off her headset and threw it onto her desk.

"Someone *please* tell me what the hell is going on!" she shouted to the room.

Next to her, Rick mumbled to himself as he tapped and swiped furiously on his screen, paging through the ship's monitoring systems, looking for the problem. Every head in Mission Control was lowered as the technicians worked frantically.

Kate turned to find Frank, but he was gone.

Noah Bell stood a few feet behind her desk with his arms crossed, chewing his bottom lip as he stared up at the display wall.

"Are the astronauts okay?" he asked.

"They seem to be fine," Kate said. "For now. Can you think of anything that might have happened?"

He rubbed his forehead. "I need a workstation."

"Take mine," Kate said, stepping aside.

Noah sat down quickly and began typing. He accessed the real-time monitoring schematic for the thermal antimatter drive on the workstation screen and zoomed in on the ignition chamber. There were no alerts on any of the equipment.

"Looks good here," he muttered.

Someone from across the room shouted, "Kate, could be a leak in the secondary fuel line! Confirming now."

"Then why don't I hear a warning alarm?" she shouted back. Then, quietly, she added, "It would be a damn short trip if that was the case."

Noah swiped the workstation screen, panning over to the longest run of fuel lines at the bottom half of the craft.

The secondary fuel line pulsed with a red glow.

Kate's mouth went dry. She picked up her headset with shaking hands and slipped it on.

"Do – do they need to separate from the antimatter drive?" she asked, unable to keep the image of an exploding *Explorer I* from her mind.

"Mission Control, what's the story down there?" Riley asked over the headset. *"Are we about to be barbecued?"*

"S-stand by, Explorer," Kate said.

"Ah-ha!" Noah said, pounding the desk. "It's not a leak."

"Then what is it?"

"A simple sensor malfunction. You see here?" he jabbed a finger at a small string of yellow numbers tagged to the pulsing red fuel line on the screen. "That's the identification code for the fuel line sensor. The last two numbers should always be zero-one, which means it's communicating with the ship's computer."

"Those numbers are zero-zero," Kate said.

"Exactly. The main fuel line is reading just fine, but the sensors monitoring the *secondary* line aren't talking to the computer."

"So if it's a sensor issue, why can't they start the engine?"

"It's a failsafe protocol," Rick interjected. "Computer won't let them fire it up until the error is cleared."

"That's right," Noah said, nodding with satisfaction. "We built multiple fail safes into the ship. Engine lockouts for an unsealed airlock door, auto-closing hatches if we detect massive pressure differentials–"

"Explorer," Kate said into her microphone, cutting him off, "we're looking at a sensor error in the secondary fuel line. Can you confirm?"

"I'm pulling it up now," said Jeff.

Kate resisted the urge to ask him if he was doing alright.

"Copy that, Canaveral," he said a moment later. *"We can confirm a bad sensor on secondary fuel line."*

Kate turned as the doors from the hallway slid open and Frank came running into the room. He stopped next to Noah, breathing hard.

"Is it the fluid chamber?" he asked urgently.

"No, Frank," said Noah, leaning back casually. "It's not your darkest fear. It's a faulty sensor on the secondary fuel line."

Kate didn't know as many details about the TAP System as Noah or Frank, but she had picked up some of the broader strokes during meetings and while thumbing through the seemingly endless reams of mission-related technical documents. The fluid chamber was a conical compartment with a refractory metal core near the aft of the antimatter rocket that heated propellant to generate thrust. Judging from the bits of information she gleaned from overheard conversations, it had been a constant thorn in Frank's side since its installation.

"They're going to miss their departure window," Kate said, glancing up at the clock above the display wall. If they didn't launch soon, Titan wouldn't be there when they arrived at their destination. Instead, it would be with Saturn on the other side of the gas giant's orbit around the sun.

"It's not too late to abort," Rick said quietly.

"No offense, Canaveral," Riley said, *"but we'd rather not come home just yet."*

Frank wiped his sweaty face. "We could, uh, reroute the sensor stream to bypass the secondary fuel line. Temporarily, of course, until we can figure out the root problem."

Noah rapped his knuckles on the counter while he rocked in Kate's chair.

"How many spare sensors did we give them?" he asked.

"Two of each," Rick said. "But one of the crew would have to go outside the ship to replace it."

"They don't have time for that right now," Frank said.

"We never planned an EVA while the ship was en

route to Titan," Kate said. "They're not supposed to be outside the ship until they start building the research station."

"It's possible," Noah said, staring thoughtfully at the ceiling. "The TAPS burns in cycles. There's a long stretch a little more than halfway when the engine is cold." He turned in his chair to face Rick. "If I remember correctly."

"Checking on that now," Rick said. He grabbed a thick binder of course printouts from beneath his desk and flipped through the pages.

Kate turned off her microphone.

"Just so we're clear," she said softly enough that the other mikes couldn't pick up her voice, "you're talking about sending them off without a functional sensor on the secondary fuel line. You want one of the crew to go extravehicular while the ship is at maximum speed to replace the sensor."

"They'll be traveling the same rate as the ship, Kate," Frank said. "There's no reason it won't work."

"It's an unnecessary risk. Not to mention insane."

Noah looked at Frank.

"The only other option I see is to abort," Frank said. "Pull them back now and try again next year."

Kate wanted to slap him. She knew what he was doing. If Noah waited a year, his main competitor, MarsCorp, would likely patch up their problems by landing a deal with NASA and get to Titan first.

Rick paused while reading from his binder and looked up. "We can wait until they get to Titan."

"Explain," Frank said.

"There are four fuel pumps shared between the primary and secondary lines." Rick typed rapidly at his keyboard and pulled up a schematic of *Explorer I* on his screen. With a few keystrokes, he zoomed in to a cross-section of the fuel lines running side-by-side through a wall-mounted fuel pump. "Each of those pumps has a flow-rate sensor so we know fuel is physically passing through the pumps."

"But the pump sensors don't differentiate between what's coming in from the primary or secondary lines," said Frank. "It reads the aggregate."

"So we keep an eye on the last pump sensor before the lines hit the engine," Rick said, tapping the small wireframe box on his screen. "If the flow-rate sensor registers the same amount of fuel that's leaving the tank farther upstream, then the secondary fuel line is perfect. If we get a faulty reading during the journey, *then* they can go outside. At least this way, they have a choice."

Kate crossed her arms nervously. "How long would it take for us to know if there was a leak?"

"During a big burn, fuel passes through those lines in less than a tenth of a second," said Frank. "We'd know almost instantly, and we could shut the engine down so they could go extravehicular."

To Kate's surprise, Noah looked uncertain. He squinted and rubbed his jaw, using no small amount of brainpower on the problem. Then he looked at Frank.

"Yes, it's a risk," Frank said carefully, maintaining eye contact with Noah. "But we didn't start this because it would be easy. The crew can handle it, and so can the ship."

Noah cleared his throat and turned on the microphone built into the workstation.

"Commander, this is Noah Bell."

"Good morning, sir," said Riley.

"We have a way to proceed with the mission, but I want to run it by you first. If you don't approve of the plan, then it will not be executed. We'll have you come home so we can get the mess sorted out. Understood?"

There was a pause.

"Understood."

Noah laid it out for him, describing the details of the problem and the potential EVA that would be required to fix the sensor if another red flag popped up along the way.

"So that's it," said Noah. "What do you think?"

Another pause.

"Give us a minute," said Riley, and the line went dead.

Riley turned to face the others. He reached up to scratch his face and bumped against the clear faceplate of his helmet, then shook his head in frustration.

"As you heard, those planet-huggers below have managed to screw something up," he said. "I want to hear your thoughts."

"The secondary fuel line is used during the two major burns on the way there," Jeff said. "The microburns use only the main line."

"So four chances for something to go wrong," Gabriel said.

"We can't dock with the space station to fix the problem," Ming said. "That would take too long." She thought for a moment. "Is it legal to continue the mission when something like this happens?"

"This isn't NASA," said Riley. "There is no regulatory agency breathing down Bell's neck to make sure he's following every safety protocol. We're in uncharted territory."

"When's the next departure window?" Gabriel asked.

"Thirty-six days," Riley said. "But we wouldn't hit that one either. Prep work on the ground for another launch would take longer."

"I say we go," Ming said, "and fix the sensor when we get to Titan."

"Hmm," said Gabriel. "Are the guys who built the fuel line the same guys who built the sensor?"

Jeff smiled. "No. Different companies."

Gabriel thought about it a moment, then nodded inside his helmet. "Okay. Then I say we go."

"It's really Dolan's decision in the end," said Riley.

"Why me?" Jeff asked.

"Because you know the guts of this ship better than the rest of us. You're the one who would have to go outside."

Jeff sat back in his seat. He hadn't been thinking about who would draw the short straw to go extravehicular en route to Titan.

"If Mission Control gives us the green light," he said, "then let's go. If I *had* to go outside before we got to Titan, the chances of being hit by a piece of space debris are astronomically small, if you'll excuse the pun."

Riley turned back around to face the front of the ship and reactivated his microphone.

"Canaveral, we are badass adventurers, and we're going to get this show on the road."

"Copy that, Explorer," Kate said, her smile evident in her voice. *"You have the go-ahead. Bypassing secondary fuel*

line sensor now."

"They can do that from down there?" asked Gabriel.

"Some of the ship's functions are mirrored in Mission Control," Jeff said, "in case all of us are incapacitated and somebody needs to flip a switch. They would have to deal with the same delay as our uplink the farther we get from Earth, but it should work all the way to Titan and back."

"Eighty-three minutes is a long time to wait for help when you really need it," said Gabriel.

"Better than nothing," Ming added.

"Sensor bypassed," Kate said. *"You should be all set."*

"Copy that," said Riley. "Lieutenant, let's try this again."

"Yes, sir," Ming said.

They rested their hands on their controls while Riley counted down the steps to ignition.

"Now."

Riley and Ming pressed their ignition buttons and nothing happened.

"Oh, come *on!*" Riley shouted.

"No wait!" Jeff said. "It worked. The engine is on. Can you hear it?"

They all stopped breathing while they listened.

"I hear a hum," Ming said.

"That's it," said Jeff. "It's burning propellant in the fluid chamber. It happens a lot faster on Earth, but up here–"

The back-end of the ship ignited in a giant blue ball of fire and the crew slammed back into their seats as

Explorer I shot forward.

"*Woooohooooo!*" shouted Gabriel.

Jeff glanced over at him. His outline was blurred by the rapid shaking that gripped the entire ship. Jeff clenched his teeth to stop them from rattling.

"Passing first marker!" Ming said with a tremor.

"Throttling back!" shouted Riley.

He twisted two dials counter-clockwise simultaneously, and the shaking ceased.

"Burn scheduled for another twenty seconds," Ming said, breathing hard.

"Copy that," said Riley. Then he whistled. "Sweet Mary, would you look at that?"

He pointed at the small monitor on his control panel. It showed a brilliant blue trail of light flowing behind *Explorer I*. The light narrowed to a sharp point at the very end. It was so bright that its radiance blacked out all the stars, and Earth itself. It looked as if the ship was flying away from a pitch-black void.

Ming adjusted a dial. "Terminating burn in three...two...one."

With the push of a button, the thermal antimatter drive cut out, and *Explorer I* soared through the vastness of space, toward Titan, without even a whisper.

PART II

THE VOYAGE

_DAY 3

Kate leaned back in her chair, exhausted. She slowly pulled off her headset and tossed it onto her desk. The large red numbers of the clock above the display wall told her it was just after midnight.

"I guess that's it, then," Rick said. He pulled his glasses down the bridge of his nose and rubbed his bloodshot eyes.

"Hardly," said Kate.

"Well, for this portion of the mission. Next it's five months of boredom followed by two months of high stress, then another five months of boredom as they head back." He reseated his glasses and sniffed. "I think you did a great job."

She looked down and smiled.

"You never could take a compliment," Rick added.

"I'm just exhausted."

"Let me ask you something," he said. He turned in his chair to survey the room before continuing. Kate followed his gaze. Frank and Noah were nowhere to be seen. Rick rolled his chair a little closer and spoke quietly. "Does it seem odd to you that the guy who put this whole project together and the other guy who's responsible for overseeing that same project aren't spending a whole lot of time on the operations floor?"

"I don't think Noah Bell has a lot of free time," Kate said. "And he was just sitting *right here*, Rick, in my seat."

"I mean besides that," Rick said. "Don't you think he'd want to be here for more of it? Isn't that weird? Listen." He wheeled a little closer and his voice dropped to a barely audible whisper. "Someone came to visit me last night."

"Rick," she said coyly, "did you finally get a girlfriend?"

"No, nothing like that," he said hastily, waving the topic away with agitation. He bristled quickly whenever she didn't take him seriously. "It was a guy claiming to have worked for Diamond Aerospace in the past. He told me that the company had a facility near Russia. He used to work there before they shut it down."

"Michael Cochran," said Kate.

Rick leaned back suddenly, looking at her in surprise.

"How in the *hell* did you know that?"

"He was on my doorstep when I got home the other night."

"And did you talk to him?"

"Of course not! I chased him off with a baseball bat."

Rick threw his hands up in frustration and hissed,

"Someone comes to you with the mother of all bombshells, and you pick up a blunt object?!"

"Something wasn't right about him, Rick."

"He was running for his life!"

"Wait a second," said Kate, eyeing him suspiciously. "Did *you* talk to him?"

"You're damned right I did! Something's going on around here, and I'm going to find out what it is."

"Oh, please. Like what?"

"Well, that's what I have to find out, isn't it? Shh shh shh! *Here he comes here he comes!*"

Rick quickly turned around in his chair and wheeled back to his desk. Frank walked over, beaming.

"Other than that initial hiccup," he said proudly, "I'd call that a resounding success, wouldn't you, Ms. Bishop?"

She smiled, hoping it would make her look less weary. "Absolutely."

"A proud day for all of us," Frank continued. He slapped Rick's back, nearly knocking his glasses from his face. "Good job, everyone!"

Kate suppressed an internal groan. It seemed as if he had chosen to use that moment to give one of his ineffective motivational speeches.

"But there's still a long road ahead of us," Frank said loudly, addressing the room. Employees with heavy eyelids looked up at him slowly. "We are on the first leg of a historic mission. In a year's time, what you all did here today will go down in history. It will take hard work and perseverance to get there. I promise you, though, we will get there together."

He waited a moment for a clap or a cheer. There was none. He lowered his voice and said to Kate, "Can we talk for a minute?"

"Of course," she said. Then, to Rick, "Buzz me if anything comes up."

"You got it."

She followed Frank away from the display wall, past the rows of workstations. He led her up the stairs and across the viewing platform, toward the conference room. He held the door open for her as she walked in and waited until it was completely closed behind her before he started talking.

"I know about your relationship with Jeff Dolan," he said.

She looked at him sharply, trying to figure out what he wanted.

"I get it," he continued. "You were worried we'd put you on different teams if we found out. We probably would have, for the exact reason I'm talking to you now."

There was no shred of the pride or satisfaction he had just been showing out on the operations floor. Now he was all business; stern and direct.

"Okay..." she said.

"I need to make sure your relationship with one of the crew isn't going to affect any decisions you have to make in the future."

"What do you mean?"

He sighed and seemed to relax a little. "I'm only saying that sometimes accidents happen, and those of us here, on the ground, have to make difficult decisions regarding those up there."

"I have absolute confidence in the crew," Kate said. "Should I be worried about something else, Frank?"

She watched him closely, gauging his reactions. He wouldn't make eye contact.

"Of course not," he said, as if it were the most ridiculous notion in the world. "Look, it isn't the first time something like this has happened. A relationship of this nature, I mean."

"Would you have fired me if you found out before the launch?" asked Kate.

"I knew two months ago," he said simply. "I never had to bring it up because you're a professional, and it wasn't affecting your job."

"It isn't affecting my job now, either."

"Look, I just had to put all the cards on the table. If something goes wrong up there, I need to know you'll make the right decision, no matter the consequences."

"The mission comes first, sir," Kate said stiffly, putting a little too much emphasis on the *sir*. "It always has and it always will."

He smiled, and the weariness showed in the lines of his face. "Glad to hear it."

"Frank, I've been thinking about that fact that no one covered the launch. Usually we have press inside the building, and I'm really struggling to find a reason they weren't invited for this one."

He rubbed the back of his neck and looked away.

"Will it be the same for the rest of the mission?" she persisted.

Frank looked at her, his irritation obvious. "Due to

the safety concerns of launching a new rocket system, we decided it was a good idea to wait before publicizing the event."

"Well, that was a canned response if I ever heard one. You mean you wanted to make sure the rocket wouldn't blow up in our faces while the whole world was watching."

He shrugged. "More or less."

"Will the world be watching after we get to Titan?"

Frank crossed his arms and faced the glass wall of the conference room. He looked down at the employees on the operations floor of Mission Control.

"They'd better be," he said. "These days, space exploration is a hard sell to much of the public. They don't care about the details of our mining operations. Their interest starts and stops right here, on the ground. As long as we keep sending back natural resources, people don't give an iota of thought about where it came from. We need a solid victory right out the gate if there's any hope to achieve our ultimate goal of colonizing the stars."

Kate's eyebrows went up slowly. She had never heard such a direct mission statement from him before. "Colonizing the stars? Bit lofty, don't you think?"

"Well," he said with a slight grin, "no one said it would be easy."

Later that day, Noah's sixty-million-dollar Gulfstream G950 jet skimmed the top of a field of clouds over the Atlantic coastline. The pilot made a slight course adjustment to avoid some major upcoming turbulence, then ran her new trajectory through the piloting computer to make sure she was still on the fastest route possible to New York.

Noah stood next to her in the cockpit, one arm resting casually on the headrest of her seat, watching the clouds slide underneath the plane.

"Could be a little bumpy up ahead," said the pilot.

She was in her late-twenties and fresh out of flight school. Noah had hand-picked her along with four others to be the pilots of his growing fleet of private jets. This was her first outing in the G950. So far, he was impressed.

"Will it affect our arrival time?" he asked. He had a meeting in Manhattan with the visiting Emir of Dubai to discuss the building of a titanium processing plant on the outskirts of the Emir's native soil. The dignitary was notorious for canceling meetings if the other party was even a few seconds late.

"No, sir," she replied. "But I would hold on to your martini with two hands, just in case."

Noah patted the top of her seat, and said, "Thank you, Carol."

"Anytime, sir."

He left the cockpit and returned to his seat – a plush leather recliner, one of only four in the forward section of the plane. The other three were blissfully unoccupied. A divider separated the forward section from the rear, where three of Noah's aides were likely on their phones, deep in the cloud with their significant others and catching up on the latest pop media gossip. He also always flew with two business advisors, who he imagined were eyeing the younger aides with a mixture of contempt and jealousy.

The thought made Noah smile as he settled into his recliner. He grimaced at a sharp pain in his back, then reached behind him and pulled out a hardcover edition of *The Glories of Solitude* by Arjay Gupta. Mr. Gupta was one of Noah's personal heroes. The man had built himself a shack on the side of a mountain in Nepal and had lived there a full year without any human interaction whatsoever. He had grown his own food and fetched his own water from a stream a mile from his shack.

He had done it all on his own, then he wrote a book about the soul-searching he accomplished during his sabbatical.

For Noah, it was as close to fantasy as he could imagine. If he decided to take a year off, his companies would crumble in his absence. After the money dried up, the boards of investors would inevitably default to infighting, double-crossing, and hostile takeovers.

Noah sighed as he opened the book to the page where he had left off.

He read the words at the top of the page carefully, forcing his mind to slow down in preparation for new knowledge.

"Chapter Eight," he mumbled. *"Realizing the New Me."*

This should be good, he thought, settling deeper into his seat.

The plane hit a small pocket of turbulence and the walls shook slightly. Empty glasses clinked together on a drink cart in the rear section. Carol had suggested Noah hold on to his martini, just in case. He didn't drink. Alcohol seemed to have the opposite effect on him that it had on most people. It made him feel anxious and sick to his stomach. His brain became a clouded mess even after one light cocktail.

Oddly, he never regretted his abstinence. He still threw one hell of a party, and of course booze was always present. He didn't feel like he was missing anything without it, so he listened to his body and avoided it. Noah was struggling to adopt that policy with more aspects of his life, especially his business. He was now so successful that he could afford to follow his gut more than his financial planners.

It seemed to be paying off with the mission to Titan. Four out of five of his closest advisers had warned him not to go. Regardless of the long-term possibilities, they saw the mission as a financial black hole from which Noah would not be able to escape once he launched the rocket.

He could not tell his advisors about the object, of course. There were so few people who knew, and it wasn't as if <u>he</u> could squeeze it into one of the company's projected earnings charts without alerting the world to its existence.

Noah wasn't even sure there would be any monetary gain as far as the object was concerned. He *felt* like there would be – he felt it in his gut. And so, he had taken a leap and continued to fund *Explorer I*.

He pushed those thoughts from his mind as he lifted his book and began to read.

"Mr. Bell?" one of his assistants, Trevor, asked from behind.

Noah lowered his book slowly. "Yes?"

"I just received a call from the plant manager in Illinois."

"Chicago?"

"Freeport," Trevor replied.

Industrial venting systems, thought Noah.

"And?" he prompted.

"There's been another accident."

Noah closed his book and set it on the empty drink table next to his chair.

"How bad?" he asked.

"A worker's hands were caught in one of the aluminum cutters. He's expected to lose everything up to both of his elbows."

Noah frowned and shook his head. It was the third

major accident in as many months at that factory. They coincided with the major equipment overhaul. Some of the older machines had been updated, but most had been scrapped and replaced with brand new models built by a company just outside of Los Angeles. Apparently, they had sold Diamond Aerospace several trucks' worth of faulty equipment. And now his employees were paying the price.

"Shut it down," said Noah.

"The machine, sir?" asked Trevor.

"The factory. I want every piece of new equipment loaded onto cargo trucks and sent back to Bulowski's factory in Los Angeles. Call our lawyers in California and have them meet me there after I'm finished in Dubai. Pay the workers their normal wages during the next overhaul."

Trevor cleared his throat. "Sir, I already had the financial advisors run the numbers for shutting down the Freeport plant. We would be operating at a loss of one-point-seven million per day until operations were up and running again, in addition to new equipment costs."

"You had them run the numbers," Noah repeated.

"Yes, sir."

"And what do *you* think we should do, Trevor?"

"Sir?"

"What would you do if you were in my shoes?"

He thought about it for a moment. "I would keep the factory running and settle the inevitable lawsuit out of court. Long-term profit will outweigh any potential lawsuits."

"I see. Keeping your eye on the bottom line at all times. What's his name?"

"Whose name, Mr. Bell?"

"The man who lost his hands."

Trevor paused while he checked his notes. "Lewis Carter."

"Send him ten million dollars, in addition to a promise that he won't ever have to worry about medical bills ever again. Shut down the Freeport plant. Send back the equipment. Contact my lawyers."

And you're fired, he thought. That would come later, Noah decided. After this trip to New York.

"Yes, sir," Trevor said reluctantly as he retreated to the rear section.

Noah gazed out the window at the vast blue ocean below, lamenting that he wouldn't have time to call on Elena Riley while he was in New York. He genuinely felt there had been a spark between them – a spark he would one day like to coax into a towering bonfire.

He looked down at his hands, and shuddered at the thought of losing them the way Lewis Carter had lost his. Some days he hated his own success. It afforded him the frequently brazen opportunity to take a risk that occasionally got other people hurt.

Yet he still took the risk, every time. He *had* to. He needed to keep going, to keep pushing farther. It was the only way to reach a place like Titan before anyone else. If he didn't take the risks, someone else would, and Noah couldn't stomach the idea of sitting out the next big phase of humanity's history.

_DAY 10

The microwave-sized rehydrator hummed softly while it suffused Jeff's beef cubes with enough moisture to be technically qualified as edible. There was a block of mashed potatoes in the packet as well, but no green vegetables. Those remained in the vacuum-sealed pouch in the latched cabinet above the rehydrator, along with enough other meal pouches to get the crew to Titan. Food for the return journey was stowed in the six-meter-long cargo hold behind the crew module. Radiation shielding lined the cargo hold – enough to deflect the small amount of residual gamma ejecta from the antimatter drive that wasn't funneled into the ship's wake by the cone-shaped engine-wash shield on the tail-end of *Explorer*.

The dining area and kitchen were in the narrowest sectional ring of the centrifuge, just after the crew quarters. The kitchen was a small cubby between two section walls, with barely more than half a meter on one side to slip past. Besides the food rehydrator, there was a water station for filling plastic bottles and a supply cabinet for moist towelettes and disposable plates. No oven. No microwave. All of the food was pre-cooked for the journey and had to be kept at ambient temperature for the duration, which meant it was always cold.

The crew were going to be helping themselves to the perishables first: the meat and potatoes, so to speak. They expected the meals to become less appetizing as the mission progressed.

Jeff chose to defer the veggies until his dinner – partly because he could, and partly because their consistency favored packing foam. The mashed potatoes were barely better. What they lacked in flavor, they made up for in structural integrity: they never lost their boxy, pre-packaged shape, even with the three-quarters Earth's gravity generated by the spinning centrifuge.

Resilient to the end, those spuds, Jeff thought.

The rehydrator beeped and he removed his food packet. He emptied the contents onto a square disposable plate and plucked a square, reusable fork from the utensil pouch stuck to the side of the rehydrator.

He looked down at the literal square meal he'd just prepared. Every meal aboard *Explorer I* was a little too symmetrical for his taste. It lacked the ordered chaos of an organically-prepared dish – a meal with just enough of the haphazard, characteristically *human* element that proved you made it naturally, with your own hands.

The lessened gravity slowed his walk as he followed the wall of the centrifuge – or the floor, as it became when the cylindrical component was spinning.

It helped for Jeff to think of the crew module centrifuge as a series of sectional rings aligned from the vessel's nose to its tail. Each ring was separated from the others by a low wall. The first ring held the crew quarters – four claustrophobic bunks tucked head-to-foot against the forward centrifuge wall. Each bunk had a small reading light and a privacy screen. They were all empty at the moment.

The remaining floor space in the first sectional ring was dedicated to a hygiene compartment, which was more or less the size of a cramped phone booth with a drip shower, a ream of moist towelettes, and a mirror.

The next sectional ring contained the kitchen. Along the curved floor of the centrifuge next to the kitchen cubby was a small, bolted-down table. Four undersized, bolted-down metal seats, like insufficient barstools, surrounded it. Gabriel occupied one of them. Dark circles hung under his eyes and he looked about ten seconds away from falling asleep sitting up. He sipped from a packet of apple juice as Jeff walked over.

At three-quarters of Earth's gravity, walking in the centrifuge added a slight bounce to his step. The sensation was reminiscent of being just barely weighted enough to walk on the ocean floor, but without the water resisting any movements.

"Eventually we'll be eating insulation painted to look like a pork loin," Gabriel said as Jeff sat down next to him.

His empty plate was secured to the table by one of the four elastic loops on its surface. He took one last sip of his apple juice and let the packet fall from his lips. It dropped more slowly than it would have on Earth. Instead of catching it, he batted it up toward the central pillar which ran through the core of the centrifuge.

The packet slowed at the peak of its arc, as if it were preparing to drop back down. Instead, it crossed the gravitational boundary near the pillar and hung there, spinning in place.

Gabriel watched it while Jeff chewed his beef cubes, wishing for all the world that the folks in the nutritional department at Diamond Aerospace had dumped more beef flavor into the cooking vat.

"Ming still up front with Riley?" Jeff asked between chews.

Gabriel nodded. "Prepping for a microburn."

"Another one? We just burned this morning."

"Order came through while you had your head stuck in the wall."

Jeff had just finished maintenance checks on the oxygen filters lining a cylindrical, closet-sized tube in the wall at the back of the crew module, just past the centrifuge. It was the last crew-accessible area inside *Explorer I* without going EVA. The tube was aligned with the central pillar, and there was no gravity within. Part of Jeff's job was to float in that tube for three hours every other morning while he checked the oxygen filters and dependent systems.

"How's that lima bean coming along?" Jeff asked.

Gabriel grinned tiredly. "For now, it's just a seed in the soil. But it's a strong seed. The problem up here will be the root system in such a narrow pot."

"Lucky it has you," said Jeff. He took a bite of mashed potatoes and instantly regretted it. "I didn't think the root system was something you had to worry about. Plants have been grown in space for decades."

Gabriel shrugged. "No one's ever tried it around Titan before. Gravitropism doesn't function as a universal constant up here. The bean would be a nice present for the first crew of the orbital space station, but I'd rather not gift them something with a root system that will siphon nutrients from more necessary plants. The seeds we brought were modified to have less-invasive root structures so they could be planted closer together, in smaller pots."

"Well, even if the root system doesn't end up cooperating, you're still giving them a greenhouse that produces oxygen *and* a replenishable food source."

"And maybe lima beans."

Jeff chuckled. Gabriel tucked his empty tray into a garbage pouch attached to the low wall next to the table. Later those bags would be collected and emptied into a small trash compactor. The compactor would crush the trash into half-meter cubes, which would be jettisoned toward the sun when *Explorer I* reached Titan.

"Well," Gabriel said with a sigh. "I'm going to grab some shut-eye."

"You want to wait until after the burn?"

"I could sleep through anything right now." He wiped his fork down with a moist towelette and put it in his personal cubby within the small kitchen. "See you in a few hours."

"See you."

Jeff heard Gabriel brushing his teeth in the hygiene compartment. There wasn't a whole lot of privacy on the ship, unless you happened to be alone in one of the modules. There were no real walls in the crew module, just flimsy screens on the bunks that couldn't do anything to keep out the sound.

That's why music was such an important part of the journey, at least for Jeff. His headphones helped to block out the others' noise. Sometimes he even managed to successfully pretend he was by himself on *Explorer*, sailing the cosmos on some grand solo mission.

Then he would think about Kate, and it would become impossible to imagine anything other than the warmth of her body pressed against his. He was glad *Explorer* would only be gone a few days shy of a year. Before he left Earth, in the quieter moments when there hadn't been much else to think about, Jeff worried that Kate would forget about him.

Nothing like a few hundred million kilometers between people to make them realize their true feelings, he thought.

He tucked his empty plate into the garbage pouch next to the table and wiped down his fork. Unlike Gabriel, whose shift had just ended, Jeff's was only halfway finished. He still had a nice, long list of maintenance checks and systems analysis to work through before he could get some sleep.

A low hum filled the crew module – the microburn. Jeff felt no apparent change in velocity, just a gentle rumble in the floor of the centrifuge. A few seconds later, the floor was still again. Small retrorockets would have fired during the burn if necessary, keeping *Explorer I* on the proper trajectory toward Titan, but these adjustments were made automatically and would have been undetectable by the crew.

Jeff went over his work list in his mind. Checking the vehicle monitoring systems at the various stations in the next section of the centrifuge wasn't scheduled until just before dinner, but he decided to bump it up because of the burn.

One of the good things about being so far from company headquarters, he decided, was not having numerous bosses constantly looking over his shoulder.

Frank stood right behind Kate's chair, watching her workstation monitors while she cycled through the data feeds from *Explorer I*. He was an annoyingly heavy breather, and he would occasionally click a silver pen that he fondled whenever he was thinking. Each successive click was like a hammer tap on her spine, making her wince. Sometimes when she was very tired, sharp sounds gave her a massive headache.

Click.

Kate spun around in her chair to face him. "Everything's looking good," she said, trying to hurry him along. She glanced longingly at Rick's empty chair, wishing he was around to run interference so she could focus.

"Mmm," said Frank. He didn't seem to be in any kind of a rush. "Why is that graph spiking?" he asked, pointing to the crew biometric readout on the display wall. There were four thin lines on the graph, each one like the silhouette of a unique, jagged mountain range.

"Riley's probably exercising," Kate said, turning back to look at the screen. "Yep, he's on the treadmill. Gabriel's asleep, and Ming and Jeff are wide awake. She's in the command module and he's near vehicle monitoring systems."

She frowned and picked up a clipboard, studying the daily schedule.

"Jeff isn't supposed to check vehicle systems for three more hours."

"I'll have a little chat with him about that when he gets back," said Frank.

"Ha, ha," she said flatly.

Frank let out a tired whoof of air as he sat in Rick's seat, clearly not intent on leaving her alone anytime soon.

"How's the secondary fuel line?"

"No change," said Kate.

"Nothing peaking on any of the nearby sensors?"

She shook her head. "Nada. If I see it, you'll see it."

Frank and Noah were linked into the data stream with their cell phones. Any anomalies came through instantly as alerts containing a coded description of the problem.

"Just kicking the tires," Frank said soothingly. "Making sure we don't have a leak." He grunted as he wheeled Rick's chair a little closer to her. "I heard you had a visitor a couple weeks back."

"Visitor?" she asked, momentarily confused. "Oh, you mean the creeper on my front porch. That was just some space wacko trying to get his story in the news. He sounded even more paranoid than Rick." Her brow furrowed. "How did you know about that?"

He shrugged nonchalantly. "My daughter is dating a guy from the Sheriff's Department. I've discovered it can be very beneficial to cozy up to his commanding officer."

"You're keeping tabs on your daughter's boyfriend through his boss?"

"It helps to know if she's headed in the wrong direction before she gets there."

"Isn't that something she should figure out on her own?" Kate asked.

"I'll never stop worrying about her, even after she gets married. If I can soften any emotional blow that's headed her way, I will."

"So the commanding officer told you about my midnight visitor."

"Correct."

"Isn't that private information? I didn't sign any information release waivers."

"We were having a simple discussion over drinks."

She eyed him skeptically. "And it just came up."

"He knows what I do and where I work. It was casual conversation. You know, Kate, if you ever feel unsafe, the company can have someone watch your house. I've spoken with Noah about it."

"No," she said, a little too quick and forcefully. "Thank you, Frank. I'll be fine. I'd just like to wrap up my paperwork so I can go home and get some sleep."

He held up his hands in concession. "Fair enough," he said. "Just thought I'd ask."

She shook her head as he walked away, offended

that he had stuck his pointy nose so far into her personal business. Still, he was just an employer looking out for his employee, right? He was just being a little overprotective, that was all.

As soon as Frank's footsteps had faded, Rick scurried to his chair and sat down quickly. "I thought he'd never leave."

"*There* you are!" Kate said. "Could have used you a few minutes ago."

He looked over his shoulder nervously as he pulled his cell phone out of his pocket.

"Catch the news this morning?" he asked.

She sighed, already weary of his circuitous way of arriving at whatever point he was trying to make.

"Well," he continued, "if you *did* turn on your TV, I'm pretty sure you wouldn't have seen this."

He handed her his phone. The screen glowed with the image of a dead man in a dumpster. The man's clothes were splashed with blood from multiple stab wounds.

"Oh my God," said Kate. "Why would you show this to me?"

"Look closely."

She pushed the cell phone back into his hands. "No way."

He huffed in annoyance and held out the phone again, then lowered his voice and said, "It's Michael Cochran."

She opened her mouth to speak, then stopped.

"Yeah," said Rick. "*That* guy." He must have seen something in her face, a manifestation of the crawling dread she felt in her stomach. "What?" he asked. "What is it?"

"Frank was just asking me about the time Cochran showed up at my house."

"How the hell does he know about that?"

"He claims to have a contact at the Sheriff's Department," Kate said. She hesitated before asking her next question, knowing it would trigger Rick's conspiracy gene. "You think the company is watching us?"

Rick grunted. "Wouldn't surprise me. Did he ask about yours truly?"

"Why would he?"

"Because I talked to Cochran," Rick reminded her.

"No, he didn't mention you."

"Good."

Kate took the phone back and scrolled down past the picture, reading the attached article. "It says he was a local vagrant. No name."

"His teeth and fingertips are missing."

Kate frowned in disgust and swallowed hard. "What website is this?" she asked as she scrolled up to the top of the page. The site's logo was a cartoon fist raised in defiance, clenching a magnifying glass.

"The Daily Glass," Rick said. "It's a vigilant alternative news source that's not afraid to print the truth. You'll never see a story like this on regular television. To mainstream news he was just some homeless guy."

"Death is always news," she said.

"Not if someone pays to keep it quiet."

Kate's brain seemed to be working slowly. She was having a hard time wrapping her thoughts around the fact that the man who had visited her home, albeit briefly, was now dead in a dumpster.

Murder, she thought, and shivered.

"Who would pay to keep this off the major networks?" she asked.

"I don't know about you," Rick said, "but I'd rather not find out. I'm perfectly fine with all of my teeth, and I like my fingertips on the end of my fingers where they belong." He leaned in close. "But *something* is going on."

"You mean…a *conspiracy?*" she said mockingly. Despite the unsettling circumstances, she couldn't bring herself to admit the matter went beyond one man's murder.

"Laugh if you must, but when I come back with evidence, try not to act too surprised."

"*What* evidence?"

He leaned back in his seat and shrugged. "Don't worry about it," he said guardedly.

"Don't do anything foolish, okay?" He shrugged and looked away. She would have to press him. "*Okay, Rick?*"

"Define foolish."

"Whatever it is you're thinking about doing."

He rolled his eyes dramatically. "Fine. I'll just sit here and do my job like a good little boy, and pretend that *nothing* is going on behind the curtain."

Kate smiled, ignoring his sarcasm. "Good. Now help me run a check on the vehicle monitoring systems. It got bumped up on the schedule."

Rick grumbled as he put on his headset and wheeled his chair up to his workstation. Kate spun sideways in her chair and looked casually up at the viewing platform at the back of the room.

Frank was staring right at her. He smiled slowly and gave her a thumb's up. She returned the smile and spun back around. When she reached up to adjust her microphone, she couldn't stop her hand from shaking.

Noah stood at the large redwood desk in his office, arms crossed, staring at the image on his computer monitor: a dead man in a dumpster, his torso punctured by multiple knife wounds. The photograph was taken earlier that morning when a local sheriff's deputy left a coffee shop and heard a little girl scream from a nearby alley. The girl lived across the street and was about to climb into the dumpster to retrieve a toy her brother threw away. Instead, she found the corpse of Michael Cochran.

Noah picked up a manila folder on his desk and studied the file inside. It was an employee record of Cochran, who had worked for Diamond Aerospace five years ago, back when the company still operated a facility at Baikonur, just outside of Russia.

How far we've come, thought Noah.

He pushed the intercom button on his desk phone and said, "Trevor?"

"It's Neil, sir."

"Right. Sorry, Neil. I'll get it eventually. Is Frank Johnson still in the building?"

A slight pause, then: *"Yes, sir. He's at his desk in Mission Control. Shall I send for him?"*

"No, thank you. I'm going to take a walk. Back in a few."

"Yes, sir."

Noah turned to face a recessed wall mirror and checked his appearance. He fastened one button of his gray tailored suit jacket and adjusted his scarlet pocket square.

A man who used to work for you has been murdered, he thought as he stared into his own eyes in the mirror. *How do you feel about that?*

He shook his head and walked away. He was doing it again: playing the role of the press as they grilled him for any small morsel of evening news fodder. It was a technique he employed to minimize the chances of being caught off guard by hard-hitting questions.

Yet the report of Cochran's murder had come to Noah through the private security detail he maintained for just such occurrences. The team was a safety net for his companies, keeping an eye on the countless ways any part of his empire could be damaged, whether it was by slander or sabotage.

He stepped into his private elevator and descended toward the ground floor.

Doubtless a small rumor regarding Cochran's past involvement with Diamond Aerospace would eventually leak to the press. Somehow information always got out, especially when death was involved.

Noah briefly reflected on how strange it must be to have a job as a news reporter. One moment you had to pretend to be deeply hurt by the untimely death of someone you had never met, and the next moment you were all smiles while you told your viewers about a surfing bulldog.

Still, Michael Cochran hadn't done anything to garner sympathy before his passing. The file on Noah's desk stated he had been homeless for the last six months, drifting in and out of halfway homes and struggling with a severe alcohol problem. He had even voluntarily committed himself to a mental facility two months ago just outside of Dallas, Texas.

In other words, even if mention of his death somehow reached the pages of a larger newspaper, it would, tragically, be forgotten as quickly as it appeared. He was no celebrity to mourn for months after his passing.

The fact that his company's most aggressive competitor, MarsCorp, was headquartered in Dallas didn't bother Noah as much as Frank would tell him it should. Cochran had not been allowed access to the engine schematics of the vessels constructed inside the Baikonur facility, and therefore would have no useful knowledge to sell to an interested competitor. He had done little more than solder together stripped wires and make sure the comm systems wouldn't black out after launch.

Weighing on Noah's mind was the fact that Cochran had checked himself out of the mental facility two days before showing up on Kate Bishop's front doorstep in the middle of the night. The puzzle of what the two of them discussed during their brief encounter occupied his every resting thought.

With a gentle bounce, the elevator stopped and the door opened onto a dim hallway. Noah swiped his security badge at the lock of the door on the far end, then pressed his thumb against the fingerprint scanner. The scanner beeped and the door slid silently open. The door leading to the hallway was made of the same dark paneling as the rest of the room, difficult to identify for anyone who didn't know exactly where to look.

He walked out onto the viewing platform at the back of Mission Control. Frank sat at a large desk on the platform, watching the slowly ticking data on the display wall. He had apparently chosen that location to set up an improvised, open-air office.

The desk had suddenly shown up one morning after a long weekend. It was a monstrous thing of metal and glass, seven feet wide, pushed right up against the railing that overlooked the operations floor. Frank had five transparent monitors on the desk, arranged in an arc so they could all form one continuous display if he pressed the right button.

"Frank, you're giving me desk envy, and that's not easy to do," Noah said as he walked past. "Join me in the conference room?"

Frank pushed back from his desk and followed. Noah scanned the operations floor below as he strolled across the viewing platform.

Everything down there was quiet. The Ground and Flight Teams Manager, Kate Bishop, leaned back in her chair at her desk, watching the display wall readouts at the front of the room. Several members of her team were engrossed in their duties at other workstations.

Frank was right on his heels as they entered the glass-fronted conference room.

"Is this about Cochran?" Frank asked as he pushed the door shut behind him.

Noah held up a finger for him to be silent, then leaned over the edge of the table and inspected the conference phone in the middle. There was no glowing red light, which meant there were no active outgoing lines in use.

"Yes," Noah answered.

"Poor man," Frank said, shaking his head. "What an awful way to go." He turned to look out through the glass wall. "And abysmal timing on top of it. We're trying to keep a lid on things until the team gets to Titan, and Cochran goes and gets himself killed." His cheeks flushed red and he looked down at the floor. "I'm sorry," he added quietly. "That sounded very…inhuman."

"Do you have any idea what he and Ms. Bishop could have discussed at her home?"

Frank put his hands in his pockets and thought about it for a moment.

"Nothing of significance," he said. "If it was about the company, then maybe he dropped some veiled hints about the Baikonur facility where he used to work. At worst he told her outright lies about the stability of the Thermal Antimatter Propulsion System. I caught a glimpse of Cochran's file from the mental institution.

'Unfounded Paranoia' ranked very high on his list of quirks."

Noah frowned. "Why do you think he would mention the TAPS specifically?"

"Hell if I know," Frank said with a shrug.

"He could talk about any one of a hundred other systems, electrical first of all, since that was his main focus."

"The engine is the biggest target for scrutiny, Noah, not the damned wiring. We're the only company in the world to have this technology. Maybe Cochran landed himself a job with MarsCorp, or another company we haven't even heard of yet. He could have been trying to scare Kate into revealing some details about our project."

Noah looked at him evenly. "Would he have a valid reason for warning Ms. Bishop about the TAP System?"

"Of course not! You have the same documentation that I do. The system has been cleared for practical application many times over."

Noah joined Frank by the glass wall and looked down at Kate. She seemed to sense that she was being watched, for she spun in her chair and glanced up at the conference room. Noah nodded at her, and she gave him a weak smile in return before turning back to her workstation.

"I'm going to be staying close for a while," said Noah, "just in case anything else comes up."

"What about the tech conference in London?" Frank asked. "You're the keynote speaker."

"I'm sure they have a long list of billionaires to fall

back on if I were to suddenly become unavailable. I feel like this is the best place for me right now."

"Well, then," said Frank, "I'll let the team know."

_DAY 41

The asteroid belt's only dwarf planet, Ceres, orbited the sun at a distance of four-hundred million kilometers. With an equatorial diameter greater than 950 kilometers, it was the largest object in a circumstellar donut of rocky space debris that looped, for the most part, between the orbits of Mars and Jupiter.

By sheer coincidence, the dwarf planet was barely visible as *Explorer I* shot past at seven-thousand kilometers per second.

Jeff sat strapped into his seat in the command module, looking out through the narrow window in front of the pilots' seats. He was alone.

Most of the time, the window at the nose of *Explorer* showed nothing more than a horizontal strip of pinpoint lights over a dark background. Now there was a small globe of brilliant light off to the left – a spherical object roughly a thousand kilometers in diameter that wouldn't pass that way on its orbit again for another four-and-a-half years.

From that distance, Ceres had the apparent size of

a bead of water. It was only visible for a few seconds. *Explorer I* traveled onward, and the reflection of the sun's light against the bone-white surface of the dwarf planet vanished.

Diamond Aerospace had spent weeks making sure *Explorer* wouldn't bump into Ceres as the ship zoomed through the asteroid belt. It was a simple fluke of timing that the flight team had to consider it at all. With an average distance approaching a million kilometers between objects in the belt, the chances of a collision with *Explorer I* were astronomically small.

Jeff unbuckled his straps and floated up from his seat. He waited there a few moments, enjoying the weightlessness. His blue cargo pants and white t-shirt were brand new, fresh out of a vacuum-sealed pack. He and the others swapped out their underwear every four days, their shirts every seven, and their pants as needed for identical sets that had been pressed and infused with a freshly-laundered scent before leaving Earth. The soiled garments went into the garbage alongside their food scraps.

Jeff smiled as he remembered Kate's disgusted reaction when she learned the dirty details of life aboard *Explorer I*. Yet what he told her then had turned out to be true: the controlled environment of a spacecraft was much cleaner than a workstation in Mission Control, and he and the other crew members rarely exerted themselves to the point of sweating.

He grabbed the top of his seat and pulled himself toward the back of the command module. Drifting through the T-junction that separated the modules, Jeff stayed close to the floor, anticipating the shift in gravity when he passed the barrier into the centrifuge.

Gravity pulled down on his chest as he grabbed hold of the ladder at the entrance to the crew module. He swung his legs around in slow motion and climbed down the ladder, gravity slowly and inexorably squeezing the air from his lungs as he descended. Even when he was expecting it to happen, he found he couldn't hold onto his breath during the transition, not until he was at the bottom of the ladder, standing upright in the three-quarter's gravity of the centrifuge.

He walked through the sleeping quarters and went into the kitchen. He prepared his rehydrated meal robotically, his mind back on Earth, with Kate.

Monotony. Routine.

Those were the two words that constantly tumbled around Jeff's mind as he went about his daily work. Keeping an advanced piece of machinery like *Explorer I* running smoothly meant repeating the same maintenance procedures over and over again; pushing the same buttons on the same console; wiping the oxygen filters in the same direction so particulates didn't get wedged in the tight vent flaps. It only followed that the remainder of his time would mimic that pattern. Showers, meals, even sleep – all of it was routine by that point.

He only knew it was a Tuesday because Gabriel had put a page-a-day calendar in the kitchen on top of the food rehydrator. There was a picture of a sunflower with the words "Brighten Up Your Life" in cursive type over it. Jeff stared at that sunflower for a long time, long after the rehydrator beeped to let him know his chicken casserole was ready.

After lunch, he went aft, through the sectional ring containing communications systems access and vehicle monitoring systems, where he spent most of his time. The two divided areas after that belonged to the science lab and to space suit storage, which was the last section in the centrifuge before the cargo hold.

Multiple workstations filled much of the floor space in the science lab, dedicated to the various experiments the crew had been and would be running throughout their voyage. With no cryostorage, any samples they brought along had to be freeze-dried and then thawed later. There was a small refrigerator next to one of the workstations for temporary sample storage until an experiment was complete. For the most part, Jeff and the others were stuck with ambient-temperature project material.

Not that he had the science background to delve into the specifics, but Jeff would have loved to run a test on extremophile organisms in deep space. He knew it sounded too much like science fiction, but he hadn't stopped hoping that a breakthrough in the understanding of such tough and adaptable little creatures like the vacuum-surviving tardigrade could lead to the advent of cold stasis for long-term space travel.

Ming sat staring into a microscope at one of the workstations, still as a statue, a stylus gripped loosely in one hand. The tip of the slender instrument hovered over her glowing PDA. Gabriel sat two tables away, muttering to himself while he made notes in a leather-bound journal. A small, narrow pot rested on the table in front of him, filled only with black soil.

The crew had been operating in such close proximity to each other and for so many days that small talk had mostly fallen by the wayside. Jeff left Ming and Gabriel to their projects and walked around the centrifuge until they were directly on the other side of the central pillar. He was essentially on their ceiling, and they were on his.

Jeff ran his usual checks on the medical equipment. He patched the biometric computer into the communications mainframe so it could sync crew data with Mission Control. The company wanted to ensure Mission Control was getting medical data accurate to the millisecond until the growing comm delay rendered live monitoring impractical.

Jeff watched rhythmic EKG blips flash on the screen as the system sent a data packet toward Earth, then he disconnected the biometric computer from the comms and reattached it to the mainframe.

Next, he was scheduled to run a diagnostics test on an experimental piece of equipment called the doctor pod. Diamond Aerospace had leased a few square meters of floor space aboard *Explorer I* to a Swedish company named Vitus, who had then installed a coffin-like medical unit with a clear acrylic lid. Once a patient laid down inside the pod, the hinged lid would close, and the pod would be able to perform a vast array of automated tasks, from something as simple as applying antiseptic bandaging for a minor cut to setting a broken limb. The idea behind it was to eventually eliminate the need for any kind of medical training amongst the crew.

The doctor pod was still in beta testing. Despite reassurances from the Vitus representative that the product was ready for use, Jeff and his fellow crewmates still received advanced medical training before leaving Earth, enough so that they could handle most emergency situations that might arise while en route to Titan. For anything more severe, they only needed to suffer through the small radio delay to and from Earth while waiting for instruction.

Needing medical assistance from Earth was not an expected scenario, however. His training instructors had admitted that, in space, there was a very thin line between marginally injured and outright dead. If things went wrong, they tended to go wrong in a big way, and no amount of medical advice from Earth would make a difference.

They went on to assure him that, as long as he was being careful, there would never be a need to get inside the doctor pod.

The acrylic lid of the pod opened slowly as Jeff approached. Thick steam rolled out and quickly evaporated, revealing Commander Riley lying atop a stiff, padded mat. He wore only a pair of exercise shorts and a neon green pair of opaque goggles. Tucked up next to him, one to each side, were the jointed robotic arms that performed most of the pod's operations.

Riley groaned from within as he sat up, his legs dangling over the side. He peeled off his goggles and blinked at the harsh white light of the crew module.

"You know this thing has a UV setting?" he asked when he saw Jeff. Two strips of blue lights running down either side of the mat dimmed slowly until they darkened completely.

"I hadn't gotten that far in the manual yet."

Riley stood up and tapped a few keys on a control panel at one end of the pod. The machine beeped and the lid lowered slowly until it sealed shut. He grabbed his folded clothes from a small cubby cut into the plastic molding of the pod.

"There's a lake about a ten-minute walk from my house," said Riley. He pulled on a pair of blue sweatpants and tied them off at the waist.

"In Colorado?" Jeff asked.

Riley nodded. "Thing I miss most when I'm up here is being able to just…lie there on the shore, taking in the sun and listening to the birds." He looked thoughtfully at the doctor pod. "I didn't realize I missed it so much until I found out this thing had a low-powered UV setting."

"Now all you need is a soundtrack of bird calls."

Riley pulled on his white t-shirt and grinned ruefully. "That might be a little too real for me. I don't like to forget I'm up here. It's important to stay focused on the job."

"Of course it is," Jeff agreed. "But everyone needs to blow off steam from time to time."

"Not us." He looked at Jeff seriously. "That's not why we're up here."

"We all had the same psychological profiling, Commander."

What Jeff didn't have to say, and what everyone on the ship knew, was that each of them had been chosen because they conformed to a very strict set of psychological guidelines.

As individuals, they needed to be perfectly content being alone for very long periods of time. They needed to be self-motivated, self-driven, and self-reliant. If any of them was the last person remaining on board the ship, they had to be mentally resilient enough to handle the rigors of extended solitude. The qualifying system of psych tests had been in place since humanity first punched its way out of Earth's atmosphere, and had been refined to near-perfection over the following decades.

As a team, the crew needed to remain calm under pressure, to trust each other completely, and to be astute conflict resolvers. In other words, they needed to not act like a bunch of yahoos with a spaceship.

None of them would be on *Explorer I* if they hadn't met all of those qualifications.

"Anyway," Riley said with a contented sigh, "you should give it a shot." He patted the lid of the doctor pod. "A few minutes on the UV setting followed by a good night's sleep, and you'll feel like you were back home again. Speaking of which..."

He excused himself and left for the crew quarters. Jeff would be seeing him again before his own shift ended. Riley's idea of a good night's sleep was four hours of light slumber followed by a brisk cold-water splash-off in the hygiene compartment. The guy never seemed the worse for it, though. Jeff felt groggy with anything less than six hours of sleep, which often made him wonder why he had thought it would be a good idea to allow himself to be sealed in a spaceship and sent so far from Kate's warm bed.

Because we're making history, he thought.

He had realized that long before the launch, and he had increasingly pushed himself to the limit during his last few weeks on Earth. He stayed longer in the simulations, and he studied when he should have been resting. He *knew* he was better prepared for the Titan mission than any of the other potential flight engineers, and that's why he believed Noah and Frank chose him out of the pool of remaining applicants.

Jeff knelt next to the doctor pod. The machine was still warm from Riley's UV bath. The heat felt good in the slightly chilly crew module. Jeff called up the pod's digital manual on the glowing control screen at the head of the machine and navigated to where he'd left off three days ago: suturing of minor lacerations.

He pressed a button and the two robotic arms within the pod moved in a demonstration, as if sewing up a cut on an invisible patient. Jeff checked his watch. Four more hours until dinnertime, and then he could record a five-minute video for Kate. There weren't too many free bandwidth spots between all the expected outgoing scientific data where he could squeeze in a quick message.

Jeff could barely wait to see her. He had even shaved that morning after letting his stubble grow for days. He hated doing it back on Earth, and in space the procedure was aggravating to the point of madness.

There didn't seem to be an easy, clean way to get the job done.

He had noticed that the other crew members tidied up more than usual for their short video messages with their loved ones back home. In the end, Jeff knew it was a good thing, because it kept them all from letting themselves go. It was good for morale, but more importantly, it kept the lived-in, unwashed odors from permeating too deeply into the insulation.

Jeff still smelled slightly of soap after his shower that morning, mostly because it was difficult to rinse off all the suds in the small hygiene compartment with nothing more than a drip faucet. His shirt was a little sticky against his skin, but he knew from experience that the uncomfortable sensation would fade. Of course, Kate couldn't smell him over the video feed, but he thought the clean residue made him feel peppier and fresh for conversation. He didn't want to betray any hint that he was very lonely without her, and he didn't need anyone listening in on the conversation to hear how much he wished she were there.

Jeff could barely wait to see her. He had even shaved that morning after letting his stubble grow for days. He hated doing it back on Earth, and in space the procedure was aggravating to the point of madness. There didn't seem to be an easy, clean way to get the job done.

He had noticed that the other crew members tidied up more than usual for their short video conferences with their loved ones back home. In the end, Jeff knew it was a good thing, because it kept them all from letting themselves go. It was good for morale, but more importantly, it kept the lived-in, unwashed odors from permeating too deeply into the insulation.

Jeff still smelled slightly of soap after his shower that morning, mostly because it was difficult to rinse off all the suds in the small hygiene compartment with nothing more than a drip faucet. His shirt was a little sticky against his skin, but he knew from experience that the uncomfortable sensation would fade. Of course, Kate couldn't smell him over the video feed, but he thought the clean residue made him feel peppier and fresh for conversation. He didn't want to betray any hint that he was very lonely without her, and he didn't need anyone listening in on the conversation to hear how much he wished she were there.

Kate stared at herself in the bathroom mirror. She wore a lacy purple blouse tucked into a dark gray, knee-length skirt. Stopping short of high heels when she got dressed that morning, she instead chose her more comfortable black flats. Besides, the high heels wouldn't have been visible in the video message she'd be sending to *Explorer I*.

She anxiously checked her watch. Five minutes until she could watch Jeff's message and record her response. An errant strand of hair fell across her forehead, and Kate impatiently tucked it behind her ear. She had let down her seemingly perennial tight bun that day, allowing her brunette hair to dance over her shoulders.

Anyone who had been paying attention would notice the eye makeup and lip gloss she almost never wore. She felt a little silly getting all dolled up for a brief recording, as if she were in high school again, trying to capture the attention of a boy she knew she would only pass in the hall a few seconds of each day.

Kate smiled to herself. Before her mother had passed away, she told Kate it was a good sign if she still had feelings like that after being in a relationship with someone for a while. She only needed to start worrying when one of them stopped putting in the effort.

Her mother had been a font of advice, unwanted right alongside the welcome.

Kate pressed her lips together one last time to smooth the gloss, and nodded her own approval, reluctant though it was. She left the bathroom and walked through the empty break room.

Things were quiet on the operations floor. The team had been going about its business with about one-third of the usual amount of personnel for several weeks running. During those quiet days of the mission, only five to seven technicians were at their stations during any given shift. Rick had the day off, and Noah rarely came down from his office, if he was even in the building at all. Frank spent most of his time at his overseer's desk up on the viewing platform.

Kate didn't like having an overseer. She felt as if she were a line worker on a factory floor, her every movement scrutinized.

Coming back in to work after Rick told her about Michael Cochran's murder had been surprisingly easy. She simply weighed the unlikely possibility that her company had something to do with the incident against leaving Jeff out in the cold on his mission. He would have survived without her, of course, but it wasn't just about him. Kate needed to stay in contact with the ship for the sake of the entire crew.

Rick dropped the subject of the murder almost immediately after it happened. He had been strangely silent the last few weeks as *Explorer* barreled uneventfully toward Titan, the steady routine slipping into clock-watching monotony. Typically, he was full of chatter about the latest conspiracy theory to cross his desk on any given morning. Yet, recently, he had been just like any other employee in Mission Control. He kept his nose to the grindstone, put in his hours, and went home each day without a fuss.

His quietude disturbed Kate more than his default endless banter. She tried not to let the thought bother her too much as she walked to her workstation.

"Juan, how are we looking for that microburn?" she asked as she passed one of the Flight Operations desks.

"Everything's A-okay, Ms. Bishop," the stocky department head answered with a smile. His dark brown eyes twinkled jovially. "Lieutenant Ming is going to initiate the burn on our mark."

"And the commander?"

The flight surgeon, an aging man named Walt, spoke up from a different workstation farther down the row. "Sleeping like a baby. You want me to wake him up?"

"Let him sleep. The guy doesn't get enough as it is. Lieutenant Ming can handle this one."

Walt smoothed his wispy, unruly white hair and leaned back, looking up at the display wall.

The crew had performed four microburns so far, each one providing small course adjustments to ensure *Explorer* remained perfectly aligned with its target destination. The burns had all gone off without a hitch. It wasn't that Kate wanted to let her guard down when it came to safety, but they really didn't need two pilots in the command module to push one button for the microburns.

She sat at her workstation and arranged a stack of papers to one side. She interlaced her fingers together on top of the desk and stared at the blank monitor of her station. Then she readjusted the stack of papers and interlaced her fingers together again.

"Ms. Bishop," said Juan. "Message coming in for you."

"Thank you," she said professionally.

She cleared her throat and glanced around the room. Everyone pretended to be deeply involved in their work, presumably out of courtesy for her. It had been impossible to keep the fact that she and Jeff were in a relationship from the rest of the ground crew forever. After their first face-to-face video chat shortly after departing the ISS, when he wouldn't shut up about missing her, the cat flew right out of the bag. She was grateful her coworkers respected her enough to not tease her about it, and to turn their heads the other way whenever she recorded a message to Jeff.

She reached out and pushed the ship's feed button next to her monitor, and suddenly she was looking inside *Explorer I*. Jeff grinned into the camera. His short black hair was getting a little longer than she knew he liked. He stood in the centrifuge of the crew module, at one of the vehicle monitoring stations.

Kate smiled. "You shaved," she said, even though she knew it was a recording.

"Hi there, beautiful," said Jeff. "I'll get the boring

stuff out of the way first. Everything's fine here. The system has been running like clockwork ever since the little hiccup at the ISS. But it's quiet, and I miss you." He smiled. "Nothing new there. Gabriel's lima bean still hasn't sprouted, so I get to hear about that every blessed minute he's awake. The rest of the crew is still in high spirits."

He was silent for a moment and he looked away from the camera. Kate could tell something was troubling him. She hated the signal delay that forced them to record their conversations.

"I'm sticking to the routine," he continued. "Things will pick up when we get to Titan. Hopefully I won't even have two seconds of free time to rub together."

Ming's voice came over a speaker off-screen and Jeff looked up at the source.

"Jeff. Gabriel. Initiating microburn in one minute. Twelve second duration."

Kate looked over at Juan, and he nodded. "Should be seeing it soon," he said, tapping his monitor with a pen.

"How's Rick?" asked Jeff. "Every time I see him sitting there in Mission Control, he's wearing the same shirt. I'd love to hear about his latest conspiracy theory."

Kate laughed. Just the other day, Rick told her that NASA had been operating a base on the moon since the early 1970s, and they were currently building one on Mars as well. The top brass at Diamond Aerospace was under contract with NASA not to spill the beans. She thought Jeff would get a kick out of that.

"Guess I'm running out of time," Jeff said in the

recording. "I meant to ask you this during the last message, but it didn't feel right. Now it does. What do you say we move in together when I get back?"

Kate raised an eyebrow.

"Could be your place or mine," said Jeff. "Doesn't matter to me." He grinned. "Mine's not on the beach, though. At least with yours–"

The screen shook and there was a loud bang from somewhere within the ship. An alarm blared in the background. Kate's workstation lit up red with errors.

On the screen, Jeff looked around the module, wildly trying to find the source of the problem.

"Kate?" he shouted. "The walls are shaking! It's not a–"

The video feed cut out and Kate's monitor went blank.

"Jeff?" she said loudly. She leaned forward and smacked the blank screen of her monitor. "*Jeff!*"

"Full burn, full burn!" Juan shouted from his workstation.

"*Canaveral, this is Explorer One,*" said Ming over the speakers in the operations room. Her voice was strained but calm. "*TAPS is at full power and I cannot shut down. Repeat, I cannot shut down power to the engine.*"

"It's supposed to be a microburn!" Frank roared from the viewing platform. "What the hell is going on?!"

"Juan, can we shut it down remotely?" Kate asked.

"We're on a delay," he said. "Whatever happened is probably over already."

"Do it anyway!" said Frank. "And figure out what went wrong."

Kate brushed off his last comment with an aggravated shake of her head. *Of course we're going to figure it out,* she thought.

A gruff, tired voice came over the line. *"Canaveral, this is Riley. Lieutenant Ming and I are at our stations."* Something rattled loudly in the transmission background.

"Commander," said Kate, "we're sending an engine kill command remotely. I know you won't get this right away, but…hang in there."

"They're going too far off-course," Frank said woefully. He stood behind his desk, shaking his head.

"Canaveral, we are deviating" Ming said. *"Firing retrorockets now."*

"Juan," Kate said, "what happens if we do the full burn now, instead of later when it was scheduled?"

He wiped sweat from his brow. "We, uh, we'd have to run the calcs, but I would guess they'd arrive at least a month early."

"That's not so bad," said Walt.

"Titan won't be there when they show up," said Juan. "But that's not even the biggest issue," said Juan. "We do the big burn at the end because it's easier to maintain course when the ship is that much closer to its destination. The deviations closer to Titan don't make as much of an impact on the ship's trajectory. At this distance, every micrometer of deviation is amplified exponentially if it isn't corrected immediately. They'll burn more fuel staying on a new course, and they run the risk of overshooting Titan by millions of kilometers if we screw up the calculations."

"We're going to make sure that doesn't happen," Kate said sternly. "Understood?"

Juan nodded shakily. Then he squinted at his monitor. "Kill signal is still on its way to Explorer."

"Uh, Canaveral," Riley said over the line. *"We have exhausted our options for engine shutdown from the command module, and we are still burning hot. Repeat, the engine is still hot."*

"They'll eat up their reserves," Frank said solemnly.

Kate looked up at the display wall. In the fuel monitoring section, the gauge visibly dropped as the TAP System continued its burn.

"**T**he walls are shaking!" said Jeff. He looked up. The central pillar of the centrifuge vibrated like a struck tuning fork as the engine roared to life. The floor under his feet rattled loudly. "Kate, it's not a microburn!" he shouted over the noise.

Then the force of the acceleration hit him like a giant's fist and punched him toward the back of the crew module. His feet banged against a table as he flew over the science lab and slammed into the back wall of the centrifuge.

There was more banging and a scream, followed by a heavy thud. Jeff looked up. Gabriel groaned as he tried to sit up after being plastered against the back wall.

"It's a…major burn!" Gabriel managed to shout from above.

"It's too early!" Jeff yelled.

A deep vibration coursed through the walls of the module. Jeff heard the squeal of twisting metal and the unmistakable *ting* of something heavy popping off its equipment rack.

"Head's up!" Jeff shouted as a bulky display monitor tumbled through the air toward the back of the ship.

He and Gabriel rolled away as the monitor

crashed into the back wall of the centrifuge, cracking into a hundred pieces.

Riley's voice came over the intercom, calm but urgent. *"Get up here, you two. We have a situation."*

"We're stuck!" yelled Gabriel.

"Use the tether track on the central pillar," Riley said impatiently.

Gabe looked down at Jeff. "Did you hear that?" he asked, his voice shaking from the vibrations in the wall. "It's so simple."

"You're closer," Jeff said.

Gabriel rolled over onto his stomach and yelled as he strained to push himself into a crawling position. Fighting the constant pressure from the burn, he inched down the back wall of the centrifuge and made it to the central pillar.

He opened a small compartment and unspooled two long tethers, identical to the ones used outside the ship to secure a crew member to the hull during a spacewalk. The slide-tracks were embedded forty-five degrees apart around the circumference of the pillar. Gabriel handed the end of one tether to Jeff, who quickly looped it around his chest and clipped the hook to the line over his sternum. Gabriel did the same, then snapped the other ends of their tethers into two of the four slide-tracks that ran the length of the entire central pillar.

"All the way to the front?" Gabriel asked loudly. Jeff nodded.

Gabriel typed a command sequence into a small digipad next to one of the slide-tracks. A motor at the other end of the pillar engaged and began slowly pulling their tethers along the slide-tracks, toward the front of the ship.

Jeff relaxed as best he could and allowed himself to be pulled off the back wall of the centrifuge like a pancake being peeled from a sticky griddle. He and Gabe bumped against the pillar as they were pulled forward. The tether dug into his armpits and pinched the skin on his back.

Gabriel floated a few feet away as the two of them were hauled like dead weight toward the command module at the front of the ship.

Jeff heard a constant whooshing noise in the floor below him, loud enough to break through the rattling of the ship.

"What's taking so long?" Riley asked over the intercom.

"Not easy to move against full thrust, Commander," Gabriel said.

"Are we going to blow up?" Jeff asked.

"You tell me," said Riley.

Jeff and Gabriel were halfway along the central pillar. Below them, a vibrating display monitor showed bright blue engine wash trailing behind *Explorer I.*

"All systems in the green," Ming reported.

"You still can't shut it down?" Jeff asked.

"Sure we can, Dolan," Riley said. *"We're just having fun up here."*

"We tried," said Ming. *"Override controls are unresponsive. The microburn should have ended two minutes ago."*

184

"But even the major burns aren't supposed to last this long." Jeff's stomach dropped when he realized the implications of a longer burn: less fuel for the return trip.

"*Dolan,*" said Riley, "*can we cut off the fuel supply to the engine?*"

"Not if the pumps are still running," Jeff answered. "The fuel would back up and eventually burst the lines."

"*So what happens if you shut off the pumps?*"

Jeff stared blankly at the central pillar as his mind raced to wrap itself around the problem.

"*Dolan!*" Riley prompted.

"I would…well I would have to work my way from the front of the ship to the back, stopping the pumps one at a time," he said, speaking quickly. "It would be like squeezing the last bit of toothpaste out of a tube, but it wouldn't be instantaneous."

"*Do it,*" Riley said. "*Silva, help him.*"

"You think it will work?" asked Gabe.

"It's our only option short of damaging the engine to turn it off," Jeff said. "I don't know about you, but I'd like to get home eventually."

"Right *now* sounds good to me."

"Yeah, me too."

The tethers reached their terminus at the front of the crew module. Jeff and Gabriel hung from the lines ten feet back. Straining against forces that were trying to send them flying to the back of the ship, they slowly climbed the central pillar ladder to the front wall of the module.

"This will be tricky," Jeff said, breathing hard. Gabriel nodded. "Let's do it."

Four one-meter-wide square panels were in the floor of each ring section of the centrifuge except the crew quarters. While the fuel lines themselves were inaccessible from inside the vessel, the pumps had been built "maintenance-friendly" – which was another way of saying an astronaut didn't have to spend two hours getting into a spacesuit to go EVA just to flip a switch.

Jeff typed a sequence of commands into a digipad at the front of the pillar. As he climbed down the ladder on the forward wall of the centrifuge, hooking his heels behind each rung so his legs wouldn't be pulled behind him, the anchor point of his tether remained locked at the front of the pillar. The line was taut, but unspooled with some resistance as long as he moved slowly. Any sudden jerks on the line would cause it to lock up. Gabe followed just above him, almost stepping on Jeff's fingers.

The curved floor of the centrifuge had enough barriers so the two of them could let go of one secure handhold and slide along the floor until they banged into the next obstacle, moving back through the module in a series of controlled falls.

Jeff grabbed a small electric drill from a tool box stuck to the dividing wall next to the kitchen and knelt near one of the floor panels. The tether loop around his chest rubbed the skin under his thin t-shirt raw. Vibrations in the floor shook him to the bone.

He unscrewed four large fasteners and handed them to Gabriel, who crouched next to him, eager to help.

"Thanks," said Jeff, his teeth clattering. "Help me lift this. Careful when you let it go."

He gestured a few feet away, at a dividing wall where the panel would most likely hit when he and Gabe released it.

Gabriel nodded and dropped the fasteners into the pocket of his black exercise pants. He grabbed the left side of the floor panel. With a grunt, the two men lifted the heavy piece of paneling and set it flat on the ground. As soon as they let go, it slid toward the back of the ship, gaining momentum until it slammed into the dividing wall.

The compartment beneath the floor was packed with insulated cable, electrical meters, and a piece of machinery in the center that looked like a flattened, oversized, four-stroke scooter engine.

"This is the control valve," Jeff shouted over the noise from the open compartment, pointing to a small red toggle on the side of the fuel pump. "Right now it's open. If I do this, and then this," he added, miming a clockwise turn and pretending to push the toggle into the pump until it was flush with the side, "the pump will force whatever fuel is inside farther down the line but won't draw any more from the tank."

"Won't that cause a pressure backup?" yelled Gabriel.

"Temporarily. But the sensor in the tank will register the build-up and stop the outbound flow to the first pump. Once we start the process, we have to move quickly, because the next three pumps will still try to draw from the ones we shut down. Bad things happen when they run dry for too long. Got it?"

"Got it."

"There's another drill at the next panel. You get started on that while I shut this one down. We'll worry about replacing the panels later."

"Okay."

Gabriel half-crawled, half-slid to the next section, gripping his tether line firmly with one hand and holding the other in front of him in case he began to fall.

The centrifuge was still spinning, which it wasn't supposed to do during a full burn. Otherwise the two of them wouldn't have been able to stay on the floor. Jeff was grateful, yet the fact that the centrifuge still spun was symptomatic of a much larger problem: the ship's systems weren't talking to each other.

He reached into the floor compartment, turned the toggle on the fuel pump, and pushed it in flush. The pump groaned in protest and seized up violently.

"Um..." said Jeff.

"Everything okay?" shouted Gabriel from the panel in the vehicle monitoring section of the crew module.

The fuel pump wheezed, then sputtered and fell silent again. Jeff put his hand close to the pipe seals but couldn't detect any leaks.

"Yeah!" he said loudly. "I think we're good."

He slid-crawled to the next section as Gabriel

pocketed another set of fasteners. They lifted the floor panel and let it slide down the floor to bump against a dividing wall, revealing a compartment identical to the one in the kitchen section.

"I'll go to the next one," said Jeff. "You know what to do?"

Gabriel was already reaching into the compartment for the toggle.

"It might buck a little," Jeff added as he crawled toward the science lab, his tether quivering like a plucked guitar string behind him.

He knelt beside the third panel and worked quickly, his confidence growing with each passing second.

It's going to work, he thought. *We're going to be fine.*

There was a loud clank from behind him. The second fuel pump was off. Jeff dropped the four fasteners into his pocket and lifted one side of the floor panel on his own without waiting for Gabriel.

He held up the panel and reached into the compartment. Cold air rushed past his hand. The fuel pump whistled like a boiling teakettle.

"Hey," said Gabriel, "you didn't wait for–"

"*Get back!*" Jeff screamed.

Metal groaned and the fuel pump shook in place. Jeff grabbed and twisted the toggle, then pushed it in. As soon as it clicked into place, the pump exploded. Shrapnel burst upward, piercing his face and chest. The force blew him backward into an anchored table. His head cracked against a sharp corner and he tumbled toward the back of the ship, unconscious.

A terrible silence hung in the air of Mission Control. Kate stared up at the display wall, urging something positive to happen. She hated not having instant communication with the ship. She hated guesswork. For all she knew, *Explorer I* could have blown into a billion pieces, and she wouldn't find out about it for another ten minutes.

Frank breathed out heavily as he walked over to her workstation.

"We've done all we can for now," he said. "We just have to wait." He turned to address the room. "Someone want to tell me why the *hell* our automated shutoff system didn't work?"

"It did," Juan said from his desk. "Well, the *signal* worked. I'm not reading any errors in communication between the ship and our relay on the ground."

"You're saying Explorer's computer received the kill command?"

"Yes, sir. It looks that way."

"So why wasn't the damn thing activated?" Frank demanded. "Kate, any thoughts?"

She took a deep breath, attempting to regain some semblance of composure.

"If Jeff and Gabriel manage to shut off the fuel pumps soon," she said, "they'll barely have enough juice to get home. It will take longer than we planned because they wouldn't be able to squeeze out as many burns."

"Would they have enough food supplies?"

"We'd have to ration their meals."

Walt cleared his throat. "They're getting the minimum amount of protein as it is, like I mentioned earlier."

"They'll have to get by with even less if they want to make it back home," said Frank.

Kate anxiously rapped her knuckles on her desk. She felt helpless. *I can't do anything from down here*, she thought.

"Can I talk to you for a moment?" Frank asked.

She looked at him, confused. "What, you mean *now*?"

"Yes, now," he said gently. He gestured to one side of the room, out of earshot of the other employees.

Kate went reluctantly, not keen on leaving the monitor readouts at her workstation. Frank followed close behind.

"Listen," he said. He leaned casually against the wall with his hands in his pockets. "It's going to be harder than it has been from this point on."

"Stop," she said, holding up a warning hand. "Stop

right there. Just because Jeff and I are in a relationship, that doesn't mean I'm going to have some kind of emotional breakdown if I can't hear from him right away."

"It's not a short delay," he continued. "Any number of things could happen during the time it takes for a signal to travel between the ship and Earth."

"Are you trying to make me feel worse?"

He shifted uncomfortably and looked around for help, but found none.

"I'm just saying that it's no use worrying until we're sure. I saw you over there. You nearly chewed your bottom lip right through."

"I did not," she protested. Kate tongued the inside of her bottom lip surreptitiously. It hurt, and she thought she tasted blood.

"We trained our people well," said Frank. "If anything happens up there, they can handle it. Okay?"

She hesitated, then nodded. "Okay."

"I got a red light on fuel pump number three!" Juan shouted from his workstation.

Kate ran over to him, Frank right on her heels. Juan's monitor screen showed a digital schematic of the crew module. He tapped the blinking red symbol of a fuel pump.

"We're not getting any readings," he said. "It's completely offline."

Static burst over the comm line. Kate pressed her headset harder against her ear and adjusted her microphone.

"Explorer One, do you copy?" she said urgently,

knowing her message would be delayed. "Commander Riley, are you there?"

Another burst of static.

"Canaveral, this is Explorer One," said Riley, his voice exhausted. *"Fuel pump three is gone. There was an explosion in the crew module. Dolan was...he was standing right on top of it. He's been badly injured, over."*

_DAY 43

Laughter echoes under cotton sheets, limbs intertwined. Golden sunlight spills in from a dusty window, flowing over the two bodies like water.

They slept in on a warm Saturday morning. Beach later, then a picnic at the park, then–

Jeff's eyes popped open and he gasped.

He was lying in a small chamber, a plastic lung with light coming from beneath him and a cold robotic arm next to each of his. It took him a moment to realize he was inside the doctor pod. The air in the confined space was thick and humid. His lungs felt damp and heavy, as if he were breathing beneath a thick blanket. Yet all he wore was a pair of bloodied blue workpants and a blood-streaked white t-shirt that had been precisely cut down the middle from neck to waist.

He tried sitting up and an invisible knife stabbed his chest. Wincing, he pushed against the lid of the doctor pod.

Locked.

"Get me out of this thing!" he croaked. His throat felt as if it were lined with sandpaper.

Ming appeared a moment later, leaning over the pod to look in at him as if he were an experiment.

"Just a second," she said, her voice muffled.

She tapped a few buttons on the pod's control panel and the lid hinged open automatically. Jeff sat up, ignoring the stabbing pains in his chest, and took a deep lungful of the ship's cold, metallic air.

He gingerly probed his chest through the cut shirt and felt a thick bandage over his sternum. It crinkled with dried blood.

Ming tucked her short hair behind her ears and raised an eyebrow. "How are you feeling?" she asked.

"Like I just got out of a blender."

She nodded. "Sounds about right. You took most of the blast over your sternum and the right side of your ribcage. Those bits of shrapnel were easier to remove. Took the doctor pod half a day to pull the smaller pieces out of your neck and face. I'm sorry to say you will have massive scarring on your chest."

Jeff touched his burning cheek, and felt another bandage there.

"But otherwise, you seem okay," said Ming. "Unless you're not."

"I'll be fine," he said. "I think."

He stood cautiously, testing his weight on one foot, then the other.

"Floor's cold."

"Your shoes are over there," she said, pointing to a nearby table, "along with a fresh set of clothes."

Jeff walked slowly to the table, keeping one hand on the doctor pod for support until he was forced to let go and take the last few steps on his own. The reduced gravity made it easier.

At least the centrifuge is still spinning, he thought.

He sat in a bolted-down metal chair with a pained groan and began the laborious process of slipping on his shoes.

"How long was I unconscious?" he asked.

"Almost thirty hours."

He froze with his toes half in the shoe. "Are you serious?"

She nodded.

Jeff listened to the faint hum of the ship's electronics systems. The TAP System wasn't in operation.

"What happened after the explosion?"

"Gabriel shut off the last fuel pump," said Ming.

"Is he okay?"

"He's fine. There was no fire," she added quickly, answering the question any astronaut fears having to ask. "It was a pressure blast. Some minor damage to the interior insulation of that section of the centrifuge, but it was mostly superficial. The TAPS burned for another thirty seconds at full output before shutting down. I did my best to keep the ship on target. Mission Control is tracking a new course for us to meet up with Titan, but so far it looks good. The full burn lasted three minutes longer than it was supposed to."

"And occurred way too early. What does that mean?"

"It means we'll be at Titan in twenty days instead

of eighty."

Jeff laughed, then quickly sobered. "Wait a second. That doesn't add up. Even with a longer burn it would take us at least sixty days to arrive."

Ming hesitated a moment, then said, "Canaveral authorized another full burn before we get there."

Jeff shook his head and chuckled humorlessly as he finished slipping on his shoe. "Sure. I mean, why the hell not?"

"They say we still have enough fuel to get home, even with the extra burn."

"But the return trip will take a lot longer if we use more fuel now."

Another hesitation. "Ten months instead of five, if we're careful," said Ming.

"That's too damn long," Jeff said. He winced as he put on his second shoe, then he stood. "I need to talk to Riley. There's no reason to keep us out here longer on the tail-end if we only have to wait an extra few weeks to get to Titan."

"The burn is already complete," Ming said as Jeff walked past. "We've begun our deceleration process."

He stopped with his back to her and slowly crossed his arms.

"You were in the doctor pod," she continued. "Canaveral said there was no reason to wake you because you'd just have to go back in after the burn."

"How thoughtful."

"For what it's worth, both Gabriel and I both were against the additional burn."

"And Riley?"

She shrugged. "He said he's following orders."

"Well, hey," Jeff said sarcastically, "what's an extra few months out here, right? Not like Earth is going anywhere while we're gone. Oh wait, it's going to be on the far side of the *sun*. So not only do we have a longer return trip, we have to wait months for Earth to swing back around to our side of the solar system."

"Mission Control is working on a solution."

"I won't hold my breath," said Jeff.

His cheeks flushed with heat as he clenched his jaw, then his vision got blurry and his knees buckled.

Ming hurried to his side as he crumpled, easing him to the floor.

"You still have a lot of painkillers in your system," she explained. "Best to take it easy for a while."

"I need to go lie down," he said.

"Let's walk together."

He nodded as she helped him to stand. He leaned more heavily against her than he intended, but he didn't have the strength to ease up. His legs were like rubber and his head spun as if he were doing barrel rolls in a jet.

She guided him into his bunk and covered him with a blanket. He shivered and his teeth chattered. Ming turned out the light and closed the privacy screen, leaving Jeff curled up in darkness.

Kate sipped tepid coffee and watched the little green blip representing Jeff's delayed heartbeat on her workstation monitor. He was awake, but he hadn't checked in. Riley sent a progress report a few hours ago, letting her and the others in Mission Control know that the remaining fuel pumps were fully operational and that the final big burn of the outward journey went smoothly.

Communication with the ship would be sporadic now that the signal delay was steadily increasing. They had scheduled check-in reports along the way, but the remainder of the journey to Titan, short as it was, would be mostly radio silent unless there was another emergency – and even then, Kate wouldn't find out what was going wrong until it was maybe too late.

She set her coffee cup on a stack of papers, creating yet another moisture ring. She had been rifling through that particular stack of data printouts for several days, trying to figure out the malfunction that caused *Explorer*

I to perform a primary fuel burn instead of the minor one that was scheduled. Neither she nor the engineering techs could come up with an answer. All of *Explorer's* systems checked out. Besides the ruined fuel pump, every piece of equipment on the vessel was operating beautifully.

This wasn't how she expected things to go when she accepted a job with Diamond Aerospace. Her last work environment at Boeing had seemed much more corporate, for lack of a better word. As a local operations manager working out of the Boeing building at Kennedy, Kate had only to keep up with detailed schedules and actionable plans that were outlined years in advance.

There was no real mystery to the job, because she knew what was around the corner every step of the way. It was comforting, for the most part. She had been fortunate to take part in several spacecraft design initiatives that more than made up for the monotony of her administration job – namely the Starliner capsule and Space Launch System rocket programs.

When Noah Bell personally offered her a job at Diamond Aerospace, her immediate internal reaction was to decline. Accepting the offer would have felt like leaving solid ground to step out on a chasm-spanning narrow footbridge with no railing.

Leaving solid ground was exactly his intention.

She had been safe at Boeing, and she saw a clear and uncomplicated career trajectory in the years to come. Boeing had stood the test of time as a company, and would be around long after she retired. Diamond

Aerospace, a relative infant in the space industry by comparison, was not the sure bet.

Yet they were going to Titan.

And now she was in Diamond Aerospace's Mission Control at Kennedy, wondering what else could go wrong that she hadn't seen coming. There had been a formal plan, but it was rapidly crumbling as *Explorer I* got farther and farther from Earth. Apparently, there was a room full of geniuses in Houston in direct contact with Noah trying to figure out the best way to get the astronauts home after their stay in Titan's orbit. Kate had been assured that safety wasn't the issue – it was time. Each day, the ship's target return date was pushed back. What was supposed to be a roughly eleven-month voyage had now ballooned to fifteen. If it extended much farther, the crew would run out of food before they got back.

"*Pssst*," someone hissed from the side of the room.

Kate swiveled in her chair, looking for the source. Rick stuck his head out of the break room door and impatiently waved her over.

Kate wasn't in the mood. She shook her head, no.

Rick huffed impatiently and hurried over to her workstation. He leaned down and whispered, "You'll definitely want to see this."

"Is it a new espresso machine?"

"We wish."

He attempted to stroll back to the break room inconspicuously and failed. She glanced around the room. No one was watching him anyway. Why would they? Rick took more coffee breaks than anyone else who worked in the building. Seeing him mosey across the operations floor, mug in hand, was a common sight.

Kate reluctantly stood up and followed him, taking her time. Rick scanned his thumb, swiped his security badge over the electronic lock, and pulled open the door when the lock clicked open and the light over the handle turned green.

"I still haven't figured out why there's a lock on this door," Kate said.

"Want to know what I think?" Rick asked.

She held up her hands. "No. No I do not."

"Did you know," he said, his voice lowering as they entered the break room, "that my unique badge code was just stored in a central database on-site because I unlocked the door? If something were to happen inside the break room after I swiped my badge, the security team would know it was me."

"Uh huh…" said Kate. She smelled another conspiracy rant coming on.

They were alone in the room. Black tiles covered the floor, touching black walls that led up to a ceiling that was a solid rectangle of soft light from edge to edge. There were vending machines and a microwave on one side, a table with magazines and newspapers on another, and doors leading to the bathrooms across from the entrance. Several build-it-yourself black tables were in the middle, each one surrounded by plastic chairs, the backs of which bent back too far if you weren't careful.

Rick led Kate to a closed laptop on one of the tables. He sat down and opened the lid, then pulled an empty chair next to him and patted the seat.

Kate sighed. "Come on, Rick. Is all this cloak and daggers nonsense really necessary? I need to be out there watching the feeds."

"Jeff is fine," he said gently. "He is surrounded by the most competent people we could send into space. You can't do anything for him down here that they can't do for him up there, except worry a lot harder. And like I said, you'll want to see this."

She softened a little.

"They keep records of everything that happens inside this building," Rick said, finally continuing his earlier monologue. His clunky laptop booted up slowly. Lines of text scrolled up the screen. He was running some kind of Linux system on an older machine. "They log badge swipes, keystrokes, fingerprint and retinal scans, and outbound signals...including access requests to the remote system on Explorer One."

The welcome screen on his laptop popped up. Big letters in a faux spray paint font were printed over a brick wall background image: NOT YOURS, ASSHOLE.

"Just to deter any snoops," Rick explained.

"Ah." Kate sat next to him and folded her arms.

He typed at the keyboard, and several console windows appeared, each one rapidly scrolling through hundreds of lines of small text.

"It's a smart system," Rick said as more text scrolled up the screen. "If something goes wrong, they wouldn't have to waste time checking every line of code. Instead, they could just go directly to the source and solve the problem."

Kate leaned back in her seat slightly, her eyes narrowing. "Except...you don't have *access* to those systems," she said.

He hit the Enter key and gestured to the screen.

"I do now."

"Rick–"

"I know," he interrupted. "I had a hunch and it turned out to be right. No one would prosecute me for finding this out."

"Finding *what* out?"

He nodded toward the screen. "See for yourself."

Kate shook her head as she tried to make sense of the myriad streams of data in the console windows.

"This one here," Rick said, pointing to a window at the top.

She recognized what looked like a long string of computer IP addresses and security badge codes, each one followed by a time stamp starting three days earlier and ending five minutes ago. Below that information was a block of text listing various systems, everything from the alarms to network access for a security upgrade.

"You can match the time stamps with the system that was being accessed," said Rick. "For example, this one here registered five minutes ago and shows my unique badge code." Kate followed his finger to the list of accessed systems and saw that the time stamp corresponded with something called INT_SEC 017. "It's saying I accessed the internal security locking system, door number seventeen. That's the door to the break room."

She leaned back suddenly, finally understanding where he was heading.

"But it was a malfunction," she said, referring to the primary engine burn that should never have happened. "It *had* to be. No one here would have triggered a primary burn remotely. It could have ruined the entire mission."

"Yet that's exactly what happened," Rick said, pointing at a line of text. "Here's the remote access system code for Explorer One."

The code was REM_SYS EXP-1, and the time stamp next to it logged an access request two minutes before the primary burn. Below that line of text were the names of the two users in the system when the burn was initiated.

JOHNSON_F and *BELL_N*.

"Oh my God," Kate whispered. "They could have killed everyone on the ship."

"We don't know if it was both of them or not," Rick said. "Keep in mind that you followed me into the break room after I used my badge. If I left and you bashed in the microwave, I'd be the first one questioned by security." He shifted nervously in his seat. "I went back through the logs, and Frank is logged in to the remote system a hell of a lot. Now, that could just be a precautionary measure so he doesn't have to waste time logging in if something terrible happened and he needed to take control. But Bell...he hardly ever logs in. The last time he was in the system was for the first big burn, shortly after the ship left the ISS."

"Okay," she said. Her heart beat faster and her

breathing was noticeably quicker. "We might be working for one or two psychopaths. What should we do?"

"We certainly don't confront either of them until we know more," Rick said.

"Isn't this enough?" Kate demanded, pointing at the screen.

"Diamond Aerospace owns this information. It lives on their servers. I am *not* a welcome guest in their digital fortress. We would only get ourselves fired if we told anyone. Or worse. Remember Michael Cochran?"

"We can't just sit back and wait for them to jeopardize the mission and the lives of the crew again."

Rick slowly closed the lid of his laptop.

"We could leave," he said.

Kate looked at him. He was serious.

"Honestly, it would be easy," he continued. "We yank the money out of our 401k accounts before the company can stop us and head for South America until Noah and Frank commit career suicide because of their own mistakes."

"It's not that easy," she said. "I...I can't leave Jeff. Or the others. I don't know what's going to happen once they reach Titan, but I *do* know they're going to need all the help they can get. Especially if someone here is working against the mission."

Rick crossed his arms in thought and stared up at the ceiling. He rocked quickly against the flimsy back of the chair, then stopped suddenly.

"Okay, then," he said. "We'll stay. But I'm going to do some more digging."

Kate looked at him skeptically. "What does *that* mean?"

"The less you know, the better. Let's just say I have another hunch."

"And if it turns out to be right, like the one you just told me about...?"

"Then we have more to worry about than who initiated a primary burn."

Kate swallowed. Her throat was dry and scratchy. "Like what?"

"Like not ending up in a dumpster."

_DAY 52

Jeff floated in the maintenance tube at the rear of the crew module, staring into an open wall panel. He had an electric screwdriver in one hand and a length of stripped wire in the other, yet he could not for the life of him remember what he had been about to do.

He was dizzy from his morning painkiller. For some reason, the reaction to taking one had lasted longer than usual, causing a cold sickness in his stomach and dryness in his throat. After breakfast, he had caught a glimpse of himself in the mirror. His pale cheeks were shaded green.

Must not be getting enough sleep, he thought. *Or maybe the beef cubes are finally doing me in.*

Jeff shut his eyes tight and worked backward, remembering that he ended every visit to the maintenance tube with a ship-wide check of the electrical systems.

Batteries, he thought, a dim light of revelation gleaming deep in his mind. He unscrewed a short wire from an electronics panel and replaced it with the one he was holding, then he pushed the old wire into his pocket to dispose of later. It was the last stage of his bi-weekly process to make sure the electrical systems were properly balanced. Any lopsidedness in the charge would reveal itself in one of the little wires on the main panel. They acted as early-warning fuses, and would melt before a serious piece of equipment became compromised.

He replaced the cover of the wall panel but didn't exit the maintenance tube. Instead, he floated in silence, his eyes closed, and listened to the hum of the ship.

Getting his bearings had been tough after the accident. If it hadn't been for the fact that the other crew members weren't trained to do his job, he would have liked to stay in his bunk until *Explorer I* made it back to Earth. Ming had enough knowledge to keep the oxygen systems running and to perform maintenance on the computer mainframe, but she had only been superficially trained in propulsion and electrical.

The urge to stay in his bunk and ride out the rest of the mission was only temporary. He quickly found that the best way to keep his mind occupied was to embrace his daily routine. And so he pretended that the ship hadn't suffered a serious malfunction. He felt a little queasier in the mornings after taking his painkiller, and he seemed to tire out a couple hours earlier than usual. Those symptoms would only last another couple of days, Walt assured him.

"Dolan."

Jeff jumped at the sound of Riley's voice. He looked

down the maintenance tube. The commander floated near the central pillar of the crew module, holding on to the ladder with one hand.

"Join us for a meeting in the lab," he said, nodding down to the floor of the centrifuge below him. "Got a mission update, and it's a doozy."

His face was red and sweaty. Jeff figured he had just wrapped up one of his longer UV sessions in the doctor pod.

"Be right there."

Riley coasted toward the wall just outside the maintenance tube, whistling to himself, then he climbed down a ladder just under the tube opening and disappeared from sight.

Jeff checked to make sure all the panels in the maintenance tube were secure because he couldn't remember which ones he had accessed over the last few hours, then he followed Riley down the ladder to the floor of the centrifuge.

Gabriel was already sitting at one of the lab tables when Jeff arrived. Ming walked over from the crew quarters a few moments later, yawning and stretching. She eased down onto a secured stool next to Gabriel and rubbed her tired eyes. Jeff took a seat at the table next to theirs. Riley remained standing, his arms folded, leaning against another table.

"I just received two messages," he said stiffly. "One from my demon of an ex-wife, which I will not recount because I already complain about her too much…"

Gabriel chuckled. He had borne the brunt of a vast majority of the commander's polemics denouncing the unsavory antics of his former bride – diatribes that came to be known affectionately amongst the crew as 'Riley's Rants'.

"…and one from the man himself, *Mr.* Noah Bell," he continued. "He wanted me to congratulate all of you on your excellent work thus far. He's very proud that you're part of the crew taking humanity's first steps into a wider universe."

Gabriel's eyes opened wide. "Wow," he said. "I didn't know you were a robot."

Riley breathed out heavily, clearly relieved to be done with the speech. "I agree, rhetoric usually isn't my thing."

"Did Bell tell you to say that?" Ming asked.

"More or less. I may have left out some of the more effusive paragraphs, but I couldn't help it. The guy sounded like a giddy little kid who thinks he has to tell everyone else that he's excited." Riley's face went suddenly red with anger, and it looked like he wanted to punch someone. Jeff thought there might be something else going on behind the curtain, some detail about their conversation that Riley was dwelling on but not divulging.

"Why is he softening us up?" Jeff asked.

"Because you all have a monumental task ahead of you," Riley answered. His posture relaxed slightly and he breathed out evenly as his anger retreated.

Gabriel chuckled. "All we're doing is bolting together a few pieces of scrap in orbit around Titan."

"Laying the groundwork for a space station is not a trivial undertaking," Ming said.

"That's correct," Riley agreed. "Bell wants the station fully staffed and operating within five years, which is a tall order. It will mean multiple trips to Titan with crews that won't do anything more than add another section to the facility." He paused for a moment. "But that's not what I wanted to talk to you about."

"Are we going to be on Sesame Street or something?" asked Gabriel.

Jeff laughed unexpectedly – the first genuine laugh since his accident.

"Unfortunately, no," Riley said with a grin. "I think you'll like it better. Bell showed me a picture in the video message he sent. A picture of Titan."

"I have one of those in my bunk," Ming said.

"Not with an alien artifact in it," Riley added.

The three of them stared at Riley for a long moment, then looked at each other. The slight hum of the air filtration system was the only audible noise in their small, pressurized universe.

"Did Noah really send you a video message?" Jeff asked.

"He really did."

"And he showed you a picture of an alien spaceship on Titan," Gabriel stated.

"Not on Titan," Riley corrected. "In orbit around it. And they're not calling it a spaceship. It's an artifact."

Another silence. Jeff sat with his mouth half-open, hung up because he wanted to ask a dozen questions, but wasn't sure where to start.

"Did they know about this artifact before we launched?" Ming asked.

Riley hesitated, then said, "I believe so."

"But you only learned of it in the message from Bell."

Riley shrugged. "We're ten days from Titan. I think he wanted us to be prepared for what we're going to see."

"And he's clearly in a hurry to get us there," said Ming.

"What do you mean?" asked Gabriel.

"I went back over the logs preceding and following the 'accidental' primary burn. It was triggered a few seconds before I was about to initiate a microburn. I checked who was logged into the remote access system at the time. Only two people, Noah Bell and Frank Johnson."

"You think one of them scheduled a big burn at the same time they knew you would perform a smaller one?" Jeff asked.

"It wasn't an equipment glitch," Ming said. "It wasn't pilot error. What does that leave?"

No one had an answer.

"So what the hell do we do when we get there?" Gabriel asked a few moments later, throwing up his hands. "I'm supposed to install incubators for greenhouses on a space station!"

"You'll do exactly that," Riley said calmly. "Just like Dolan and Lieutenant Ming will install the central computer systems, and I'll operate the extension arms."

"Surely they want us to take a closer look at whatever's out there," Jeff said.

Riley nodded. "Absolutely. Since we're arriving early, we'll run our scans, take enough photos and videos to fill a mainframe, and wait for instructions. When Mission Control says it's time to go home, we go home."

They were silent for a long time. Riley watched them stew in their own thoughts.

"What's it look like?" Gabriel asked.

"The picture was blurry. Black and white. It was a

dark object. Ovoid, I would say, like a slender egg."

"How do they know it's alien?" Jeff asked,

"They don't. Bell admits it could be a hoax from one of his competitors, or some kind of new satellite system the government is testing."

"How did Bell get the picture?" Ming asked.

"Beats the hell out of me," said Riley. "I didn't ask.

But we're still the only ones with the TAP System, or anything close to it. Anyone else would have needed to launch years ago to beat us here."

"So the bottom line is that there's no way to know what we're walking into," Jeff said.

They sat together in wary silence as the ship hurtled toward its rendezvous with Titan.

_DAY 61

Kate stood in the open doorway at the back of her apartment, sipping hot lemon tea and watching the orange clouds of sunset over the ocean. The soft but powerful glow came from behind the building, illuminating the beach that stretched from her backyard fence to the water's edge. Beachgrass wavered in the warm, gentle evening breeze. A man and woman walked barefoot in the wet sand, laughing and flirting. Kate watched them until they passed, then took another sip of tea.

It felt good to be away from Mission Control. She had been putting in such long hours recently that it felt like she was only ever home long enough to fall asleep and wake up. If she had been forced to admit the truth, she didn't need to be at work that much in the first place. She mostly just sat at her workstation, watching the data feeds on the display wall and waiting for the next message from *Explorer I*.

What else am I supposed to do? she wondered. *Jeff's return date keeps getting pushed back, but it's not like I'm going to hit the bars and find a replacement because he's a little late.*

Still, she had to admit to herself that she could use a friend or two to help distract her from her daily worries.

Kate went into the apartment, to her small kitchen, and rinsed out her tea cup. She was turning over names in her mind, trying to decide which of her local friends she could call to get things moving, when tires squealed on the road outside. She hurried to one of the front windows, hands still wet from the sink.

A blue Jetta, older than her Mustang, had mounted the curb of her front yard and sat parked half on her grass and half on the road. Rick was behind the wheel, looking scared. Amid a symphony of honks from stopped drivers, he backed off the grass haltingly, then pulled into the small parking lot.

Kate opened the front door and leaned against the doorway, arms folded, mentally steeling herself for whatever craziness was headed her way. Rick got out of his car in a hurry, clutching a thick blue file folder to his chest with one hand and a half-gallon fountain soda with the other.

"Nobody knows how to drive around here!" he exclaimed as he hustled from his car, gesturing toward the road with his large soda. "They act like they've never seen a turn signal before."

"It might help if you stuck to veering into driveways instead of onto lawns," Kate offered. "You ruined my future rose bushes."

She pointed to the two deep score marks left in the grass by the Jetta's tires. Rick turned back and winced at the sight.

"Good thing you hate gardening, right?" he said hopefully.

"Yeah, right. Anyway, what's the rush?"

Rick tapped the blue folder hesitantly, then gestured into the apartment. "You mind if I come in?" he asked breathlessly. "Feels a little awkward standing out here on the porch."

Kate waited a moment, then stepped aside and gestured for him to enter.

"Thanks," he said as he walked past.

Kate sighed, regretting not calling one of her friends sooner.

Careful what you wish for, she thought.

Rick sat at the dining room table with the folder in front of him. He tapped his fingers on it nervously. Kate remained standing, hoping his visit wouldn't last long.

"Are you going to tell what's in there, or do I have to guess?" she asked.

He regarded her intensely, as if scrutinizing her ability to handle whatever he was about to say.

"Before I spill the beans," Rick said, "I need to be sure you can detach any feelings you might have for certain people on the mission from the actual mission itself. What I have in here," he continued, resting his hands on the folder, "will change everything."

"Enough with the suspense!"

She held out an eager hand for Rick to give her the folder. He held it tightly against his chest, eyeing her suspiciously. Finally he relinquished it, looking as uncertain as a new mother who just handed her baby to a stranger.

Kate flipped open the thick folder. It was filled with computer printouts detailing the construction of a Diamond Aerospace launch facility in Kazakhstan, near the Baikonur Cosmodrome. The Baikonur spaceport had been the primary launch site for all of Russia's space missions until the country built the Vostochny spaceport on their own soil. It was still used occasionally by the Russians when launch conditions to the International Space Station weren't favorable from the newer facility.

"Rick…" she said slowly. "I've never seen this. I doubt anyone has. Where in the *hell* did you get it?"

"Archives," he said.

"You mean the locked and *sealed* archives inside the Diamond Aerospace building?"

"Yes."

"The archives to which we don't have any legal access?"

"Yes, yes! Fine, so I wasn't *supposed* to go inside. Was anybody *supposed* to ask Nixon about Watergate?"

She snapped the folder shut and dropped it on her dining table with a dull thud.

"I don't care about Nixon," said Kate. "I care about my job."

"Well, you should care about the people on the spacecraft, too," he said. "There is a lot more in that folder besides building schematics."

"Like what?" she asked hesitantly.

"Like evidence that the antimatter propulsion system wasn't ready for real-world flight."

"Don't be ridiculous," Kate said dismissively. "That system was subjected to more tests than any other piece of equipment in the history of spaceflight."

"And the test results were faked." Rick leaned in close. His voice dropped to barely a whisper as he said, "Explorer One is not the first ship Diamond Aerospace has sent to Titan."

She sat down hard, unable to make her eyes focus on the data in front of her.

"That can't be right," she whispered weakly. "I...I've been with the company for two years, ever since they opened the Canaveral facility. The only launches before Explorer were near-Earth commercial satellites for third party companies."

"Launches from Cape Canaveral, yes," said Rick. He pushed his glasses up the bridge of his nose and pointed to the blueprint of a large warehouse facility. "But not from Baikonur."

"We never partnered with the Russians. China won all of our Titan contracts."

"Look," Rick said. He shuffled through the papers in the folder until he found one with a list of dates and coordinates. "Six probes in three years, launched from Baikonur. All of them but one malfunctioned on the way to Titan because the engine was faulty. The one that made it all the way disappeared when it got there. They think it probably disintegrated in the atmosphere, but not before snapping a single photo and sending it back to Earth. There's a record of it here," he added, tapping a line of text on the page.

"Where is the photo?"

"Not in the folder," Rick admitted begrudgingly. "I may have missed something while I was snooping around in the archives."

Kate stared at the folder. "You said the TAPS malfunctioned…"

"It habitually blew up on the way to Titan."

"…Oh."

"I was trying to break it to you gently. According to these records, each probe completed two successful primary burns en route before losing all contact with the Diamond Aerospace facility near Russia. The engineers suspect that something happened during the ignition process of the third and final primary burn."

"But Explorer has already completed *three* primary burns!" Kate said urgently.

"And the crew will need another two to get home, if their fuel levels hold."

"We already know they don't have enough fuel for two more major burns."

"Then they're safer taking it slow. It's not a question of *if* the engine will fail, but *when*."

"Do the reports show the cause of the malfunction?"

"The engineers never figured it out," Rick said, "but not for lack of trying. The company sank millions into the problem and came up with nothing."

"How could they *do* this?" she asked. "How could the company send people into space using unproven technology?"

"Explorer was only supposed to initiate four primary burns total," Rick said. "Two there and two back. My guess is that as soon as the probe sent that picture back from Titan, Bell decided whatever's in the photo was worth the risk of rushing to green-light the TAP System."

"It's *murder*."

"*Legal* murder," Rick corrected. "There are copies of the crew contracts in the folder. Everyone on Explorer, including Jeff, signed an agreement not to hold the company liable for any risks, known or unknown. The contracts are riddled with dense verbiage, but the bottom line is that there has always been a high chance of failure. The crew knew that from the beginning."

Kate shook her head slowly as she tried to think of a way to rage against a seemingly helpless situation.

"But...what about Michael Cochran?" she asked.

"Now that most definitely *was* murder."

"Cochran worked for Diamond Aerospace, right?"

Rick nodded. "He was on the operations floor of their Baikonur facility during the probe launches."

"Then let's take this to the cops. We'll show them the folder and everything that's in it. We'll tell them about Cochran."

Rick held up his hands to slow her down. "Just hold on a second."

"I don't want to wait anymore, Rick!"

"You told me that Frank might know someone at

the Sheriff's Department–"–"

"So?"

"If we take this information to them, who's to say they won't squash the story…and *us*…before it gets out?"

She fidgeted nervously with a corner of the blue folder. "What are you suggesting?"

"Just give me one more day to work some magic," he said. "I know a reporter who would *kill* to broadcast this kind of a story. Not literally, of course. If we can get the story out, then Diamond Aerospace would be forced to play by the rules. They've been free from public scrutiny throughout this entire ordeal, and it's time that changed."

"You want to force them to be accountable for anything that happens next," Kate said.

"Exactly."

"You're not talking about a reporter from The Daily Glass, are you?"

"They ran that picture of Cochran when no one else would!" he said defensively. "These are noble people sticking it to Big Media any chance they can."

She was silent for a long moment. "We might be working with a murderer, Rick."

He nodded slowly. "What do you think we should do?"

"I have to go back to work," she said helplessly. "I don't have any other choice."

Rick reached across the table and squeezed her hand. "I'm going to try and arrange a meeting tonight with that reporter. Hopefully we'll have to wade through a sea of them to get inside the Diamond Aerospace building tomorrow morning."

"Just…be careful," she said.

It was dark when he collected the papers into the blue folder and said goodbye. Kate watched from the front doorway as he backed out into the street in his beat-up Jetta and drove away. She turned around and went inside, not seeing the heavily tinted black SUV without a license plate following after him.

PART III

THE ARTIFACT

_DAY 62

Jupiter was on the far side of the sun when *Explorer I* passed the boundary of its orbit on the way to Titan. The crew had originally been promised a distant glimpse of the largest planet in the solar system as the ship hurtled toward its destination, but everything changed with the early and unexpected primary burn.

Now the only object worth seeing through the narrow window of the command module was a pinpoint light three-hundred million kilometers ahead.

Saturn.

In a matter of hours, that pinpoint light would grow to a small disk the size of a dime. The planet's rings would be clearly visible at that distance as a wire-thin equatorial halo. *Explorer I* would get no closer, because Titan's orbit would soon after bring the moon to the waiting ship 1.2 million kilometers away from its ringed parent.

Saturn was a gas giant, like Jupiter, comprised mainly of helium and hydrogen that surrounded a hot, soupy liquid core of various metals and rock. Ammonia crystals in the gaseous outer layers of the atmosphere gave the planet a pale ochre hue much like that of its sixth moon. Though where Titan appeared as a hazy billiards ball without a pattern, Saturn was layered with horizontally-stacked pale stripes from pole to pole.

Yet the gas behemoth held no interest for the nascent space industry of Earth. At the dawn of their burgeoning space empires, those in the industry knew it would be far more lucrative to focus on the many moons of the planet – moons which held the possibility of countless natural resources untapped by the greedy fingers of Earth. They existed as worlds without regulation, with no protection except for the moral code of whoever got there first.

During one press conference, Noah Bell called it "a bold new frontier for industry", and "a powerful spark for the collective imagination of humanity".

There was no doubt in Jeff's mind that Noah was just as much of a dreamer as he was a businessman. Attaining such goals as those grasped at by a man like Noah demanded not only a cunning worldly acumen, but also the capacity for improvisation, adaptation, and creative needlework on a vast scale.

Jeff stood in the lab section of the centrifuge, cycling through the on-screen menus of the doctor pod. He had already run his routine maintenance of the equipment earlier that morning. Now he had a few minutes of rare private time. Instead of taking it in his bunk, he decided to see if he could figure out a way to use Riley's UV program.

Most of the pod's protocols were focused around healing minor external traumas, such as cuts and abrasions. The robotic arms could set broken bones and expertly stitch and staple deeper flesh wounds. Jeff found a menu for automated ultrasounds, but there seemed to be a necessary piece of equipment missing within the pod for that particular function. The menu screen for that process was grayed out, inaccessible.

He swiped to the next menu and paused as he read the descriptive text.

Targeted gamma radiation treatment.

None of Jeff's maintenance protocols had required him to check that specific setting. It was mentioned nowhere in the documentation he had been referencing since he began servicing the doctor pod, and it certainly wasn't in the stock manual he had recently been sifting through.

He pressed the button for more information and continued reading.

According to the documentation, localized bursts of gamma radiation could inhibit the growth of Stage 1 cancer tumors. Higher doses of radiation could theoretically have a greater effect on later stages of cancer, but the doctor pod was unable to produce that much energy output.

Ideally, none of the crew would need such a feature in space. The voyage held inherent dangers in the form of constant radiation bombardment, both from the sun and from the cosmic fabric of the universe itself. The heavily shielded hull of *Explorer I* worked to mitigate most of that radiation, and bumped what remained down to survivable levels. Much like the missing apparatus for ultrasounds, there should have been no reason to include the gamma radiation functions of the doctor pod. If Jeff were reading the on-screen information correctly, it had required the installation of two heavy, low-frequency emitters within the pod, greatly increasing the flight weight of the equipment.

Jeff swiped through the rest of the on-screen menus, searching for the UV setting.

"So you figured it out," said Riley from behind.

Jeff snapped around, his heart skipping a beat. Riley must have come along the central pillar and silently climbed down a low dividing wall as Jeff paged through the pod's menus.

"You have cancer," Jeff said. He looked around the lab. Gabriel and Ming were elsewhere.

Riley stuck his hands in his pockets and frowned. He nodded once, gravely. "Took you longer than I thought," he said. "Pancreatic. They found it early, but that doesn't matter. It got my old man, and his." He stepped forward and rested a hand on the doctor pod, eyeing it appreciatively. "This chunk of metal and plastic is stalling the tumor's growth, but the little bastard will quickly take over once we get home."

"But…" Jeff started, trying to form his jumbled thoughts into words. "But you knew about the cancer before the mission."

Riley nodded.

"And you volunteered anyway," Jeff said. "They let a terminal patient command the first mission to Titan."

"That's right."

"No, that's *crazy*. Unless..." He paused as realization slowly crept to the front of his mind. "Unless you know something the rest of us don't. Are we in trouble, Commander? What are we going to find out there?"

"Nothing has changed except our timeline," said Riley. "Trust me, Dolan. Everything is going to be fine."

Kate hadn't been able to sleep the night before *Explorer I* was scheduled to enter Titan's orbit. She tossed restlessly in bed for several hours before finally giving it up for a midnight walk on the beach. The sand was pleasantly cool between her toes, and the gentle waves, their white crests glowing in the moonlight, had given her something to focus on besides the mission.

She showered before the sun came up and sat at her dining room table at six o'clock with a cup of coffee, staring at nothing while she tried to think of a way to send a secret message to Jeff. She wanted to warn him about the potential instability of the antimatter engine – that multiple uses increased the risk of catastrophic failure.

Seven o'clock rolled by, and she still hadn't come up with a single usable idea. Then, like every other morning for the past few months, including the weekends, she packed her day bag, grabbed her Diamond Aerospace security badge, and left for work.

Kate didn't feel like crying. She wasn't afraid. There was a sustained anticipation inside of her, like a taut violin string on the verge of snapping. Soon the crew of *Explorer I* would begin construction of the first phase of a new space station in orbit around a distant moon, and she was a part of it.

As she drove north on Atlantic Avenue, up the narrow barrier island that led to the Space Center, the image of Michael Cochran's dead body flashed in her mind. She shut her eyes against the memory. Another driver blared their horn. A Mercedes roared past, mere inches from Kate's side-view mirror. She had drifted over the center line.

Her eyes were open wide the rest of the way to work, even when the grisly image of murder crept back into her thoughts.

Like every other morning, she stopped at the guardhouse gate and waited to hand her security badge to the stocky security guard, Ed.

Except Ed wasn't there. Instead, a tall, muscular man ten years younger sporting aviator sunglasses accepted Kate's badge with a nod before disappearing into the guardhouse. He wore the same dark blue uniform as Ed – kind of a spin on a traditional police officer's blues. Yet where Ed threatened to bust through the buttons over his stomach, the new guard strained at the seams over his chest and biceps. It gave Kate the impression he had borrowed the uniform from a smaller friend.

He emerged from the guardhouse and returned her badge without a smile.

"Where's Ed?" Kate asked as lightly as she could manage. "He didn't catch that bug that's going around, did he?"

The guard stared at her a moment.

"I'm afraid I have to ask you for your cell phone, Ms. Bishop."

"My what?" she asked. "Why? No, I'm not giving you my phone."

"Then I can't raise the gate, ma'am. Everyone must relinquish their cell phone before entering the building. Strict orders."

"From who, Noah? Frank?"

The guard's lips tightened.

Kate snatched up her purse from the passenger's seat and rummaged through the contents. For the first time since she had joined Diamond Aerospace, she thought she should never have taken the job.

She found her phone and tossed it at the guard. He caught it deftly, his face an unreadable stone mask. A moment later, the gate lifted.

"Have a nice day, Ms. Bishop," said the guard.

He watched her drive past the guard house, her cell phone gripped like a child's toy in his meaty hand. Kate glanced up at him in her rear-view mirror and noticed something she had never seen when Ed worked the front gate: a large pistol strapped to the guard's belt.

"So what's next?" Jeff asked. He rapped his knuckles against the doctor pod's acrylic shield, rattling the robotic arms within, and Riley frowned. "Sorry."

"The lieutenant and I park this ship in orbit around Titan," Riley said, "and we see why Bell was so hell-bent on sending us out here before he should have."

"What about fixing the secondary fuel line sensor for the TAPS?"

"I want to take everything real slow and act like the smallest mistake could kill us all."

"...Because it could."

"First we'll enter orbit," said Riley, "then we'll shoot a message home and wait for instructions from Canaveral. You'll probably perform the mission's first EVA after we hear back from home base."

"I'll start prepping my suit," Jeff said.

"You have time. We won't get their response for a couple hours after we're in orbit. Slow and steady."

"It'll help keep me occupied. My daily maintenance

is almost finished, anyway."

Riley left to go to the private hygiene compartment in the crew section. Jeff stood next to the doctor pod as he looked around the interior of the crew module. The crew members' four bright orange Constellation Space Suits were laid out in shallow, molded compartments in the floor of the last centrifuge section, beyond the science lab.

He stopped by Gabriel's lab station on his way to the suits. The small, narrow pot containing Gabriel's sprouting lima bean was the centerpiece of the desk, surrounded by grimy petri dishes, an array of metal and plastic tools, and binders packed with laminated pages.

Jeff leaned over the desk to look inside the small pot, a curious half-smile on his lips.

The plant had wilted.

The small, hopeful bud that Jeff saw when he had awoken after his accident no longer held the promise of life. Instead, it was a brown and withered thing; a dried husk that could not be saved.

Jeff turned when he heard footsteps approaching. Gabriel walked over to the desk and looked down at the wilted plant with a sad smile.

"I don't think it's a bad omen," he said.

"What do you think it is?" Jeff asked.

"Bad soil. Not enough oxygen. I should have put it in one of those new zero-g microgreen boxes, but I had already maxed out my weight limit for the mission. The rest of them are doing fine."

He gestured to a rack of potted plants nearby, vibrant with fresh, green foliage.

"I thought I could get the lima bean to grow the normal way with a few old tricks," he continued. "It seems you also need some new ones if you want to conform to a strict design plan in a low-gravity greenhouse."

"At least it sprouted."

Gabriel scratched his black and gray stubble thoughtfully. Shaving hadn't been one of his top priorities for a while now. He glanced behind him to see if anyone else was around.

"I've been thinking about the fuel pump explosion."

Jeff rubbed the center of his chest and winced at the pain. He could feel the rough stitching that sealed one of his more grievous lacerations. "Yeah, me too," he said. "What about it?"

"First the fuel line, then the pump. I have to wonder what else will fail."

"You're not the only one."

"You think it's still a good idea to go outside the ship?"

"I need to swap out that sensor before another primary burn. We're already pushing our luck."

He grinned. "Yes, but that's what space exploration is all about, isn't it? We created a rulebook, a guideline of best practices. But nobody has ever been here before. We are the first."

"Are you saying we throw out the rulebook?"

"I'm saying we should be writing a *new* one. If you go outside the ship, and another piece of equipment blows up underneath you, you won't just be thrown back across the centrifuge. You'll be pushed out into space."

"I know the risks. Besides, we need the TAPS to get home, so I don't really have a choice."

"No," said Gabriel, "we need it to get home *quickly*."

"I'd rather take the chance of using it instead of spending years on the return trip."

"I wouldn't."

Because you don't have anyone waiting for you, Jeff almost said, but he caught the cruel jab before it slipped out, then cursed himself for thinking it. Gabriel's parents lived in Brazil with his younger siblings. Jeff was tired and on edge, and that combination muddied his thoughts.

"I'll get the sensor patched up and we won't have to worry about it," he said. "A couple months late is better than nothing. I'm sorry about your lima bean."

Gabriel picked up the small pot and stuck his finger down on the withered bud, crushing it into the soil.

"It's only a bean," he said.

Static crackled over the intercom and they both looked up at a speaker embedded in the central pillar.

"All crew to the command module. We have visual on Titan."

Kate looked into the retinal scanner and swiped her security badge at the door to Mission Control. The lock chirped and the doors slid open. Movement caught her eye and she stopped. She stood with one hand by her side, the other gripping her day bag, watching.

Frank walked among the workstations on the operations floor, talking loudly with the operations technicians, a big grin on his face and a chocolate donut in his hand. He slapped Juan on the back a little too hard. Juan chuckled until Frank walked away, then his smile turned to a scowl as he rubbed his hurt shoulder. He spun in his chair to face the display wall, shaking his head.

The operations floor was busier than it had been since launch day.

With good reason, thought Kate. There were a lot more moving pieces in play that morning, and each one of those pieces represented an entirely new and different way to fail.

She squared her shoulders and entered Mission Control.

"Ms. Bishop!" Frank called down happily from the viewing platform at the back of the room. "Good morning! Coffee and donuts in the conference room." He waved her up to the platform and walked out of sight, presumably to get another chocolate donut.

"Why's he in such a good mood?" Kate grumbled to herself as she plopped her bag on the seat of her chair.

"We're ahead of schedule," Juan said without emotion, reciting a recurring workplace mantra. "And saving time saves–"

"–lots of money," she finished for him. "Yeah, yeah. That's one of his favorites. If I had a dime for every time Frank quoted himself, I wouldn't have to work here."

"Anyway," said Juan, shrugging. "We got donuts."

"Better than that early pension I was hoping for," she joked.

Rick wasn't at his workstation. Kate checked the clock on the display wall. He should have arrived shortly after her, if he was sticking to his habit of being several minutes late for every shift.

Kate walked up the aisle between the center workstations, saying her good-mornings as she made her way to the stairs leading up to the viewing platform. The multiple monitor screens on Frank's unnecessarily massive desk all showed different angles of the exterior of *Explorer I*. The camera looking over the nose had a clear view of Titan as the craft approached. Saturn's moon appeared as a hazy, yellowish marble in the distance. In another hour or so, the view would get *really* impressive.

She joined several others in the conference room.

They were huddled around one side of the table, where several ravaged boxes of donuts awaited her. Frank had his mouth around another chocolate donut. He gestured at the boxes enthusiastically.

Kate took a relatively unsquashed jelly donut to be polite, then filled a coffee cup halfway and ducked out of the room before Frank could swallow his bite and start up a conversation.

She went to the railing of the viewing platform next to Frank's desk and looked down on the operations floor. Still no Rick. Noah was absent, as well, though Kate had been getting used to not seeing him around. She figured he watched everything from his office and only came down when he thought it was absolutely necessary.

Kate went back to her workstation and checked her desktop phone for messages from other department heads, in case Rick had tried to contact one of them. Nothing. She asked the other techs to see if anyone on *Explorer I* had said anything to her in their last nightly recap. Sorry, Ms. Bishop, just a routine check-in.

She sat at her desk, gently spinning in her chair as she surveyed the room, deep in thought.

Michael Cochran was murdered. Diamond Aerospace had sent six probes to Titan before launching *Explorer I*. Who else in the building with her at that moment knew about the other D.A. facility? Who else knew that all of the probes but one failed on the way to their destination?

Kate was left wondering how she could send a message to Jeff without everyone else in the building knowing what she said. The system screened and logged every incoming and outgoing message. She and Jeff had never needed to invent a way to exchange coded messages.

More important than being eavesdropped upon by a bunch of gossips was the fact that her message would quite clearly indicate that she or someone she knew had broken into the sealed archives and read classified information about the company. At the very least, it would result in her getting fired, possibly along with Rick. At worst, the two of them might end up like Michael Cochran.

I'm starting to sound as paranoid as Rick, Kate thought. *I bet he would say I still wasn't half as paranoid as I should be.*

Regardless of the consequences to herself, or even to Rick, she needed to warn the crew of *Explorer I* that there was a potentially lethal problem with their engine, not just a glitch with the secondary fuel line sensor.

She kept repeating the question in her mind: *How can I get a coded message to just one person on a ship hundreds of millions of miles away without everyone in Mission Control knowing what was in the message?*

And if she *did* manage to send a message, what could she say? What kind of code would she use? How could she be sure Jeff would understand what she was sending him? Telling him not to initiate another antimatter burn would mean another few years before she saw him again. Yet, the more times the system ignited, the greater the risk of catastrophic failure. If the crew had to come home without the antimatter engine, they wouldn't have enough food to last them the journey. Gabriel might be able to supplement their diet if he could manage to rig a makeshift greenhouse for vegetables, but even that may not be enough for four people.

I have to let him know the risk, Kate painfully realized, *even if they're ordered to use the engine anyway.*

Her eyes landed on Walt and lingered there. The flight surgeon sat at his workstation, contentedly chewing on a glazed donut and sipping his coffee as he halfheartedly kept an eye on crew members' biometric graphs on the display wall. The lights from the high ceiling penetrated his thin, white hair and reflected off his shiny scalp.

Kate felt a shiver of revelation. All the little gears in her mind clicked into place as Walt ate his donut with steady chews.

She checked her watch. There was still time.

She accessed the cloud on her workstation computer and started researching.

Titan was the size of a nickel when Jeff first saw it.

The hazy, pale ochre moon was positioned in the center of the narrow command module window. All four crew members were buckled into their seats, sitting quietly and staring.

"I don't see Saturn," said Gabriel.

"It's behind Titan at the moment," Riley said, tapping at his controls. "She'll pop out soon enough."

Ming called up the status display of the orbital systems on her control panel and checked the settings.

"Entering orbit in fifty-eight minutes," she said. "All systems in the green."

"Thank you, Lieutenant," said Riley. "Orbital thrusters only from this point."

Ming nodded and flipped a switch to lock out some of the engine controls. "Copy that."

Jeff watched Titan as *Explorer I* approached. As fast as the ship was traveling even during the deceleration process, it was still mind-twistingly far from the moon, and it would be a while until it appeared as large as a quarter.

He hadn't given a second thought to the fact that none of them were going down to the surface until he saw the moon from the command module. Before, he had been perfectly content with the original plan to remain in orbit and assemble the skeleton of what would become the farthest manned space station from Earth. Perhaps in twenty years or so, he expected, the company would send a few brave souls down to the surface to explore. Jeff and the rest of the crew of *Explorer I* were the plumbers and electricians; the architects of that potential future who built and then vacated.

At roughly half the size of Earth, Titan had a little over one-tenth of its gravity. Each day was as long as sixteen Earth days. The moon had a fixed orbit – the same side always faced Saturn. If it were possible to stand on the surface and see through the thick atmospheric haze, Saturn and its rings would fill roughly a third of the sky.

Jeff knew it was dangerous down there on the surface. The haze masked a frigid world of hydrocarbon lakes and methane rivers fed by torrential downpours of the same volatile chemical in liquid form. Cryovolcanoes dotted the hostile landscape. Being the only moon in the solar system with a dense atmosphere, it had taken a long time to discover what was really happening beneath the fog.

Despite the methane, a visitor wouldn't need a pressure suit to explore, just an oxygen mask and protective clothing that could withstand the moon's temperatures that could plunge to negative 290-degrees Fahrenheit. With slightly less gravity than Earth's moon and an average surface pressure 1.6 times that of Earth itself, walking around on Titan would be more like bouncing through thick soup.

None of that deterred Jeff from wanting to set foot on the surface. It was torturous to know he would be so close without the chance for further exploration.

A green button flashed on the pilot's control console. Riley pressed it, then put a finger to his ear while a message came in over his headset.

"Dolan," he said, "Canaveral wants you to run a diagnostic on the biometric equipment."

"I just went through the whole routine this morning."

"They said something about a calibration error on our end, and it could screw with their readings."

Jeff hesitated, not wanting to miss the approach to Titan.

"It should only take twenty minutes, right?" Gabriel offered.

"Yeah," Jeff conceded. He unbuckled his straps and hovered over his seat. "Fine. But if anything happens, call me back."

"Will do," said Riley.

Jeff pushed off gently from the back of his chair and floated down through the open hatch in the floor, reluctantly leaving the others to enjoy the view.

The biometrics monitor in the science lab was already on when Jeff arrived, which meant that someone on Earth had sent an automated power trigger over an hour ago. The black screen was sectioned into quadrants, each displaying the biometric data of a crew member in glowing green letters, numbers, and lines.

"Must really want me to run this test," Jeff mumbled as he swapped wires on the back of the monitor.

He temporarily routed the ship's communications mainframe into the narrow-field biometrics equipment so it could listen to more from Earth than the simple automated trigger that had switched it on in the first place.

Then he waited.

He leaned against a lab desk, his arms folded, and watched the data on the biometrics screen. A thin line at the bottom of each of the four quadrants blipped with the heart rate of each crew member. The three in the command module watching the approach to Titan had noticeably quicker heartbeats, beyond the normal resting rates for individuals in great condition.

No wonder, he thought, looking longingly toward the command module. *I bet they're getting a great show.*

His own EKG readout was a steady fifty-two beats per minute. He yawned as the data from Mission Control flowed into the monitor. The EKG lines went flat temporarily, then spiked rapidly during the initial testing cycles.

Jeff pushed off the desk and started walking toward the command module. He was supposed to babysit the equipment during the tests, but he had just run the same routine that morning, and he would be damned if he was going to miss the reveal of Saturn.

The biometrics monitor beeped three times and he froze in his tracks. Three beeps during a test cycle meant there was an error in the system.

It can't be too bad, he thought as he hurried back to the equipment. *All of the readouts were perfectly fine.*

All of the EKG lines were flat at the bottom of each quadrant. Jeff frowned and patted his chest, feeling for the small suction cup monitors that had been attached to his skin since he left Earth. He lifted his shirt and inspected the four flexible discs. They were still there. The wireless data nodes, like small beads of mercury, were still embedded securely in the center of each cup.

It might be possible for one sensor to fail, but not all four on the same person. And *certainly* not all four on each member of the crew.

Jeff reached for the keyboard to run a diagnostic

and the screen flashed off.

"Oh, come on," he whispered.

The screen popped back on and Jeff shook his head in frustration. Only a single flat line showed on the screen instead of the usual quadrant display.

A moment later, the line began to pulse with a heart rate. Jeff watched the beats and checked his own pulse, trying to match the two. The beats on the screen were erratic and came in short bursts. It wasn't a heartbeat at all.

It was Morse code.

He translated the message and forgot all about missing the approach to Titan.

Gabriel's jubilance could barely be contained. His legs bounced anxiously and he sat on the edge of his seat, straining against his straps as he leaned toward the window.

One of Saturn's rings appeared from behind Titan, rising steadily from behind the moon as *Explorer I* drew near.

"You almost missed it!" he said as Jeff floated into the crew module. "Can you believe it? We are the first people in history to see Saturn with our own eyes!"

"No, I really can't believe it," Jeff said darkly as he strapped into his chair.

Ming noted the tone of his voice and cast a sideways glance, but remained silent. The edge of Saturn peeked out behind Titan; a sliver of the striped and sand-colored gas giant from which projected its trademark flat rings.

"How's the equipment?" Riley asked as he stared out the window.

"The biometric scanner is fine," Jeff said. "Probably

the only piece of this ship that wasn't broken before we launched."

Riley twisted in his seat and stared at Jeff with a furrowed brow.

"What the hell does *that* mean, Dolan?"

"Mission Control didn't want me to run another diagnostic on the equipment. It was Kate sending me a message using Morse code."

"The EKG readout," Ming said. "Clever."

"Why didn't she just send you a video?" asked Gabriel.

"Because she knows it would be seen by others before it left Earth," Jeff said.

"What was in the message?" Ming asked.

"Kate said the antimatter engine was unstable. During all the tests, the system would only get two or three uses before something went wrong. They never solved the problem."

"They wouldn't send us out here if that were the case," Gabriel said. "Besides, we made it just fine."

"She said 'fake results'," Jeff replied. "Noah or Frank had to know. Maybe both."

"You don't know that, Dolan," Riley said.

"What are we supposed to do if she's right?" Jeff asked. "Disconnect the primary engine and paddle home?"

"If we don't use the antimatter drive again," Ming said, "it will take us years to get back."

A third of Saturn had emerged from behind its moon. Jeff watched the slow reveal with regretful detachment.

"But all the tests were conducted on Earth," said Gabriel. "The only way to know if the system was unstable would be to launch a prolonged mission, and we are the first."

Jeff shook his head. "Diamond Aerospace sent six probes to Titan before we launched. All of them failed except one."

"That must have been one hell of a long message if she used Morse code," Riley said.

"It was."

Ming's control panel beeped, and she pushed a button. Lines of data scrolled across her screen.

"What is it, Lieutenant?" Riley asked.

"I'm picking up a strange signal from Titan."

"Radiation interference?"

She shook her head. "Our scanners are set to ignore the moon's natural emissions. This is…something else."

"Elaborate," Riley ordered. He turned to his own control panel and called up the same information.

"It's in the audible spectrum, sir." She pressed her headset against her ear and listened. "Sounds mechanical."

Jeff put on his headset and patched it into what she was hearing: a deep, constant thrumming.

"It's an oxygen compressor," he said. "This is exactly what our ship would sound like in low-power mode. Most of the electronics would switch off, but the atmospheric regulators would constantly churn out breathable air."

"You're telling me there's another ship out here?" Riley asked.

"Look!" Gabriel shouted, pointing at Titan.

They were now close enough to the hazy moon that a rectangular segment of it completely filled the narrow crew module window. Jeff struggled to find anything out of place on the pale yellowish swath of atmosphere he could see.

Then, from the edge of the window, a black speck appeared. It was locked in orbit around Titan, circling the moon quickly, moving from one side of the crew module window to the other.

"That's not what was in the photograph," Riley said.

"It's another ship," Jeff whispered.

"No way."

"What else *could* it be?" Gabriel insisted.

"An asteroid caught in the moon's gravity."

"Not with that audio signature," Ming said. She studied her control panel. "Sir, at our current rate of deceleration, we'll begin entering orbit in less than twenty minutes."

Riley squinted at the black speck as it moved over Titan. It disappeared past the edge of the window, and he slowly leaned back in his chair.

"Stay the course, Lieutenant," he said. "Our primary mission is to build a space station, and that's what we're going to do."

"We were supposed to be the first ones here," Gabriel said with disappointment. His face instantly brightened as a thought occurred to him. "What if it's just one of the probes? The one that didn't blow up? Those were unmanned, right?"

"They wouldn't need an oxygen system," Jeff said.

Gabriel's shoulders sank. "No, I guess not."

The four crew members sat in silence, looking out through the window.

Jeff kept expecting to see a variation in the surface of Titan, some kind of pattern in the methane atmosphere. There was none. The crew module window had turned from a solid strip of black space to a solid strip of foggy yellow.

"Ready those orbital thrusters," Riley said a few minutes later.

"Aye, Commander," Ming replied. Her fingers moved rapidly over her console. She paused and looked out the window. "Here it comes again."

Jeff didn't realize he was holding his breath until the object appeared at the edge of the window. In the few minutes since the speck was last visible, *Explorer I* had covered half its own distance to the moon. Now the speck had grown to the size of a bullet, and its features became more distinguishable.

"It *is* a ship," Jeff said finally. "You can clearly see the design of the fuselage, there, and the engine shield."

"It looks a hell of a lot like Explorer from here," Gabriel said.

"It sure does. There's writing on the side."

"Sweet mother," Riley said grimly. "I'd bet my ex-wife's purse collection that's the MarsCorp logo."

"There's something else, sir," Ming said.

"How can there *possibly* be anything else?!" he roared. He forced his shoulders to relax and took two deep breaths. "Apologies, Lieutenant. Please continue."

"There's a pocket of interference that *looks* like it's coming off the other ship, but when I try to zero in on the pocket, our scanners slip off and give me a reading from Titan."

"Maybe they used a different kind of engine," Gabriel offered. "Something we've never seen."

"Wait a minute. It's coming from about a hundred meters off the nose of the ship," said Ming. "Not from inside."

"I don't see it," Riley said, squinting.

Jeff leaned forward. "I do," he said. "Barely. It's like a shadow, a short distance in front of the ship."

"Do you think they're building a space station, too?" Gabriel asked.

"I'm not reading anything like that on my equipment," Ming said.

She cycled through the menus on her console monitor, bombarding the orbiting ship with every type of scan at her disposal.

"I see it, too," said Gabriel. "Jeff is right. It's just off the nose."

"I wish we could magnify this stupid window," Riley said angrily.

The ship and whatever it chased disappeared from view as it orbited the far side of Titan.

"It will be back soon," Ming said.

The time passed quickly. Jeff drummed his fingers on the arm rests of his chair, eagerly awaiting the ship's return. When it finally showed up, as large in the window as his own thumb, he sat back in surprise.

The other ship was parked in front of a large torus

– a hoop twice the diameter of the MarsCorp vessel made of a black, non-reflective material. The crew of *Explorer* hadn't been able to see it clearly because they were looking at the relatively thin object from its side, so it appeared as the whisper of a black line, only truly detectable at a closer distance. The ship and the object were locked in orbit around the moon, their velocities matched so perfectly that they appeared to be attached by an invisible connector.

As the pair traversed the space above the surface of the moon, the torus rotated, always keeping one edge of the hoop toward Titan. It gave Jeff and the others a clearer view of the strange object as it followed its course.

It wasn't like anything he'd ever seen before. He could think of no practical reason MarsCorp, or any other company for that matter, would want to install such an object in orbit around one of Saturn's moons.

"MarsCorp didn't put this here," he said. "It *is* the artifact, isn't it?"

Looking at the design of the torus, he could not see any seams in its construction. It was just a guess at that distance, but Jeff would have said it was cut from a single piece of material. The costs would be astronomical, and the transport unthinkable over such a distance.

All those considerations led him to believe, beyond the shadow of a doubt, that the torus wasn't made on Earth at all.

"Should we try to contact the other ship, sir?" Ming asked, breaking the prolonged silence.

Riley clenched his jaw while he thought about it.

"No," he said at last. "Let's send Canaveral a picture and see what the hell they want to do. This is above my pay grade."

Noah stood in his dark office, holding a printed picture with white-knuckled hands – a picture of another company's spaceship in orbit around Titan. His eyes blindly searched the surface of his desk as he strained for a way to make sense of the fact that someone else had beaten him to his goal.

He sank down into his chair. The anger faded only to be replaced by heartbreak.

I didn't get there first, he thought.

He looked again at the picture. Someone downstairs had enhanced the image sent by *Explorer I*, zooming in on the other ship and cleaning up the slight blur that was in every photo taken while the ship was in motion.

MarsCorp, thought Noah. *How did they do it?*

He lingered on the design of the ship, noting its similarities to *Explorer*. Granted, it was possible that two separate companies working independently might arrive at a similar design. There were only so many ways to skin a cat, to state it crudely.

Yet there were certain elements of the MarsCorp design that so blatantly mirrored the ship built by Noah's company that it would be foolish to blame everything on coincidence. The placement of the centrifuge was identical on both ships. If Noah looked at a similar photograph of *Explorer I* taken from the same distance, he wouldn't be surprised if the diameters matched up perfectly.

The communications arrays for both ships were easily recognizable and likewise in the same position: behind each crew module in two identical clumps of delicate machinery, like twin metal tumors stuck to the sides of the vessels. It was a redundant design in case one of the groupings should fail.

Noah had always been wary of industrial espionage, ever since the beginning of his optimistic space endeavors. He had taken all the necessary precautions to safeguard his company's secrets. Outgoing communications were monitored. Each employee had to sign a waiver agreeing to a spontaneous polygraph test should the need arise.

So far, it hadn't.

As Noah looked at the picture, he realized he had been much too lenient with security. There was no real way to know how badly his proverbial ship was leaking. It was money, of course. Someone on his staff had taken a payout, and MarsCorp got his ship design. Judging by the fact that they beat him to Titan, they also stole his antimatter engine.

His phone rang and he scooped it up.

"Yeah."

"Video feed's coming through in five," said Frank.

Noah hung up and stared at the receiver. He slowly crumpled the picture into a ball.

What about Frank? he wondered.

Aside from Noah, no one knew the intricacies of what went on at Diamond Aerospace better than Frank Johnson. He had been there since the beginning, back when Noah was still building models to try and impress the media.

Frank was the most dedicated employee Noah ever had, and it didn't sit right that he would sell the company's secrets to a competitor.

He isn't the last person on the list of possibilities, Noah reminded himself as he rode the elevator down to Mission Control.

He forced his mind onto the artifact – the torus, as Riley called it.

Technically speaking, Diamond Aerospace had more of a claim on the object than MarsCorp. It was Diamond Aerospace's probe who first made it to Titan and had sent back the blurry photograph. It might be a stretch to say the torus was a clear match for the blur in the first photo. Yet no one could deny the fact that MarsCorp had stolen Noah's engine design and only knew about the torus because of D.A.'s groundbreaking antimatter engine.

The question was if MarsCorp would agree with that assessment. Noah doubted it. The next question then became whether or not he could convince a judge to side with his company. Past experience told him it was possible to sway a verdict, given the right amount of compensatory guidance.

He tried to console himself by admitting that, whichever way the chips fell, he stood on the precipice of a historic moment. How that moment played out was solely up to him.

Kate sat at her workstation, her eyes glued to the display wall, nervously chewing on the end of her pen. Rick had yet to show up for work. His empty chair was like a void at the edge of her vision, tugging at her every conscious thought. She hadn't heard from him since he left her house with the folder he'd taken from company archives. Normally, not hearing from him wouldn't have made her think twice. At the moment, things at Diamond Aerospace were far from normal.

The display wall in Mission Control had been reconfigured to give precedence to the main exterior video feed coming in from *Explorer I,* pushing the continuously streaming ship and crew data to the edges of the massive screen.

The ship was holding position a mere five-hundred kilometers from the outermost border of Titan's atmosphere. The moon filled most of the display wall – a hazy, pale yellow disc suspended in the inky blackness of space. As Noah watched, two dark objects moved steadily across the screen, orbiting the moon. At that distance, the MarsCorp ship appeared to be the size of a bullet, and the torus was no larger than a wedding band.

Kate was having a hard time forcing herself to accept that she was looking at an alien artifact. Her initial reaction when the object came within visual range was that the MarsCorp crew was constructing some kind of satellite or docking station. As *Explorer I* approached, however, the logical possibilities for the artifact's shape and function ground down to nil, at least as far as Kate's own knowledge was concerned.

Within only a few minutes of seeing the torus on the display wall for the first time, it became easy to accept that it had not been built by human hands.

Noah walked briskly up the middle walkway between the rows of workstations and stopped next to Kate's desk, a spot he frequently occupied while observing the display wall from the operations floor. Frank hurried to his side and stood beside him, red-faced and steaming as he glared up at the image of the other ship.

Kate studied Noah's face and saw mostly anger, which, despite such an awesome discovery, led her to guess that he had only known about one of the objects in orbit around Titan. Kate assumed it was the torus, and the appearance of the MarsCorp vessel was an absolute and unwelcome surprise. Noah had shattered deadlines and expectations to be the first man to send a crew to Titan, and he had just discovered someone beat him to it.

"What's our status?" he asked.

"We're almost at peak delay for audio and visual," Frank answered, slightly out of breath. "Everything we're seeing now, Explorer saw seventy minutes ago."

"Is there any way to get a closer look?"

"Juan," Kate said, looking over at the tech, "zoom it in a little."

Juan nodded and straightened up in his seat. "It'll get blurry," he said as he tapped on his monitor.

The area of Titan the objects were traversing became magnified, and the objects themselves turned into blocky representations of basic shapes over a muddy yellow background.

"Not much use at this distance," Frank offered.

"Zoom back out, please," Noah said. Juan complied and the image on the display wall reverted to its actual dimensions, with Titan looming large in the center. "How far are they from the ship?"

"Holding steady at about eighty kilometers," said Kate.

Noah crossed his arms. "Let them get a little closer."

"How close?" Frank asked.

"I'll leave that to Commander Riley's discretion. Ms. Bishop, have Explorer contact the other ship and ascertain what they're doing at our moon."

"What about the torus?" Frank asked.

"We'll figure that out after we talk to the other ship."

Kate adjusted her microphone. "It'll be more than an hour before we hear back from them," she reminded Noah.

He nodded. "I don't think we're going anywhere before then."

"Explorer One," she said, "this is Mission Control. Your orders are to match orbital velocity with the MarsCorp vessel and attempt communication with its commanding officer. We'd like to know what they're up to. Let's take this nice and slow, Commander."

She turned off her microphone and leaned back in her chair. A few seconds later, the room speakers crackled to life.

"Copy that, Mission Control," Riley said. "We will match velocity with MarsCorp vessel and let you know if we hear anything back."

All of the various clicks and creaks in the room ceased instantly. The only sound was a distant hum from an air conditioning unit somewhere in the ceiling.

Noah grinned slowly. "The torus is boosting the signal," he said, his voice filled with wonder. "It *has* to be. How extraordinary! Ms. Bishop, please tell the commander that we acknowledge his last message."

On the display wall, the MarsCorp ship and the alien artifact continued along their orbital path.

Jeff and the other three crew members in the command module of *Explorer I* stared at the console in front of Riley's chair after Kate's last message. Riley cautiously reached forward and pushed a comm button on the console.

"Uh...Mission Control?" he said.

A few seconds passed before Kate answered. *"Go ahead, Commander."*

He glanced around at the others. Jeff imagined he looked as confused as everyone else.

Riley pushed the button again. "Just confirming that communication between Earth and Explorer One is now instantaneous."

Noah's voice came in over the line. *"That appears to be the case, Commander, although it's not quite instantaneous yet. I suspect as you approach the artifact, we'll lose the last remaining seconds of delay."*

"Copy that," Riley said. He looked at Ming and she nodded. "Commencing maneuver."

They began a fluid, synchronized ballet of movement as they flipped switches, pushed buttons, and twisted dials, performing the same functions simultaneously. The hull of the command module shuddered slightly as the small orbital thrusters fired. A moment later, the engines cut out and *Explorer I* drifted silently toward Titan.

"Preparing for turn," Ming said. She reached over her head and pushed three glowing red buttons, then hovered a finger over a fourth. "Ready."

Riley typed a long numerical code into a keypad in the wall next to his shoulder. A button on his console lit up green.

"Hit it, Lieutenant."

The view of Titan began to slip sideways as *Explorer I* turned. They still drifted toward the moon, but small bursts of air from lateral stabilizing thrusters had begun slowly spinning the ship until it was parallel with the surface.

"And there goes the show," Gabriel said as the last sliver of Titan disappeared from the command module window.

"Retro burn to match ship velocity in thirty seconds," Riley said.

"Copy, Commander. We'll catch up with them after they make one more full orbit."

Jeff was no longer able to tell how close they were getting to the moon's surface. His own console allowed him a detailed overview of every function aboard *Explorer I*, but he wasn't patched in to the navigational computers. Anything he couldn't see through the window was only trackable from the pilots' chairs.

"Initiate retro burn," Riley said.

The boosters fired and Jeff was pushed back against his seat. It was nothing like the bone-flattening crush he felt while under thrust to break free of Earth's atmosphere – more like the gentle pressure one experiences on a commercial airplane during a banking maneuver shortly after takeoff.

"The ship and the artifact are about to overtake us, Commander," Ming said.

"Final burn to match velocity," he replied.

With the flip of a switch, the boosters gave one last push, then cut off. Ming tapped on her console screen and called up a radar display that showed two objects in near proximity to *Explorer*.

"Confirmed we are locked in Titan's orbit along with…well, with whatever else is out there."

"Lieutenant…" Riley said.

"Yes, Commander?"

"What would you think about swinging our caboose back around to where it was?"

"You want to face Titan again?"

"We've matched velocity with the other ship. I think I'd like to see it out the window instead of only on these tiny monitors."

Ming tapped on her screen, parsing lines of dense text. At one point, she briefly pulled up a schematic of the pneumatic lines.

"We can do it. It would be safer to pre-program the maneuver so we don't swing too far."

"The less I have to do, the better," Riley joked.

"Mission Control, what do you think?"

Kate spoke a moment later: *"Stand by."*

Ming started punching keys, recording an operations macro that the ship's computer would activate when ordered. Even if Mission Control came back with a negative, she could simply delete the operation from the queue.

"Explorer," Kate said, *"if you want to see it with your own eyes, you are more than welcome."*

"Copy that, Canaveral. We are grateful."

He gave the go-ahead to Ming, and she initiated the maneuver. Stabilizing thrusters at the back of the fuselage spurted air, and the aft of the ship swung away from Titan, the command module acting as a pivot point. A few more pops of air from thrusters on the opposite side of the fuselage, and *Explorer I* was steady once more, only this time with a better view.

Riley had ordered them within three kilometers of the MarsCorp vessel and the torus. At that distance, details of both were clearly visible. The one that immediately stood out to Jeff was the open hatch of the MarsCorp ship.

"Their airlock is open," he said.

"See if you can get them on the horn, Lieutenant," said Riley.

Ming twisted a dial on her console. "MarsCorp vessel, this is Explorer One. Looks like we're going to be neighbors out here." The line was silent. "MarsCorp vessel, do you copy?"

Noah broke in over the comm line. *"Anything, Commander?"*

"Negative. No response from the crew of the other ship. I can confirm their airlock is wide open."

"I understand. Jeff, you are to proceed with EVA repair of the secondary fuel line sensor. Retrieve a backup fuel pump to replace the damaged one while you're at it. Commander Riley, Dr. Silva...I want you both outside as well. Check that other ship. See if anyone over there needs our help."

"What about the torus?" Riley asked.

"Under no circumstances are you to approach the artifact," Noah said. *"We're going to take this slowly, one step at a time. We will consider the torus only if it becomes obvious there is no immediate danger."*

Jeff couldn't help but crack a wry smile. *Immediate danger,* he thought. *What about long-term danger? Guess that doesn't matter as much.*

Gabriel peeled off his headset. "Easy for *him* to say. He's not floating around out here with a broken engine. All we are doing is wasting more time."

"Stow that talk, Silva," Riley said. "Let's just get it done."

Noah strode purposefully into his dimly lit office from the elevator, rolling up his long shirtsleeves as he approached his palatial desk.

"Desk lights, business call," he said to the room.

A narrow, rectangular hole opened in the middle of his broad desk, and a video conference screen rose silently from within.

Recessed lighting in the ceiling, and more so in the floor, illuminated to cast a warm glow on his desk and leather chair – a preprogrammed setting which lit Noah's face mostly from underneath, giving him a faintly ominous appearance. The desired effect was a hint of intimidation and a gentle psychological reminder that the scales were balanced in Noah's favor.

He dropped into the firm leather chair and jabbed at the intercom button of his desk phone.

"Neil," he said.

The response came back almost immediately: *"James Whitaker on the line for you, sir."*

A small green light gently pulsed on top of the

video screen. He shifted in his seat, leaned back into the leather, rested his elbows on the armrests, and steepled his fingers in front of him.

"Join call," he commanded.

The video screen flicked on, showing a man in his early fifties seated in a black office chair. The blue sky over downtown Chicago lit his capacious penthouse suite through the wall-sized window behind his desk.

MarsCorp's CEO cleared his throat and adjusted his navy-blue tie. His piercing gray eyes alighted on the camera for a split second before darting away. Noah thought James Whitaker had always seemed out of place in his position. Stark white hair trimmed in the flat-topped military style contrasted his perpetually-sunburned, bulbous face. Rugged lines creased his leathery skin. Retirement on a sailboat in Florida certainly wouldn't treat the man better than what he'd already been doing, but at least it would get him out of Noah's hair.

"Noah," he said. "What can I do for you?"

"How about telling me how your company acquired the designs for my ship?"

Whitaker grunted laughter, his eyes sparkling. "Can't say I know what you mean. We're still slapping our ship together, remember? We took quite a hit when you snatched the Chinese contract out from under us."

Noah leaned forward slightly. "Let's not play this game, Jim. The ship in orbit around Titan is a replica of Explorer, and it has your company's name smeared all over the side."

Whitaker stared into the camera, his eyes

narrowing, his hard frown just another line lost in a road map of creases.

"So you made it to Titan," he said.

"You knew I would."

"Not with that engine of yours. I thought my boys would be picking up the pieces of your ship on their way back to Earth."

"Then your ship had a crew, after all," said Noah.

"What the hell are you talking about? Of *course* North Star has a crew."

North Star, thought Noah. *How vain.*

"We can't raise anyone on comms. I'm going to play a hunch and say you haven't heard from them in a while."

Whitaker hesitated, then said, "We lost all audio and video contact with the crew as soon as they arrived at Titan. But there could be any number of reasons for radio silence, not the least of which is that they saw *you* coming." He looked away, searching for answers. Noah thought he noticed a hint of vulnerability and decided to act on it.

"North Star's hatch is open," he said.

Whitaker looked sharply into the camera. "You're lying."

"Why would I?"

Whitaker smiled without humor. "Why do *any* of us do what we do, Noah?"

"On behalf of Diamond Aerospace, I'm willing to offer any and all assistance to North Star and her crew."

"I bet you are. I got there first, Bell. The spoils are mine."

Noah smiled tightly, fighting to keep his jealous anger from boiling to the surface. "Unless you have an orbital station in the hold of your ship, along with the crew to build it, I beg to differ."

"Bah," said Whitaker, waving a dismissive hand toward the camera and turning away from the screen. He looked out his window at the glimmering Chicago skyline. Noah thought he would have to press the matter further, but Whitaker said, almost too quietly to hear, "My nephew is on North Star."

Noah scooted forward, gripping the edge of his desk, sensing victory just around the corner. *Pull the line too soon*, he imagined his deceased father instructing, *and the hook won't pierce deep enough to catch the fish.*

"If I don't agree to your *generous* assistance, then what?" asked Whitaker. "You leave my crew to rot?"

Noah spread his hands in a casual shrug, expecting at any moment for the other man to call his bluff. Riley and Silva were already heading over to the other ship, and would do what they could for the other crew, regardless of how the conversation with Whitaker concluded. "We're stretched for time as it is, Jim. You understand."

The older man stewed in his own thoughts, trying in vain to uncover a different path. Finally, he growled, "What do you want?"

And the hook is sunk, Noah thought. Apparently, Whitaker thought him vicious enough to follow through on his threat not to investigate.

"Don't interfere with our operation," Noah said.

"And?"

"Tell me how you got the plans to build North Star."

Whitaker tugged at his collar, as if it had suddenly tightened around his neck. "I'll send over the designs right now, if that makes you feel any better."

"It would."

Whitaker typed hastily at his embedded desktop keyboard, then pointedly tapped the transmit key.

"You should have it."

Noah opened his cloud server and saw the file waiting for him. He opened it and began skimming through the pages. At first glance, the documentation was identical to *Explorer's*.

"But how did you *get* these in the first place?" he asked.

"Michael Cochran sold them to us."

Maybe that's what ultimately landed him in a dumpster, Noah thought.

He continued scanning the documentation, then stopped abruptly when he came across a schematic for the antimatter drive. "You changed the engine configuration. Why?"

Whitaker sighed. "Cochran's plans came with a special warning regarding the antimatter drive. My engineers convinced me to listen."

"Our engine works perfectly."

"Not if it was built from the plans I bought off Cochran."

Noah thought about the five failed probes Diamond Aerospace launched toward Titan, and the improvements to them that were made after each failure. The sixth probe snapped the picture of the artifact. "We fixed any design flaws before Explorer left the ground."

Whitaker laughed. "No, you didn't. I saw your engine firsthand. It's a blind miracle the ship made it to Titan in one piece."

"The only way you could have seen the engine was if you went to the ISS yourself."

"Or had someone who was already on the station take a few simple photos. The same someone who helped slap the antimatter drive together while waiting for your crew to arrive."

Alexei, thought Noah. Then another loose cog in his brain clicked into place.

"You partnered with Russia."

Whitaker nodded. "When the Russian Space Administration lost your company's contract to the Chinese, they went looking elsewhere."

"And found MarsCorp. *That's* why you didn't tell anyone about the artifact. Russia isn't supposed to launch anything other than low orbit satellites and capsules to the ISS."

"Yes, their new head of state is a real pain in the ass."

"Imagine what would happen to your company if someone found out you were violating a national mandate."

"I know, I know!" Whitaker said, agitated. Then he sighed. "Everyone's been happy with the status quo, until now."

"You stole my designs, Jim. You didn't innovate.

You never would have made it so far on your own. Doesn't that bother you in the slightest?"

Whitaker smiled knowingly. "It doesn't matter how you get there, Noah, only that you get there first. I thought you would have learned that by now."

Kate joined the other department heads in the conference room at Noah's request. A nervous energy permeated the room as she sat in one of the high-backed chairs that ringed the circular table. Four department heads occupied chairs around the table, including Kate. The aging flight surgeon, Walt, looked to be the most nervous of all. His wispy white hair stuck out as if he'd jammed his finger into a light socket. One of his legs bounced vigorously, causing his whole chair to shake.

Juan from Flight Operations nodded in her direction. He wiped sweat from his brow and blinked hard, as if a bright light were shining into his eyes.

Allison Jones sat next to him, her short gray hair tucked neatly behind her ears, looking just as bewildered. Like Walt, she was an industry holdover from the '20s, back when NASA was still gearing up for the first manned mission to Mars. She ran System Logistics and worked closely with Juan's team to certify that when a crew member flipped a switch, the ship returned the desired response. If *Explorer I* were a living organism, then Allison and her team were the doctors tasked with ensuring the disparate parts of the spacecraft functioned in tandem with each other.

Noah himself was not there yet, but Frank stood at the back of the room, leaning against the dark wood-paneled wall, staring out through the glass at the display wall. The video feed currently showed Riley and Silva in the spherical airlock, donning their bright orange Constellation Suits for the trip over to the MarsCorp vessel.

Kate was about to excuse herself when Noah pushed open the conference room door and strolled in waving a stack of papers.

"The North Star," he said bitterly. He dropped the stack of papers on the table with a dull thud. "The central point in the sky around which all other objects rotate. That's what they named their ship."

"Who, MarsCorp?" Kate asked, leaning forward to look at the top sheet of the stack. It was an official press release from the other company, outlining the details of the *North Star's* mission to Titan. According to a stamped redaction over the primary content, the press release had never been made public.

"There are ship schematics in there, too," Noah said. "It confirms that their ship is nearly identical to Explorer in every way."

"Where did you get those?" Kate asked.

Noah shrugged off her question and turned to look out at the display wall, waiting for his assembled brain trust to provide some answers.

Lucius Howell from Propulsion pulled the stack over and began thumbing through the pages with precise movements. His dark, sharp eyes darted over the words, scanning them like a machine reader. Lucius had designed engines for Northrop Grumman straight out of college before moving over to the private sector in his early thirties. His calculated pedantry made him somewhat of a social pariah, but Kate would rather have a brilliant outcast on her team than a popular doofus. In addition, she would vote him least likely to lose his cool in an emergency.

He adjusted his wireframe glasses and frowned deeply after pausing halfway through the stack.

"It's our engine," he said, "right down to the curvature of the wash shield."

Noah nodded, as if he already knew. Kate saw him cast a quick, icy glance at Frank. Something passed silently between the two of them, and Frank looked away.

Lucius held up a cautionary finger. "Except," he added, "They added extra shielding around the fuel ignition chamber and–" He paused and raised an eyebrow as he read farther down the page. "And this is interesting. The antimatter doesn't interact with liquid fuel until it's almost flushed out the back of the ship."

"What does that mean?" asked Juan.

"To put it simply," Lucius said, "in Explorer, antimatter reacts with liquid fuel in the ignition chamber and swirls it around as the magnetic coils speed it up even faster. MarsCorp removed the magnetic coils. The engine might burn more fuel, but it takes less time for a reaction to occur."

"How does that help them?" Walt asked. He looked between Lucius and Noah, struggling to follow the conversation.

"The fuel ignition chamber is built to contain an explosion," Lucius replied. "The less time energy from an explosion resides in your ship, the greater chance you have of not blowing up."

"We tried removing the magnetic coils," Frank said, finally joining in. "In the simulations, we never had enough fuel to get home. And I would guess that MarsCorp was more concerned with getting there before us. They didn't care much about getting back in a hurry."

"So they copied our ship design," Kate said. "I don't see how that has any impact on our mission."

"Their presence might push back the timeline," Frank said. "If Explorer lingers too long, the crew will miss their return window. Months of delay could turn into years."

"We no longer *have* a departure window," Kate countered. "It doesn't matter that we got there early if we don't have an antimatter drive to get us back. The problem now is their supplies. With an extended return journey, they're going to run out of food before they get home. Look, you want to send Riley and Silva over to the other ship. Fine. All they have to do is give it a cursory glance and offer medical assistance if anyone needs it. Jeff will repair the fuel line sensor and the broken pump. Great. After that, they stick to the mission parameters, which state they begin construction of the orbital station."

"What if the other crew is stranded out there?" asked Allison. "Maybe they ran out of fuel, too."

"We didn't run out of fuel," Juan corrected. "There's enough for one more major burn, plus a little extra."

"Let's take things one step at a time," Frank said.

"We can't ignore the artifact," Noah said quietly. Kate thought he was almost pleading for someone to convince him he was right. "It's a monumental discovery, not just for the company, but for the entire world."

"That depends on its function," Lucius said, pushing up his glasses. He glanced around the table. He had everyone's strict attention as he continued. "Either it's decorative, which I doubt, or it serves a very specific purpose."

Kate hesitated, not sure she wanted to hear the answer to her next question. "How do we learn its purpose?"

"The crew of North Star probably figured it out," said Lucius, "but they're not exactly answering our calls, are they?"

After seeing Riley and Gabriel safely to the airlock, Jeff coasted down the central pillar of the centrifuge, tapping ladder rungs to stay on track, until he reached the aft-most section. He descended the wall ladder at the back and began the process of unbuckling his bright orange Mark IV suit from its shallow compartment in the floor. Ming's suit was in the cutout next to his, a few centimeters shorter and slightly thinner. Several meters away in the same section of the centrifuge, a rat's nest of open straps and buckles represented the spots usually occupied by the other two suits.

In moments like those, when Jeff had to wrestle with a hundred-pound spacesuit, he was especially thankful for the slightly reduced gravity in the centrifuge.

After he released the last buckle, he opened a small floor panel and pressed a button inside. A telescoping arm in the floor extended upward, hoisting the suit by a quadruple-stitched nylon loop on the back of its neck.

The suit rose slowly, as if an invisible occupant were rising to his feet.

Jeff opened a nearby wall cabinet, grabbing a blue pair of long thermal underwear and a black unitard. He peeled off his clothes and pulled on the underwear, making sure he didn't have them inside-out. If he did, the small silver strip over his left hip wouldn't be able to interface with his suit through the unitard, and he wouldn't reap the benefits of its auto-cooling system. Things got hot when one layered up for a spacewalk. He remembered scoffing at auto-cooling underwear during mission training, then quickly changed his tune after spending only an hour in one of Diamond Aerospace's deep training pools without them, at his instructor's insistence. He hadn't quite passed out from heat exhaustion after they opened his suit following the dive, but he promised himself never to turn down any piece of clothing the company told him to wear, no matter how exotic.

He wiggled into his unitard, taking care that the wicking fabric didn't bunch up in any of his crevices, and pulled the hood up over his head, leaving only his face uncovered.

The telescoping arm stopped when the open ankles of the Constellation Suit pants barely brushed the floor.

Ming's voice came over the intercom: *"You doing okay, Jeff?"*

"Fine," he said, speaking to the room. One of the embedded microphone arrays in the central pillar would pick up the sound. He plucked the fabric of the unitard. "Just getting ready for the ballet."

"Ah yes, a performance of 'The Ugly Duckling'. It's a classic."

Jeff grinned as he began the complex unzipping procedure to open the outer layer of his suit. "Maybe you want to do this instead."

"What do I know about fuel line sensors?" she replied.

"Apparently not as much as old ballets."

"You need some help?"

He unzipped the last zipper and peeled open the outer layer of the suit. "I can manage until you meet me at the airlock. Thanks, though. How's it looking with the other two?"

"Looking good. They're about halfway to the other ship."

"Taking their sweet time, I guess," Jeff said.

"Yeah, I guess so."

The telescoping arm acted as a stabilizer while Jeff stepped first into one pant leg of the Mark IV, then the other, tugging up until his unitard-covered feet poked out. He leaned back to slip his arms into the sleeves and the suit enveloped his body, trying to deflate to its storage configuration. Jeff worked the various zippers, clasps, dial-locks, and seals blindly, having memorized the procedure during countless training exercises. The gloved fingertips of the unitard contained small tactile sensors which transferred dull electrical current to the skin of the wearer, simulating tactile pressure. It wasn't entirely necessary while only wearing the unitard, but it helped to feel what he was doing after putting on the bulkier Constellation Suit gloves.

After he was as fully dressed as he could get on his own, Jeff toed the button in the floor. The telescoping arm lowered a few centimeters and stopped just long enough so he could shrug the nylon loop at the back of his neck off the hook.

There would be no jumping up to the central pillar for easy coasting through the crew module. With the extra seventy-five pounds of weight on his shoulders, the best Jeff could manage was a lumbering stroll toward the front of the ship.

He began to sweat as he climbed the ladder at the front of the module. The internal cooling system wouldn't kick in until the suit was a closed loop. For that, he needed gloves, boots, helmet, and pack. With each successive rung, gravity lessened. Finally, blessedly, he passed into zero gravity and felt the weight of the suit slip away like an iron-filled blanket being lifted.

Ming waited for him by the airlock door as he drifted into the T-junction, sitting motionless in midair with her legs folded meditation-style, her dark hair wavering slowly around her head.

"Oh, sure," Jeff said. "Show up for the easy part."

"Careful," she warned. "I don't have to tighten your boots all the way if I don't want to."

Ming keyed a set of numbers into a wall panel. After a loud solenoid clunk, the inner airlock door slowly opened.

Jeff followed her into the spherical airlock, being careful not to bump the sides of the hatch with his suit. The room was washed out with bright white light coming from a single hole in the ceiling. To Jeff, it looked more like a sterile clean room one would find in a medical research facility than a ship's pressurization chamber.

The remaining suit components were kept in a cabinet within the airlock. Ming opened it and put on Jeff's boots and gloves, sliding the locking rings into place until they sealed with loud, satisfying clicks. The maneuvering and support system pack weighed as much as the suit in full gravity. In zero-g, Ming was able to help Jeff shrug into its straps without a grunt of effort. She hooked the pack up to the interface panel on the back of his suit.

"Give it a whirl," she said.

Jeff checked the data pad on his forearm, pressed a button to start the initial test. Moments later, he got a green light.

"Looks good," he said.

She handed him his Snoopy cap. "Ready for your helmet?"

"You trying to get rid of me?" he asked, strapping on the Communications Carrier Assembly.

"Any way I can."

"I'm ready."

She lowered the protective pressure helmet over his head until the lock at the bottom slipped into the grooved ring around the neck of his suit. With a slight twist, the gold-visored helmet locked into place. Ming slid another lock over the neck seal, closing the system. Jeff felt a cool hiss of air as the pack activated. A red Heads-Up-Display bordering the edges of his face shield told him he was now breathing the suit's air, and had four hours remaining. His tongue tingled for a moment, just as it always did during training after the first few breaths of metallic atmosphere.

Other small displays at the corners of his face shield HUD showed his relative distance to nearby objects, his vital readouts, and remaining suit power. Directional nitrogen jets positioned around the pack would allow him to navigate easily once outside the ship, but drained his power more quickly.

Ming knocked on the top of his helmet.

Jeff pushed a button on his wrist pad and the golden visor sheathed up, leaving only the clear polycarbonate bubble.

She touched a finger to her ear and looked at him questioningly. Another few taps on his wrist data pad with bulky, gloved fingers, and Jeff patched his suit comms into the ship. Ming drifted over to the curved airlock wall and held down a button on the comm panel as she spoke.

"You hearing me okay?"

"Loud and clear. All readings in the green."

"Glad to hear it. I'll get out of your hair so you can get to work."

"Gee, thanks."

She gave him a thumb's up and pushed off the wall, coasting through the inner airlock door. Once she was through, Jeff keyed a number into the wall panel, and the door slowly closed. He saw her floating down the T-junction through the small polycarbonate porthole in the center of the door.

With a gentle tap on the wall, he spun around to face the outer door. There was no window in the round slab of metal, just a smooth exterior which hid a complex series of locks and seals. He reached out and pushed a sequence of buttons on the control panel. Two of them lit up: one green, one red. He pushed the green one.

The powerful white light in the ceiling dimmed instantly and was replaced with a pulsing yellow hazard strobe as the air was quickly sucked from the room. Jeff saw the evidence of this as streaks of cold air flowed down the walls of the room and disappeared into floor vents. He heard nothing from within his suit except his own breathing.

The yellow strobe painted the room in flashes, flicking on and off. The two buttons lit up again. Jeff pushed the green one. The outer airlock door swung slowly inward, opening up a hole in space. Stars dotted the infinite blackness – tiny pinpoints of light glimmering with an intensity that astronomers on Earth could only imagine. Titan was behind him, on the side of the ship opposite the airlock.

Jeff stared into the void beyond the hatch. For a brief moment, he was convinced he would fall to eternity if he crossed the barrier separating the two worlds. It would be like jumping into a hole over an endless chasm – some kind of gravity well would seize hold of his body and pull him on and on, away from the ship.

The sensation passed. He tapped a command on his wrist data pad to extend the flight control stick attached to the underside of his left forearm. With the smallest amount of pressure on the stick, the jets on his pack let out tiny bursts of nitrogen, and he coasted forward, out of the airlock and into space.

There was nothing to see but the sparkling pinpoint lights of a billion distant stars, and the sight took Jeff's breath away. A few seconds ago, he still had the solid walls of the airlock to reassure him he was still in a physical realm. Now there was nothing below his feet but an emptiness that had no end.

"I'm clear of the airlock," he said.

"Copy that," Ming replied over his headset from inside *Explorer*. *"I see you."*

He manipulated the flight control stick with his left hand, jets in his pack spat nitrogen, and he turned around slowly.

"Are you recording?" he asked.

"Of course."

The command module at the front of *Explorer I* came into view as he rotated, as sleek as a polished bullet except for the narrow black window cut into the top of its tapered nose.

"No bugs on the windshield," Jeff said. "Clean as a whistle, from where I'm standing – er, floating."

"Excellent."

"Maintenance panel for secondary fuel line access is port-side, directly behind the cargo hold," he said, speaking for the benefit of the official record rather than to Ming, who already knew the panel's location. "Heading there now."

He navigated away from the front of the ship and drifted aft, staying parallel to the cylindrical crew module. Inside, the centrifuge was divided into sectional rings, each with a distinctive function. Outside the ship, the crew module was a smooth piece of seamless metal, adorned only with the three-meter-tall Diamond Aerospace logo and the words *Explorer I* in sweeping, triumphant lettering.

"Can you see the others?" Ming asked.

"Negative. Crew module's too wide. Maybe when I get past the hold. How're they looking?"

"They're at the hatch of the other ship. Looks like there was a minor explosion from inside the airlock."

"We heard the oxygen compressor."

"Yes, the interior is still pressurized. They're trying to close the outer airlock door now."

Jeff studied the spartan HUD readout in his helmet as he continued to drift farther aft. "Is there any way to pump a video feed into the helmet? I don't remember that from training."

"They never mentioned it, but give me a second," Ming said. *"I'm pulling up that model's documentation."*

"It came with an instruction manual?"

"Not exactly. Looks like it was written by someone from the coding department. Hold on...I found something. I'm giving your suit permission to access the ship's video feeds, but you have to manually patch in."

She read off a long string of letters and numbers, which Jeff dutifully typed into his wrist data pad.

"Get all that?" she asked.

A new option appeared along the bottom of his HUD, at the lowest edge of his face shield: a button-style object with, naturally, the word *VIDEO* in the middle. He used the arrow keys on his wrist pad to activate it. A small picture-in-picture video box popped up in the lower left corner of his HUD, slightly transparent so it wouldn't fully block what was behind.

"I got it," Jeff answered. "Thanks, Lieutenant."

The feed showed *Explorer*'s view of North Star. Riley and Silva appeared small at that distance as they crowded the airlock of the other ship. Jeff cycled through all the available feeds until he found one from Riley's helmet camera.

"–tried that already," Riley was saying. *"Damn thing's stuck."* It seemed the system fed both video *and* audio to Jeff's suit. Riley's camera showed the interior of a spherical airlock identical to *Explorer*'s. Melted black streaks gouged the smooth metal walls, originating from the interior side of the sealed inner airlock door. He had a bottle-sized multipurpose hex driver in his gloved hands, and was working to open a panel in the charred wall.

Gabriel said, *"But if that's not the manual override for the outer door–"*

"Wait a sec," Riley said, grunting. *"Almost there."*

The tool slipped out of its groove and he cursed – but the panel popped open.

"Gotcha!" he said, pushing the loose panel aside. He drifted down to shine his helmet's light into the open panel. Another curse. *"Explorer, are you seeing this?"*

"Copy, Commander," Ming replied.

Jeff saw it, too. The manual door override was fried – melted and fused to the wall.

"Must have been one hell of a fire," said Riley. *"Explorer, it seems we're unable to pressurize the airlock."*

Jeff floated past the end of the crew module where it tapered down to the narrower cargo hold. "If that ship was built like Explorer," he said, "there should also be an exterior manual override."

"We know about the other override, Dolan," Riley said testily. *"But then we couldn't get back inside."*

"I could close the door with the manual override outside the airlock."

"Do it," Kate said suddenly, and Jeff jumped in his suit.

"Hi, Ms. Bishop," he said, grinning from ear to ear. "Have you been listening this whole time?"

"Hey, Dolan," Riley said. *"Stop flirting and just let us into the ship."*

"Say please."

"What did you just say to me?"

"Play nice, boys," Noah interrupted from Mission Control.

"And you stay out of this," spat Riley.

"Ease up on the hostility, Commander," Frank said.

"It's not benefiting anyone. Jeff, you are approved for task deviation. Close North Star's outer hatch, then continue with your repairs as planned."

What the hell was that about? Jeff wondered. He'd never heard the commander snap like that. Riley was a tough guy when he needed to be, sure, but he had always kept his cool during tense moments of training.

Explorer dropped away below Jeff as he maneuvered toward North Star, revealing the full disc of Titan ahead. The hazy, yellowish moon filled his field of vision, and he craned his neck up to take it all in.

The surface wasn't distinguishable beneath Titan's thick, nitrogen-rich atmosphere – the only one of its kind in the solar system.

Since Explorer matched orbital velocity with North Star, the two ships were seemingly stuck in the sky together, as if connected by an invisible, rigid pole.

The alien torus floated a hundred meters off North Star's bow, silent and still, as all three objects circled Titan. Jeff stared at it as he accelerated away from Explorer. Its diameter was larger than North Star's, and there was nothing in the middle. It was just a hoop comprised of deep black material, with no visible machinery.

Nothing in the middle, Jeff thought as he looked more closely at the empty space inside the torus. He had crossed half the distance to North Star, and was now looking at the artifact obliquely, instead of directly from the side when it would appear as a solid line.

He set his comms to wide broadcast.

"There's nothing inside the torus," he said.

"*Of course not,*" Gabriel said, amused. "*It's a circle.*"

"I mean there's *nothing*. No stars, no Titan. If you look through the middle, it's just a black disc."

Jeff had been watching Gabriel's video feed from his own HUD. Riley and Silva were both visible within the darkness of *North Star*'s airlock – even so far from the heart of the solar system, there was enough sunlight to cast dim shadows in the spherical room. Riley turned to Gabriel and did his best to approximate a shrug.

"*Silva and I ogled that thing on the way over, Dolan,*" he said. "*We both saw stars through the middle.*"

"You might want to look again."

Gabriel drifted out of the airlock and turned toward the torus.

"*My God,*" he said reverently. "*It's empty.*"

"*I'll be damned,*" Riley said, floating next to Gabriel. "*Dolan's right. That's kind of creepy, actually. Canaveral, do you have a visual?*"

"We see it," Kate said.

"*Silva and I were looking at it from the other side,*" Riley continued. "*From over here, the stars on the outside go right up to the outer edge of the hoop. Then it's almost as if there's a black sheet covering the interior of the torus. I should be able to see a little bit of Titan in the lower-left quadrant, but now it looks like something took a perfect little bite out of it.*"

Jeff reset his comms to send only to *Explorer*.

"Hey, Ming?"

"*Yeah?*"

"Can you stop recording my feed for a minute?"

He heard a few clicks on the other end of the line. "*Done.*"

"I'm starting to feel a little unsure about this whole thing."

"You and me both."

"What would happen if we left early?"

"What do you mean?"

"If we left without building the orbital station."

"You mean right now?"

"Sure, now. What would happen?"

"They're already saying it's going to take almost twice as long to get home. I would say it's up to us whether we wait a few extra weeks in orbit around Titan or wait closer to Earth."

"In other words, we're screwed either way, so it doesn't matter."

"Right. What about Space Station Glory?"

Gabriel and Riley maneuvered back into the ship as Jeff neared the airlock. His HUD counted down the distance in the upper-right corner of his face shield.

"I'm not saying I want to vote on it just yet," Jeff continued. "But I am saying my reasons for sticking around are quickly evaporating. It's hard to stay confident in a company when it becomes increasingly obvious they're merely improvising on a large scale...especially when that same company sent you halfway across the solar system in a ship that could blow up with each ignition."

"I don't owe the company anything else," Ming said. *"If it comes down to it, you have my vote."*

Jeff smiled. "Thank you. Okay, I'm patching back into main comms now."

"Reactivating recording. Hope we can get the glitch

figured out so we don't lose your comms again."

Twenty meters out from *North Star*, Jeff no longer maintained any doubt that it was mostly identical to *Explorer*. If the company logos were swapped, he may have even found it impossible to tell the difference.

He slowed his approach with a few forward bursts of nitrogen from his pack, then bumped gently into the side of the ship, next to its airlock. Jeff hooked his pack's retractable safety tether into a welded loop on the hull. He had almost thirty meters of line to work with, if he needed it.

"Hang tight, guys," he said as he used his multipurpose hex driver to loosen the bolts of a square panel in the hull.

The panel hinged outward from one side, revealing a gray lever shielded by a plastic cover. A sticker bright with yellow stripes warned him that it was the emergency door release. If he pulled the lever, the pneumatic governors that lowered the outer airlock door at a controlled speed would open and the door would slide shut like a spring-loaded guillotine.

Below the emergency door release were two hexagonal holes side by side labeled INNER and OUTER. The tool that fit the holes resembled a T-shaped tire iron. Jeff pulled it from its clamp next to the holes and inserted the long end into the hole labeled OUTER. With a forceful twist, he managed half a turn.

"The outer hatch just dropped a few centimeters," Gabriel said.

"There's some resistance," Jeff said, already breathing a little heavier. "Give me another few hours and it will be down all the way," he added jokingly.

He gripped the handles and gave the tool another turn, working to seal the outer airlock door.

Kate watched Jeff's progress from her chair on the operations floor. He had succeeded in fully closing the outer hatch, and was now inching the inner door open, slowly letting the ship's atmosphere bleed into the airlock. It wasn't the ideal method, but without power to what remained of the airlock control panels, there wasn't much choice.

A smaller window on the display wall showed Riley's camera feed. He and Silva were hooked to welded metal loops on the airlock wall in case the outer door failed.

"*Ten more minutes,*" Jeff panted between turns. "*Hope you… can get the… power back on.*"

"*It is on,*" Ming said. "*Well, the air system seems to be functioning, at least. Looks like the rest of the ship's systems were suspended.*"

Kate turned in her seat to ask Rick a question, then stopped short when she remembered he had never shown up for work. She glanced to the back of the room.

Frank and Noah were engaged in a heated conversation in the conference room.

Farther down her row of workstations, Juan sat staring intently at the video feeds. Kate walked over to him and touched his shoulder.

"Juan," she said.

He jumped in surprise, his concentration severed from the display wall.

"Geez, you scared me," he said.

She sat in the empty chair next to his. "Sorry about that. Can I borrow your cell phone?"

He shook his head. "The guard took it from me this morning."

"Mine, too," she admitted.

She turned when Noah burst out of the conference room and disappeared into his private elevator. Frank stayed behind, aggressively jabbing numbers into the dial pad of the conference phone.

"I'm worried about Rick," Kate said.

"Why?"

Frank spoke quickly to someone on the other end of the conference phone line, then jabbed a button to terminate the call. He walked out of the conference room and stopped at the viewing platform railing, gripping it tightly.

"Just a bad feeling," Kate answered distractedly.

Moments later, the door leading from the front of the building to the operations floor slid open to admit a dozen security guards in dark blue uniforms. They all resembled the same bulked-out guard who had taken Kate's phone when she arrived at work that morning.

Like him, they all wore guns in their belt holsters.

Every tech on the operations floor stopped what they were doing and watched the guards as they took up innocuous positions around the outer edges of the room, standing in the shadows when they could, as still as statues.

"What's happening, Ms. Bishop?" Juan asked.

"I don't know," she replied. "But let's find out."

She stood and walked toward the stairs at the back of the room, heading for Frank, half expecting for the security thugs to stop her. He was joined by the very same guard she'd met that morning, and the two of them entered Noah's private elevator.

"Alright," said Riley in the feed on the display wall. *"We should be able to squeeze through. Thanks, Dolan."*

Kate looked at the closed elevator door for a long moment, then reluctantly turned back to watch the screen.

"No problem," Jeff said. *"If you can't get the power working, give me another call and I'll let you out. Maybe."*

"Ha, ha."

The nearest security guard stood in a wide stance, his thumbs hooked lightly in his belt. He kept his eyes locked on Kate as she approached.

"Hi," she said. "You mind telling me what you're doing here?"

He didn't give any indication that he heard the question. Kate was just about to turn away when he said, "Just extra security, ma'am. There's nothing to worry about."

Then he winked.

Noah walked briskly to his desk from the elevator.

"Lights full!" he shouted. White light flooded his office as he sat at his desk and pounded the intercom button. "Neil, get the head of Blackbird security on the line. I have a situation." Silence on the other end of the line. Noah smacked the button again. "Neil!"

"I sent your support staff home," Frank said as the elevator door opened. "You won't be needing them for the duration of the mission."

Noah picked up his phone and started dialing a number. He looked at the receiver in confusion when he didn't hear a dial tone.

"No internet," Frank said. "No outgoing phone calls. I'm sorry, but I have the only communication link anywhere in the building."

Noah sprang up from his chair and stormed toward Frank, intending to let him know, in vitriolic detail, what he thought about his presumptuous interference. He slowed to a stop when Frank stepped out of the elevator, followed closely by a muscular security guard who wore a satisfied smirk on his face and a heavy pistol on his hip.

"What's this about, Frank?"

"Hand over your cell phone."

Noah stuck his hands in his pockets and lifted his chin. "You're fired. I want you out of here immediately."

Frank gestured to the security guard, who stepped forward eagerly. He rested his hand on the butt of his holstered pistol. Noah sized him up, then pulled his phone from his pocket and tossed it to the guard.

Frank nodded. "Thank you. I was hoping to avoid this uncomfortable situation, but you leave me no choice. As I said earlier in the conference room, we don't have time to do things your way. I know your methods, Noah. You'll get right up to the edge, then pull back if it looks too dangerous. I can sense it happening even now. It's not a fitting trait for a man who strives to accomplish as much as you. To be honest, sometimes I'm surprised you've gotten so far."

"I'm not pulling back from anything."

"Not yet, no. But what if everyone on North Star is dead? You'll order the crew of Explorer to break away from the artifact and build the station on the far side of Titan, if you let the project continue at all. You don't risk lives when risking lives is the only way to progress."

"And what would you do?"

"Study the artifact, even if means the crew lingers at Titan past their departure window."

"They can't stay out there indefinitely, Frank."

"True. Yet they signed up for this mission, and by extension, for any exigent circumstances that arise along the way. Gleaning every iota of knowledge from the torus being chief among them."

"We can always go back for it."

Frank snorted. "What if it's gone? Would you risk it? The artifact enables instant communication across half the *solar system*! What if that were merely a hint of the object's vast capabilities? What manner of propulsion is it using? What kind of power source? We *have* to know these things. Progress at any cost, Noah."

"That was never my motto."

"No, but you knew it was mine. That's why you hired me. Don't lie to yourself – you rely on me to make the uncomfortable decisions. Well, this is one of them. Explorer stays at Titan until we figure out a way to drag the torus back to Earth or to replicate its technology."

Noah looked at him as if he were an undesirable sample in a petri dish. "You really did alter the test results for the antimatter drive."

"You're damn right I did. We were sinking millions into solving the stability problem. Each successive probe we launched proved we were *almost* there. Then came number six. All the way to Titan, and it even managed to take a picture. That's all the proof I needed that a manned vessel could make it."

"You buried the real results. You withheld crucial data from me, Frank."

"Yes."

"You put the crew on the launch pad, knowing full well it might explode. That's the *real* reason you kept the press away during the launch, isn't it? They could have been invited to a barbecue."

Frank glared at him defiantly.

"Did you have Michael Cochran murdered?" Noah asked.

A shadow crossed Frank's face, and he scowled. "You're changing the subject."

"What about Rick Teller? He didn't show up for work this morning. I have security footage showing him breaking into the sealed archives. What did he find in there, Frank?"

Frank waved away the questions. "Enough. Here's how it's going to work. I assume full command of the mission. I don't want to lock you in your own office, Noah, but I will if I must. Are you going to behave?"

Noah glanced at the muscular security guard standing behind Frank. He looked like a man who wanted people to disobey.

"Yes."

Frank nodded sagely. "Good. Then there's no reason to confuse everyone on the operations floor with the details of our new arrangement. You're going to thank me for this, in the end. I'm doing something you couldn't. Deep down, I'm sure you'll agree this is the way it should be."

Noah crowded into the elevator with Frank and the security guard. For perhaps the first time in his career, he couldn't begin to guess what awaited him in the hours to come.

It would take Jeff just under five minutes to get back to *Explorer*, moving at what the Flight Op techs in Mission Control called the 'nominal speed' – a veritable snail's pace of about three meters per second.

Jeff was toying with the notion that the ship had been launched without a crew – that perhaps MarsCorp had decided on a rushed, automated mission in the hope that the mere presence of their vessel at Titan would signify a binding ownership of its resources. When he asked if that were the case, Silva told him there were signs that *North Star* had indeed been crewed until quite recently. Eating utensils clumped with food floated slowly in the dark command module as Riley tried unsuccessfully to pull up the flight record. Without power to the main systems, the centrifuge couldn't rotate, and anything unsecured floated freely throughout the ship.

The video feed window of his HUD kept Jeff's full attention until he was nearly back to *Explorer*. Riley and Silva hadn't seen any sign of *North Star*'s crew on the other side of the airlock, nor in the T-junction leading to the command module.

Jeff muted and shrank the video feed window, leaving it as only a thumbnail in the lower left corner of his HUD. He decelerated early, giving himself plenty of room to maneuver safely into position just aft of the cargo hold, over the secondary fuel line access panel. The insulated, two-meter-long panel opened onto a mere snippet of the overall fuel line, but also onto most of the sensors monitoring the complex system.

He hooked his safety tether to an anchor loop on the hull, then grabbed the multipurpose hex driver strapped to the side of his pack and unscrewed the panel's fasteners. Small rivets on the end of the fasteners caught against the underside of the hinged panel, preventing them from floating away.

Two thick fuel lines ran the length of the compartment, propped up from the hull several centimeters. A dozen small, black boxes surrounded it, bolted to the hull. Multicolored braids of wire connected the black boxes to the fuel lines.

Jeff shined his helmet light into the compartment. Silver labels on the black boxes gleamed as he searched for the one containing the faulty sensor.

"There you are," he mumbled to himself.

He popped a latch on one corner of the box and pried open its stiff plastic cover. Inside was a five-centimeter copper cube etched with fine, geometric lines. If he were to yank out all the sensors monitoring the fuel line, the pumps wouldn't be able to regulate the flow on an active system, and the engine would overload, triggering a catastrophic explosion. A temporary loss of one sensor was still considered safe. Losing more was an unacceptable risk.

Inaccessible to Jeff were the contents of the copper cube: a delicate sensor array, the components of which were suspended independently of each other in a clear gel. He pulled out the cube and ran a gloved finger inside the empty black box, checking for any sign of leaks or corrosion. It was clean, as was the copper surface of the cube. He tucked the cube into a Velcro pouch on his right thigh.

"Canaveral," he said, "the faulty fuel line sensor has been removed. No signs of corruption. Sensor array was probably scrambled inside. I'll replace it with a new sensor now."

"Copy that, Jeff," Frank said over his headset. *"Proceed to the cargo hold for that replacement fuel pump after you wrap it up."* Jeff paused for a second – he had been expecting to hear Kate's voice. Frank sounded different somehow – world-weary, as if he had shouldered an enormous burden since he'd last spoken to the crew.

The spare sensors were inside a latched compartment set into the hull between the fuel lines. Jeff retrieved one of them and gently pressed it down into the empty black box. After he resealed the box, he said, "Sensor replaced. What's the verdict?"

"Clearing error code," Ming said. *"Looks like you did it. Good job."*

"Yeah," Jeff said. "At least now we'll know we're going to blow up a few seconds before it happens."

"Cherish the small things."

"I'm headed to the cargo hold."

"Copy that," Ming replied. *"Don't forget to–"*

She cut off suddenly and gasped.

"Ming? What's wrong?"

"Oh my God," she said slowly.

Jeff was going to ask her what she was talking about, then he looked down at the small video feed box in his HUD and got his answer.

"They found the crew," Ming said.

He quickly magnified his HUD's video feed and unmuted the audio, but heard only the quick, stopping breaths of Riley and Gabriel.

Riley's camera looked from the end of the T-junction at the crew module extending toward the back of the ship. He and Gabriel had apparently given up on the power problem and left the command module to explore the rest of the ship.

The only lights came from Riley's and Gabriel's helmets – wide halogen beams flowed over every surface as they looked around. The floor layout of the centrifuge was identical to *Explorer's*, with low walls compartmentalizing specific areas. A central pillar ran down the axis of the ship, extending from above the camera's field of vision to the back of the module.

A red Mark III Constellation Space Suit, slightly bulkier than the Mark IVs, floated into view, filled out as if it contained a person. The bright, sealed space suit reflected the powerful beam from Riley's helmet light. The Mark III rotated slowly to face the camera, and Riley's light spilled over its helmet, revealing a vibrant splash of blood on the inside of the clear face shield.

Gabriel's helmet light played hesitantly around the module, landing on three other sealed red Constellation Suits, adrift in the darkness.

"*Mother Mary,*" he whispered, followed by a string of rapid Portuguese Jeff didn't understand.

Riley spoke with grim determination. "*Canaveral, Dr. Silva and I are going to check for survivors. Stand by.*"

The four bodies of the *North Star* crew drifted casually within the crew module.

If you can even call those bodies, Kate thought. She clenched her abdomen to fight down a rising sickness that had been working its way up into her throat since Riley had shined his light directly into the clear face shield of the first suit.

There had been no distinguishably human characteristics of what he'd discovered inside. The suit was still sealed and pressurized for EVA activity. Every molecule of whoever was in the suit during the violent, terminal event was still in there now – only changed. Kate had looked away as soon as the light hit a warped mass of red that had no particular shape, yet still projected what looked like a screaming mouth.

Riley started slowly making his way to the second suit, intending to illuminate whatever macabre scene awaited within. Kate forced her eyes over to Gabriel's camera feed. He was mercifully trying his best not to look at the suits, instead studying the kitchen area of the centrifuge, above which he floated, holding on to the central pillar.

Some or all of the crew had been eating immediately before putting on their suits. In addition to the floating eating utensils, meal trays rested securely under elastic straps on top of the round dining table. The hinged rehydrator door hung open, an unopened meal pouch slowly spinning within.

The crew had stopped mid-meal to don their suits, which meant they had known something was coming for them. Helmets and gloves were kept in the airlock, so the crew would have had to collect them and bring them *back* to the crew module. Kate wondered if someone in the crew had detonated an explosive device in the airlock to try to fend off whatever had gotten inside. It had been a small-yield bomb, yet powerful enough to immobilize the internal manual override and warp the doors, making it nearly impossible to crank them open.

Riley looked into the helmet of the second suit. Kate saw two bulging eyes staring at her from a congealed and silently screaming horror.

She grabbed the small trash can from under her desk and dry-heaved into it. She had lost whatever food had been in her stomach earlier, after acknowledging the very real possibility that Jeff might not make it home.

Kate wiped saliva from the side of her mouth and kicked the trash can back under her desk, expecting to need it again soon. She wasn't quite ready to look back at the display wall, so she tapped the touchscreen on her workstation monitor and called up a video replay from Gabriel's camera feed when he had been in the airlock.

After Riley had popped open the override access panel, Gabriel shined his light into the compartment containing the fused lever. Kate paused the video replay and leaned in closer to her monitor, studying the black, blooming gouges emanating from the compartment, as if the walls of the airlock had been shredded by the talons of some terrible, clawed beast.

"Looks like they put the bomb inside the panel," Noah said from behind her, and she jumped in her chair, her heart pounding. "Sorry," he added, moving to stand next to her. "Didn't mean to scare you."

Kate looked warily over her shoulder. Frank sat alone in the conference room, his legs up on the table and fingers locked behind his head, engaged in a casual conversation with someone on the other end of the conference phone line.

She turned back to look at the still image on her workstation monitor, glancing around the room in the process. The mood was subdued, yet busy. Like her, the others had realized something was different – that there had been a shift in the weather. To their credit, they hadn't let it interfere with their work.

"What's going on?" she asked.

"Just a slight change in management," Noah replied stiffly. "I'll be taking a more... traditional role for a while."

"Can't you fire Frank?"

"I tried. One of his big friends was there to help me

change my mind."

"They took all of our cell phones."

Noah nodded. "I believe we're stuck here, Ms. Bishop. I'm just trying to distract myself until things get back to normal."

He looked down at Rick's empty workstation. Kate followed his gaze and stopped on Rick's chair. In that moment, she realized he was probably dead. She had willfully dodged the possibility until then, pretending instead that he was holed up in some doomsday bunker of his own construction, until whatever shadowy group pursuing him lost his scent.

Noah gripped the top of Rick's chair. Regret and sadness tugged at his face in turns.

Kate looked at the old picture of herself taped to her workstation monitor. Back then she had just been slapping ship components together while other teams worked real magic – slinging humanity to the stars. The room at NASA had been a closet compared to Mission Control at Diamond Aerospace. Before her current job at D.A. and a year at Boeing before that, Kate had worked four of her six years at NASA in an entry-level position for entry-level pay. She'd come a long way since then.

Her eyes in the picture looked eagerly into the camera, the hopeful naivety plain for all to see.

Maybe I'll see you soon, Kate thought, *if none of this works out.*

"I know about Michael Cochran," she said softly. "And the unstable antimatter drive." Noah's grip on the chair tightened, and his frown deepened. He nodded again, giving silent assent for her to continue. "I sent a message to Jeff. By now the rest of the crew will know they shouldn't risk any more major burns. Did you know about the engine?"

"I promise you, I knew nothing about the instability. If I had, we would never have launched."

"So Frank remote-triggered the major burn we all thought was a glitch?"

"I believe so, yes."

It was Noah's turn to look back at the conference room. Frank now paced near the table, a smile on his face, waving his hands enigmatically as he spoke.

"I tried sending an email," Kate added. "He's blocking all outside communication."

"Not from the conference room," Noah said acidly.

Kate hated the inconvenient tears that brimmed to her eyes as she stared at Rick's chair.

"Noah?" she whispered.

He turned to her. "Yes, Ms. Bishop?"

"What happened to my friend?"

"If Frank knows, he isn't telling me anything," Noah replied. He gestured to Rick's chair. "May I please sit?"

Kate drew a sharp breath, then forced a nod. As soon as Noah sat, a flood of relief washed over her. He put on Rick's headset, glancing at her to gauge any resistance to his actions. Finding none, he reached over and squeezed her hand.

"We're going to work together, Ms. Bishop. Frank clipped our wings, but we can still get the crew home."

On the display wall, Riley turned away from the

fourth and last suit.

"Mission Control, this is a ghost ship," he said. *"We confirm there are no survivors aboard the North Star."*

Kate looked back. Frank stood at the railing of the viewing platform.

"Our responsibility to that ship is done," he said. "Get our crew out of there."

She faced the display wall and pushed her microphone closer to her lips. "Copy no survivors, Commander. Jeff, you mind letting our boys out?"

His video feed was in the upper right corner of the display wall, squeezed smaller to accommodate Riley's. He had been preparing to access the control panel on the hull which would allow him to open the cargo hold.

"Then I come back for the fuel pump?"

"That's the plan," Kate said.

In his video feed, she watched *Explorer* drift away as he maneuvered toward *North Star*.

"Copy that, Ms. Bishop. Heading over now."

"Jeff?"

"Mm-hmm?"

"Call me Kate."

There was a long pause.

"Copy," he said at last, his voice a little shaky.

Then his line clicked off, and Kate heard only muted silence.

The bulk of *Explorer I* extended behind its cargo hold: 85 meters of engine wrapped in a 6-meter-diameter hull, its surface dimpled with rivets all the way back to the flared engine wash shield. After opening *North Star*'s airlock doors for Riley and Gabriel, Jeff had returned to *Explorer* and performed a cursory check of the twin communications arrays clinging to the hull immediately aft of the crew module.

Heavy impact shielding covered the clumps of machinery except for two large holes, from which protruded delicate radio antennae. Several small craters dented the surface of both arrays' impact shielding – evidence of micrometeoroids that had struck *Explorer* en route to Titan. Satisfied that both arrays were still in working order, Jeff proceeded to the cargo hold door a few meters aft.

His suit beeped at him. Bright red numbers flashed in his helmet HUD, telling him he only had an hour of oxygen remaining – more than enough time to retrieve the backup fuel pump and make it to the airlock.

The notification served as a motivator, and Jeff worked more quickly to open the access panel than he would have otherwise. After loosening the panel's ten fasteners, Jeff typed a command into his wrist pad. A few seconds later, the wrist pad screen pulsed green and the cargo hold door hinged upward. With another few taps on his data pad, halogen lamps flicked on within the six-meter cylindrical compartment.

Jeff pulled himself hand-over-hand through the opening and into the hold. Thick straps secured the hold's contents to its walls – supplies which Diamond Aerospace had shuttled up to the ISS in the months prior to launch.

Material for the foundations of the orbital station occupied most of the wall space. Long support struts lay in a tightly-stacked pyramid. Next to those were the square gray panels which would form the walls of the only complete module *Explorer*'s crew would construct on that mission – the greenhouse.

A half-dozen three-meter spheres took up a quarter of the hold. Tight rubber straps bound each sphere – inflatable modules which would serve as temporary shelter until more paneling arrived with the next mission. The idea was that the inflatable modules would slowly be replaced with permanent additions, serving future crews until the space station was completed – a process Diamond Aerospace expected to take about five years.

On the wall opposite the orbital station materials was the section of the hold dedicated to parts for

Explorer. The square section resembled the surface of a large, curved circuit board, with various tools and parts neatly arranged in a grid. A quarter-second burp of nitrogen from Jeff's pack was enough to propel him to the wall.

As he worked to loosen the straps pinning down one of the replacement fuel pumps, a box he didn't recognize caught his eye. He freed the shoebox-sized fuel pump and left it spinning slowly in place as he used the other secured parts as handholds to pull himself over to the box.

"Ming?" he asked.

"I'm here."

"Patch into my video feed and tell me what I'm looking at."

The box was roughly one meter on each side, and solid black. A complex series of latches sealed its lid, and a thick yellow band of tape covered the seal. The tape would be ripped if someone opened the box.

"That's one of the items I moved from command module storage to the cargo hold when we were docked at ISS."

"Do you know what's inside?"

"I didn't have a reason to check during the transfer. Does it have a number?"

Each part in the cargo hold, no matter how small, was assigned a ten-digit designator for easy tracking and cataloging.

"Negative. It has no markings."

"I'm not seeing it on the manifest," Ming said.

"Because it isn't," Kate cut in. *"That must have been Frank's last-minute addition just before launch. You can*

thank him if you run out of ketchup, by the way. He removed some of your condiments to allow for the extra weight."

"Is he nearby? Let's ask him."

A pause, then Kate replied: *"He says don't worry about it."*

"Of course he does." Jeff moved to unstrap the box so he could open the lid. "I'll just have a look myself, then."

"Don't touch it, Dolan," Riley said suddenly. *"I just pulled up your video feed. That box looks a hell of a lot like the kind the Navy uses to store explosives for underwater detonations."*

"Explosives," Jeff repeated.

"Most likely modified Semtex."

"Modified how?"

"No trigger required. Hit that sucker with any kind of detonation and BOOM."

"So...they put a bomb on our ship."

"Is it wired to anything?" Ming asked.

"Not that I can tell. Maybe it's not a bomb, then."

"No, Commander Riley is correct," Frank said, his voice loud on the line. *"The box contains explosives. Consider it insurance."*

"Insurance for what, exactly?"

"I had no way of knowing if the artifact was hostile."

"It's a *circle*, Frank."

"I thought it best to be prepared for any eventuality. What are you worried about? It turned out to be an unnecessary precaution. The artifact is just a circle, as you say. Better to have it and not need it, right?"

"Know what I think?" Jeff said. He put some

distance between himself and the inert bomb. "I think it had nothing to do with potential hostility. I think you would have had us blow up the artifact if there was even a chance of another company getting its technology."

Jeff's HUD flashed red: thirty minutes of oxygen remaining.

"I'm fixing the fuel pump," he said, "then we're getting the hell out of here."

"That is not your decision to make, Jeffrey," Frank said.

"Buddy," Jeff replied, "if you think I'm listening to anything you have to say, you are sadly mistaken."

He retrieved the floating fuel pump and jetted for the exit of the cargo hold.

Kate stared at the display wall, dumbfounded. Jeff's video feed showed him sealing the cargo hold door. The feeds from the other two space suits were blank – Riley and Gabriel had gone back inside *Explorer*.

She slowly turned to Noah, who looked just as confused as she felt.

"Did you know about the bomb?" she asked.

"Of course not," he said. There was no defensive edge to his voice, only a hint of defeat. "Frank had full access to the command module before launch. He could have put anything he wanted into storage." Noah looked back at the viewing platform. Frank sat at his wide desk, oblivious to their conversation. "I trusted him."

"Look, Noah," Kate said, drawing his attention back to her. "We have to do something here. I honestly feel like if I tried to leave to get help, one of those guards would shoot me."

"You could try."

"I can't leave them out there," she said, looking to the display wall.

Noah smiled sadly. "Nor can I."

Kate noticed that several of the security guards stationed around the room stared in her direction.

"What Frank's doing is illegal, right?" she asked.

"Technically he hasn't broken any laws yet," Noah said.

"Besides probably murdering two people."

"Frank's clever. I doubt it would be easy to trace those crimes back to him."

Kate turned in her chair and locked eyes with Frank, who watched her from the viewing platform. He yawned and looked away.

"What if we could get him to admit to the murders?" she asked.

Noah frowned in thought. "It wouldn't matter unless he confessed to the police."

On the display wall, Jeff floated in the sealed airlock as he waited for the pressurization process to complete. Riley's and Gabriel's suits were tethered to the wall of the airlock, hooked up to oxygen and power feeds. Jeff's helmet camera looked down at his wrist pad as he typed in a command, then the video feed went blank.

"Everybody's back inside," Kate said. "It will take about three hours to recharge the suits."

Frank called down from the viewing platform, "I want Riley and Silva back outside as soon as their suits are ready."

"You need at least three of them to start on the orbital station," Noah said.

"They won't be working on the station. Not yet."

Frank leaned over the railing and beckoned the nearest guard to him – the same guard who had winked at Kate earlier.

"I guess he's done with the conversation," Noah said.

"Looks that way," Kate agreed.

The guard went up to meet Frank. They spoke for just a moment, then the guard nodded and returned to the operations floor, heading for the break room. He swiped a security badge at the door and pushed his thumb onto the fingerprint scanner, then waited still as stone until the lock clicked open and he could push open the door.

Kate stood and walked toward the break room.

"Where are you going?" Noah asked.

"Grabbing a snack. Want anything?"

He looked confused again. "Um…no thank you."

The guard had his wide back to her when she entered. He stood by the coffee maker as it percolated, the acrid smell of bad roast filling the room. Kate noticed the barely-perceptible twitch in the muscles of his neck and the slight tilt in the angle of his head as the door closed behind her. Then his ears rose slightly as he smiled.

"You again," he said.

The coffee maker hissed out the last few drops of tarry brew.

"Me again."

Now that she was alone with him, some of her stored bravery leeched away, leaving an emptiness in her chest. He turned and leaned back against the counter, folding his arms over his barrel chest.

"You want coffee, too?" he asked.

She collected what remained of her courage and strolled casually across the room to stand next to him at the coffee maker. "I can get it myself."

The guard grunted. "More than I can say for your boss."

Kate plucked a styrofoam cup from a stack and lifted the full coffee pot. The guard picked up a blue mug and held it out. It looked like a piece of a child's tea set in his massive hand. To her credit, Kate kept herself from shaking as she filled his mug, then her own cup.

"How does your boss take his coffee?" asked the guard.

"With cyanide."

He grinned maliciously. Kate held his stare as she took a superficial sip of her coffee. It tasted more sour on her tongue than usual.

"Something on your mind?" he asked.

"I was wondering if you would stop someone if they tried to leave."

"Why? You thinking about leaving?"

"Just curious," Kate said.

He held the blue coffee mug with an iron grip. The surface of the liquid within was as flat as a lake on a windless day. Then he nodded.

"I'd stop them."

Kate took another sip of her coffee. "Did Frank order you to stop people who try to leave?"

"He hired us to enforce a communications blackout

in this facility. That also applies to employees."

"You and the rest of the goon squad aren't real police officers," Kate said. "If someone wanted to leave, there's technically nothing you could do, right?"

He grinned again as he set his coffee mug on the counter. "Officially?" he said. "No. Unofficially..."

His hand shot out and grabbed her throat. The styrofoam cup slipped from her grasp and hit the floor, splattering coffee against her pants. He lifted her off her feet with barely a grunt. Kate pounded on his forearm as he lifted her higher.

"Unofficially," he continued, his eyes as soulless as a shark's, "you only have to string up one villager to keep the rest of them in line."

Kate tried to get her fingers under his to pry his hand from her throat. Her eyes bulged and her feet kicked his shins.

Then he released her. Her feet hit the floor and she stumbled, but didn't fall. She gripped the counter for support while she choked for air. The guard picked up Frank's coffee and took a sip, grimaced, and spit it back into the mug. Kate managed to take a deep, painful breath of air.

"If you have any more questions," said the guard as he walked past her, "I'll be around."

As he reached for the door, it was pushed open from the other side, cracking into the guard's hand. Juan stood there, panting, his eyes wide with fear. He held his breath and backed away when he saw the guard, who shook his head angrily, cursing under his breath. As soon as the guard had passed, Juan hurried into the break room.

"Kate!" he said urgently. "You have to see this!"

She coughed and rubbed her throat as she straightened up.

"Kate?" Juan asked. He looked back at the closed door, then back at her. "What happened? Are you okay?"

She nodded and tried to swallow. It felt like she was attempting to force a dry stone down her throat. "I'm fine," she said hoarsely. "What is it?"

"It's Rick," Juan said between quick breaths. "He's on the news."

Juan eagerly led the way back to his workstation. The display wall showed nothing out of the ordinary, just a grid of data feeds from *Explorer*. The coffee-fetching guard was unhurriedly climbing the steps to the conference room.

Kate stood behind Juan's chair as he sat and typed on his workstation keyboard. She prepared herself for what she was about to see, hoping that whatever fate had befallen Rick, it happened fast enough that he didn't suffer.

Juan tapped the enter key and leaned back, gesturing toward his screen.

Rick stood in front of a public building, maybe a library, and was talking to a group of reporters. He wore dark sunglasses and a tan jacket over a new shirt that said KISS ME, STUPID in big letters. Kate laughed and quickly covered her mouth as she watched him. Tears welled in her eyes, and this time she welcomed them.

"How did you get this?" she asked.

"Frank neutered the internet," Juan said, "but there's a UHF antenna on the roof he forgot to manually sever from the system. I think he was more worried about outgoing signals than incoming anyway. I rerouted the television feed to Mission Control's servers and patched it to my workstation. I can even get ESPN and HBO on this thing."

"What's he saying?"

"Let me start it from the beginning," Juan said, tapping at his keyboard again.

"You recorded it?"

"I started as soon as I realized it was Rick."

"—when it became clear I was being followed," Rick told the reporters on the recording. *"The documents I obtained led me to believe that someone at Diamond Aerospace doctored safety records which would have otherwise prevented the launch of Explorer One and its crew. I think it's obvious Michael Cochran discovered the same information, and he was murdered because of it."*

"Who altered the reports?" asked one of the reporters.

"Was it Noah Bell?" asked another.

Rick smiled knowingly, and Kate shook her head. He always relished owning secret information. *"Through some careful digging of my own,"* he said, *"I found that the last call Michael Cochran received was from Frank Johnson, Mission Director of the Explorer mission."*

"That's not proof…"

"Not by itself," Rick said loudly, suppressing the murmurs of disagreement from the reporters. *"But it was enough, along with my fervent insistence, to get the local Sheriff's Department to send a few units out to the Diamond*

Aerospace building, which is currently on internal lockdown."

"You said you were being followed by the same men who killed Michael Cochran. How did you get away?"

"Fortunately and unfortunately, I have had special training that Cochran did not." Kate shook her head and couldn't help but allow a small hint of smile. *"This allowed me to evade my would-be murderers."*

The video of Rick cut away to an exterior helicopter shot of the Diamond Aerospace building. Four patrol cars were in the parking lot. Details were difficult to make out at that distance, but Kate thought she could see two officers pinning down the guard who had been working the security gate.

"Cut if off," Kate said, her mind racing. Juan complied and the video froze. "Is that real-time?"

"Looks like it," Juan replied.

"Has Frank seen it?"

"Hell, no."

She nodded. "Then let's keep it that way for now."

"What are you going to do?"

"Turn the tables. What else?"

Jeff sat alone at the small, round table in the kitchen section, slowly breathing in the rich aroma of pepperoni and green peppers; of melted mozzarella and buttery crust. Dehydration had sapped both moisture and color from the toppings of the small, square pizza, leaving the pepperoni crusty and slightly orange, and the green peppers more white than green. Despite the fact that no one had ever succeeded in making anything that resembled an edible pizza while outside the Earth's atmosphere, Jeff was compelled to admit the experiment was a success.

His stomach rumbled forcefully enough to shake the fabric of his shirt as he stared down at the steaming pizza, yet he couldn't bring himself to eat. He kept thinking about the dead crew of the *North Star* – about their horrid, twisted faces.

He pushed the pizza away as Gabriel walked into the kitchen section. He sat opposite Jeff and looked at the pizza for several long, silent moments.

"How did you do it?" he asked. "It's too big for the rehydrator."

"UV setting on the doctor pod."

Gabriel nodded slightly. His short, black hair was matted on top from his suit helmet. "Solar cooker. Very good. Riley might not like that his tanning bed was used for an oven."

"He can sue me. Want some?"

Gabriel hesitated. "I can't." Dark half-moons cradled his eyes from below. He scratched at the black and white stubble covering his chin. "Aren't you going to eat? You brought it all this way."

Jeff shook his head. "They ruined it," he said.

"Ruined what? Your pizza?"

"Everything."

"Who?"

Jeff shrugged. "Frank. Noah. MarsCorp. This was supposed to be our next big step. Mars has been the barrier of our interests, until now. It took monumental tenacity to get this ship off the ground, let alone to send it to Titan. That by itself is a feat worthy of the history books. The mission was...it was *pure*. Research and exploration and discovery. The foundations of the space industry."

"No," said Gabriel. "Those are only side effects. Far more practical gears turn this machine, gears so large they would pulverize any monkey wrench we could toss inside. Yet without them, we wouldn't be here. It is the very definition of the term 'necessary evil'."

"I used to believe that, but Noah changed my mind. He made me believe he wanted something different for all of us, not just another mining outpost."

"Maybe he does. But he can't get there without industry."

Somewhere in the walls, an oxygen compressor thrummed. Cold recycled air from vents in the central pillar wafted through the kitchen section. Steam no longer rose from the pizza.

"They told us we would be the first ones out here," Jeff said.

Gabriel studied him. "You wanted a byline?"

Jeff met his gaze. "I wanted awe and wonder."

"You haven't gotten it yet? That's an alien artifact out there, Jeff, orbiting a moon no human has ever seen with their own eyes."

"And yet it's tainted, isn't it? Everything about the mission feels wrong."

"That's on you," said Gabriel.

"You don't agree?"

"I'm scared shitless. But for now, my curiosity is so overpowering that I ignore my shaking hands. Let me show you something."

Jeff left the pizza cooling on the table and followed Gabriel to the science lab.

"I saw this as soon as I came back inside with Riley," Gabriel continued.

He led Jeff to the shoulder-high racks of plants he had cultivated on the journey from Earth – oxygen- and food-providing specimens intended for the orbital space station's greenhouse.

Five stacked rows of once-verdant foliage now hung limp on graying stalks, their leaves brown and wilted. Jeff hesitantly reached out and touched the nearest leaf. The dried husk broke and crumbled under his light touch. The shriveled lima bean sprout was a disheartening end piece on one of the rows.

"They were alive this morning," he said. "Well, except for the lima bean."

"Thriving," Gabriel agreed.

"I should check atmospheric. Maybe the composition is off."

"I already looked. You run a tight ship, Jeff. The readings are normal."

"What was it, then?"

Gabriel raised an eyebrow. "What, indeed?"

Jeff looked at him. "You don't think it was the artifact."

"What else? Consider instant communication with Earth. What if the torus generates some kind of field that makes such communication possible? Explorer could be piggybacking on that system. Reversed electrostatic fields interfere with plant growth, and if the torus can produce a strong enough field to instantly send messages halfway across the solar system..." He shrugged.

"Or the soil is bad," Jeff said.

"I'm just saying there are other possibilities. *That's* why I'm not giving up. I don't care how we ended up where we are, my friend. I care that we're here, now, and I plan on making the most of it."

"What does that mean?"

Gabriel rested his hand on Jeff's shoulder and smiled. "It means I have a mystery to solve."

Half the pizza was gone by the time Jeff made it back to the dining room. Riley stood by the small table, holding a piece of crust and chewing methodically, staring at nothing.

"It's cold," he said between chews as Jeff walked over to him. "But good."

"I used the doctor pod to heat it up. There might still be some melted cheese inside."

Riley stopped chewing. His eyes tracked over to Jeff, then he swallowed. Despite the cool temperature in the crew module, sweat ringed the neck of his white shirt.

"You know, Dolan," he said, "I'm surprised you made the final cut for this mission. Your test scores were solid, but I would have thought they wanted someone with–"

"A little less personality?" Jeff interrupted.

"I was going to say a grander sense of duty. Your attitude changed pretty quick once things went south."

"Is that why you're pissy? Should I be happy about the way things are turning out?"

Riley dropped the uneaten crust on the table and jabbed a finger in Jeff's direction. "You should keep your mouth shut and do your job, like the rest of us."

"You're scared," Jeff said suddenly. "I just realized it."

"Of course I'm scared! I saw those people up close!" he yelled, pointing in the direction of *North Star*. "We have a job to do and you sit around bitching about life being unfair and you're making pizza–"

"That you just ate!" Jeff said heatedly. He took a step forward and said, loudly, "If you think for one second that I don't take my job seriously then–"

He stopped as Gabriel strolled into the dining area from the direction of the science lab, whistling. Gabriel smiled at Jeff and Riley. They watched him pass through the crew quarters, climb the ladder at the front of the crew module, and float down the access tunnel leading to the command module.

The tension that had been building inside of Jeff slowly dissolved in the electric silence that hung in the air.

"I'm angry," he said at last.

"I know you are," Riley said. "We *all* are, for God's sake. I mean, look at *me*. I haven't been this upset since my divorce. But being angry does nothing for our current situation."

"Maybe take your own advice on that one."

"I need to. Look, you hate the fact that there was an engine problem before launch. I get that. You hate the fact that the company lied to you. No one can blame you. Bottle that anger until we get home, *then* do something useful with it. Out here…we need you to keep the ship running, no matter how screwed the situation becomes. We *depend* on it. It will take all four of us to build that space station. Frank is sending us outside now to get started, but we're going to put some distance between us and that torus first. So, what do you say? Want to help build it, or not?"

Blood rushed to Jeff's cheeks again, triggered by shame instead of anger. He was getting ready to respond when yellow caution lamps flicked on in the central pillar, casting a sickly glow on the floor of the centrifuge.

"What the hell?" Riley said, looking around in confusion. Then he bellowed, "Who's in the airlock?!"

"It's Gabriel," Ming said over the intercom. *"He just started depressurizing."*

With surprising speed given the reduced gravity, Riley took two big leaps to the nearest dividing wall and scaled it without slowing, launching himself to the central pillar. He grabbed the nearest ladder rung and pulled the rest of his body into zero-g, then coasted the short distance to the T-junction separating the modules, mumbling curses as he went.

The kitchen was only the second section from the front of the centrifuge. Jeff hurried as quickly as the reduced gravity would allow and climbed the ladder leading to the T-junction. Gravity vanished and he floated freely off the top of the ladder, then used handholds on the walls of the passageway to pull

348

himself to the airlock. Riley was already there, smashing his fist against a control panel.

"Can't open it in the middle of a cycle," he growled.

Jeff turned on a monitor screen next to the control panel and saw Gabriel inside the airlock, fully suited up, waiting patiently for the outer airlock door to open. The other two suits that had been EVA were still tethered to the wall. With a miniscule spurt of nitrogen from his pack, Gabriel slowly spun in midair and waved to the camera, smiling calmly.

"What is he doing?" Riley asked, squinting at the monitor as if, through scrutiny, he could force out an explanation.

Jeff mumbled, "Going to solve a mystery."

"What?" Riley barked.

"I think he's going to the torus. Ming, can you close the door from up there?"

"I'm trying, but... hang on. I've been locked out of the system."

"What are you talking about?" Riley asked.

"The remote system had been activated. I can't control anything. I couldn't even fire orbital thrusters if I wanted to. Someone back home doesn't want us to move."

"Gabriel's in the airlock!" Juan shouted from his workstation.

"Vitals are steady," Walt added.

Because that's my primary concern at the moment, Noah thought with a hint of irritation. He stood up and made eye contact with Frank up on the viewing platform.

"You locked them out remotely?" he asked loudly.

"I had to," Frank said, crossing his arms. "They were going to leave the artifact."

"To finish the damn mission!"

Frank shook his head. "First the artifact, then the station."

Noah growled in frustration and sat back down. Beside him, Kate watched the video feed of the airlock on the display wall with something akin to stunned fascination.

Noah tried to access the remote system mainframe from the workstation, but was denied every time. Frank had changed the password on him, probably even before his coup. Noah keyed the command to patch his station in to the Constellation Suit comms.

He forced himself to calm down as he watched the display wall, then he said, "Hey there, Gabriel."

Gabriel looked around in his suit. He typed a few buttons on his wrist pad and said, *"Hi, Noah."*

"Going for a little stroll?"

Gabriel chuckled. "Thought I might go knock on the door and see who's home."

Noah sat up straighter. He had expected an edge of uncertainty to Gabriel's voice, or at least a hint that he was becoming unhinged. Instead, he sounded borderline serene.

Kate looked over at Noah and he shook his head.

"That is ill-advised at the moment, Gabriel. We still don't know what we're dealing with."

"We should find out," Gabriel said confidently. "We'll have to go eventually, anyway. Waiting another day is pointless."

With that, the white floodlight in the ceiling dimmed and was replaced by the pulsing strobe of the yellow hazard lamp. The outer airlock door split a seam at the bottom and began to open.

A quick turn of Kate's head caught Noah's attention. She looked back at Frank, who watched the display wall from the railing of the viewing platform. Then she looked at the stairs leading up to him. Noah followed her gaze – the security guard usually stationed at the bottom was gone.

"I need a distraction," she said to Noah.

"What, *now?*" he asked, incredulous.

"Yes, now!" she whispered loudly.

He gestured to the screen. "I think you already have one."

She rolled her chair over to Rick's workstation and opened a drawer, then she palmed something Noah couldn't identify and stuffed it into her pocket.

"I need more," she said. "Try to get Frank down here for a couple minutes, then tell him I went into the conference room."

Noah was about to ask her what she was planning when Riley's voice came over his headset.

"Mission Control," he said, *"what is your recommendation?"*

"Tell him to proceed outside with Silva and investigate the artifact," Frank boomed from the viewing platform.

Noah thought about it for a moment. "I think I know just the thing to keep him busy."

He stood and adjusted his headset microphone. Then he turned around to face Frank, making sure to catch his attention before he started to speak. Frank, sensing what might be coming, stood up attentively.

"Commander Riley and crew of Explorer One, this is Noah Bell," he said into his microphone. "By show of force, Frank Johnson has assumed full command of the mission." He paused, and Frank signaled two nearby guards. The men peeled away from their positions on the perimeter of the operations floor and threaded their way across the room, heading for Noah. "He will attempt to keep you at Titan well beyond your return window," Noah continued. "His priority is not for your safe return. In other words, he considers you expendable."

"Shut him up!" Frank shouted, pointing down at Noah.

The two guards were nearly to his desk. Kate slipped away under the pretense of avoiding a confrontation. She paused to whisper something to Juan as she passed his workstation.

"Commander Riley," Noah said, "with that knowledge, I urge you to ignore any order he gives and return to Explorer with all available speed. I repeat: do not listen to Frank Johnson. If you could–"

His next words were silenced by the sharp crack of a guard's pistol against his temple. A collective gasp rose from the other employees as he crumpled from his chair to the floor. He reached up to touch his numb temple and felt the slick wetness of blood.

But he still wore his headset.

"Riley," he said, breathing hard as he lay on his side, half in the center aisle of the room. Frank glowered at him, commanding him to stay put with a stare as cold and hard as granite. "Riley," Noah said again. "Get them back to the ship. Don't listen to Frank."

Frank left the viewing platform and scuttled down the stairs, hurrying down the center aisle of the room.

Noah said, "Commander Ri–"

Crack!

Another blow to the temple, bouncing Noah's head off the carpeted floor.

"Leave him alone!" someone behind him shouted. It sounded like Walt, the flight surgeon.

Good man, Noah thought in a dazed stupor.

His vision cleared from black to blurry and he was looking at Frank's unpolished loafers. Frank crouched down and snickered.

"It really shouldn't have come to this," he said with believable regret.

"Riley," Noah whispered. "Get them out of there."

Riley said, *"Sounds like somebody finally put you in your place, Bell."*

"What?" he whispered stupidly.

"Frank, did you hurt him?"

Frank looked at the guards, unsure how to answer. Then he pulled off Noah's headset and held the microphone to his lips. "Yes. He's on the floor, bleeding."

Noah could hear the grin in Riley's voice as he said, *"Good. I'd rather take orders from you than from the sonuvabitch who slept with my ex-wife. Yeah, Bell, I know about that. She sent me a nice little message after we left Earth. Classy, isn't it? She always did know where to hit me. Besides, my loyalty is to the mission, not to some pantywaist with delusions of grandeur. We'll do it Frank's way."*

"Well, I'm glad to hear that, Commander," Frank said, clearly surprised. "I hope the rest of your crew agrees."

There was a pause, then, *"They will."*

Noah tried to speak but one of the guards pressed the bottom of his black boot on his mouth and pushed down, hard.

"Good," Frank said as he stood. "Suit up and go with Silva. Let us know what you discover."

"Copy that, Director."

Noah's glazed eyes wobbled in their sockets. He forced them to focus at the back of the room, beyond the raised viewing platform. Kate looked out at him through the glass wall, and gave him a thumb's up.

"Kate," Noah rasped from under the guard's boot.

"What did he say?" Frank asked. He waved the guard away.

"Kate's in the conference room," Noah said softly.

Frank looked at Kate, then back down at Noah suspiciously. Without another word, he left him lying there, bleeding from a deep cut in his temple. The guards left silently, and soon after, Noah felt hands under his arms, pulling him up to his chair and setting him down. Someone – Walt, probably – shined a pen light in his eyes and dabbed at his cut with a white cloth.

"I'm alright," Noah said, mustering as much verbal strength as he could manage. Walt pushed a cold compress into his hand. "Thank you. I'm alright."

Slowly, the others left him alone, walking defeated back to their own workstations to don their headsets and wait quietly for the next disaster. Noah wasn't sure how much time he spent in the chair, wavering in and out of consciousness. He snapped alert when someone near him gasped sharply.

On the display wall, Noah watched Silva traversing the distance between *Explorer I* and the torus. Riley's video feed showed that he was in the airlock, already suited up and waiting for the outer door to open. Ming sat on her hands in the crew module, looking like a scared child, leaning forward against the chair straps to stare out the narrow window at *North Star* and the artifact.

Jeff floated unconscious in the zero-g of the T-junction, still as a corpse but for a slight rotation. Blood dripped from a cut on his scalp, creating a widening spiral halo of floating globules around his head. His arms were outstretched slightly over his head. They passed through the blood spiral and the globules platted gently against his skin.

What a mess this is, Noah thought drunkenly, wondering what happened to Jeff. He held the cold compress to his temple and turned slightly until he could see Kate in the conference room. Frank pushed open the glass door and joined her. *Whatever she has planned,* he thought, *I hope it really knocks him for a loop.*

Frank came alone, without one of his bulky security guards.

Kate took it as a good sign.

He slowed as the door closed behind him, and he looked around the conference room like a cautious animal searching for the mechanisms of a trap. His gaze lingered on the black conference phone in the middle of the glass table. Seeing no glowing lights which signaled an outgoing signal, he deigned to look at her.

"What are you doing in here, Ms. Bishop?" he asked.

"I wanted to talk," she said.

"What could you possibly have to say?"

"I want you to tell me why you're doing this. What happened between you and Noah to spark your mutiny?"

"Mutiny?" he asked with a sour face, as if the word were bitter on his tongue. "Don't be so melodramatic. This is business, and it's how our relationship works.

Noah toes the line, and I push him over it. He'll thank me when it's over."

"I doubt he'll thank you for bashing his skull in."

He held up a corrective finger. "I didn't do that. That was the guard."

"Just like it was a guard who killed Michael Cochran?" she said. Annoyance flashed across his face and he waved her away as he prepared to leave the room. "I think you had him murdered" Kate added. "Along with Rick Teller."

Frank stopped in his tracks and turned back to her, a barely-suppressed fire behind his eyes.

"And what makes you think I didn't do the deed myself, if you're so sure?"

"Because you'd get blood on your hands," Kate admitted. "And you're not the type of person to stick the blade in yourself. Why else would you hire an army of thugs?"

Frank let out a long, exhausted sigh. "Rick Teller is a nuisance of an employee, beyond question," he said. "Yet his truancy does not make me a murderer."

"Having one of your mercenaries kill Michael Cochran does."

He laughed. "What do you want to hear, Ms. Bishop? Shall I say that Michael Cochran sold company secrets to our competitors? Or that he tried to sabotage this mission by disseminating false information to key staff members before launch?" He clasped his hands behind his back thoughtfully and began to pace around the circular table. Kate matched his movement, keeping the table between them. "Perhaps you'd like to hear that it takes a hell of a lot more blood than rocket fuel to get a ship like Explorer off the ground. You think permission from the government for our kind of operation is cheap? I'm not just talking about money, Ms. Bishop. I'm talking about owing big favors to fat cats who sharpen their claws on the bones of men just like me every morning before breakfast." He ticked off numbers on his fingers as he said, "The moon. Mars. The asteroid belt. And now Titan. Diamond Aerospace baked the biggest pie in the history of mankind, and everyone wants a piece. If the hand reaching in is small, I chop it off. But the larger hands always get their share. *That's* the system."

He stopped pacing and fixed her with a steady glare, eager for a challenge.

"Sounds like you have it justified, then," Kate said.

"It isn't about justification. It's about adapting my thoughts to rules that were chiseled in stone long before I ever came along. That's your problem, Ms. Bishop. You keep expecting the rules to change, yet you yourself remain unaltered. And you will always fall short because of it. We are expanding the horizon for all of humanity with what we're trying to accomplish." He smirked. "Who can blame us if we make a little money along the way?"

She stuck a hand in her pocket and felt the circular object within. "And who could blame you for eliminating a few people who caused trouble?" she asked.

He snorted. "If you think Cochran's the only one who got in the way, you're more naive than you look."

"A child found him in a dumpster, Frank."

"Yes, I warned them about that." He looked up at her sharply, realizing he'd said too much, and she grinned. "Why are you smiling? Tell me now!" he demanded.

Kate pulled the circular object out of her pocket and tossed it to him. He caught the roll of black electrical tape and stared at it, dumbfounded. She leaned over the table and peeled off a small square of the tape from the black conference phone. A red light glowed solid underneath.

"Say 'hello', Ada," Kate said.

A woman with a deep voice spoke on the other end of the conference phone line. *"Hello, Frank."*

"What is this?" Frank asked, his expression a mixture of rage and confusion. The roll of tape crumpled in his crushing grasp. "What the hell are you doing?!"

"I'm recording your confession," Ada said.

"Ada Quinn works for Channel 8 News in Chicago," Kate said. "She's an old friend of mine. Focuses on corruption in high places. Thanks, Ada."

"Always happy to help," she replied. *"This is going to be a great headliner for tomorrow."*

The line went dead and the light blinked off.

Frank's eyes narrowed. "You're lying."

Kate shrugged. "Wait and see, then. In the meantime…"

She walked past him and left the conference room. It was the single most terrifying moment of the whole encounter for her. She could *feel* his anger as a palpable force when she passed. Her racing mind showed her how easy it would be for him to lash out and snap her neck.

He didn't lash out. Seething with bubbling rage, he followed her out of the conference room and to the railing of the viewing platform.

"Juan," Kate called down to the operations floor.

He looked up at her and she nodded. Juan typed at his workstation keyboard and the display wall blinked off. Several of the guards looked up at Frank expectantly, no doubt hoping this would be another opportunity to bash someone's skull. Frank ignored him. He stared at the display wall, eyes searching.

A video popped up, filling the entire wall from edge to edge. It was the tail-end of the same footage Juan had shown Kate earlier. Frank watched as officers took down the guard at the gatehouse.

"Can't lie about that," Kate said.

Now the security guards on the operations floor were watching the display wall instead of waiting on an order from Frank.

The screen changed to show a real-time exterior feed of the Diamond Aerospace building. A dozen patrol cars with spinning red and blue lights now occupied the parking lot. A group of officers in dark green uniforms conferred near the main entrance. One of them spoke into a phone and nodded. It seemed that a tip from a paranoid like Rick was only enough to subdue a cocky gatehouse guard and sit on the front stoop of the building, not enough to institute a full-force raid.

There was a sharp whistle from one of the security guards on the operations floor. The rest of them turned to look, and the whistler signaled silently. Then as one, they unhooked their heavy belts and let them drop. Holstered pistols thudded heavily to the floor.

"What..." Frank started, looking down in horror. "What are you doing?!"

They didn't answer. They formed up on the whistler and walked single-file from the operations floor, through the door that led to the main entrance. Kate watched the display wall. The officers near the entrance grabbed for their weapons when the front door opened, keeping them trained on the security guards as they filed outside with their hands up. The whistler slowly offered a badge of some sort to one of the officers, who studied it and passed it to the officer who had been on the phone.

The lead officer pulled out his phone again and dialed a number read from the card. After a few seconds of nodding to whoever was on the other end of the line, he handed the badge back and told his men to stand down. The officers holstered their pistols and the guards jogged toward the parking lot, out of range of the security cameras.

"Looks like your boys get a pass," Kate said.

Frank stood with his mouth agape, sucking air like a fish.

"I don't..." he said. "I don't..."

"You don't stand a chance," Kate finished. "Ada recorded your confession."

Frank looked at her, a question in his eyes. All his

rage had vanished along with the security guards. Now he was weakened, and he grabbed at the railing of the viewing platform as if Mission Control were the deck of a heaving, storm-battered corsair.

"Yes, she really is a reporter," Kate said. "Leave now, Frank. Tell the officers what you did." She took a deep breath, filling her chest. "If you do that, I won't call them in here to drag you away. I know you'd find that undignified, as if it matters now."

He tried to speak one last time, but only managed a barely-audible whisper. Without looking her in the eye, he trudged downstairs and left the building. To Kate's everlasting surprise, the feed on the display wall showed him walking outside with his arms raised, speaking to the officers. One of them approached warily, and with lightning speed grabbed Frank's wrist and twisted it, forcing him to his stomach on the ground. Frank was sobbing, his mouth wide open and the veins in his neck bulging. With a knee in Frank's back, the officer handcuffed him, then pulled him up by the cuffs. Kate grinned. If the feed had an audio component, she bet she would hear Frank howling in pain.

"Noah Bell!" she called down from the viewing platform. He looked up at her from Rick's chair, holding a compress to his bloodied temple. "You have your mission back. Let's get our people home."

Her smile faded as the display wall flicked back to its normal configuration. In one of the screens, Jeff floated unconscious in the T-junction, a galaxy of blood droplets encircling his head.

"What happened?!" she asked the room.

Juan turned from his workstation and called up to her, "Riley hit him with a spanner and choked him until he passed out."

Kate hurried down the steps to the operations floor, her flats clicking on black tile.

The display wall had Noah's complete attention as he sat at Rick's desk, holding the compress to his temple. With unblinking eyes, he watched Gabriel's video feed as he drew closer to the torus.

Kate stopped behind Walt and gripped the back of his chair, mentally urging Jeff to wake up as her eyes scanned the video feed. A wrench-like torsion spanner drifted lazily into view behind Jeff, slowly tumbling end over end, until it tapped the wall and hung in the air as if stuck in some invisible webbing.

"What's his condition?" Kate asked.

"He's stable," the flight surgeon replied, studying Jeff's biometric data on his workstation monitor. "Just out cold."

"And the others?"

Walt tapped on his screen, pulling up more data. "Green across the board, though Silva's heart rate is elevated."

"You think?" Juan said.

"What about Riley?" Kate asked.

"Steady as a metronome."

Outside the ship, Riley was a couple minutes behind Gabriel, heading for the torus. In his video feed, the artifact waited silently in the distance.

"What should we do?" Juan asked, looking at Kate.

She glanced at Noah, but he seemed disinterested in anything but Gabriel's video feed.

"We tell Ming to prep the ship for departure," Kate said.

"Frank locked them out of the system," Juan said.

"So unlock it."

"Can't," Noah said, shaking his head. "Need Frank's password."

Kate ran her fingers slowly through her hair, gripping it hard, wanting to rip it out and scream.

She looked up at the display wall at the front of the room. That time she didn't see individual monitor frames displaying various mission functions – she saw the whole: a grid-like tapestry of data and moving images showcasing discovery alongside borderline absurdities, all conflated to present her with the singular impression that the crew of *Explorer I*, let alone the rest of humanity, obviously wasn't ready to go knocking on Titan's door.

Jeff awoke slowly, with a groggy uncertainty of displacement. Despite realizing he was floating in zero-g, it took his mind a moment to register his surroundings and remind him he wasn't on Earth – instead, he was farther from it than anyone else had ever been.

The memory of Riley hammering him in the skull with the prong-end of a spanner woke him fully, and he breathed in sharply, blinking to focus on the flat spiral of blood droplets in the T-junction corridor. One kissed his cheek and he rubbed at it with the back of his hand, leaving a crimson streak. His scalp throbbed just above his left ear, but he was no longer bleeding. He touched his throat and winced at the pain where Riley had held him vice-locked in the crook of his elbow, squeezing out his consciousness after he tried to stop Riley from leaving the ship.

"Ming," he croaked. He coughed and tried again. *"I'm in the command module, Jeff."*

He ducked under the floating disc of blood droplets and used a handhold on the wall to propel himself to the center of the T-junction. Ming said nothing when he drifted into the command module and strapped into Riley's pilot chair. She stared out the narrow window above the nose of the module, seemingly lost in a maze of her own thoughts. The two small monitors in the pilots' control panel were blank. Jeff switched both of them on from the controls on the wall to the right of Riley's chair. He flipped through available video feeds, blinking past the empty interior of the crew module, the exterior of *Explorer*, and its darkened airlock with Jeff's Constellation Suit tethered to the wall.

Jeff found the two feeds he wanted and sent them to the pilots' control panel monitors. On the left, Gabriel's helmet camera looked toward the torus. Data pumping into the ship systems from his Mark IV glowed in blue text at the bottom of the screen. If Gabriel held his current speed, he'd get to the torus in just under two minutes.

On the right-side monitor, Riley was focused wholly on Gabriel in the distance.

Jeff stopped flipping switches and twisting dials and settled back into the chair, holding loosely onto the shoulder straps while he watched the monitors. Needles danced over the cut in his scalp, and his throat burned where it had been squeezed shut. Coupled with the occasional shooting pains in his chest from catching a grenade blast of shrapnel when the fuel pump exploded, he wasn't exactly a perfect picture of health.

"I'm sorry I couldn't stop Riley," Ming said,

breaking the silence. "I know you wanted everyone to stick together."

"Yeah, well," Jeff replied, then shrugged. "I doubt anyone would have been able to stop him."

"Mission Control still wants us to move locations before we start on the space station."

Jeff turned to her. "You really think we can last long enough out here to finish the mission?"

"Well, we have enough oxygen, and North Star probably has plenty of food stores."

"No, I mean can we last long enough with each *other?*"

Ming didn't have an answer for him.

"When do they want us to move?" he asked.

"As soon as Riley and Gabriel return to the ship. But I'm still locked out of the system remotely."

"I can regain control if I go outside," Jeff said. He looked out the window at the two small, suited figures. "But even if I do, what about the engine?"

"That's what *I* wanted to know. They wouldn't give me a guarantee. Noah said it was up to us. We're fine with orbital thrusters this close to Titan, but when it's time to go home... it will take either eight months utilizing one major burn, or four years without."

He clenched his teeth and took a deep breath, suppressing a rising anger at having to make that kind of decision in the first place.

"Rock and a hard place," he said. "What do you think?"

Ming was silent for a long moment, then she said, "I want to see my daughter again. Only one of those options maximizes my chances."

Jeff shook his head. "Four years is a long time." *Too long for Kate to wait,* he thought. It wasn't that he thought she wouldn't try to await his return if he asked – it was that he could never ask her for that kind of sacrifice.

A speaker embedded next to the monitor crackled.

"Slow down, Silva," Riley said. *"Wait for me."*

His feed showed the small figure of Gabriel as he spun around up ahead, small white jets of nitrogen geysering in quick flashes from his pack. Yet his momentum toward the artifact didn't slow.

"Oh. Hi, Commander," said Gabriel, and he waved. *"I plan to keep going."*

"Wait for backup, Silva," Riley said irritably.

The small figure of Gabriel spun away. In his feed, the torus swung back into view, nearly touching the top and bottom edges of the monitor.

"I think I will do what everyone else on this mission is doing," he said, sounding cheerful enough, *"and put my own interests first."*

"He's got a point," Ming said.

Riley let out a long string of the vilest curses Jeff had ever heard, so Jeff cut off his suit's audio. He could still hear Gabriel mutter occasionally in Portuguese as he neared the torus – what sounded to Jeff like little exclamations of surprise and wonder.

"I feel a…" Gabriel said, then paused. *"…a kind of tingling, I guess. Almost like static electricity."*

"Does it hurt?" Walt asked from Mission Control.

"Not at all."

"Jeff," Kate said. *"Is it safe to talk?"*

He cut Riley's Mark IV out of *Explorer*'s comm loop and said, "It is now."

"I wanted to let you know that things here are back under control."

He shared a quick glance with Ming. "I never realized they were *out* of control."

"Well, they were," Kate said. *"Office politics, you know."*

He couldn't help but smile. "Sounds like you've had it pretty rough down there."

"We're managing. Frank was arrested."

"Hold on while I weep uncontrollably. Okay, finished."

"I hope you'll be able to move on."

"Only time will tell." Out of the corner of his eye, he saw Ming shaking her head. "Is that why we're locked out of the system?"

"That would be it, yes. Anything you can do on your end?"

"No promises, but I can try."

"Thank you. I also wanted to say that we're glad you're alright," Kate said. *"There's no excuse for Riley's behavior."*

"I think he's convinced he's ultimately doing what's best for the mission."

"That sounds like an excuse."

Jeff said, "Call it an understanding."

"And what about you?"

"What *about* me?"

"Are you trying to do what's best for the mission?" asked Kate. He looked from the two monitors to the narrow window, then over to Ming. When he didn't

answer, Kate asked, *"Did Lieutenant Ming update you?"*

"She gave me what I imagine is the abbreviated version, yes."

"Good. I know it's a hard decision, and we're not going to pretend we can make it for you. You don't have to make it yet. There are enough food rations in Explorer's hold to last you ten months, and we're guessing at least that inside North Star."

"But it wouldn't last us four years."

She sighed in frustration, and he realized how aggravating it must be for her to relay the information to him as if she were dictating from a manual instead of saying everything she truly felt.

"If you're not planning to fire up the antimatter drive," she said, *"you'll have to check North Star for food, and ration whatever you find."*

"And if it doesn't have any extra food stores?"

"It will. If you go the other route, you'll have enough fuel for one major burn, and maybe two smaller boosts...but that's it."

An expectant pause stretched on, becoming uncomfortable.

"Please say something," Jeff said as he stared at the control panel speaker, cursing his lack of eloquence even as the words left his mouth.

At first, he thought she wouldn't answer. Then she said, with a pained voice, *"There' too much to say, Jeffrey,"* and the line went dead.

Jeff pushed the heels of his hands into his eye sockets, rubbing until it hurt.

"Damn it all," he whispered, shaking his head.

"What do you think he's going to find?" Ming asked.

Jeff slowly let his hands slip from his face. He looked at Ming with stinging, water-filled eyes.

"Who?" he asked.

She nodded toward the monitors.

Jeff relaxed a little, sinking into his seat. "I know what you're doing."

"You do?"

"Yeah. You're trying to distract me. Okay then, I'll bite. I don't think Gabe will find anything. I think he's going to walk around on the surface of the torus, then come back to the ship, disappointed."

"What about the other crew, and the instant comms?"

"If the torus is responsible for the comms, the only way we're going to figure it out is to drag that thing all the way home, and we're not doing that. As for the other crew... I don't know if we can do anything for them."

Ming suddenly sat up straighter. "We could dump our fuel into North Star," she said.

"What do you mean?" he asked.

"We could transfer our remaining fuel to the other ship and use its antimatter drive to get home."

"Why the hell would we trust an identical engine design?"

"It isn't identical," Ming said. "Bell and I talked while you were outside. The CEO of MarsCorp claims his engineers found a way to eliminate the instability in our engine."

"And you trust him?" Jeff asked.

"Bell? Yes. If the information had come from Frank, I wouldn't have mentioned it."

"What's the catch?"

"The new design burns a lot more fuel than our engine."

Jeff looked back and forth between the two video monitors quickly, without really seeing what was on them. The rust that had settled on his mind over the past several hours began to crack off as the gears of critical thought reengaged.

"Even if the North Star's tanks are empty," he said, talking faster, "we only need enough for one major burn, and we eliminate the risk of, you know, *blowing up*."

"And if we end up with enough fuel for two burns," Ming added, "we can halve our return time to four months."

He frowned. "How do we transfer the fuel?"

"With the umbilical."

"That's only sixty meters."

Ming stared at him, waiting for him to figure it out. "We don't need to do the transfer now," she said, raising her eyebrows expectantly. "But we do need access to the orbital thrusters."

"Oh," he said at last. "Right. The remote override. I'll go get suited up."

Jeff moved to unbuckle his straps. The initial stirrings of fresh hope playing at the periphery of his current state of mind evaporated when Gabriel gasped. Jeff's attention snapped down to the video feed, which showed that Gabriel was now only about five meters away from the side of the torus. The image vibrated, as if the camera were on the table of a speeding train traveling over uneven tracks.

"Is he shaking?" Jeff asked.

"Everything is shaking," said Gabriel. His teeth chattered and his voice quivered. He grunted. *"Hurts. Can feel...my chest rattling."*

"Back away, Gabe," Ming said.

He had approached the torus from the side, so that the thirty-meter-diameter hoop appeared as a thin pillar with sharp corners. Now he maneuvered sideways, drifting farther away from North Star to look at the torus from an oblique angle. The artifact morphed from a pillar to a narrow, vertical oval.

"I can see...the stars," Gabriel said shakily, forcing out the words.

An arc of pale Titan and the field of stars beyond were clearly visible in the center of the large torus.

"He's right," Ming said.

Jeff remembered the view of the torus from *North Star.* When he had been opening the airlock doors, it looked as if a solid black film permanently covered the opening, occluding the infinite reaches beyond.

Riley was still a good distance from the torus – his suit data claimed he wouldn't get there for another minute. Jeff reactivated his comm channel, but Riley was silent as he closed the distance to the artifact.

Gabriel drifted up, following the curvature of the torus. He maneuvered closer, and the shake in his visual field grew so pronounced that it was impossible for Jeff to make out any details on the four-meter-wide black side surface. He was, however, able to see that the torus appeared not to be polished into a perfect hoop, like a wedding band, but instead was flat on the front and back, as if it were only a cross-section that had been cut from a longer tube.

"*It's etched with...designs,*" Gabriel stuttered. He swallowed and grunted again, trying to focus on the discovery before him. A small laugh escaped his lips, followed quickly by a groan of pain.

"Gabe, pull back!" Jeff urged.

"*I see something...up ahead. Shadow on...the surface.*"

The outer edge of the torus rotated downward as Gabriel jetted around its perimeter, staying only a couple meters away. A quivering Titan slipped past the top border of the screen.

Despite the shaking camera, Jeff could indeed see an approaching dark patch on the surface of the torus.

"*There–*" said Gabe, and then the shadow jumped for him. His video feed cut to static.

"*Holy Moses,*" Riley said darkly. "*That thing just sucked him into the wall.*"

"Gabe!" Jeff shouted.

He looked at Riley's video feed. Gabriel had disappeared. The torus waited, orbiting Titan as innocuously as when *Explorer* first arrived.

Then, ever so slowly, it began turning toward Riley.

"**W**hat happened?!" Kate shouted from her workstation. The entire room had erupted into chaos the moment Gabriel vanished.

On the display wall, his vitals blipped weakly.

"I–I don't know," Walt sputtered as he fumbled with his keyboard. "He's gone!"

"Dead?" Kate demanded.

"No...I mean, I don't think so. I'm still registering a faint heartbeat."

The airlock video feed showed Ming struggling to get Jeff into his space suit in zero-g.

"Jeff, what are you doing?" Kate asked. No answer. "Jeff?"

Outside the ship, Riley had slowed his approach to the artifact and waited a hundred meters away. From that distance, there was no camera shake.

Out of habit, Kate readjusted her headset microphone to make sure it was properly positioned.

"Riley, can you hear me?" she asked.

"I hear you."

Noah held up a hand, asking her to wait, and said, "Commander, I advise you return to Explorer."

Riley grunted with amusement. *"Now you want me to leave someone behind? I can still read his vitals, Bell. Let me talk to Frank."*

"Frank no longer works for Diamond Aerospace. I'm in charge of the mission."

Kate expected another rebellion, but Riley grit his teeth and said, *"This damn thing is turning toward me. Can you see it?"*

"Yes, we see it."

With a spurt of nitrogen, he drifted a little closer to the torus. *"It's staying close to North Star."*

"Riley, *please* get back to Explorer," Kate said.

She looked at the airlock video feed. Jeff was having trouble sealing his Mark IV. She thought that maybe he could bring Riley back in, then she remembered what happened the last time Jeff tried to intervene.

"She's right, Commander," Noah said into his headset. "You can't help Gabriel, but you can help the other members of your crew."

"Well, look who's so quick to abandon his 'vision' of humanity's future," Riley chided.

"We'll come back to Titan," said Noah with pained finality. Kate watched him closely as he clenched his jaw and looked down, barely suppressing a simmering cauldron of varied emotions.

Riley thumbed the control stick in his left glove and glided toward the artifact, propelled by tiny streams of nitrogen from his pack.

Kate threw up her hands. "He won't listen."

"Then let's hope he can find Gabriel," Noah said.

Kate watched the video feeds from more than a billion kilometers away, feeling every micrometer of that distance as an expansive, impassable gulf separating the drama in orbit around Titan from her reality. She might as well have been watching a fictional movie for all the influence she had on the fate of *Explorer's* crew.

"Ms. Bishop," Noah said, snapping her out of the crushing chasm into which she'd fallen. He seemed to be looking right down into her soul, exposing every thought to his keen scrutiny. Somehow, it made her feel better. "Don't worry. We're not finished yet."

"Something's happening," said Riley.

Everyone in the room turned to look up at the display wall. Kate tapped her workstation monitor and enlarged Riley's video feed. The torus was facing him now, instead of its original configuration facing *North Star*.

"It's rotating," Juan said.

"Wasn't it before?" asked Walt.

Kate shook her head. "This is new."

"I'm feeling a slight vibration," Riley said.

His camera feed registered the shake. Thirty meters ahead of him, the edges of the torus blurred. Its center was a black disc. From Riley's perspective, Titan was in the immediate background, its uniform surface marred by the single, perfect black circle of the torus.

"He's feeling that much earlier than Silva," said Noah.

Riley swore as he drifted closer to the artifact. *"I'm trying to reverse, but my controls aren't responding."*

His helmet camera looked down at his gloved left hand. The thick fingers of his glove twisted the control stick and mashed the oversized buttons on its side.

"His suit systems are all in the green," Juan said, gesturing at his monitor.

"What about his pack?" Kate asked.

"I'm seeing a drain on his propulsion reserves. His maneuvering jets are definitely firing."

"Then why they hell can't I go back?" Riley asked, fear creeping into his voice. *"Oh God, I'm moving faster."*

The torus hadn't yet budged from its original position other than to face Riley. Its axial rotation increased as he drew nearer, and the shake in his video feed intensified.

He looked down at his suit. Forward-facing thrusters on his pack released steady streams of white nitrogen, flowing toward the artifact and dissipating a meter from Riley's suit. He kicked his legs, grunting in consternation.

"It's pulling me in," he said in a shaking, matter-of-fact tone. *"Help... please help me."*

The nitrogen streams jetting from his pack cut out, and he stopped struggling against whatever invisible force pulled him toward the artifact.

"Thruster reserves nearly depleted," Juan said. He blinked hard and absentmindedly wiped a bead of sweat from the side of his brow.

"Please help me," Riley repeated, his voice monotonous.

The torus loomed large in his vision, quickly increasing in size. He was heading right for the middle of the black disc. The data from his suit system relayed a distance counter that rapidly approached zero.

"Please help me," he begged. "Please help me... please help me–"

The torus itself slipped out of sight past the borders of the display wall monitor. Riley was now so close that all his camera saw was the solid black surface of whatever filled the space between the artifact's inner edges.

He gulped air and let out a terrified whimper.

"*Someone, please,*" he said. "*PleasehelpmeeeEEEEAAAGGH!!!–*"

He screamed for another six seconds as he passed through the center of the torus. The wall speakers crackled and strained at the very peak of their playback capabilities.

Silence chopped off the end of his scream, and his vitals flat-lined. Kate sucked in air, realizing she'd been holding her breath.

"Riley?" she asked softly.

"His camera's still working," Juan said. He sounded on the verge of passing out.

Riley's video feed panned gently over vast reaches of space as his suit rotated. He retained a small percentage of the momentum that carried him through the center of the torus, and he drifted away from it slowly, like he was sinking deeper into a black ocean.

Explorer I moved in and out of his camera's view, then Titan rolled up from the bottom edge of the screen.

North Star was revealed aft-first, and then came the torus. There was no black disc to cover its opening when viewed from that side, only the stars and a slice of Titan.

The torus slowly turned to resume its original configuration, facing *North Star*.

Numbly, Kate tapped on the screen of her workstation monitor, switching the focus on the display wall to an exterior view from one of the cameras in *Explorer*'s comm arrays. *North Star* and the torus appeared exactly as they had when *Explorer* first arrived in orbit around Titan.

The only new addition to the scene was the motionless, suited form of Commander Riley, drifting steadily away.

Yellow light strobed in the relative darkness of the airlock, flashing briefly inside Jeff's sealed helmet with each pulse. The outer airlock door rose slowly as he floated weightlessly within the safe confines of the metal sphere.

According to his HUD data, the suit had only been charged halfway since his last excursion. He had just over two hours of oxygen remaining and barely enough power to last him that long.

Silently, the door locked into place at the terminus of its rise, but Jeff didn't move. After what he'd just heard over comms, he was finding it difficult to hurry.

He took a long drink from his helmet's water straw to soothe his desert of a throat, then said, "I'm, uh...I'm open to suggestions."

Without hesitation, Noah said, *"Go back inside and get the hell out of there."*

"Can't," he said reflexively.

That admission was enough to make him leave the

airlock, anyway. He coasted gently forward, passing the threshold into space.

"I'm clear. Seal her up, Lieutenant."

"Be careful, Jeff," Ming said over his suit comms.

Behind him, the outer airlock door slid closed.

Ming had tried to talk him out of his EVA the entire time she reluctantly helped him suit up. Only when she had turned the final seal lock on his helmet collar did she acquiesce to his unalterable decision.

Now that he was outside *Explorer*, he looked upon the distant torus, and at the intermittently reflective speck that was Riley's slowly tumbling form. Beyond the cold confines of the ship, he felt more inclined to pay heed to thoughts of retreat.

"What's the hold-up?" he said aloud.

Gripping his pack's control stick, he aligned himself with Riley's receding space suit and set off at three meters per second. The HUD data overlaid around the edges of his face shield informed him he'd get to Riley in over six minutes, considering he'd be chasing a moving target. Jeff thumbed the control stick, increasing his speed to four meters per second, and was satisfied when a minute was shaved from his rendezvous.

"Okay, Lieutenant," Kate said from Mission Control. *"Looks like it's on you. If you're willing, I'll talk you through the remote system override process."*

"Excellent," Ming said. *"Jeff and I have another idea, as well."*

She explained the plan to Kate, such as it was, outlining her intentions for the ship-to-ship fuel transfer for the crew's return voyage aboard *North Star*. It went unsaid that the crew were no longer being asked to stick to the original mission plan.

Ming finished with, *"What do you think?"*

"I think your plan puts Explorer too close to the torus," Kate said.

"They have a long umbilical," Noah offered over the comms. *"If she parked Explorer at max distance from North Star on the side opposite the artifact, she might not trigger a response."*

"What do you mean by trigger?" Jeff asked.

"Noah thinks it reacts to stimulus," Kate said.

"Care to elaborate?"

"It woke up when Riley got too close," Noah said. *"Perhaps it was designed to respond to objects that passed some arbitrary proximity barrier."*

"But it didn't react at all to Gabriel," Jeff reminded him.

"Until he disappeared. Speaking of which…what exactly do you plan to do out there, Mr. Dolan?"

Jeff had been trying to decide that himself. "After Riley, I'll…I guess I'll improvise," he answered. "If I can help Gabe, I will."

"Riley's gone, Jeff," said Kate.

"I still have to try."

"Requesting permission to leave the ship," Ming said.

"You no longer need our permission, Lieutenant," Noah said. *"Not for anything. Do what you need to do."*

"Copy that. I'm going EVA to override the remote system."

"I should warn you that we will no longer be able to take control from here after the override, Lieutenant," Noah said.

"I understand."

"I'm two minutes away," Jeff said, referencing his HUD data. "Commander, can you hear me?"

No static on the other end of the line. No breathing. Riley's suit held the unmistakable pose indicative of an unconscious occupant: arms loosely reaching forward, legs slightly bent at the knees. Jeff periodically tried to raise him on comms as he drew nearer.

When he was a few seconds from intersecting Riley, Jeff slowed his speed to match the commander's. Riley faced the other direction, tumbling sideways. Their suits bumped into each other and Jeff grabbed hold of the stitched nylon loop on the back of Riley's suit, at the base of his helmet.

"Got him," Jeff said.

He spun the suit around, instinctively closing his eyes and suppressing a gag reflex when he saw the bloody smear across the inside of Riley's face shield.

"How is he?" Kate asked, the finality in her voice betraying that she had already seen the video feed from Jeff's helmet camera.

Jeff forced himself to look at Riley. He could see nothing beyond the mess on the inside of the helmet.

"I think we know what happened to the crew of North Star."

"The artifact passed over their ship," Noah said.

"They managed to get their suits on before it happened," Jeff added, looking at what remained of Riley. "Not that it made a difference."

He turned the commander around and programmed a collision course with Titan into his wrist pad. Then he gave the suit a gentle push toward the moon, drifting farther away himself in the process. No one in Mission Control asked him why he wasn't bringing Riley's body back to the ship. They already knew the answer. It wasn't out of bitterness or some twisted idea of revenge. It was because Jeff thought Gabriel still had a chance, and he couldn't do what he needed to do while dragging around so much extra mass.

A few seconds later, the nitrogen thrusters in Riley's pack fired, and he gently accelerated toward the pale yellow moon.

From Jeff's position, Titan filled most of the starry landscape to the right of the artifact and the two ships. Using his wrist pad, Jeff programmed an arc-shaped trajectory toward the torus which would ultimately place him on its side. He would be looking at it from the same angle as Gabriel had been when he disappeared. Yet Jeff would maintain a greater distance, planning to traverse a complete rotation around the perimeter of the artifact before heading to the ship.

His plan was predicated on the hope that the damned thing wouldn't turn to face him, as it had done with Riley. If that happened, Jeff didn't intend to wait until his vision began to shake; he would turn-tail and make for *Explorer* with all possible speed.

He finished programming the maneuver and executed the command with one final press of a button. The pack system took over, firing jets of nitrogen to send Jeff in a wide arc, swinging out from the torus to deposit him a hundred meters away to look at it from the side.

The artifact did not turn.

Now in position, Jeff regained manual control of the pack and began coasting around the diameter of the torus, focusing on the hard, black material. Gabriel had mentioned etchings in the surface, but Jeff could see no markings at that distance.

He drifted a little closer.

"Jeff…" Kate warned.

He had drifted past ninety degrees of the outer diameter, then he said, "I see a shadow on the surface."

Jeff squinted hard. It was difficult to see the black smudge outlined against the black material of the torus…but it was definitely there.

He risked a small spurt of nitrogen from his pack, nudging closer to the artifact.

"Jeff, that's far enough," Noah said.

"I don't feel any vibrations."

"That doesn't mean you won't."

The borders of the shadow solidified into a shape that would have been obvious to anyone looking at it.

"It's a door," Jeff said with surprise. The edges of his vision began to shake as he drifted closer to the torus. "I feel it now." He fired his forward-facing pack thrusters and halted his acceleration. "It's not pulling me in."

"Jeff, please don't go any closer," Kate said.

The sound of her voice struck his core, and his thumb hesitated over his flight control stick. She was afraid.

"I can't leave him," he said.

"And I can't lose you," she pleaded.

He felt a piece of his soul rip off from the whole and stay behind as he coasted closer to the artifact and farther away from Earth.

It was the hardest decision he had ever made.

His teeth chattered as he approached. He seemed to be falling now, accelerating toward the shadow on the side of the artifact as he gained momentum. The laser-precise edges of the torus became dancing waveforms as the vibrations rattled his skull. Jeff's extremities went numb, turning into icy blocks heavy in his suit. If he was receiving tactile feedback from his gloved left hand, he couldn't feel it. He sent the motor commands to his fingers anyway, attempting to perform the rote motions that would slow him down before he splatted against the outer surface of the torus like a bug on the windshield of a speeding car.

Broken voices sputtered from his helmet speakers – clipped fragments amid hissing static.

His original trajectory toward the shadowy door had been slightly skewed, he realized as he drew closer. When he was ten meters from the torus and still gaining momentum, he suddenly lurched to the side without the aid of his pack, as if an invisible giant had yanked him sideways, aligning him perfectly with the shaking shadow below.

Then he was upon it, and was sucked into a darkness so complete that had the stars themselves vanished from the sky, the remaining void would have seemed bright by comparison.

Kate ripped off her headset and fell back into her chair, staring blankly at the display wall.

Jeff's vitals had diminished to almost nothing, the same as Gabriel's. The video feed from his helmet camera flicked to static. Kate felt the eyes of her coworkers during the silence that followed.

"I could use a little help here," Ming said.

Her helmet camera showed that she was outside *Explorer*, waiting near an access panel in the hull.

Kate felt as if everyone in Mission Control was waiting for her to speak. When she didn't, Noah said, "Stand by, Lieutenant." He swiveled his chair to look at Juan. "Help her unlock the system. Once she's finished with the fuel transfer, we'll need to prep North Star for the return voyage."

"You got it," Juan said with a nod. He wheeled his chair closer to his workstation and called up the designs.

"Where's Propulsion?" Noah called, searching the usual workstations but finding them empty.

"Back here," said Lucius Howell. He stood and pushed his wireframe glasses farther up his nose, waiting impatiently with raised eyebrows.

"We need an updated timeline for their arrival."

"Using what departure window?" Lucius asked, not missing a beat.

"Give me estimates for each hour over the next ten hours."

Lucius nodded and sat back down.

Noah sighed. "That should get us started."

"Where's Allison?" Kate said, standing up slowly. Noah watched her, a faint smile tugging at the corner of his mouth.

"Here," Allison Jones replied from her System Logistics workstation farther down the same row as Kate's. Her usually-neat gray hair had been hastily brushed back.

"Pull up North Star's schematics, as well," Kate said. "We need to know ahead of time if we're going to run into any surprises after making the switch. Pay special attention to comms. I want to make sure we won't get stonewalled by an encrypted system."

"My team will handle it," she replied.

Across the aisle, Juan began to talk Ming through the process of bypassing the remote system.

"Looks like we're in business," said Noah.

Jeff slammed against the hard floor, unable to breathe. White lights danced across his darkened vision. He finally managed to suck in air as if he were breathing through a pinched straw.

Despite his pressurized suit and more than an hour's worth of oxygen remaining in his pack, the air had been crushed from his lungs as soon as he passed into the shadowy door. The only explanation that came to his oxygen-starved mind was that he had passed through some kind of gravity barrier and had barely survived the transition.

The fact that he was firmly on the floor instead of floating weightlessly in zero-g supported his theory. He managed to painfully suck in a lungful of air, then he was seized by a fit of harsh, rasping coughs that contracted his body into a fetal position.

When the coughing subsided, he slowly unfolded, lying on his side, breathing heavily. The dancing white lights in his vision faded, and the fog of darkness lifted.

He was looking directly at the back of Gabriel's suit.

Jeff sat up as quickly as his suit would allow, wincing at the stabbing pain in his chest. He pulled himself over to Gabe's prostrate form, noticing a soft blue-green glow emanating several centimeters beneath the hard, semi-translucent floor wherever he touched.

"Gabe?" he asked, his words strained as he focused on pulling stinging oxygen into his lungs.

He grabbed Gabriel's shoulder and hesitated. Then he pulled Gabe onto his pack to face the ceiling, and a wave of relief washed over him when Gabe's eyes popped open wide.

"Can you hear me?" Jeff asked.

Gabriel coughed and spasmed, thrashing on the floor. Jeff held him down, gripping the padded chest of his suit. Gabriel's booted heels bounced off the hard floor, triggering bursts of blue-green light under the translucent surface.

"Easy, buddy!" Jeff said loudly, hoping Gabriel could hear him. "I'm right here!"

Gabe reached up for the seal of his helmet lock, scrambling to slide it open.

"Hey!" Jeff yelled, pulling Gabe's hands away. He sat on one arm and held the other to his own chest as Gabriel tried to twist free.

Eventually Gabriel's resistance subsided and he relaxed, his face beaded with sweat.

"Explorer, I've found Gabriel," Jeff said. A moment passed without reply. "Ming? Kate?" He heard nothing but silence on the other end of the line. "Anyone?"

Gabriel blinked hard and his eyes snapped into

focus. His body spasmed once and settled. He looked up at Jeff.

"Where the hell are we?" he croaked, his voice loud inside Jeff's helmet.

"Inside the torus," Jeff answered. At least the suit-to-suit comms were functioning.

"Now I remember," Gabriel said. He cradled his helmet as he sat up. *"You know something? That* hurt.*"* There was a sucking noise over the comm line as he drank from his helmet straw. Then he looked around and whistled appreciatively.

"You just had to see it up close," Jeff scolded. "Couldn't wait."

"I'm sorry." He looked around.

They were in a wide corridor that curved gently out of sight in both directions, apparently following the curvature of the torus. The entirety of the floor was comprised of the same hard, green-tinted translucent material Jeff had smacked down upon during his violent arrival. Soft pulses of brilliant blue-green light glowed to life and danced below the surface, moving without any kind of noticeable pattern before fading out and reappearing half a meter away.

The ceiling and walls were a half-moon arch made of the same dark material as the exterior. The arch was roughly four meters across at its base. A narrow, unbroken spine, like a smooth tube, lined the corridor at its peak, running parallel to the floor. A spherical, spinning purple-green light appeared inside the spine at one end of the corridor and shot past overhead, disappearing farther down its hollow track.

There was no sign in the ceiling of the shadowy door through which the two of them had arrived.

Jeff stumbled to his feet and stood up slowly, for some reason expecting to be knocked back down at any second.

Gabriel panted hard on the floor. *"I thought...I left asthma...in my childhood,"* he said.

"Can you walk?" Jeff asked.

Gabriel held out his gloved hand. *"Let's find out."*

Jeff strained to pull him upright, but eventually the two of them stood next to each other, breathing hard in their heavy space suits as they studied the corridor.

Gabriel tapped the chest of his suit with closed fists. *"Something...pushing down on my chest."*

Jeff nodded. "Gravity is different."

"Where's Riley?" Gabriel asked.

"He's dead. Followed you to the torus, but it sucked him into the black hole."

"Oh my God," Gabe said, shaking his head. *"Oh, no."*

Jeff gestured farther down the corridor. Under normal circumstances, he would have wasted air to say something as superfluous as *We need to find a way out of here.* Now, though, he saved that air for breathing.

Jeff chose a direction without deliberation and started walking. Blue-green light bloomed within the floor under his boots like the phosphorescent glow of a deep-sea organism. Gabriel wandered to the smooth wall and held his gloved palm to it as he walked.

"Same etchings as outside," he said.

The walls looked unadorned from Jeff's track in the middle of the corridor. Then the spherical purple-green light shot past in the ceiling, and he briefly glimpsed a shimmer of superficial gossamer lines.

"Any ideas?" Jeff asked. He had to breathe hard after the simple exertion of talking.

"Looks like a circuit diagram." He paused to breathe. *"Probably just decoration."*

I wouldn't be too sure about that, Jeff thought. Whatever the torus was, it had been constructed with a clear and specific purpose. In Jeff's experience, that left little room for extraneous aesthetics. On the other hand, humans still painted their cars. Go figure.

"What if there is no exit?" Gabriel asked as they walked on, following the interior curvature of the artifact.

Jeff didn't have an answer for him. The real answer was that, without an exit, they were doomed. Ming would eventually leave, and Jeff and Gabriel would die of thirst or starvation – but not boredom. Jeff glanced down at his HUD data. Fifty minutes of air left. He doubted he could walk a full circuit of the torus corridor before his oxygen ran out.

"Look," said Gabriel. He pointed down the corridor.

A shadow split the smooth wall up ahead. Jeff increased the pace of his belabored shamble, struggling against the increased gravity. He was sweating freely, soaking his clingy unitard, by the time he discovered it wasn't the exterior door after all, but a square-cut opening in the wall.

He and Gabriel left the corridor and stepped through the opening, entering the cube-shaped room beyond.

The walls and ceiling had been constructed with the same translucent component as the floor. Thin tubes of solid-colored light threaded every surface, occasionally converging behind bowl-shaped cutouts in the wall. Small, red squares of light were embedded in the wall beside each cutout.

Each of the cutouts contained a small amount of foreign material. In one, a slick of black goo undulated within the confines of the vertical cutout, attempting to crawl beyond the bowl's edge. Every time it came close, the lights behind the cutout grew brighter, and the goo folded back into itself, retreating to the center of the cutout.

In another, bright red algae hugged the curving wall of its cutout. Gabriel held his gloved hand a few centimeters away, and the algae extended a geometric part of itself, like a tiny skyscraper extending from a single-story city.

"*Remarkable,*" he whispered. Then, more loudly, "*You know what this is?*"

"Specimen lab," Jeff guessed.

"*Right.*" Gabriel moved from cutout to cutout with wide-eyed wonder. "*That's exactly right.*"

"Gabe, we need to go."

Gabriel held up a delaying hand as he continued around the room. Jeff was about to grab his arm and haul him out to the corridor when one of the square red lights on the wall caught his eye. It pulsed enticingly, like a big button aching to be pushed. The cutout next to the pulsing light only had a small sample within, as if it hadn't had as much time to mature as the other specimens.

Jeff walked to the wall and stood before that particular cutout. The little square light illuminated the inside of his face shield with a red glow. The light wasn't a protruding button, just a patch of red embedded flush with the wall. Jeff stroked it with a gloved finger, and the light expanded. He took an awkward step back as the square of light grew to be half a meter on each side.

At first, the square appeared to be comprised of solid red light. Jeff leaned in closer and realized it had a textured, almost organic quality. Hair-thin black filaments twisted circuitous paths across the surface of the square. The filaments seemed to be shaping themselves into a very specific pattern.

He snapped upright, not entirely believing what he saw.

Gabriel lumbered over and stood next to him, panting. "*What is it?*"

"Look closely."

Gabe leaned in, squinting against the bright red

light. Then he laughed. *"It's a picture of a human!"*

The black filaments were indeed shaped to resemble the rudimentary Vitruvian form of a human being, arms and legs splayed proportionally. Fine braids of filament represented the core body shape, and special focus was paid to the anatomically neutral area between the figure's legs, where animated threads of the wire-like substance interlaced to weave a denser, more active pattern.

Jeff looked at the shallow, muddled black and gray pool of cells in the cutout next to the red square of light. Almost at the edge of perception, he could tell the cells were multiplying – synthesizing impossibly fast and spreading to cover every allowable centimeter of their bowl-shaped prison.

Gabriel started to speak, then stopped. He leaned in close to the weaving filaments, then to the slowly filling cutout.

"Those are cancer cells," he said.

"And these..." Jeff said, motioning to the other cutouts in the room. Not one of them was empty. "These are all the samples it's collected. That one's a liver."

He pointed to a cutout nearby. Inside the vertical bowl, a glistening human liver fluttered gently. In the cutout next to that was a human eye, its optic nerve splayed out behind it in a gruesome asterisk. The eye's gold-flecked, dark brown iris stared out at nothing as a netting of fine red veins wove sluggishly between the glistening stalks of the optic nerve.

Gabriel turned in place, mumbling numbers under his breath. *"Barely a hundred,"* he said.

"Must be more rooms." Jeff took a moment to suck in a lungful of air. "It assimilated them," he said. "It must have...copied somehow..." He had to stop to breathe.

"I guess it didn't need anything from us," said Gabriel.

Jeff caught his breath and said, "I've seen enough."

Gabriel's gaze lingered on the light-tubes criss-crossing the walls and ceiling. *"I could spend a lifetime in this one room."* Finally, he nodded. *"Let's find the door."*

Jeff led the way out, feeling somewhat relieved when he stepped onto the light-blooming surface of the corridor.

"Wait," Gabriel said after he had left the room. *"I was broadcasting visual, but I want to record. The ship probably isn't getting any of this."*

Jeff shook his head. "I'm moving on."

"One second," Gabriel said, pretending not to hear him as he turned away.

"Come on, man, we can't–"

Gabriel stepped back into the room and disappeared.

Jeff reached out and stumbled, pulling up short just outside the opening to the room. He peered inside, seeing no one.

"Gabe?"

Static on the suit comms. Jeff's HUD beeped at him: thirty minutes of oxygen remaining.

"Damn," he muttered as he walked into the room.

It was different. The configuration of lights in the walls and the ceiling had noticeably changed, following curving paths instead of straight lines. Nearly half of the bowl-shaped wall cutouts were sealed by plastic domes, containing the writhing specimens within. Still others contained asymmetrical lumps of solid matter resembling more familiar materials such as copper and iron.

Jeff hurried out of the room, and Gabe was suddenly standing next to him, shouting Jeff's name.

Grabbing a fistful of Gabe's suit, Jeff pulled him away from the room, farther down the corridor. They passed and ignored the square-cut openings to other specimen rooms.

"Fold-space," Gabriel huffed between strained breaths. He grinned as he allowed Jeff to haul him down the corridor. "Stacked rooms…"

He tripped and fell to the floor, landing hard on his side. For half a minute, he lay there wheezing while Jeff stood next to him, hands on his own knees, trying to catch his breath.

"Getting…worse?" he asked.

Gabriel nodded, blinking sleepily. *"Heavier."*

Jeff was fast-approaching the limits of exhaustion, seeing nothing that signaled a way out of the torus. He hoisted Gabriel back to his feet and they set out down the corridor, encountering more sample rooms and no exits.

The spherical, purple-green light running a track along the spine of the corridor reappeared on the horizon. It slowed as it approached, then halted, shimmering and swirling overhead, casting thin shafts of light in all directions.

A disembodied voice filled Jeff's mind, as if he were

thinking the words himself.

"COME-the-real-DOWN-you," it said.

The unseen speaker used an amalgam of different voices – words stolen from the staff in Mission Control and the crew of *Explorer*, then stitched together to form broken sentences. At first it was Riley's voice, then suddenly Kate's, and even Jeff's, as if someone had recorded every communication during the mission and spliced the words together. Each word had the tinny overlay of a voice piped through a small comm system to be played from inadequate speakers.

"Do you hear that?" Gabriel whispered, looking around the corridor for the source of the voice.

"I hear it," Jeff said. "It's *us*."

"COME-the real-DOWN-you," the voice repeated. After a moment of confused silence, it said, using Gabriel's voice, "Oh. Hi, Commander."

Jeff turned his helmet slowly to look at Gabriel, who shrugged.

"Hello," Jeff said to no one in particular.

The ball of light in the ceiling twirled faster, then slowed.

The rotating cast of voices said, "TAKE-the long-HOME-system-system-CAREFUL."

"I think it wants us to leave," Gabriel said.

Jeff gestured helplessly with heavy arms. "We're trying!"

"Hello," said Jeff's disembodied voice.

He groaned in frustration and pulled Gabriel down the corridor. The ball of light in the ceiling followed above.

"We're running out of oxygen," Jeff said. "No more games."

"No more games," the voice mimicked. Then it switched to Noah's voice to say, "Looks like they put a bomb inside the panel."

Screams tore the air, piercing Jeff's mind like knives. He and Gabriel buckled to their knees, gloved hands pressed to their helmets. There was an explosion, and then someone Jeff didn't recognize said, "It didn't work!" Another yelled, "Here it comes!"

The screaming stopped. Jeff knelt on the glowing floor, breathing like a spent marathon runner.

"Both-NOTHING-NOTHING-without the object," said the symphony of voices. Then it played a series of beeps, long and short.

Morse code, Jeff thought. He waited for silence from the voice, then said, "Per aspera ad astra."

"*'Through hardships to the stars'*," Gabriel translated breathlessly. "*What's it mean?*"

Jeff stared up at the light at the top of the ceiling, watching it spin, as if it were part of a larger program waiting for an input response.

He said, "It means the universe just got a lot smaller."

The light spun faster, then shot away down the spine of the corridor arch and disappeared. As soon as it vanished, a shadow blossomed in its place. The shadow slid over the ceiling like water over tile, whispering toward Jeff and Gabriel.

They stood, grunting against the heavy gravity, to face the oncoming shadow.

"Well," Gabriel said, *"I guess–"*

With a violent jerk, the shadow yanked them up to the ceiling and they were slammed into crushing darkness once more.

Red light flashed rhythmically through Jeff's closed eyelids. He opened them to see his angrily-blinking HUD, informing him he had less than twenty minutes of oxygen remaining. He was in space, outside the torus. Gabriel floated a couple of meters away, eyes closed serenely.

They had been deposited – or had drifted – a little over a hundred meters away from the torus, on the side opposite Titan. It was very close to where *Explorer* had been before Ming parked it near *North Star*.

Jeff did a double-take of the ships. When he had gone into the torus, *Explorer* was still where it had been when the crew first arrived. Now it was only sixty meters from *North Star*, connected to it by a long fuel umbilical.

Jeff saw Ming's suited form in the distance, maneuvering into *North Star*'s open cargo hold.

"Gabe?" he said, testing his own voice. It was markedly easier to speak and breathe outside the confines of the torus. He took a long drink of tepid water from the straw positioned near his mouth as he coasted over to Gabriel and checked his vitals from his wrist pad – all in the green. "You gotta stop passing out on me, bud, or I'll start taking it personally."

He clipped the end of his safety tether to the nylon loop on Gabe's suit, then thumbed his control stick toward *North Star*.

Gabriel bounced at the end of the tether when it snapped taut, jerking Jeff backward. With no slack in the line, their momentums synced and Jeff was able to tow Gabe behind him without feeling a strain on his own system.

"Ming?" Jeff asked as he coasted forward. "Kate? Anyone listening back home?"

No answer.

He checked his wrist pad, noticed that his comm system was off, and rebooted it with a few taps on the small screen.

"–hear me, Jeff?" Kate was saying after the system turned on with a static pop. *"You need to get back inside now. Your oxygen levels are almost critical."*

"You weren't worried about me, were you?" he asked with a grin.

"There you are," she said, sighing with relief.

"I'm headed to the ship now."

"How's Gabriel?"

"He looks alright. The transition from the torus knocked him out."

"It's no wonder. The thing spit you two out like bullets from a gun."

"How'd we stop?" he asked.

"No idea. We thought you'd know."

"I'm still trying to process everything we saw inside."

Static crackled, and Noah said, *"You were conscious inside the artifact?"*

"Wide awake." Jeff adjusted his course, and Gabriel tugged slightly against the tether as it went slack and snapped taut again.

"What did you see?" Noah asked, excited.

"Can't spare the oxygen for the details just yet," Jeff said.

After a pause, Noah, sounding crushed, came back with, *"I understand."*

"I bet if you stopped flirting with Kate," Juan said eagerly, *"you could at least tell us something."*

"Is that Juan?" Jeff asked, still smiling. "Who gave you a microphone?"

"I've always had one."

"Two words," Jeff said. "Fold-space."

Kate and Juan simultaneously said, *"What-space?"* while Noah replied, *"You're joking."*

"Ask Gabe about it when he wakes up. Just say 'stacked rooms' and I bet he'll chatter all the way back to Earth."

"Speaking of getting home…" Ming said.

Jeff was happy to hear her voice. "Leaving so soon?"

"No point in sticking around. I was just waiting for you to wrap up the reunion."

"I appreciate that," Jeff said. "What's the status?"

His flashing red HUD beeped urgently: fifteen minutes of air remaining. *No problem,* he thought. *I'll be in the airlock with Gabe in less than three.*

"I transferred all the fuel I could to North Star's empty tanks," Ming said. *"She'll give us one major burn, two max. Should get us home within six months at the most."*

"No fuel at all left in Explorer?"

"There's probably enough sloshing around at the bottom of the tank for a quick burn. The umbilical couldn't suck up the dregs. Not that we need it."

"Could be worse," Jeff conceded.

As he approached *North Star* and watched Ming coasting back and forth in the hold, a half-remembered thought tugged at his brain. Then he looked toward the front of the ship, at the open airlock door.

"Actually," he said, "it *is* worse."

"What do you mean?" Ming asked.

"The airlock," he said. "I forgot about the damn airlock. Someone has to manually close the outer door or the ship won't let us fire the engine."

"Oh," she said without concern. *"That's not a problem."*

"You can override the system?"

"No, but I worked out a different solution while you were dinking around the artifact."

"Dinking?"

"That's right," she said.

"How long were we inside?"

"Three hours."

"What?!"

Jeff looked at his HUD again. According to his

oxygen reserves, he had only lost ten minutes.

"*Tell me about it,*" Ming said. "*If your vitals hadn't been coming in, I would have left.*"

"Right."

"*What gets me is wondering why the crew would set off an explosive in their own airlock.*"

Jeff remembered the recorded screams he heard inside the torus. "They were afraid," he said.

"*Lieutenant,*" Kate said over comms.

"*I'm here,*" Ming replied.

"*According to North Star's manifest, the three of you should have enough food in the crew module to last you eleven months.*"

"*So I can stop untethering this crate of dehydrated soy steak?*"

"*By all means. You'll also be pleased to know the computer systems on both ships are analogous. You should have no trouble accessing North Star's controls and communicating with us in Mission Control.*"

"*Excellent. I'm going to seal the hold.*"

"Maybe grab one box of soy steak," Jeff said. "You know, for Gabriel."

"*Right,*" said Ming. "*For Gabriel.*"

The distance meter in Jeff's HUD ticked down to zero as he bumped into *North Star's* hull next to the airlock. He grabbed a welded handhold and turned sideways to allow Gabriel a cushioned halt against his padded shoulder. After the soft impact, he noticed the access panel to the manual door override was open. He was certain he closed it after he'd let Riley and Gabriel out of the ship earlier.

Jeff held onto the tether near the nylon loop in Gabe's suit and kept him close as Ming maneuvered over to them, the cargo hold door closing automatically behind her.

"*Got your fake steak,*" she said, tapping the rectangular box she held to her chest.

"Perfect. Now what do you say we get the hell out of here?"

"*Sounds good to me.*"

Streams of nitrogen slowed Ming down before she bumped into Jeff. She met his gaze then searched his face thoughtfully.

"What is it?" he asked, stuck halfway between amusement and concern.

"*Just thinking about how we ended up here.*"

"Let's do that after we get inside, okay?"

She hesitated, then said, "*I'm glad you were part of the mission.*"

He nodded. "Feeling's mutual."

She pulled herself into the darkened airlock and let go of the box, letting it spin toward the wall in slow motion as she fiddled with the fused and melted door controls. Jeff followed her inside, pulling Gabe after him. He unclipped his own tether from Gabe's suit and released it to automatically spool into his pack.

"So what are we doing?" he asked.

She kept her back to him and didn't answer. He drifted closer to look over her shoulder when she lifted her legs to plant her boots against the wall and pushed off, ramming her pack into Jeff's chest. They coasted backward across the width of the spherical airlock as if falling through water. Jeff's pack hit the opposite wall and fresh warning lights flashed in his HUD as if he were standing under the psychedelic lights of some midnight carnival.

With a grunt, she stepped on his thighs and pushed off again, flying with extended arms toward the open outer door.

Jeff let go of Gabriel's suit and reached out, grabbing her ankle when she was halfway outside. He jerked forward with her momentum but slowed her down.

"There was never any workaround, was there?" he said as he reeled her back into the airlock. He pulled her close and turned her around so he could look into her steely eyes. "You were going to seal us in."

"One of us has to close it from the outside," she said. *"It's the only way. I tried to reactivate the automated controls."*

Jeff shook her shoulders. "What about your family?"

"What about your family?" she said. *"What about Gabriel's?"*

Left unattended, Gabriel floated freely around the airlock. One of his arms drifted into Jeff's peripheral vision, and he noticed the wrist pad, its screen still aglow with power. While holding Ming's shoulder with one hand, he used the other to pull Gabriel between them, facing Ming.

"Jeff, what are you doing?!"

"Hug your daughter for me," he said.

Jeff tapped a string of commands into Gabriel's

wrist pad and executed the sequence. He jammed Gabe's gloved hand forward against his control stick, and nitrogen blasted from the back of his pack, pushing Gabe and Ming deeper into the airlock and Jeff toward the open door.

"*Jeffreeeeey!*" she screamed.

He scrabbled at the threshold as he drifted out of the airlock, grabbing a welded rung on the exterior and swinging his body around to bounce against the hull.

The manual override access panel was right in front of him. He flipped up the plastic shield over the spring-loaded manual release, then pulled the lever. The outer airlock door slammed shut, and he was alone.

His HUD beeped.

Ten minutes of air remaining.

He planted the soles of his boots against the hull and inserted the T-shaped tool into the hexagonal hole labeled INNER. Pain stabbed the wounds in his chest as he struggled to twist the handle. He paused after only half a turn, leaving time for the main cabin pressure inside *North Star* to leak under the crack at the bottom of the inner airlock door.

"*Jeff...*" Kate said, her voice heavy with sorrow.

"Hey, don't worry," he said, trying his damnedest to sound upbeat. "I still have Explorer, right? It'll be a slow journey home with just the orbital thrusters, but you guys can pick me up on the way."

"*We'll find you,*" Noah said resolutely.

"See, babe?" Jeff said. "It's just a little delay."

"*Airlock pressurized,*" Ming said remorsefully.

Jeff gripped the handle of the T-shaped tool and twisted, breathing hard and exerting what little energy remained in his tired limbs. The oxygen meter in his HUD skipped a minute, dropping from nine minutes remaining to seven.

"Door is halfway open," Ming said, and Jeff let go of the handle.

"Sorry," he breathed, clenching his aching hands. "Hope it's enough."

"We can slip through." A few moments later, she said, *"We're inside."*

Aided by mechanisms within, closing the door to its resting state was easier. Afterward, Jeff returned the T-shaped tool to its clamp within the access panel with shaking hands, knowing whoever picked up *North Star* on the other side of the solar system would need it to open the door.

He kicked off from the hull and jetted toward *Explorer*, leaving *North Star* and the torus behind.

Just you and me, honey, he thought.

"Hope you eggheads back home can talk me through the flight procedures," he said.

"We'll be with you every step of the way," Kate replied.

Ming's helmet camera was still active. She hadn't bothered removing her suit as she sat inside *North Star's* command module. In his flashing red HUD, Jeff could see her working the ship controls, powering up all the necessary systems. The star field outside the narrow window shifted as the ship slowly peeled out of orbit under minimal thrust.

"I want to put some distance between us and the artifact before I warm the antimatter drive," Ming said.

Jeff turned back to look as he continued toward *Explorer*.

The torus followed *North Star* as it left orbit, matching the ship's velocity.

"You have company," he said.

On the little video feed in his HUD, he watched Ming page through *North Star*'s external video feeds until she was looking back at the pursuing torus.

"Full stop," she said, manipulating the controls.

Forward-facing thrusters spit air, and the ship slowed to a halt, hanging in space like a forgotten relic. The torus maintained its distance, waiting silently behind the ship.

"That thing is going to follow you all the way home," Jeff said.

"Maybe that's not such a bad thing," Noah said. *"We could learn so much from its composition alone."*

"Did you forget what it did to Riley?" Jeff asked. "And to the other crew?"

"But not to you and Gabriel. Regrettably, I agree that it's too dangerous to bring back."

Jeff bounced gently off *Explorer*'s closed airlock, using his pack thrusters to stabilize himself after impact. He grabbed onto a handhold and stared at the door's control panel, his gloved hand hovering centimeters from the access button. Then he looked over to *North Star* waiting to be swallowed by the torus, should it so choose.

"Any suggestions?" Ming asked.

"Yeah," Jeff said reluctantly, pulling his hand away from the control panel. "I have one."

But you're not going to like it, he thought.

Jeff opened the maintenance panel over the main fuel line, hinging it up after loosening all the fasteners. He studied the organized layout of wires, tubes, and black boxes within.

His HUD beeped: five minutes of oxygen left.

"Hey," he said thoughtfully as he began opening black boxes. "Someone want to remind me about the reserve oxygen tank you put into these suits?"

"There is no reserve tank," Kate said. "The meter is accurate. If you don't get inside right now, Jeff, you're going to suffocate."

"I was kind of hoping it was like a car," he continued, "where if the meter hit empty you could still squeeze out a few more miles."

After he flipped up the lids to all of the black boxes, he began pulling out the copper cubes within and pushing them out into space. They tumbled slowly, catching the reflected light of Titan and glimmering like tiny stars.

He didn't bother closing the panel as he

maneuvered down the fuselage, drifting toward the back of the ship. Halfway down the ship's 130-meter length, he found the panel he needed. Using his multipurpose hex driver, he unscrewed the fasteners and pushed the loose panel away.

"Jeff," Kate pleaded. *"What the hell are you doing?"*

He looked over at *North Star* and the torus behind it. "Just fiddling with Ming's fine handiwork. I have to tweak it a little."

He was still for a moment, then he nodded to himself and reached into the open compartment to pull out a hard, silver circuit sheet from a tight slot in a rack filled with more than a hundred similar boards.

"I'm syncing the remote system with my suit computer," he said.

"Why?" Noah demanded.

Jeff didn't answer. With the arc-torch setting on his multipurpose hex driver, he burnt the circuits used for connecting the remote system to the ship's comm arrays. He replaced the silver board and pulled out another from farther down the rack. Embedded in its surface was a small, transparent screen. Jeff activated the screen and scrolled through a list of commands. He tapped the right one and held the board close to his wrist pad. A second later, the screen flashed, signaling it had paired with a new master system.

He replaced the silver board and said, "Almost there."

"Jeff, you can't," Kate said.

He paused, caught off-guard by the honest pain in her voice – a tone that triggered some ancient protective mechanism deep in his core. If he had more time to think about it, he probably would have abandoned his plan and retreated inside *Explorer*, clinging to the minuscule hope of seeing her once again.

But he didn't have more time. His HUD flashed that he only had a minute of air left. He pushed away from *Explorer* and thumbed his control stick, jetting away at max velocity.

"Ming, you're going to want to punch it as soon the torus turns my way."

"How do you know it will?"

"Because if it doesn't," he said, "we're *all* screwed."

Jeff turned around as he put more distance between himself and *Explorer*. Using his wrist pad, he sent a command to the ship's mainframe to warm the antimatter drive. Orange light glowed from within the flared engine wash shield at the back of the ship. At the same time, he triggered orbital thrusters to fire, pushing *Explorer* closer to the torus.

Two hundred meters out, Jeff coasted to a stop, floating motionless in space as *Explorer* inched toward the artifact, which remained firmly aimed at *North Star*.

"It's not moving," Ming said.

Jeff swiped his finger over a slider on the screen of his wrist pad, bumping up the power flowing to the drive. The orange light emanating from the flared engine wash shield brightened to a star in its own right.

The torus swiveled in place, turning to face *Explorer*.

There we go, Jeff thought. *Come get your new sample.*

He pushed the ignition button on the screen of his

wrist pad, engaging *Explorer's* antimatter drive. Fire belched from the tail-end of the ship as fuel ignited in the engine chamber, sparking the reaction that would propel the ship forward at inhuman speeds.

Yet the ship didn't budge.

It shook in place as it tried to tip free of some invisible force. Behind it, the torus approached, its frame rotating around the black disc in its center.

"Now, Ming," Jeff said loudly. "Go now."

Orbital thrusters fired, and *North Star* pulled away from the artifact, heading away from Titan.

"Jeff," she said, *"the antimatter drive is priming. I can't stop it or else we'll lose the fuel."*

"I know."

A silence grew, then she said, *"Thank you."*

Explorer shook so violently it threatened to snap apart at the seams. The torus closed in, now only thirty meters behind. Its frame rotated more quickly, and flashes of transparency skittered across the surface, revealing the corridor within. A sphere of purple-green light shot past inside the corridor, then again and again as it traversed the interior perimeter, moving faster and faster.

"Firing engine," Ming said. *"See you, Jeff."*

"Good luck," he answered.

Light bloomed from the tail of *North Star*, and the ship accelerated quickly, shrinking in apparent size until it was only a pinpoint light in a sea of stars. Its light blinked out in the distance.

His HUD stopped flashing and switched to solid red. His oxygen meter read zero, but he didn't yet feel the strain of a failing air system.

Between him and Titan, the torus engulfed the tail-end of *Explorer*, swallowing the belching flames, then the engine wash shield, moving as methodically as a snake consuming a large rat. The back of the ship disappeared briefly into the void strung between the inner edges of the torus.

A few seconds later, the engine wash shield emerged from the other side. The flames had been extinguished. It emerged a few meters below and much more slowly than the front of the ship was being consumed. Seen from the side, it looked as if one ship were entering, and another ship were exiting at decreased speed and slightly off-center.

"Mission Control," Jeff said, "we'll probably lose instant comms very soon. Kate..." he added, "...I'm sorry."

Explorer snapped in half under the tortuous pressures rending its hull. The outer walls of the torus were completely transparent. The purple-green light within zipped around the perimeter so quickly that it was a solid ring of glowing energy.

"No trigger required," Jeff whispered, remembering Riley's exact words.

The torus passed over the cargo hold, and the box of modified Semtex within.

Boom.

The explosion tore open the twisted hull of *Explorer* and licked briefly into space, blasting forth a shockwave that cracked the wall of the torus, splitting it open.

The torus wobbled in its rotation like an uneven

bike tire. Jagged shards of black material spun away. The crack in its surface widened, and a chunk of the artifact broke from the whole, tumbling out into space. The black disc of its interior blinked out, and Jeff could see Titan through the broken loop.

Drifting away from the remains of *Explorer*, the torus wobbled toward the atmosphere of the moon.

Explorer itself was in two mangled pieces. The aft twenty percent was mostly intact up to the laser-clean cut at its forward-most end. The front half wasn't swallowed by the torus. It had become a twisted clump of metal, terminating at the cargo hold, which was peeled open by the explosion like a metal flower. The rest of the ship – the part that constituted the length between the surviving pieces – had vanished along with the black hole of the torus.

"Kate?" Jeff said.

His comms crackled.

"I know you can't hear me," he continued. "Without a ship, this message will take years to find you, even if I'm pointed in the right direction. I might be sending this to Pluto for all I know."

Staring at the glowing number zero inside his HUD's oxygen meter, Jeff wondered how many breaths he had left. Sometime during the explosion, pulling air into his lungs had become increasingly difficult.

"I guess I might have a couple minutes left. Figured I'd spend them talking to you." He took a deep breath before continuing. "Didn't get a chance for a proper goodbye. Maybe there *are* no proper goodbyes when I'm so far away." Jeff shook his head. "Listen to me yammering. Maybe it's because—"

A burst of static cut him off. The HUD indicator for his comm system blinked out. Jeff stared into deep space, toward the direction of Earth, yearning.

He switched off his dead comms and turned to fully face Titan, gazing upon its full disc unaided, drinking up every detail of its surface. His face and the tears which streamed down his cheeks were clearly visible in the red reflection inside his helmet.

Warning alarms beeped loudly, and his HUD went dark. Jeff tapped on his blank wrist pad screen, then looked at Titan. He decided to watch it until the very end, when he could no longer keep his eyes open. There was no desire to reflect back on his life, except upon those warm weekend mornings in bed with Kate.

That was happiness, he thought contentedly.

His eyelids grew heavy.

Just as they were about to close, he thought he imagined a dark shape just beneath the outer layers of Titan's atmosphere, moving toward him.

He forced his eyes open.

The shape was mostly occluded by the thick gases hugging the moon. Then it broke free of the atmosphere suddenly, leaving sworls of pale gases in its wake. Immediately after, a second object followed behind the first, bursting from the hazy atmosphere at a terrible speed.

Not just one torus, but two, the center of each a solid black hole, like widening circular blemishes on the surface of Titan.

The first one shot past in a blur barely three meters

to Jeff's right, heading in the direction of the receding *North Star*. Its passage didn't affect the vacuum around Jeff in the slightest. He comforted himself in the knowledge that it would never catch up to Ming and Gabriel even at that impressive velocity.

As the second torus approached, Jeff became increasingly certain it was coming right for him. It was moving so quickly and growing so rapidly in apparent size that he hardly had time to think that yes, it was going to swallow him up just as it had Riley.

He didn't have the oxygen to scream, or he would have. Instead, he was silent as he was engulfed by the black hole of the torus.

He emerged in the atmosphere of Titan, falling toward the surface.

Turning back, Jeff saw another torus – or the same one – disappear behind him in thick yellow smog. At one-tenth Earth's gravity, he knew he shouldn't be plummeting so quickly. It felt like he had jumped off a ludicrously tall building on Earth.

As he turned back around, dark, massive shapes moved in the fog on both sides. The thick yellow haze parted briefly to give a hint of hard black material, much like that on the exterior of the torus, yet on a gargantuan scale, as if the impossibly tall skyscraper from which Jeff imagined himself jumping had uprooted and floated freely in the upper atmosphere.

With his powerless suit, there were no HUD lights to cast reflections on the interior of his face shield. There was also no temperature regulation. Jeff's thin breaths fogged the polycarbonate in fleeting blooms. It pained him to breath the diminishing oxygen trapped inside the suit, his chest stabbing with each inhalation and burning every time he exhaled.

The atmosphere thinned, transitioning from a yellow soup to a flowing ochre mist.

With increased visibility, Jeff could see why he was falling so quickly. Another torus awaited him below, its walls transparent and spinning around its black core.

He fell into it silently and popped out of another one a kilometer above Titan's glistening white surface. Anything in his stomach would have lurched its way out of his mouth from the way his organs twisted every time he passed through one of the artifacts, yet all he could do was fight back a gag reflex and waste precious air by breathing heavily for a few seconds.

The surface was as clear as Earth's on a cloudless summer day, despite the blanketing atmosphere. Light from the distant sun refracted off nitrogen crystals trapped within the yellow smog, illuminating the ice-covered surface.

A vast hydrocarbon lake stretched out directly beneath him, its gray edges touching razored shores of water-ice tundra. In the distance, a towering cryovolcano spewed ice and water high into the air.

Jeff's rate of descent slowed noticeably half a kilometer above the hydrocarbon lake. He was close enough to see white-capped waves on its surface, formed by a strong, westerly wind.

Dark structures dotted the landscape of Titan, and moving among them were many tori, hovering over the surface, unimpeded by the moon's reduced gravity. The structures were clusters of various-sized black arches all criss-crossing and lying on top of each other, as if gigantic atoms had frozen half-out of the ice.

The tori tended to the structures, adding arches here and platforms there. Jeff watched as one rested parallel to the surface, then gently rose into the air. Threading from its black core was the arch of a structure. As the torus moved along its curved path, the arch appeared from its center, as if being sketched or molded into existence.

Many of the structures were clustered near the shore of the hydrocarbon lake. From his vantage point, Jeff thought it looked like a small village.

He was only able to manage a breath every couple of seconds. His lungs compressed with each exhalation, and darkness played at the edge of his vision. The hydrocarbon lake slowly drew closer. If he didn't slow down, he thought dreamily, he would hit it soon.

Focusing on the nearest structure on the shore's edge, Jeff saw a figure in an orange suit walking on one of the arches. He tried to rub his blurring eyes but his hands thumped against his face shield. The orange figure pushed off the arch and drifted into the air in a prolonged jump, deftly alighting on a taller arch. It knelt down and opened some kind of panel, then dropped inside, out of sight.

Two more orange suited figures crawled over the arches of another structure. Another emerged from the void in the center of a torus. It was joined by additional figures wearing red. Some of them walked on the arches, others hovered about, seemingly propelled by whatever mechanism powered the tori. Looking around at the structures that dotted the wind-swept dunes of the icy tundra, Jeff counted dozens of orange and red suits.

One of the orange-suited figures pushed off the icy surface and hovered across the lake, moving toward a rising structure on the other side. It was only a few meters above the water, and the closer Jeff got, the more it looked like he was going to crash into its back.

He didn't.

He passed right by the figure, who wore an orange Mark IV Constellation Suit. The helmet had a darkened face shield instead of the usual golden sun visor. Etched in clean black letters in the nameplate over the face shield was the name RILEY.

The figure ignored Jeff as he dropped into the lake feet-first, swallowed by an abyss far more terrifying to him than the cold vacuum of space. The liquid attacked his suit, hammering him with ungodly cold.

As he took the last gulp of oxygen in his disintegrating suit, a torus materialized in the black depths below, rising slowly like the eager maw of some alien nightmare.

_DAY 63

Noah slowly pulled off his headset and dropped it on Rick's workstation. He had been watching the display wall for hours, waiting with diminishing optimism for some word from Jeff Dolan.

A lonely representative from the Sheriff's Department poked around the conference room, the last of a cadre that had swept through the building after Frank was arrested. The excitement of their inspection quickly abated once the officers scanned Frank's computer and found archived messages regarding Michael Cochran, Rick Teller, and another employee who had disappeared under mysterious circumstances from the old Diamond Aerospace facility near Baikonur.

Kate left shortly after most of the officers had departed, as soon as Ming called in from *North Star* to say that she and Gabriel were safely through their first major burn and probably had enough fuel for half of a second. Now that they were back on a standard delay, Mission Control only buzzed to life every other hour or so during the status updates.

Noah stood and cracked his back, looking around the disheveled room. Food wrappers and empty overturned coffee cups littered the floor. Half the workstation monitors rested at crooked angles, and the other half were dark.

The display wall showed two sets of vitals: Lieutenant Ming's and Dr. Silva's. Both were in the green. Silva had awoken briefly to hydrate and ask about Jeff before passing out again.

Noah took stock of the present employees as he walked to the back of the room and climbed the stairs to the viewing platform. Most of them had stayed through the debacle with Frank Johnson, no doubt spurred on by the perseverance and loyalty of their department heads. Noah would have to remember to give everyone a raise before the next payout, even though the mission didn't go exactly as planned.

Rick Teller had called in his resignation when Riley was being turned inside-out by the torus, and Noah couldn't blame him. How Rick had evaded Frank's goon squad was beyond the grasp of his most acute guesswork.

Noah doubted he would ever see Kate Bishop again.

She had left without a word, walking from the building in a daze. She sat in her car in the parking lot for a long time, staring forward, still as a statue. Then she started her car and drove away. It was the most uneventful resignation Noah had ever encountered, if in fact it was a resignation at all. Yet something about the finality of her absence told him she was finished with Diamond Aerospace.

Noah rode his private elevator to the top floor and stood at the threshold, staring at his ostentatious desk. He had ordered Frank's to be broken apart and hauled away shortly after his arrest. Not that he needed the extra space on the viewing platform – he just didn't want any reminders of such a dark time for his company.

Yet hadn't Frank been doing what he thought was right? It was certainly true that he had pushed Noah to make uncomfortable decisions in the past – decisions which ultimately ended up benefiting the company.

He stewed over the moral conundrum as he walked to his desk and sat down, feeling as if he were acting out predetermined motions instead of doing something purposeful. There was no real reason for him to be in his office – he simply didn't want to be on the operations floor. The image of the broken torus haunted his mind, as he knew it would for years to come. He had been so close to something with Titan – so close to altering the course of human history for the better with new technology that he could smell the changing winds.

Then it had slipped through his fingers like so much sand.

He didn't regret choosing the crew over the mission, even though only two of them survived. Anyway, the damn torus probably would have swallowed half of Earth before he could figure out a way to unravel its mysteries.

The words *fold-space* stuck in his mind like darts in

a wall – a tease from Dolan after exiting the torus. The lost prospect of near-infinite storage rooms occupying the same physical location sent shivers of wonder coursing through his body. Whoever had built the torus had somehow harnessed the ability to manipulate dimensional space. Remarkable.

He sighed, remembering the old adage about spilled milk.

What's done is done, he thought.

Already his mind raced as he strained to reassemble the pieces of a shattered puzzle. The preparation for future launches to Titan had long been underway – missions that were meant to build on the foundation laid down by Riley and his crew.

The entire skeleton of Space Station Glory had been lost with *Explorer*, and would take time to replace. Noah could extend the next launch date, if he had to. The crew of *Explorer II* would arrive for training in less than a month as that ship inched toward completion, updated engine and all. If they backed down, there were doubtless many previous applicants who would be all too eager to accept a fresh invitation from Diamond Aerospace, despite the company's recent setback.

His desk phone beeped, and he pushed the intercom button.

"Sir, Riley's helmet camera was still active when North Star left Titan," said his assistant. "The ship was able to record and relay the last few minutes of his video feed after linking up with Mission Control."

"I'd rather not look at the shattered torus right now, Neil, but thank you."

"I think you should see it, sir. It's not what you think."

Earlier, Noah had banished Riley's feed from the display wall in Mission Control. He thought it rude for so many others to look through the lens of a dead man. Now, he instructed Neil to patch the feed to his monitor, and he sat before it, mouth agape at what was on the screen.

Apparently, Riley's camera was recording as the commander's body fell through the dense yellow fog surrounding Titan.

"Restrict this file," Noah said quickly. "Top-level access only. Transfer it to my private server and delete it elsewhere. That means from your server, too, Neil."

His assistant grumbled, then said, "Yes, sir."

Noah severed the call.

In the recording, Riley's body emerged from the lowest barrier of Titan's atmosphere, his camera panning across the alien landscape below.

Noah's breath caught in his throat as he leaned closer to the monitor, his eyes filled with wonder.

_EPILOGUE

Kate sipped coffee on her back porch, a warm, salty breeze teasing her hair. It was a cloudy day in Cape Canaveral. The usual afternoon storms had rolled in early, leaving behind wet sand and a gray horizon.

She didn't let her gaze drift too high into the sky – she wasn't ready to look up that far quite yet. Instead she focused on what was right in front of her. Since she had left Diamond Aerospace, she started a garden. Kate hadn't been able to think of anything else to do. She didn't want to look for another job so soon, though she had several interesting leads. Rick had promised to introduce her to his new boss over at Deep Black, an upstart private space company that was rumored to be gunning for investor capital.

She took a sip from her mug and rubbed a tomato plant leaf between her fingers. The rest of her meager garden was faring well enough, but the tomatoes really seemed to thrive.

The wind picked up and blew stinging sand against

her cheek. She turned away, closing her eyes. When she looked out toward the ocean, she noticed people running. Even in Florida's stormy weather, you couldn't keep a tourist from their day at the beach.

A family of four, two parents and two young girls, had gathered around something on the shore. Gray waves lapped over the splayed orange form of–

"Oh my God," Kate whispered.

She dropped her coffee mug and leaped over the low fence hedging her garden, pounding across the wet sand with bare feet. The wind plastered her blue t-shirt to her skin. Sand sprayed up from her feet and splattered against her jean shorts.

The two girls were pointing at the helmeted, orange-suited figure and talking loudly to their parents. The father knelt next to the figure as Kate burst forward, nearly bowling him over.

"Please!" she said.

She fell to her knees in the wet sand. The face shield was too dark to see through. With shaking hands, she touched the nameplate on the helmet that read DOLAN. She pushed against the *Explorer I* mission patch on the shoulder of the suit, terrified there would be no occupant.

Someone was inside.

"Daddy?" asked one of the girls, an edge of fear in her voice.

The parents hurriedly led the young girls away.

The tide washed in, pushing Jeff's orange space suit a few inches farther onto shore. Kate probed the seal of his helmet with shaking hands, feeling that it was intact.

She slid the helmet's seal lock to the side and gently pried it off. Water dripped from the inside, spattering against Jeff's peaceful face.

His eyes were closed; his face ashen. She touched his cold cheek with the back of her fingers. He wasn't breathing. Then she covered her hands with her mouth, knowing she was about to cry.

Jeff coughed and spasmed, his limbs thrashing in the surf, and Kate backed away, unsure what to do. He sucked in air and his eyes popped open, looking around wildly. He noticed Kate and went still, panting as if he'd just awoken from a nightmare. She knelt at his side and he blinked up at her, squinting in the daylight.

Kate bent lower and pressed her forehead against his, tears dripping down her cheeks to splash against his as she laughed through her sobs. Jeff reached up and held the back of her head, pressing them harder together. She finally sat up so she could look at him. His short hair was soaking wet.

Jeff looked down at himself as the tide washed over the legs of his suit. It looked brand new, as if he had just put it on for the first time.

"I thought I was drowning," he said. "How did I get here?"

Kate shook her head, looking over his suit in disbelief. "I thought you'd tell *me*."

"Where are the others? Ming and Gabriel."

"On their way home. You made it back first."

"But they're okay?"

"Last I heard, yes. They still have five months to go."

He sat up, patting the neck of his suit.

Kate found the zipper for him and ran it down one side of his torso before it took a right turn over his stomach. He twisted three dial-locks embedded in the coarse fabric and peeled open the outer layers of the suit to reveal his bare chest. He looked down in confusion as he probed the unscarred flesh over his ribcage.

"What's wrong?" Kate asked.

He looked behind him, at the ocean, then at his left arm. His wrist pad was missing. "I was falling."

Lightning cracked in the distance, spiderwebbing over the Atlantic.

"Toward Earth?" she asked.

He shook his head. "Titan. The torus, it – it *took* me…" He squeezed his eyes shut and held a palm to his temple. "I can't remember." Then his eyes popped open. "Wait. Yes, I can. I fell into a lake."

"A lake on Titan?"

"A torus came for me. They function as builders, or gateways…I don't really know how to describe it."

"They?" Kate asked.

His eyes darted back and forth as he became excited. "I was pulled through the atmosphere by a series of them. I saw…oh, Kate, you won't *believe* what I saw!"

She helped him shrug out of his pack and stand on unsteady legs, surprised he'd been able to get off the ground wearing the heavy suit. Water dripped from the orange fabric as he took his first steps in the wet sand. He put his arm around her shoulders, and she wrapped hers around his chest.

"Tell me everything," she said as they slowly walked toward her apartment. Lightning split the sky over the ocean, followed by a rumble of distant thunder.

Behind them, Jeff's helmet floated in the surf, its darkened face shield looking out to sea.